FINDING COLIN FIRTH

Mia March, also the author of *The Meryl Streep Movie Club*, lives on the coast of Maine. To learn more about her visit www.miamarch.com.

FINDING COLIN FIRTH

MIA MARCH

PAN BOOKS

First published in the United States by Gallery Books, 2013

This edition published 2013 by Pan Books
an imprint of Pan Macmillan, a division of Macmillan Publishers Limited
Pan Macmillan, 20 New Wharf Road, London N1 9RR
Basingstoke and Oxford
Associated companies throughout the world
www.panmacmillan.com

ISBN 978-1-4472-5407-2

A CIP catalogue record for this book is available from the British Library.

Typeset by Ellipsis Digital Limited, Glasgow
Printed and bound by CPI Group (UK) Ltd, Croydon, CR0 4YY

Visit **www.panmacmillan.com** to read more about all our books
and to buy them. You will also find features, author interviews and
news of any author events, and you can sign up for e-newsletters
so that you're always first to hear about our new releases

For my beloved Max,
who made a mother out of me

'I'm fully aware that if I were to change professions tomorrow, become an astronaut and be the first man to land on Mars, the headlines in the newspapers would read: "Mr Darcy Lands on Mars".'

— COLIN FIRTH

Chapter 1
Bea Crane

The letter that would change Bea's life arrived while she was in the kitchen at Boston's Crazy Burger, working on four orders of Mt Vesuvius specials — three patties stacked a foot tall and layered with caramelized onions, bacon, Swiss cheese, lettuce, tomato, sour pickles and hot sauce. One of her new roommates, subletting for the summer in the dumpy three-bedroom apartment that Bea now shared with two strangers, poked her head in, said she'd signed for a certified envelope for Bea, and since she was coming to Crazy Burger for lunch, she'd brought it over.

'Certified? Who's it from?' Bea asked, taking a fast glance at the parcel as she scooped up the caramelized onions from the pan. Mmm. She'd been frying onions for three hours and still, the smell never got old.

Nina glanced at the upper left-hand corner of the envelope.

1

'Return address says Baker Klein, Twelve State Street, Boston.'

Bea shrugged. 'Will you open it up and read the first few lines to me? I need both hands to finish this burger.' Her manager, Barbara, would go nuts if she caught anyone but employees in the kitchen, but Bea was curious to know what the package was about, and Crazy Barbara, as the staff called her behind her back, was in her office, going over inventory.

'Sure,' Nina said. She slit open the envelope, pulled out a letter and read, 'My darling Bea.'

Bea froze, her hand paused on lettuce leaves. 'What?' That was how her mother had always addressed the letters she'd written to Bea at college. 'Turn it over – who's it from?'

'It says Mama.'

Bea raised an eyebrow. 'Well, since my mother died over a year ago, it's definitely not from her.'

'It's handwritten,' Nina said, 'but it definitely says Mama.'

That made no sense. But Bea's mother always signed her letters Mama. 'You can drop it on that chair, Nina. I'll just finish this last burger and read it on my break. Thanks for bringing it over.'

Bea was due for that much-needed fifteen-minute break: she'd been on shift at Crazy Burger since eleven and it was now close to two. She loved working at the popular burger joint in Boston's Back Bay, even if it was supposed to be temporary since she'd graduated from college a year ago and still hadn't found a teaching job, but her boss was driving her crazy. If Bea took sixteen minutes for her break, Barbara would dock her pay. The woman lived to dock pay. Last week, one of her Mt Vesuvius burgers was randomly measured and discovered to be only eleven inches high; Bea's paycheck was cut short five bucks.

In between each layer of burger – three of them – Bea piled on the toppings, added an extra helping of hot sauce, put on the top bun, then measured it. Just shy of a foot, which meant she had to add more lettuce. Finally, she set it on a plate next to the three other Mt Vesuvius burgers, plunked down a basket of onion rings and a basket of cheese fries, then rang the bell to alert the waitress to pick up. She called Manny, the other cook, in from his break, then took the manila envelope and went outside into the back alley. She lifted her face to the June sunshine. The breezy, warm day felt wonderful on her skin, in her hair, after being cooped up in the small kitchen half the afternoon.

She pulled out the contents of the envelope and her body went completely still. The letter was from her mother; there was no mistaking Cora Crane's handwriting. It was dated just over a year ago and attached to what looked like forms.

My darling Bea

If you're reading this, I'm gone now. A year gone. I've kept something from you all your life, something I should have told you the moment you were placed in my arms when you were just a day old. I didn't give birth to you, Bea. Your father and I adopted you.

I'm not entirely sure why, but I was ashamed that I couldn't bear a child, something I wanted so desperately, something your father wanted so desperately. When the adoption agent placed you in my arms, you were mine. It was as though I had given birth to you, and I suppose I wanted to believe it myself. So your father — God rest his soul — and I made it so. We never breathed a word to you, never told you. And you grew up believing that you were born to us.

Now that I feel myself going, I can't bear to take this with me. But I can't bear to tell you with my final breaths, either — I can't do that to you. So I'll wait on this, for both of us. But you should know the truth because it is the truth.

How I wish I'd been brave enough to be honest from that first minute. To tell you how grateful I was, how you were mine before I even met you, from the second the adoption agent called with the news.

I hope you will forgive me, my darling girl. You are my daughter, and I love you with all my heart.

Mama

Bea pulled the letter from its heavy paperclip and looked at the forms behind. Adoption papers, dated twenty-two years ago from the Helping Hands Adoption Agency in Brunswick, Maine.

Her hand shaking, Bea stuffed the letter and papers back

inside the envelope, and paced around the alley, then stopped, pulled out the letter and read it again. The words, in black ink, started blending together. *Should have told you. Adoption agent. Sorry. The truth is the truth.* If it weren't for her mother's handwriting and the good stationery she'd used for all correspondence, Bea might have thought someone was playing a trick on her.

Adopted? What?

The letter and papers had been sent by a law firm Bea had never heard of; her mother had been long-widowed and not well off, and when she died last year there was only the sparsely furnished year-round rental cottage far from the beach on Cape Cod to settle up. Bea had gone through the drawers and closets looking for every last precious memento of her mother, and if this letter had been in that house, she would have found it. Her mother had clearly arranged for Bea to hear the news well after she was gone, after the grief had subsided some.

She tried to imagine her mother, the sweetest person Bea had ever known, propped up in her hospice bed, writing that letter, in anguish, most likely. But another image kept coming: her mother, her father, twenty-two years ago, meeting Bea as a day-old newborn. 'Here's your daughter,' the adoption agent must have said. Or something like that.

Who the hell am I? Bea wondered. She thought of the framed photograph on her bedside table. It was her favourite family picture, taken when she was four, and Bea loved looking at it every night before she fell asleep and every morning when she woke up. Bea, sitting on her father's shoulders, her mother standing beside them, looking up at Bea and laughing, a tree ablaze with orange and red leaves behind them. Bea had been wearing the Batman cape she had insisted on every day for months, and the red hat that her mother had made for her. Cora had saved those old favourites and now Bea kept them in a keepsake box in her closet. Another picture came to mind, one she kept on her desk in her room, of herself and her mother at her college graduation last May, just over a year ago, and just a few weeks before her mother had gotten very sick and been diagnosed with ovarian cancer, as though she was holding on to watch Bea graduate. Two months later, her mother was gone.

Cora Crane, piano teacher with the patience of a saint, with the dark curls, bright blue eyes and a smile for everyone, was her mother. Keith Crane, handsome construction worker who sang her an Irish song before bed every single night of her childhood until he died when she was nine, was her father. The Cranes had been wonderful, doting parents who'd made Bea feel loved every day of her life. If someone else had given birth to Bea, that didn't change anything.

But someone else *had* given birth to her. Who?

A hollow pressure started building in Bea's chest.

'Bea!' Crazy Barbara came charging outside, glaring. 'What the hell are you doing? It's still lunch rush! Manny said you went out at least twenty minutes ago.'

'I just got some very strange news,' Bea said, her head spinning. 'I need a few minutes.' Her hand went to the tiny gold heart locket around her neck; her mother had given her the necklace for her sixteenth birthday and she never took it off.

'Well unless someone died, you need to head back to work – now.' Barbara started muttering under her breath. 'Taking an extended break in the middle of lunch rush! Who does she think she is?'

'Actually,' Bea said, barely able to think straight. There was no way she'd be able to get through the craze of orders. 'I need to go home, Barbara. I just learned some weird news, and—'

'You either get back to work or you're fired. I'm sick to death of all these excuses – all day long, someone has a headache, someone's grandmother's sick. Oh no,' she sing-songed, 'you got strange news. Boo hoo, Bea. Do your job or I'll find someone who actually earns their paycheck.'

Bea had been working at Crazy Burger for three years, full-time since last summer, and was the best cook in the kitchen, and the fastest. But nothing ever was good enough for Crazy Barbara. 'You know what, Barbara? I quit.' She took off her apron, handed it to a for once speechless Barbara, and went back inside to collect her bag from her locker.

She shoved the letter in her bag and walked the half-mile home in a daze, tripping over someone's backpack the minute she walked through the front door of her apartment in the four-storey brick building. God, she hated living here this

7

summer with strangers. She headed down the narrow hall, stepping on a pair of boxer briefs, then unlocked her door and locked it behind her. She dropped her bag on the floor of her room and sat down on her bed, hugging her mother's old cross-stitched pillow to her chest. She didn't move for hours.

'Wow, Bea, your entire life has been a lie.'

Slice of pizza en route to her mouth, Bea stared at Tommy Wonkowksi, star forward for the famed Beardsley College football team. A half-hour ago she'd been lying on her bed, staring at the ceiling, grappling with yesterday's bombshell, when her phone had rung: Tommy, at Poe's Pizzeria, asking if he'd gotten the time wrong for their date. She'd forced herself up and out the door and along the two blocks to the restaurant; she hadn't eaten since she'd received her mother's letter, hadn't left her room. But now, as she sat across from Tommy, she wished she'd cancelled. With her universe tilted, she needed comforting and familiar, and Tommy Wonkowski was anything but. She wasn't even sure why she'd said yes to this first date, but it wasn't every day a hot jock asked Bea out. When they'd met last week at the university's Writing Centre, where she had a part-time tutoring job (Bea had been helping him write a final paper for the freshman English class he was now bothering to take as a senior in summer session), she had been charmed by his good looks, how different the two of them were in every way, and the fact that he towered over her. Bea was five foot ten, and Tommy made her feel kind of dainty for once.

'I wouldn't go that far,' she said, wishing she'd never told him about the letter. But they'd run out of things to say to each other by the time the waitress had set down their large pizza, and she'd blurted out what was consuming her every waking thought as she'd shaken parmesan on a slice. Guess what I just found out yesterday? Turns out I was adopted.

But yes, it did sort of feel like her whole life had been a kind of lie. Friends, strangers – Bea herself – marvelling over the years at how utterly different she was from both Cora and Keith Crane. They were dark-haired; Bea was blonde. Her mother's eyes were startling blue, and her father's were hazel, yet Bea's were driftwood brown. Her parents were average height; she was an Amazon. She wasn't musical like her mother, or mathematical like her father. They were both quiet introverts and she could talk and talk and talk. More than once, Bea could remember strangers, friends, looking at her and saying, 'Where on earth did you come from?'

And her father responding, 'Oh, my father is quite tall, almost six-two,' and pictures of the late grandfather she'd never met reflecting that. Or her mother casually tossing off, 'My mother – God rest her soul – had Bea's brown eyes, even though I have blue like my father's.' And that was true too. She'd seen pictures of her maternal grandmother, who died when she was very young. Brown eyes, like Bea's.

It was as though I had given birth to you, and I suppose I wanted to believe it myself. So your father and I made it so.

'Holy crap, you must hate your mother now,' Tommy said around a mouthful of pizza. 'I mean, she lied to you your whole life about something so . . . what's the word?'

'Fundamental,' Bea said through gritted teeth. How dare you suggest I'd ever hate my mother, you oversized blockhead? she wanted to shout. But once again the image of Cora Crane, dying in that hospice bed, her hand holding Bea's with the last of her strength, was all she could think of. Her sweet mother. 'I don't hate her at all. I never could, ever.' Though if Bea let herself go there, as she couldn't help doing the past twenty-four hours, she felt a strange anger that would build in her head and start her heart pounding, then give way to a confusion that made her head spin and her heart just plain hurt. A fundamental truth had been withheld. But she couldn't be mad at her mother; she couldn't bear that. Her mother was gone. 'She explained herself in the letter. And if you knew my mother—'

'Adopted mother.'

She glared at him. 'Actually, it's adop*tive*. But no, she's my *mother*. Just my mother. That she adopted me doesn't change that, Tommy.'

He picked up a second slice and bit into it, gooey mozzarella cheese extending. 'It kind of does, Bea. I mean, someone else gave birth to you.'

Bea sat back, defeated. Someone else had given birth to

her. Someone she hadn't known existed a day ago. Someone she couldn't even conjure up. There was no face, no hair colour, no name. Last night, as her eyes were finally drifting closed at 3 a.m., she had imagined her birth mother to look exactly like herself, just . . . older. But how old? Had her birth mother been a teenager? Or a very poor older woman who couldn't feed an additional mouth?

On 12 October, twenty-two years ago, someone had given birth to Bea and then had given her up for adoption. Why? What was her story? Who was she?

'Yes, Tommy, someone else gave birth to me,' she told him, her appetite gone again. 'But that just makes that person my birth mother.'

'Just? There's no "just" about a birth mother.' He chuckled and dug into his third slice of pizza, looking out the window at the busy Boston street as though Bea was proving to be the one who needed tutoring. He turned back to her. 'Like, what if you're married and have a kid, and that kid is dying of some kind of horrible disease, and your blood and your husband's blood aren't a match? Your birth mother could save your kid's life. Man, that's epic. I mean, think about it.'

But Bea didn't want to. Her parents were Cora and Keith Crane, la, la, la, hands over her ears. Still, the more she sat there, listening to Tommy Wonkowski tell her how she should feel about all this, the more she realized he was actually right about a lot of it.

*

For a week, Bea walked around Boston with the strange truth knocking around in her head. A week ago, she'd been one thing: the daughter of Cora and Keith Crane. End of story. Now, she was something else. Adopted. She'd started as someone else's story. Ended someone's story, maybe. What was that story? She couldn't stop thinking about her birth parents. Who they were. Where she came from. What they looked like. And yes, Tommy Wonkowski, what their medical histories were.

She sat at her desk, her favourite novels, books of essays, a memoir about a teacher's first year and her laptop making her feel stronger, more like herself. She stared at the manila envelope, lying right next to a copy of *To Kill a Mockingbird*, on which she'd written her senior thesis. She was supposed to be an English teacher by now, middle school or high school, teaching teenagers how to write strong essays, how to think critically about novels, why they should love the English language. But when her mother died last summer, Bea found herself floundering for months. She hadn't gotten a single interview for a teaching job at any of the private schools she'd applied to, and the publics all wanted her to be enrolled in a master's programme for teacher education, which would mean more loans. A year later, here she was, not teaching, and still living with students. The only thing different was that she wasn't who she thought she was.

Bea stared at the photo of herself and her mother at her college graduation, willing herself to remember that she was still the same Bea Crane she was last week. Same memories, same mind, same heart, same soul, same dreams.

But she felt different. She felt different in her bones, in her cells, as though they were buzzing with the electricity of the truth. She had been adopted. Another woman, another man, had brought her into this world.

Why did that have to change anything? Why did it matter so much? Why couldn't she just accept the truth and move on from it?

Because you're here alone, for one. Her two good girl-friends had left Boston upon graduation for first jobs. Her best friends from high school were scattered across the country and in Europe; everyone was off on their summer plans, except for Bea, who had nowhere to go, no home.

She felt caged and absolutely free at the same time. So this week she'd stalked around Boston, thinking of her parents with one breath, and this nameless, faceless birth mother with the next. Then she'd come back to her room and stare at the manila envelope until she opened it and read the adoption papers again, which told her nothing.

Maybe if she did know something, just something. Something to make this tenuous grasp on the words 'birth mother' feel more . . . concrete.

'Damn it,' she said, grabbing the envelope and sliding out the papers. Before she could stop herself, she picked up her cell phone and punched in the telephone number on the first page.

'Helping Hands Adoption Agency, may I help you?'

Bea sucked in a breath and explained the situation and that she just wanted to know if there were names. Most likely there would not be. Bea had done some reading and learned that most adoptions were closed, as hers had been according to the paperwork, but that sometimes birth mothers left their names and contact information in the adoption files. There were also registries that birth parents and adoptees could sign up for, to leave their information in case the other side wanted to track them down. Bea would not be signing up for anything.

'Ah. Let me look in your file,' the woman said. 'Hold just a minute.'

Bea held her breath. Make this difficult, Bea thought. No names. She wasn't ready for a name.

Why had she called? When the woman came back, Bea would tell her thank you for checking but she'd changed her mind, she wasn't ready, wasn't ready to know anything about her birth parents.

'Bingo,' the woman said. 'Your birth mother called to update the file at her last address change, just over a year ago. Her name is Veronica Russo and she lives in Boothbay Harbor, Maine.'

Bea couldn't breathe.

'Do you need a minute?' the woman was saying. 'I'll give you a minute, no worries.' She did indeed wait a minute, and Bea's head was close to bursting when the woman said, 'Honey, do you have a pen?'

Bea said she did. She picked up the silver Waterman that her mother had given her as a graduation present. She mechanically wrote down the address and telephone number the woman gave her. Home and cell.

'She even included her employment address and phone number,' the woman continued. 'The Best Little Diner in Boothbay.'

Veronica Russo. Her birth mother had a name. She was a real person, living and breathing, and she'd updated the file. She'd left every possible piece of contact information.

Her birth mother wanted to be found.

Bea thanked the woman and hung up. She shivered and grabbed her favourite sweater, her father's old off-white fisherman's sweater that her mother had bought him while they were on their honeymoon in Ireland. It was the one her father wore in her favourite picture, with Bea up on his shoulders. She put it on and hugged herself, wishing it smelled like her dad, like Ivory Soap and Old Spice and safety, but her dad had been gone since Bea was nine. A long time. For the next eleven years, it was just Bea and her mom, both sets of grandparents long gone, both Cranes only-children.

And then Bea lost her mother. She was alone.

She walked to the window seat and stared out at the rain sluicing down. I have a birth mother. Her name is Veronica Russo. She lives in a place called Boothbay Harbor, Maine.

She works in a diner called The Best Little Diner in Boothbay.

Which had a cute ring. A woman who worked in a diner like that couldn't be so bad, right? She was probably a waitress, one of those friendly types who called her customers 'hon'. Or maybe she'd fallen on hard times and was hardbitten, a shell of a woman who set down eggs over easy and fish and chips with a depressive thud.

Maybe she was a short-order cook. That might explain Bea's ability to make an incredible hamburger, not that she could cook anything here in her kitchenless room. This past year, between her jobs at Crazy Burger and the Writing Centre, she had enough money to pay her rent. But now she'd come up short for July, and the Writing Centre was open only part-time for the summer sessions. Her last lousy paycheck, a half-week's pay from Crazy Burger, wouldn't help much either.

She had nowhere to be, nowhere to go. But she had this name, and an address.

Bea could take a drive up to Maine, make herself walk into The Best Little Diner, sit at the counter and order a cup of coffee and look at the name tags on the waitresses' aprons. She would be able to check out her birth mother from a very close distance. She could do that.

Yes. She would drive up, check out Veronica Russo and, if it seemed right, she would introduce herself. Not that she had any idea how to go about that. Maybe she'd leave a note in her mailbox, or just call. Then they'd meet somewhere, for a walk or coffee. Bea would find out what she needed to know so she could stop wondering, speculating, driving herself crazy. Then she'd say thank you to Veronica Russo for the information and drive back home to Boston and start looking for a new place to live. And a new job. Maybe she had to let go of her dream of being a teacher. She'd come home once her past had been settled, and she'd figure out what the hell she was supposed to be doing with her future.

Home. As if there were one. This room was nothing more than a big closet. And her mother's rental cottage in Cape Cod, where she and her mom had moved after her father died, had long ago been sold by the owner. But that little white cottage had been the one place left on earth that had felt like home at Thanksgiving, Christmas, summer breaks, at times when Bea was stressed or heartbroken or just needed her mama.

Now there were just memories, and this old fisherman's sweater. And a stranger named Veronica Russo, up in Maine. Waiting a long time to be found by Bea.

Chapter 2
Veronica Russo

Only an idiot would attempt to make a pie – a special-ordered chocolate-caramel cream Amore Pie – while watching *Pride and Prejudice*. Had she put in the vanilla? What about the salt? Damn Colin Firth and his pond-soaked white shirt. Veronica set down her measuring spoons on the flour-dusted counter and gave her full attention to the small TV next to the coffee maker. God, she loved Colin Firth. Not just because he was so handsome, either. This TV mini-series was at least fifteen years old, and Colin Firth had to be fifty now. He was still gorgeous. But it was more than that. Colin Firth was six feet two inches of hope. To Veronica, he represented what she'd been looking for her entire life and had never found and probably never would, at this point. Veronica was thirty-eight years old. Still not married.

'If you wanted love, really wanted love, you'd have it,' friends, even boyfriends, had said many times over the years. 'There's something wrong with you,' her last beau had said before he'd stormed out on her for not agreeing to marry him. 'Something wrong with the way your heart works.'

Maybe there was. No, Veronica knew it was true. And she knew why too. But now, at thirty-eight, friends were worrying about her ending up all alone, so she'd started saying what felt light-hearted but true at the same time: that she was holding out for a man who felt like Colin Firth to her. Her friend Shelley from the diner had known exactly what she meant. 'I realize he's an actor playing roles, but I get it,' Shelley had said. 'Honest. Full of integrity. Conviction. Brimming with intelligence. Loyal. You just believe everything he says with that British accent of his – and can trust it.'

All that and yes, he was so damned handsome that Veronica had lost track of her own Amore Pie, a pie she could make in her sleep. Her special elixir pies were in high demand ever since she'd been back in Boothbay Harbor – just over a year now. She'd grown up in Boothbay, but had bought a house far from the one she'd lived in with her parents. It had been love at first sight for the lemon-yellow bungalow on Sea Road, and the day she'd moved in, while hanging the wooden blinds on the sliding glass door to her deck, she'd heard someone crying. She'd peered her head out the door to see her neighbour sitting on her back porch, wearing only a black négligé and black leather stilettos. Veronica had gone over and asked if she could help, and the woman blurted out that her marriage was over. Veronica had sat down, and within moments her neighbour, whose name was Frieda, had shared the whole story, how she'd tried to entice her husband, who barely looked at her these days, home for lunch with exactly what she was going to do to him. But he'd said he'd brought last night's leftovers and would just have that.

'He'd rather have a cold meat-loaf sandwich than me?' Frieda had cried to Veronica. 'For months I've been trying to entice him back to me, and nothing works.' She broke down in a fresh round of tears.

Veronica had told Frieda that she was a baker and would make her up a special pie to serve her husband for dessert that night. When she gave him his slice, she was to think about how much she loved him, wanted him. And just for good measure, she could run her hands up the back of his neck.

Well, that night, Frederick Mulverson had said he didn't know what came over him, but he was back. Frieda had Veronica's Amore Pie on standing order every Friday. One word to her friends and relatives, and Veronica's phone had started ringing with orders, just as it had in New Mexico. Amore Pies were her most requested.

She made upwards of twenty special pies a week. Plus two a day for The Best Little Diner in Boothbay, where she worked as a waitress. And nine a week for three local inns. But those — for the diner and the inns — were just her 'happiness' pies, pies that tasted like summer vacation. She saved her special elixir pies for her clients around town, everything from Feel-Better Pie – which came in all kinds of dietetic-friendly varieties, such as gluten-free, dairy-free and even sugar-free – to Confidence Pie, which involved Key limes.

What she couldn't seem to do was make a Colin Firth Pie for herself. She'd made Amore Pies for hundreds of clients that seemed to attract love to them. Sure, maybe it was mostly the power of thought, but so what since it worked? 'You get what you believe' was what Veronica's grandmother used to say. At the thought of dear Renata Russo, who'd died just months before all the trouble had started when Veronica was sixteen, she closed her eyes. She let herself remember what it was like when she'd had a family, when Veronica, her parents and her grandmother would sit around the table in the house she grew up in – just several miles away from here – and have big Italian dinners. Meatballs and so much linguini in her grandmother's home-made tomato sauce that it seemed to come from bottomless pots.

She missed those days, days that had ended on an April morning when Veronica was sixteen and blurted out over a pancake breakfast that she was pregnant. She'd finally taken a pregnancy test after her period was two weeks late. Please be negative, please be negative, she'd silently prayed as she'd waited the two minutes. But when she opened her eyes and looked at the little window on the stick, the pink plus sign had been unmistakable. Positive. Her hand had been trembling so badly she'd barely been able to hold the stick steady.

She'd been so scared that she'd kept the news to herself for almost two weeks. After that, everything had changed. One minute she'd had a family – minus her beloved grandmother. The next, Veronica had been sent away.

Why are you upsetting yourself by thinking about all that? she asked herself as she turned her attention back to the TV and the Bennet sisters, Elizabeth and Jane, conspiring in their lovely white dresses about their love lives. But since she'd moved back to Boothbay Harbor, her past was all she could think about. It was why she'd come home, for heaven's sake. To face it. To stop . . . running.

She thought if she came home, if she faced her past, maybe her heart would start working the way it was supposed to. And maybe, maybe, maybe, the daughter she'd given up for adoption would contact her. Veronica had been living in New Mexico when that baby girl had turned eighteen, and Veronica had called the Helping Hands Adoption Agency and left her contact information, then done the same with the registry in Maine. She'd waited by the phone that day. And the next. But there was no call from a young woman asking if she was Veronica Russo, if she'd given birth to a baby girl on 12 October 1991 in Boothbay Harbor, Maine. For weeks afterwards Veronica had kept her cell phone close, expecting a call any time. She wasn't sure why she'd believed her daughter would contact her on her eighteenth birthday, but she had believed it.

She'd started baking then, four years ago in New Mexico,

pies that felt like hope. She'd never been much of a baker before, but she'd been watching a cooking show, a special on holiday pies, and had gone out and bought ingredients to make a pie from scratch. She loved the feel of flour in her fingers, the pale yellow sticks of cold butter, the texture of shortening, the whiteness of sugar and salt, the purity of water. Such simple ingredients for a pie crust, not that there was anything simple about making pie crust from scratch. But Veronica had persisted until she'd perfected her crusts — all kinds, depending on the pie. Just like that, she'd found what comforted her, what replaced lonely nights. She loved baking pies. And her pies felt so special to her that when she made them for friends, she'd name them for the reason she was sharing them in the first place. For a heartbroken friend, Healing Pie. For a sick friend, Feel-Better Pie. For a down-in-the-dumps friend, a Happiness Pie. For the lovelorn, Amore Pie. For the worried, Confidence Pie. Her Hope Pies were popular too. One friend had wished that her boyfriend, on his second tour of combat duty, would come home from Afghanistan in one piece, and Veronica had baked her a salted-caramel cheesecake pie that she put all her hope into and then told her friend to do the same while cutting the first slice. The boyfriend had returned with only a broken leg. Her pies had worked their sweet magic on so many people that Veronica had developed quite a clientele. How did it work, they wanted to know. Either Veronica had a little bit of magic in her or it was all about prayer. Or luck. Maybe some of each.

But Veronica had never bothered with a Colin Firth Pie in the hopes of bringing a man into her life whom she could finally love. All the magical pies in the world couldn't fix her messed-up heart. She wasn't capable of loving someone; kind as she was to others, she knew that. She'd loved once, so fiercely, and had been irreparably hurt. By her grandmother's death. By a sixteen-year-old boy. By her parents washing their hands of her. She'd tried to love; she'd tried damned hard. She'd had her share of boyfriends over the years. Some for a couple of years, some for just a few months — all kinds of men. From the cute short-order cook at the first diner that had hired her as a sixteen-year-old waitress in Florida, where she'd moved after giving birth, to the proud Marine in New Mexico who'd announced he was tired of waiting for her to say yes, he was driving them to Las Vegas to get married that day whether she liked it or not. She'd tried to explain again, said they could have a wonderful, romantic weekend in Vegas without a wedding, without talk of marriage, but he'd figured she'd cave once they got to the wedding chapel. She hadn't. Furious and shouting that he'd had it with her and her inability to commit to him, he'd left her there by the chapel and driven away, and she never saw him again. By the time she'd returned to New Mexico the next day, his few belongings were gone from the house he practically shared with her. Her heart had just never opened fully to him. It never had for anyone except Timothy Macintosh, a boy she'd spent the past twenty-two years trying not to think about.

It had been there, in front of the Little White Wedding Chapel, that Veronica had realized she had to go back to Boothbay Harbor. If she ever wanted to fix herself, she'd have to go back. Back to her home town, where she'd been shunned and sent away, where she had given birth to a baby girl she'd held for two minutes and then had to hand over. She believed if she came back, faced all those memories, her Hope Pie might work on herself and her heart would suddenly open and that baby girl would make contact.

Veronica just wanted to know that the daughter she'd given up was all right. That was all. Sometimes Veronica thought if she could just know that, she could move on. Her jagged heart would piece together, and her life would change. Could change, anyway.

So she'd come home, uncomfortable as it had been. Come home and tried to face her demons right away. Before she'd even started looking for a house to buy in town, she'd driven by the house she'd grown up in, a white saltbox that the new owners had painted blue. She'd pulled over and felt sick to her stomach and got away from there fast. But she'd driven by several times, and each time she'd had less of a reaction. Same for the place the Macintosh family had lived in, the brick cape house where she and Timothy had spent so much time. She'd even walked in the woods where she and he had set up her old Girl Scouts tent, where they'd talk for hours about their dreams, about leaving Maine right after high school and taking a Greyhound bus to Florida, where it was always warm and never snowed. That old tent was where a child had been conceived.

She'd tried to face her past, but she was obviously doing something wrong — not facing the right things, maybe — because she felt as unsettled in Boothbay Harbor as she had the day she'd moved back a year ago. She didn't even know why. No one cared about what had happened twenty-two years ago, except several folks who did remember her as the girl who'd gotten pregnant as a junior in high school, whose parents were so embarrassed they'd sent her away, sold their house and left town, left the state, leaving her behind to fend for herself. Two of those people who did remember had unfortunately signed up for Veronica's pie-making class tomorrow night — Penelope Von Blun and CeCe Allwood, who'd gone to school with her and now led perfect lives and fake-smiled at Veronica in town before whispering behind her back. Veronica's pie classes were popular; she'd taught four so far, but she limited the class to five students so that she could give individual attention to each baker. Ironic, since she'd spent most of the past year trying not to pay any attention to Penelope and CeCe.

Fitzwilliam Darcy's face filled the TV screen. 'My affections and wishes are unchanged, but one word from you will silence me on this subject for ever,' he was saying to Elizabeth, and Veronica felt something move in her chest the way she always did at this scene. God, he was intense. Intense with fierce love.

The doorbell rang, and Veronica pulled herself away from the kiss she'd been waiting the entire episode for. She wiped her flour-dusted hands on her apron, took one last glance at the TV, and went to the front door.

Officer Nick DeMarco and his daughter, whom Veronica would guess to be about nine, maybe ten. Veronica always thought of him as Officer DeMarco, even though they'd gone to school together their whole lives. Well, until junior year, anyway. He'd been friendly with Timothy. So Veronica had kept her distance from Nick, who seemed to keep something of a distance from her, as well. He was out of his police blues, wearing jeans and a Boston Red Sox T-shirt. His daughter looked just like him. Same dark hair burnished with lighter brown, and dark brown eyes with long, long lashes. She had an elfin chin, though, and there was nothing elfin about Nick DeMarco.

'We're not late, are we?' Nick asked, peering in behind her. His daughter looked up at her expectantly.

'Late for what?' Veronica asked.

'The pie class,' he said.

Pie class? Nick DeMarco had definitely not registered for her class. If he had, even staring at Colin Firth for two hours the past four nights would not let her forget it. 'Well, actually, you're early. My pie class starts Monday night. Right time, wrong day. But I don't have you on my registration list, do I?'

He winced. 'I had your flyer in my back pocket for a week

and kept meaning to call, and then I figured we'd just show up.'

The girl looked like she was about to cry. 'We can still take your class, right?' she asked Veronica.

Oh hell. The class was full. She had six people already and really did prefer to limit each four-week session to five students. Otherwise, there wasn't enough of Veronica to go around and the class got too unwieldy. Too many elbows at the counters and table.

Officer DeMarco was staring at her, pleading with her to say, 'Yes, of course you can take my class, sweet girl.'

'I happen to have a few slots open, so not a problem at all,' she said to his daughter.

She watched the girl relax and wondered why learning to make pie — and perhaps one of Veronica's special pies — was so important to her.

'What's your name, honey?' Veronica asked.

'Leigh. Leigh DeMarco. I'm ten.'

'Well, Leigh, you just turn up with your dad on Monday at six o'clock sharp, and don't forget to bring an apron.' One look from Nick told her that he didn't have an apron. 'But if you don't have one or forget, I just so happen to have extras.'

Leigh smiled and her whole face lit up.

'Is there a particular kind of pie you're interested in making?' Veronica asked Leigh. 'I'm planning on teaching apple pie for the first class, but I'll have recipes for my special elixir pies available if anyone wants to work on one of those too.'

The girl glanced sideways at her father, then at the ground. 'Apple pie is fine. I had a slice at the diner last week. It was really good.' It was obvious the girl had her mind set on a particular special pie but didn't want to say in front of her father.

'Ah, yes, my apple crumb Happiness Pie,' Veronica said.

'I did feel happy when I was eating it,' Leigh said, but her shoulders slumped.

Nick ruffled Leigh's hair. 'Well, we won't take up more of your time, Veronica. Sorry about the mix-up. We'll see you Monday at six, then.'

He looked so uncomfortable that Veronica felt sorry for him. She was pretty good at reading people; it was how she had earned her reputation with her pies. But Nick DeMarco was impenetrable beyond the obvious desire to leave. A cop requirement, most likely.

Just as Veronica turned the lock, the doorbell rang again.

This time, only Leigh DeMarco stood on the porch. Her father stood on the sidewalk. He held up a hand and Veronica nodded at him.

'Hi, hon,' she said to Leigh.

'I remembered what kind of special pie I want to learn to make,' Leigh whispered. 'But I want to keep it secret, if that's okay.'

'That's okay.'

Leigh bit her lip and turned around, as if to make sure her father was out of hearing distance. 'I want to make the kind of pie you made for Mrs Buckman. She's my neighbour. She invited me in for a snack after school last week and gave me a slice of the pie. She told me you made it for her special. She said it would make me feel better too.'

Veronica's heart squeezed. The pie she'd made for Annabeth Buckman was a Spirit Pie, a shoo-fly pie, the only kind that seemed to work for Veronica when she wanted to feel close to her grandmother. Shoo-fly pie was nothing special, just molasses and a crumbly brown-sugar topping, and rarely seen these days, but Veronica loved it. Her grandmother had grown up making shoo-fly pie during her family's poorest times, and Renata Russo had said she'd be happy never to make a shoo-fly pie again as long as she lived and had access to fruit and good chocolate and other delectable ingredients. But one day, in those early weeks when Veronica had moved back to Boothbay Harbor and was so lonesome for her grandmother, she'd made a shoo-fly pie for the first time, and at the smell of the thick molasses and the crumb topping with its brown sugar, it was like her grandmother was in the room. She felt her so close, felt her love, felt everything she'd say to Veronica now. God, how different life would have been had her grandmother been alive when Veronica had gotten pregnant. She would have kept the baby, most likely, instead of having to give her up for adoption. Her grandmother would have taken her in.

Focus on Leigh, she told herself, sucking in a quick breath. 'I know just the pie you mean, Leigh. It's my Spirit Pie – a shoo-fly pie. When you make it or eat it, you think about the person you want to feel close to. That's how it works. Shoo-fly pie got its name long ago because it was so sweet that it attracted flies while it cooled. So the bakers would say, "Shoo, fly!" And it stuck.'

'Shoo-fly pie,' Leigh repeated. Then she nodded and turned to leave, then turned back again, and said, 'Thank you.'

Her mother, Veronica realized. Leigh must want to feel her mother's presence. Veronica had heard that Nick DeMarco's wife had died in a boating accident almost two years ago.

Oh, Leigh, Veronica thought, watching her slip her hand into her father's as they started up Sea Road.

It would be no trouble at all to add the sweet girl to her class. Her father probably wouldn't last past the first session. They were likely 'doing something together', and then he'd drop off Leigh at the next class and she wouldn't have to be at such close quarters, like her kitchen, with Nick DeMarco, who clearly remembered her from school and knew she'd gotten pregnant and then mysteriously disappeared. Back then everyone had known she'd been sent to Hope Home, a residence for pregnant teenagers on the outskirts of town. The few friends she'd had had told her that everyone was talking about it and how Timothy Macintosh was telling people he wasn't the father, that Veronica had slept around on him.

How did that still have the power to sting in the centre

of her chest? she wondered as she turned up the volume on the TV. Forget everything but *Pride and Prejudice* and Colin Firth's face, she told herself. After all, she had an Amore Pie to make, and she had to be in a certain frame of mind to make that pie. She'd finish watching *Pride and Prejudice*, ogle Colin Firth, and then she'd get to work.

Chapter 3
Gemma Hendricks

Ever since Gemma had seen the pink plus sign on her home pregnancy test two days ago, she'd been in a full-blown panic. She'd kept the news to herself. The second she told Alexander, he'd grab her up in a crushing hug, swing her around the room, then call his family, order celebratory cigars by the truckload and set the plan in motion that would slowly suck the life out of her.

Gemma had lost her job last month — a job she'd loved so much that she still got teary before she went to sleep every night — and she knew that Alexander, an assistant prosecutor, would use all his considerable skill to make his argument, the argument he'd been making for almost a year now: they should get started on the three children he wanted, move to the same Westchester County town as his parents and his brother's family, preferably equidistant between their two

33

homes, and Gemma would be a stay-at-home mom, hosting play dates. 'We're *twenty-nine*,' Alexander constantly said. 'Married five years.' Then he'd stare at her, an equal measure of love and curiosity shining in his eyes, and say, 'I wonder if our little girl will inherit your honey-coloured hair. God, I hope so,' he'd add, reaching out to touch the end of her ponytail and caress her cheek. 'My beautiful Gemma.'

In those moments, she'd relax and hug him fiercely, a bit caught up herself in the very distant future. The distant future, with its vague, 'one day' quality, was fine. But then Alexander would playfully tug her hand towards the bedroom and say, 'Let's go create that baby right now,' and the here and now would splash cold water all over her.

Gemma gripped the railing of their apartment balcony, high above the streets of Manhattan on the eighteenth floor. A minute ago, she'd been okay. She'd been sitting on her bed with her laptop, making final arrangements with her friend June about what time she'd arrive in Maine tonight for their mutual friend's wedding tomorrow. Then ping, ping, ping. Seven emails from Alexander's mother. House listings in Dobbs Ferry, each annotated with Mona Hendricks' thoughts and feelings on every room, paint choices, landscaping, and a bit about the neighbours —since Mona had made it her business to scope them out in advance.

Good God. She'd been fine until that moment. Just knowing she was about to get in a car and drive to Maine for a girls' weekend, a weekend away from all pressure, Gemma had managed to calm herself, the panic abating a bit. Then the emails came from Mona, with a vision of the life Alexander would try to force her into, and she had escaped to the balcony to gulp in air.

Oh no. Now the Bessells, who lived in the apartment next door, had come out on to their terrace with their infant, Jakey. Jakey-Wakey this, Jakey-Wakey that. Gemma heard the Bessells cooing at their baby all night long. 'Jakey-Wakey needs his dipey-wipey changed!' Even at three in the morning, the Bessells always seemed thrilled to be awake and dealing with poop.

Lydia Bessell held up Jakey, clad only in a diaper, blowing raspberries on the baby's bare belly as John Bessell pretend-nibbled one tiny foot. Jacob gurgled his delight.

She full-out stared at them, trying to imagine herself with a baby, but she couldn't. She was meant to be a reporter, writing award-winning articles about life in a Brooklyn housing project, or about the effect of Hurricane Sandy on families on a particular block in Far Rockaway. She was supposed to be out there, getting the who, what, where and why, and writing articles that generated hundreds of letters and comments. She was a reporter, had been a reporter from the moment she'd stepped into the school newspaper office as a high-school freshman. It was all she'd ever wanted to do, find the truth, share people's feelings, let readers know what was really happening out there from a personal perspective. But all her hard work, all the paying of dues, all the promotions, the writing around the clock to make insane deadlines – all that came down to being called into her boss's office last week at *New York Weekly*, a long-running, respected alternative newspaper where a byline meant something. She'd been let go. Let go with 'I'm so sorry, Gem, I fought for you, but times are tough, and upstairs said anyone who'd been on staff less than five years had to be first to go in this round of lay-offs. Someone will snap you up fast, Gemma. You're the best.'

Right. The best. The best wouldn't be let go, though, right? Alexander, to his credit, insisted 'the best' had nothing to do with 'upstairs' and their nutty decisions. Policy was stupid policy and he'd assured her any of the papers in the city would grab her. Except they hadn't. 'Not hiring, sorry' was the refrain she'd heard from all the newspapers, magazines and TV stations to whom she'd sent her résumé. But then he'd started saying that getting laid off was a blessing in disguise, that it was time to start a family, to move on to the next stage of their lives.

She wasn't even sure which had been more shocking – losing her job at *New York Weekly* or seeing the pink plus sign. How had this happened? Gemma had taken her birth-control pills like clockwork, at exactly seven every morning. Six weeks ago she'd been prescribed an antibiotic for bronchitis, and when her doctor told her that antibiotics lessened the efficacy of birth-control pills, she'd made Alexander use condoms, which elicited a deep sigh from her husband.

And now she was pregnant. One stupid condom that had torn. Whammo.

She wouldn't tell Alexander until she came up with a solid plan to present to him, one strong enough that she could refute any argument of his. For two days she'd been working on it. They'd stay in the city. They would not move to Westchester — let alone the same town as the overbearing Hendrickses. She'd send out a fresh batch of résumés to her second-choice news outlets. She'd find a great new job, work until the day before her due date, have the baby then go back to work when it was three months old, a great daycare or full-time nanny long arranged. She and Alexander would draw up a schedule of who would take days off work for baby illnesses and paediatrician appointments. For the past two days, when Gemma thought about it this way, she could at least breathe a bit easier, even if the part about the baby scared her to death. She had no idea how to be a mother, how to want to be a mother, how to want any part of motherhood.

But there was no way Alexander would say yes to any of her plan. For months now, all he'd talked about was wanting a completely different life: a baby; a house in the suburbs; a safe, sturdy car like a Subaru instead of their snazzy little Miata. According to Alexander Hendricks, they could be on their second child by now, like his brother, who had a two-year-old and another on the way. Alexander was sick to death of New York City — the crowds, the noise, the car alarms, the crazy cab drivers, the subways. For the past six months he'd been reminding her, as gently as his excellent litigation skills would allow, that there were two of them in this marriage, that marriage was about give-and-take. Then she'd say the same back to him, and he'd sigh, but hug her tight and suggest a movie or going out for Thai food, their stalemate forgotten for a day or two. But just a day or two. Alexander wanted a baby.

She glanced at her neighbour on her terrace, still blowing raspberries on little Jakey's belly. But suddenly Jakey's expression changed and his face got kind of red. Lydia laid him down on the padded chaise longue and started moving his legs in bicycle formation. The baby stopped fussing.

How does she know what to do? Gemma wondered. Maybe it was as easy as Lydia always made it look. Maybe motherhood was about instinct.

But Gemma didn't have any maternal instincts. And Lydia Bessell was no help in Gemma's plan. The woman was a former Wall Street investment banker who wasn't planning on going back to work; the Bessells had already found their dream home in Tarrytown and were moving at summer's end. 'See,' Alexander would tell Gemma, since he knew she generally liked and respected Lydia. 'Even Lydia gave up her three-hundred-thousand-dollar salary to be a stay-at-home mom in the 'burbs. It's the dream life, Gemma.'

Once Alexander knew she was pregnant, he'd take over. She'd always loved his take-charge, responsible ways. But now, she couldn't even imagine how bad it would get. The hovering, the nagging, the constant calls. Did you, are you sure you, don't forget to . . . The campaign for the life he wanted. Case closed.

'Gem, if you want to get to Maine before dark, you need to hit the road,' Alexander called from his home office. 'It's past one.'

She absolutely did need to hit the road. Alone in a car for seven blessed hours. Heaven. She could think, formulate her plan, her arguments. She could figure out how she felt about being pregnant in the first place. Right now, all she had was one emotion: panic.

As Gemma turned to go back inside, her neighbour's mother, who came over practically every day, appeared on the terrace. She bee-lined for the baby, scooping him up carefully in her arms and making more baby talk at him. Gemma's heart squeezed as it always did; she couldn't imagine ever sharing such a moment with her own mother, who was cold and kept to herself. Even Alexander, who'd met some of the shadiest characters in his work as an assistant prosecutor for the state of New York, was taken aback by Gemma's mother's lack of warmth and social skills.

She went back inside the apartment and over to Alexander's makeshift office that he'd created and hated, two pressurized walls that reminded him on a daily basis he didn't have enough room and had to resort to fake walls. He was staring at his computer screen. For a moment she was startled, as she sometimes was when she looked at her husband, at how good-looking he was – tall and muscular, with all that sandy blond hair and intelligent dark brown eyes that missed nothing.

She'd loved his overbearing ways when she'd first met him, loved how his family welcomed her as though they were already married on their third date, when Alexander had brought her over to meet the loud, opinionated Hendrickses. Unused to a happy, boisterous clan, she'd adored them all. During the first month they'd been dating, his mother had called her for her opinion on everything from what colour shoes to wear with a brown dress to what she and Alex's father should get him for this birthday. Gemma loved being drawn in by the Hendrickses, loved every minute of how vocal they were with their thoughts and opinions and family get-togethers during the week for no reason at all. Her own family life had been so lonely. Her mother was a French professor who spoke French most of the time at home despite Gemma and her sister never quite picking it up, mostly because of how stilted conversations were with their mother, and how few and far between. Her mother wasn't one to feign enthusiasm over badly made papier-mâché self-portraits, leaving seven-year-old Gemma standing crestfallen in the hallway with her art project, her mother having moved on to make a phone call. Her father, more loving and attuned to children, was a businessman who travelled during the week. When her parents divorced when Gemma was eleven, she was almost relieved, thinking the dead silences would end, that both parents would suddenly become warm and loving in their separate homes. But that hadn't been the case.

So yes, Gemma had been crazy about the warm, tell-me-your-every-thought Hendrickses. But a few years into their five-year marriage, it all got to be too much, and they wanted her to change, become more like them. When she and Alexander argued, sometimes he'd strike below the belt with what he knew would help sway her to his side: 'You're acting like your mother, Gem.'

She'd been so in love with him once – and she still loved him – but she was grateful to be getting away this weekend. The timing, at least on this, couldn't be better. Maybe a weekend apart would make him miss her, make him see her again as a separate person who had her own ideas, her own opinions, her own dream life that didn't include moving to Westchester and being a stay-at-home mother.

That panicky feeling returned, and Gemma reminded herself that in about seven hours, if traffic wasn't too bad, she'd be in Boothbay Harbor, sitting on that beautiful white wooden swing on the porch of the Three Captains' Inn with June, and her smart, insightful friend would help her talk through this. Thank God for girlfriends who owned beautiful old inns in Maine.

'I'm all set to go,' she told him, eyeing his computer screen. Real-estate listings.

'You look so tired,' he said, studying her, standing up and moving a tendril of hair behind her ears.

'Just worried about not being able to find a job – a job I really want. It's been keeping me up at night.'

He hugged her. 'Everything's going to be fine, Gem. You know why?' He glanced at her, as if bracing for her reaction. 'I put in an offer on a house in Dobbs Ferry. It's practically next door to my—'

Steam circled in her ears. 'Wait a minute. What? You made an offer on a house? When you know I don't want to leave the city?'

'I know you don't. I know, I know, I know. But Gemma, something's got to change, and you're being really stubborn about this.' He held out the print-outs. 'This house is perfect for us and I didn't want to lose a shot at it. It's practically next door to my parents – that means when we have a baby, my mom can help out at a moment's notice. It's walkable to downtown. There are a few regional newspapers you can apply to for part-time work on, if you really insist on working. It's a good commute for me into the city. Just look at it, okay?'

Part-time work. If I *insist on working*. A shot of anger hit her in the gut. 'You shouldn't have made an offer without talking to me, Alex.'

'We've been talking for months now. Nothing ever changes. So we're just going to stay here because it's what you want? What about what I want?' He let out a frustrated breath. 'I don't want to argue before you leave, Gem. Just take the listing and information with you,' he said, handing her a sheaf of papers. 'Just promise to look at them, okay?'

Fury gripped her. How dare he? 'Promise me right now that you won't buy the house if your offer is accepted. Promise me, Alexander.'

'I'll promise that if you promise to look – really look – at the information.'

Let it go for now, she told herself. Just get in the car and drive away. But before she could even think it through, she blurted out, 'Alex, I think I'm going to stay up in Maine for the week instead of just the weekend. I think it'll do me some good.'

He stared at her, then his expression softened. 'Actually I think that's a good idea. All that fresh air, the beautiful cottages, the water. I think you'll see life in a small town is pretty great.'

That wasn't what she'd meant at all. She glanced at her watch. 'Like you said, I'd better hit the road if I want to get to Maine before dark.'

He gave her that look, the look that said they weren't done talking about this, but they'd both been over this so many times that there was little left to say. Alexander had gotten the thing he needed to tip the scales in his favour: she'd gotten laid off and couldn't find another job. The pregnancy would send the scale plummeting down on his side. In a flash, she'd be in that house in Dobbs Ferry, her mother-in-law breathing down her neck, Alexander making her to-do lists and creating feeding and napping schedules. Gemma pictured herself nine months pregnant, asking herself what the hell had happened to her life.

She got her suitcase, already packed, from the bedroom, wondering if she had to think about how heavy it was. She wouldn't drink at the wedding reception, of course. There were probably a hundred other little things she needed to know about how to live as a pregnant person. Foods she couldn't eat, like brie and runny eggs, she was pretty sure.

But this was Alexander Hendricks, who'd taken the morning away from work to see her off, so, upset with her or not, of course he carried her suitcase down to the garage of their building and put it in the trunk of their car. Then he hugged her goodbye.

'Please look at the listing,' he told her. 'Okay? I love you, Gemma.' He cupped her face between his hands. 'I love you so much. I hate all this tension between us.' He tipped up her chin and kissed her sweetly and gently on the lips.

'Me too,' she said.

Only when she was on I-95 did she finally exhale.

The moment Gemma arrived in Boothbay Harbor, she relaxed. She hadn't been here in years, but she knew this place; it was inside her. From the age of eleven, she'd spent a month every summer here with her father after her parents' inevitable divorce, running up and down the docks with her friends, getting crushes on boys, living for tans and new-wave music.

She'd always felt like a different person in Boothbay Harbor — carefree, light-hearted, happy, instead of tiptoeing around her mother back home on the Upper West Side of Manhattan, walking on eggshells for fear of saying something her mother would deem stupid. Here in this picture-postcard-perfect summer town, where you wore flip-flops all summer and your biggest dilemma was what kind of ice cream to choose, Gemma had always felt most herself. She'd even charmed the *Boothbay Regional Gazette* editor into allowing her a kid's column for the summers, polling people on the best fish and chips, who had the best ice cream, favourite places to jump in the bay. Gemma smiled as she drove slowly through downtown, crowded with tourists, the harbour and the boats glittering just beyond. Yes, she could think here. She could never live in Boothbay Harbor year-round — she loved New York City with its grit and beauty and eight million stories — but she was very relieved to be here now.

Gemma lowered her car windows and breathed in the scent of summer, of the Atlantic, of nature. The bay shimmered in the late-June sun as she drove up Main Street with its one-of-a-kind shops, then turned on to Harbour Hill Road. The Three Captains' Inn came into view on its perch, two winding streets above the harbour. Gemma loved the inn, a robin's-egg-blue Victorian house with white trim and a white porch swing, pots of flowers blooming everywhere.

She pulled up in the small parking lot beside the inn, her gaze on the woman on the porch swing. She held a baby on her lap and was rocking gently. A guest maybe. As Gemma carried her suitcase up the three steps the woman stood up, put the baby in a bouncy chair on the porch, then slipped on a Baby Bjorn and had the infant inside in under ten seconds. Gemma felt the usual rise of panic at how easily mothers seemed to do these things. There was so much to learn, so much to know.

The woman was smiling at her. 'Gemma, right? I'm Isabel, June's sister.'

Isabel, of course. Gemma had met the Nash sisters when she was eleven, the first summer she'd come to Boothbay Harbor with her dad. She and June Nash were the same age and had hit it off immediately, but Isabel was three years older and in a different orbit. 'Isabel! Wow, you look fabulous. I've been in my own world and completely forgot that June said you'd gotten remarried and had a baby. Congratulations.'

'Thanks. Her name's Allie. C'mon in and I'll get you settled. I manage the Three Captains'. June said she'd be by at seven to whisk you away for dinner.'

Gemma followed Isabel inside the inn, past an antiques-filled foyer and into Isabel's office, unable to take her eyes off the baby. She was so beautiful, with lots of dark hair, blue eyes and tiny bow lips. Gemma tried to imagine herself multi-tasking with a baby on her hip. She couldn't see it. 'I'm a little early.'

'No problem. We're happy to have you at the Three

Captains'. You'll be in the Lighthouse Room, on the third floor. It's a single and small, but cosy, with views of beautiful old trees. And like I tell all my guests, don't worry about hearing a baby cry in the middle of the night. I don't live at the inn, but we're very close by in town if there are any problems.'

Gemma followed Isabel up the staircase to the third floor, which held two guest rooms and a full bathroom, since the Lighthouse Room didn't have a private bath. The room was just as Isabel had said, small but cosy. It held a full-size bed with a pretty scrolled headboard, a small antique bureau with an oval mirror above it, a round braided rug on the wide-planked wooden floor, and a painting of the Portland Head lighthouse on the rocky cliffs of Maine. The one window looked out on the big back yard, trees as far as Gemma could see. Yes, she would be able to think here. It was perfect.

Isabel stopped by the door. 'Oh, before I leave you to get settled, I wanted to let you know that we're officially starting up an old Three Captains' Inn Friday-night tradition – Movie Night.'

Gemma was glad to hear that. Two years ago, when June and Isabel's Aunt Lolly, who'd left them the inn, had passed away from cancer, the sisters had put a hold on Movie Night, a weekly tradition at the Three Captains'. Every month they changed the theme. Romantic comedy. Food. Foreign. Meryl Streep. John Hughes. *Dirty Harry*, which always attracted the male guests, who usually passed on Movie Night. Gemma and Alexander had flown up for Lolly's funeral, but both had had to get back to work and Gemma hadn't been able to spend much time with June.

Isabel shifted baby Allie to her hip and leaned close to whisper: 'It's Colin Firth month, in honour of him coming to Boothbay Harbor to film scenes for his new movie. Three members of a Colin Firth fan club are in the room across from you, so hit the parlour a bit before nine to get a comfy seat. We're starting with Bridget Jones's Diary.'

Gemma's heart skipped a beat. 'Colin Firth is here in Boothbay Harbor? I love him.'

'Me too. I'm not sure if he's here yet – the fan club says there's no official sign of him, but there have been supposed sightings. Big lights and trailers have been set up over by Frog Marsh.'

Colin Firth. Here in Boothbay Harbor. Maybe Gemma could get a press pass from the Boothbay Regional Gazette and do a story on the effect of a movie set on a small tourist town, and score interviews with the stars. You can take the girl out of the newspaper, but you can't take the newspaper out of the girl.

Isabel left Gemma to settle in, and Gemma surprised herself by flopping down on her bed and staring out the window at the trees. She thought she'd lunge for her notebook to jot down ideas for the piece on the movie set to pitch to the Gazette on Sunday morning. She had to admit she was tired, though, in a way she'd never felt before. Pregnancy-tired. And she was angry and frustrated that Alexander had put an offer in on that Dobbs Ferry house when he knew how she felt.

'Gemma!'

Gemma glanced up to find her dear friend June Nash in the doorway, her arms open for a hug. June, co-owner of the inn along with her sister and their cousin Kat, who was away in France, looked as she always had – her beautiful long auburn curly hair wild around her shoulders, in a pretty cotton sundress. June had a nine-year-old son and had recently eloped to Las Vegas with her long-time love, Henry Books.

'Let's go to dinner and catch up properly. You wrote that you had something big to tell me.'

'I sure do,' Gemma said, two days of pent-up worries whooshing out of her. She'd finally share her news with someone. Someone – a mother – who'd listen, help her work through the situation, and tell her just what motherhood was really like.

Dinner with June had been as good as an hour-long deep-tissue massage, except for the texts from Alexander. *Let me know you arrived safely. Don't forget to look at the information on the house.* And a final one with a link to an article on how Dobbs Ferry, New York, was a great place to live. She'd texted back that she was here safe and sound, and ignored the rest.

Over delicious steak fajitas at a Mexican restaurant, Gemma had told June everything. About the pink plus sign. About losing her job. About Alexander putting in an offer on a house near his overbearing family. About not being ready for motherhood – and definitely not being ready for the life Alexander was preparing for her. June had understood, just as Gemma had known she would. And since June was a mother, she gave Gemma an unscary introduction to Baby 101 and stopped at the bookstore she and her husband owned for a book on pregnancy. June believed you didn't need instinct so much as love and commitment and a good book on what to expect when you were pregnant and during the first year.

'When do you think you'll tell Alexander you're pregnant?' she asked as they pulled back into the driveway of the Three Captains' Inn with just minutes to spare for the start of Movie Night at nine.

Gemma bit her lip. 'I'm not sure. I know I can't keep it secret much longer. It's too big. And I know it's unfair to keep it from him when it would make him so happy. But I just need to come to terms with it, what it means for me, us, before I tell him and get bombarded with what he wants, how he sees our future unfolding. We have such different ideas on what that is.'

June leaned over and gave Gemma a hug. 'You'll figure it out, and you two will make it work for the both of you.'

Gemma wasn't so sure. On the long drive up, one thing she hadn't even thought of before had come crashing down on her: who would hire her when she was pregnant? She'd have to disclose it at her interviews; it would be disingenuous not to. How would she ever get back what she'd had at

New York Weekly? Alexander would realize this in a hot minute and argue her into that Dobbs Ferry house before she knew it. He'd make his case until she had no arguments of her own. And once she had the baby? He'd bombard her with articles about working mothers and bad nannies and reckless daycare centres. She would morph into a copy of Alex's sister-in-law in no time.

When Gemma and June entered the parlour, it was packed with Movie Night attendees. Isabel and her elderly 'helper', Pearl, who watered the plants, were sitting on the sofa with Isabel's eighteen-year-old stepdaughter, Alexa, who was headed off to college this fall. The three members of the Colin Firth fan club, who wore HAPPINESS IS COLIN FIRTH T-shirts with his image on them, were on the love seat, and four others, including one man, were scattered around the large room on chairs. June went to get two more folding chairs and they sat down, a bowl of popcorn and a pitcher of iced tea on the antique table next to them.

The lights were turned off and Isabel slid the DVD of *Bridget Jones's Diary* into the player. Gemma had seen and adored the film when it first came out. A movie like that — warm and funny and true to life — was just what she needed. That and the company of women. And popcorn.

'I had the biggest crush on Hugh Grant a bunch of years ago,' Isabel said, sitting back down, a handful of popcorn on a napkin on her lap. 'He's so great in this movie.'

'For me, Colin Firth all the way,' June said. 'He's our generation's Cary Grant – that swoon-worthy older actor, tall, dark and handsome, debonair but still very masculine and completely epitomizing everything a woman wants in a lifetime partner.' June held up the DVD box. 'Just look at how politely good-looking he is. He's so British!'

The Colin Firth fan club rattled off a bunch of stats about their hero. That he'd appeared in over fifty films and had a few in post-production. That he'd twice been nominated for the Academy Award for Best Actor, for *A Single Man* and *The King's Speech*, winning for the latter. That as a young actor he'd been involved with the actress Meg Tilly, with whom he had a son, and had lived with her in a remote Canadian town for years before resuming his acting career. And did everyone know that he'd been romantically linked to his co-star in *Pride and Prejudice*, Jennifer Ehle, who also appeared in *The King's Speech*? He was now married to a beautiful Italian woman named Livia with whom he had two children. And, if anyone wanted to know, he was a Virgo and six foot two.

The movie began so the fan club finally hushed up.

Renée Zellweger, an actress Gemma had loved since *Jerry Maguire*, appeared on screen, woefully singing along at the top of her lungs to that old seventies ballad 'All By Myself' in her pyjamas. Gemma burst out laughing, as did everyone else. This was her, exactly how she felt, all by herself, her husband far away and as unconnected as if they weren't married at all, but the scene was hilarious, and Gemma felt herself loosening up inside. June had been right to suggest a movie – this movie, too.

Single in her thirties, bumbling but honest Bridget Jones swept Gemma out of herself to London.

'No, I like you. Very much. Just as you are,' June and Isabel repeated in unison after Colin Firth uttered those beautiful words in his gorgeous British accent.

Which was what everyone wanted, including Gemma's husband. 'This is who I am,' he'd said often over the past few months. 'You knew that. You supposedly fell in love with that. Now you want me to be someone I never was.'

The problem was that Gemma felt the same way.

'Think we'll get to see Colin Firth when he comes to film his scenes?' June asked when the credits started rolling. 'I stopped by the set yesterday, but there's not much there. Just some guy with a clipboard who told me not to blab about the set and bombard the area with gawkers.'

Isabel got up and began collecting the almost empty popcorn bowls. 'That'll happen whether he likes it or not. For a glimpse of Colin Firth, even I'll brave the crowds.'

'Me too,' June said, stacking glasses and the pitcher of iced tea on the tray. 'I loved him in *Pride and Prejudice*. That's when I first fell in love with him. *Bridget Jones's Diary* is loosely based on that book. I love that Colin Firth plays Darcy in both *Bridget Jones* and *P & P*.'

The three members of the Colin Firth fan club began listing every one of his movies, complete with co-stars and their opinions of the films, and that's when everyone else began heading their separate ways. Gemma went up to her tiny room on the third floor, changed into a tank top and her PJ pants, then slipped beneath the white-and-yellow quilt stitched with stars and moons. Her phone pinged. A text from Alexander: *Did you look at the information on the house?*

Gemma sighed and texted back a *Not yet* and that she was exhausted, then tried to will herself to sleep. But she couldn't stop thinking of Colin Firth telling Renée Zellweger that he liked her, very much, just as she was. She turned on the lamp on her bedside table and opened the book on pregnancy that June had given her, much preferring to read that than look at the real-estate listing.

Chapter 4
Bea

Bea pulled her car over on the shoulder of the road, by the huge green sign that read BOOTHBAY REGION. Her heart was beating too fast. For a moment she thought about turning around, just forgetting this whole thing. She'd almost turned around two and a half hours ago, at the sign reading WELCOME TO MAINE: THE WAY LIFE SHOULD BE at the Maine–New Hampshire border. The sign had loomed so large. Keep going this way to meet your birth mother, it might as well have read.

It had been three weeks since she'd received her mom's letter, and she wasn't even sure she wanted to be here to see her birth mother, let alone meet her. She had no idea what she wanted. Except for some kind of . . . closure. No, that wasn't the right word. Or maybe it was. Bea knew that sometimes, in order to get closure, you had to open a door.

Such as sending away for her original birth certificate, which she'd received in the mail yesterday. Just the sight of 'Name: Baby Girl Russo' made her tremble, as did the rest: 'Mother's Name: Veronica Russo. Father's Name: Unknown. Time of birth: 7.22 p.m. Issued by: Coastal General Hospital, Boothbay Harbor, Maine'.

She couldn't shake the feeling that she'd started off life as someone else entirely, belonging to other people, a different family, in a different place. She had to find out who these people were, who Veronica Russo was.

She parked in a public lot and glanced at her little notebook: The Best Little Diner in Boothbay was on Main Street, the main drag she was on now. Bea glanced out her window. Boothbay Harbor was a coastal summer town, crowded with tourists walking along the narrow, cobblestone and brick sidewalks, lined with shops and seafood restaurants, and hotels everywhere she looked.

She'd find a cheap motel for the night. She'd give herself a night here, maybe visit the hospital where she was born, walk around, think. Decide if she wanted to meet Veronica Russo. She could stick around town as long as she wanted, since she had no home any more. A few days ago she'd gone back to the apartment to find one of the new roommates having sex in the living room. Bea had had it with this apartment, these strangers. The roommate had said her sister wanted to move in, and that was that. Now, the money she'd been saving for July's rent could support her here for a while until she decided where to go next. And she could go anywhere, which was scary. The only place she wanted to go to was Cape Cod, to her mother's little cottage. But that wasn't her mother's any more. She'd have to throw a dart, or apply to every school district in the US and go where she got hired. For now, home was her car. Everything but her mother's furniture was in the trunk of her old Toyota – her clothes, her laptop and books, her parents' photo albums, the raggedy old stuffed Winnie the Pooh her father had given her on her sixth birthday. Her mother's furniture was in a cheap storage facility. When she landed somewhere, she'd get back her mother's belongings. She'd make a home as best she could.

For a bit of courage and grounding, Bea touched her gold heart locket, then headed up bustling Main Street, but didn't pass the diner or see it on the other side of the street, and she wasn't ready to. She turned onto a wide pier of souvenir shops and restaurants, the bay opening up in front of her. It was a Saturday in June, a gorgeous early evening, and the pier was packed with people, shopping, biting into lobster rolls, licking ice-cream cones, drinking iced coffees, watching the boats. She passed couples, hand in hand, arms slung around each other, and felt a stab of pure envy. She wished she had someone to tell her everything would be okay, someone to be there if it wasn't okay. The last real boyfriend she'd had, someone she'd dated for a few months, had flaked out on her when her mother had gotten sick; he hadn't even come to the funeral. She watched as a guy dipped his girlfriend for an impromptu romantic kiss; a few people clapped. Bea had never felt more wistful. Or alone.

She got herself a lemon ice-lolly from a cart vendor and stood in the sunshine, trying to orient herself, figure out where she was via the free shopper's map she'd picked up outside a store. She had no idea where The Best Little Diner was in relation to this pier. But luckily the diner was marked on the map; it was barely a quarter-mile from where she stood.

Bea put the map away, her heart beating fast again. Just like that, a snap of her fingers, and she could meet the birth mother she hadn't known existed until a few weeks ago. This was crazy. As was her sudden realization that any fortyish woman she passed could be Veronica Russo. That one, blonde like Bea, in the pale yellow sundress and flip-flops, an outfit Bea might have chosen herself. She watched the woman check her phone, then look around the expanse of pier as though she were waiting for someone. Bea's biological father, maybe. For all Bea knew, her birth parents had gotten married. Had always been married. Had other children, older or younger. Maybe both. Bea could have a sister. Twin brothers.

Bea sat down on a bench outside a weathered restaurant with a giant sign proclaiming THE BEST LOBSTER ROLLS IN BOOTHBAY. She had to stop this or she'd drive herself crazy. She'd spent three weeks wondering, speculating. How could she even begin to guess what her birth mother's circumstances were?

Veronica Russo could be the tall blonde jogging with a yellow lab beside her. Or perhaps Bea had inherited the blond from her biological father, and Veronica was the redhead who'd just walked away from the seafood shack's take-out window, eating her lobster roll while gazing at a whale that had just made an appearance in the bay. I have to know something about you, Veronica Russo, she thought. About my birth father. About my birth grandparents. I have to know who I was before the Cranes adopted me.

Bea opened her backpack and pulled out her little red notebook. *Veronica Russo. Home: 225 Sea Road. Tel: 207 555-3235. Work: The Best Little Diner in Boothbay, 45 Main Street.* According to the map, all she had to do was walk a bit up to Main and turn right.

Just go to the diner, she told herself. Just go check her out.

Bea couldn't pick her out right away. There were three waitresses, two the right age to be Veronica, and one no older than Bea. The one Bea's age was working the counter, so Bea took the empty seat that wrapped around the side by the door, giving her a view of the entire diner. The place was crowded; only one table was empty, and almost all the counter seats were filled.

She liked the diner. It was a combination of old-fashioned greasy spoon and coastal Maine, with pale blue walls displaying the pricey work of local artists, and overstuffed chairs and love seats along with the more typical tables. The ceiling was covered in a lobster net with a giant wooden lobster caught inside. Near the counter where Bea sat was a bookshelf filled with books and a sign saying READ ME.

Bea glanced at the two other waitresses and looked for name tags, but she wasn't that lucky. One was heading to a table with four plates balanced in her hands, and she was tall like Bea, but she didn't have Bea's blonde hair; none of the waitresses did.

'Sorry it's taken me so long to even give you a menu,' the young waitress said to Bea. She wore a gold nameplate necklace: Katie. 'We're crazed right now, so I'm helping on the floor too.'

'No problem.' Bea ordered an iced coffee and whatever the decadent-looking pie next to the carrot cake was.

'Oh, that's fudge Happiness Pie, and intensely good. One of our waitresses is a legend in this town for her pies.' She headed to the coffee station, glancing around until her gaze landed on a woman coming out of a back room. 'Oh, there you are, Veronica. I'm about to sell the last of your amazing fudge pie.'

Bea froze.

Her birth mother. Standing not seven, eight feet away. Had Katie not gone to get Bea her coffee, Veronica might have noticed Bea sitting there, white as her paper napkin and trembling. She closed her eyes and turned her head to look out the large picture window, telling herself to breathe.

My birth mother, she thought, turning to take another look. Veronica gave Katie a dismissive wave and a pleased smile, then went to the coffee station and filled a large take-out cup. She was no older than late thirties and tall, like Bea. Busty, unlike Bea. Her auburn hair cascaded just past her shoulders in soft waves. And her eyes were just like Bea's: driftwood brown and round. But Veronica Russo was beautiful in a lush, womanly way that Bea — who an ex liked to describe as looking like a farm girl, even though she'd grown up in Boston and Cape Cod — would never be. Still, there was something in the woman's expression that was like Bea's, something subtle.

She wore all white, a sparkly white tank top and white pants. And beaded sandals. Done with her shift, Bea figured.

You're a complete stranger, and yet my entire history comes from you, Bea wanted to shout. What is your story? What was your story?

Bea glanced at Veronica's hands as she added a packet of sugar to her coffee. No rings at all. So she wasn't married.

'Hey, darling,' a man said, and Bea glanced over to see a tall, skinny, half-balding redheaded guy wobbling in the doorway as though he were drunk, his foot stuck in the screen door. He was staring at Veronica. 'Is today my lucky day? Gonna go out with me?'

Veronica cut him a sharp look. 'Please stop asking me out. My answer is never going to change.'

'She's breaking my heart!' he shouted and mock-stabbed

himself in the chest, and those sitting around the front of the diner burst into laughter.

Bea watched Veronica good-naturedly shake her head and stir her coffee as the guy staggered away.

'Colin Firth's signing autographs at Harbour View Coffee!' a nasal voice called out from in front of the diner.

Colin Firth? The actor?

Bea's mother had adored Colin Firth; she'd gone to opening night of all his films, then bought the DVDs for a keepsake collection at home. A few years ago, Bea had come across a Colin Firth wall calendar, a large photo of the actor to grace every month, and she'd bought it for her mom as a gag gift. The next time she visited, the calendar was hanging front and centre next to the fridge, her mom's appointments jotted on the little squares.

Veronica was out the door in a shot. Along with half of everyone in the diner.

Bea had the strongest urge to get up and follow her, but her body wouldn't listen to a single command. Except for her hand, shaking around her fork, she was frozen. She set down the fork, sucked in a breath and thought about calling her good friend Caroline to tell her she'd seen her birth mother in the flesh, that she was beautiful; but Caroline was in Berlin for the summer.

Bea looked down at her untouched slice of pie, the gooey fudge, the flaky crust. Her birth mother had made this pie. She took a slow bite, letting herself savour it.

Bea wanted to chase after Veronica and throw some time-stop pixie dust on her so that she could surreptitiously study her every feature — the shape of her eyes, the line of her nose, the structure of her jawline — and search for herself in Veronica's face, her body, her mannerisms. Something to force her brain to accept that this was all true, that this woman, not Cora Crane, had given birth to her. That someone, a man whose name she didn't know, had fathered her. Who was he? Had they been in love? Was it a one-night stand? Something awful? Where did I come from? Bea wanted to know. Suddenly, she was itchy to learn Veronica's life story, Bea's own history. Who were her grandparents?

Who was Bea?

Bea put a ten-dollar bill on the table and raced out after Veronica.

Main Street was so crowded with tourists and cyclists, a dog walker with the leashes of at least ten dogs, and a bunch of children walking towards her two by two in neon-yellow HAPPY KIDS DAY CAMP T-shirts that Bea couldn't see Veronica in any direction she looked. Harbour View Coffee was five shops down. Bea went in and looked around, but there was no sign of Veronica, let alone a British actor.

'If you've come looking for Colin Firth, he's not here,' the barista called over, rolling her eyes. 'Someone obviously thought it would be funny to send every woman in town rushing in here.'

Bea saw a couple leave through the back door with their iced coffees, and she headed out to the small patio. No Veronica. A cobblestone path led to the street running perpendicular to Townsend, right along the harbour. She must have gone out this way.

Okay, now what? She could come back tomorrow – and this time perhaps she'd sit in Veronica's section. Bea headed towards the harbour and tried to think. She'd come to Boothbay to see the town, this place where she'd been born, where she'd begun as someone else's story. The plan was that, when and if the time was right, she'd knock on her birth mother's door, either literally or figuratively.

It had felt right a moment ago. But what if she had caught up to Veronica? Would she have run up to her, tapped her on the shoulder and said, 'Uh, hi, my name is Bea Crane. You gave me up for adoption twenty-two years ago.' It was clear Veronica wanted Bea to contact her; otherwise she wouldn't have updated the file. But maybe a call would be better, for both of them. A bit of distance, letting them both sit down and digest before actually meeting.

Yes, Bea would call, maybe tomorrow.

As she neared the harbour, even more crowded than the main shopping street, Veronica's features, her warm brown eyes, the straight, almost pointy nose, so like Bea's own, were all imprinted in her mind. Bea was so lost in thought that she started walking in no particular direction; if she stopped, she felt like she might tip over.

Unless Veronica had stayed out of the sun her entire life, she was no more than late thirties. Bea would give her thirty-six or thirty-seven, which meant she'd had Bea as a teenager.

As Bea wound her way through the crowd of tourists, she imagined a very young Veronica walking these same streets, pregnant, scared, unsure what to do. Had Bea's birth father been supportive? Had he abandoned her? How had Veronica's mother, her own grandmother, handled it? Had Veronica been able to turn to her? Had she been shunned? Supported?

Bea let herself wander and speculate, until she realized she'd walked around the far side of the bay, away from the hustle of downtown. Up ahead by the side of a pond, she saw a bunch of people setting up huge black lights and massive cameras, a long beige trailer behind them. Looked like a film set — she'd come across a few of those in Boston and always hoped for a glimpse of a movie star, but she never saw anyone famous, though people around her claimed they had.

Maybe this was what the Colin Firth shout-out had been about. He must be in town to film a new movie. Bea headed over, needing a distraction from herself.

'Movie set, right?' she asked a tall, lanky guy in wire-rimmed glasses standing in front of the trailer. A laminated pass hanging down from around his neck read: TYLER ECHOLS, PA.

He gave Bea something of a nod, but didn't look up from his clipboard.

A pretty teenaged girl with long dark hair sat a few feet away in a folding chair by the trailer. She had a book upside-down on her lap, and if Bea wasn't mistaken, it was *To Kill a Mockingbird*. Bea would recognize that original cover from a mile away.

'I love that book,' Bea said to her. 'I wrote my senior thesis on it.'

'I can't even get past the first paragraph,' the girl said, fluttering the pages. 'It's so boring. How am I supposed to write a paper on this book? It should be called *To Kill a Boring Bird*.'

She had no idea what she was missing. '*To Kill a Mockingbird* is a brilliant reflection of its time – of the South, of racism, of right and wrong, of injustice, all through the eyes of a girl who learns a lot about life, her father and herself. It's one of my top ten favourite novels of all time.'

The guy with the pass glanced at her then, leaning one foot up behind him against the trailer, but went back to checking things off on his clipboard.

The girl looked even more bored, but then brightened. 'Could you write my paper?'

'Sorry, no,' Bea said. 'But give the novel a chance, okay?'

The girl rolled her eyes. 'You sound like my brother,' she said, upping her chin at the guy with the clipboard.

'So is this a movie set?' Bea asked the guy again, glancing at the cameras, then back to him.

He looked up. '*Please* don't go telling everyone we're here.

66

The last thing we need is a huge crowd watching us position lights. There's no movie star here. I swear.'

'What's the movie? Colin Firth is starring, right?'

'You're trespassing, you know,' was all he said.

She seemed to be doing that a lot today.

Chapter 5
Veronica

Veronica had four plates, four coffees, four orange juices and a basket of mini corn muffins with apple butter on the heavy tray she carried over to table seven. It was Sunday morning, eight o'clock, and since the diner had opened at six-thirty, she'd served what seemed like five hundred plates of eggs — from scrambled to omelettes to over-easy — home fries, bacon and toast, maybe a thousand cups of coffee. And folks kept coming. A line had formed by the door, the counter was full, and every table was taken. The Best Little Diner in Boothbay lived up to its name and was one of the most popular eateries in town. Even the fish and chips rivalled the seafood joints, and that was saying something in a harbour town in Maine. And of course, when it came to pie, no one went anywhere else.

Of all the diners she'd worked in over the past twenty-two years, The Best Little Diner in Boothbay was her favourite. She loved how pretty it was, for one. The floors were wide-planked pumpkin originals dating back to the late 1800s, when it used to be a general store. Instead of standard vinyl seats for the booths, the seating was white-painted wood (washable, of course) with soothing starfish-printed cushions. And the tables, twenty-five in total, were polished wood and round. When the diner slowed down at off times, she loved checking out the local artists' work on the walls. And the back room was a waitress's paradise of comfy recliners, a nice restroom, even a lovely back alley to sneak out for some fresh air. The diner's owner, Deirdre, had something of a secret flower garden out back, and Veronica often spent her breaks just standing amidst the big pots of blue hydrangeas and breathing in the scent of roses.

'I see a table open right there, young lady,' Veronica heard a familiar voice snap to the hostess. Oh no. Mrs Buffleman, pointing, with her usual scowl, at the table that had just opened up in Veronica's section. Mrs Buffleman was Veronica's old English teacher from junior year. Buffleman retired a few years ago and had breakfast practically every day at the diner; Veronica had long ago told the hostess to seat her in someone else's section, but sometimes, when it couldn't be helped, Buffleman ended up in hers, like today.

'Good-morning, Mrs Buffleman, Mr Buffleman,' Veronica said as she stopped at their table, coffee pot in hand. 'Coffee this morning?'

Mrs Buffleman studied her for a moment with her usual slight shake of her head, the shake of disappointment. When Veronica had had to drop out of high school, all her teachers had received a memo about why, and informing them that her last day would be at week's end. Mrs Buffleman was the only teacher who'd brought up the subject with her. 'Darn shame,' she'd said to Veronica on her last day, when Veronica had been on the verge of tears since walking in the building that morning. Head-shake. 'What a waste.' More head-shaking. And Veronica, who hadn't thought she could possibly feel worse, had felt worse.

Veronica had never particularly liked Mrs Buffleman, but the old battle-axe had given her an A on every paper, and she had earned As on every exam. English had been her best subject, but it wasn't as if she'd planned on becoming a teacher or an editor of some kind anyway; Veronica had never known what she wanted to do. When she started baking four years ago, she thought about opening her own little pie diner, but that took a lot of money to invest in and keep up, and though Veronica had a nest-egg squirrelled away from twenty-two years of waitressing, low rents and low overheads, she was afraid to spend it on something that might fail. It wasn't as though she had anyone else, like a life partner, to rely on for half the bills, half of retirement, and even if you did have a husband, you never knew what could happen. That little pie diner was nice to fantasize about, though.

'That's the gal who dropped out of high school because

she got pregnant,' she heard Buffleman whisper to her husband, for at least the hundredth time since Veronica been back in town, as she walked away with her coffee pot.

Veronica rolled her eyes, then groaned at the sight of Penelope Von Blun and her mother sitting at a table for two. She'd have to add Penelope to the list of people not to put in her section. Penelope was one of the biggest snobs Veronica had ever met, and unfortunately she'd signed up for Veronica's pie class tomorrow night. Veronica was surprised the woman would deign to learn the art of making pies from her, but she was pretty sure there was an ulterior motive involved. Penelope likely wanted to learn the secrets of making her own elixir pie so that she wouldn't have to give Veronica her business.

Penelope's whispering to her mother started the moment Veronica began walking over with her coffee pot. Veronica had no doubt what she was saying. 'Remember the slutty girl who got pregnant my junior year and dropped out to go to Hope Home? That's her. Working at the diner. Guess we see how her life turned out.'

'Veronica!' Penelope said with fake brightness, and Veronica was struck by how different she looked from usual, toned down somehow, the hair less straight-ironed, the outfit more conservative, and just a couple of simple pieces of jewellery instead of the usual statement necklace and earrings. 'I'm so excited about pie class tomorrow night.' She turned to her mother and said, 'Veronica is known in town for special pies. Have you ever had one?'

'Oh, I don't go for that nonsense,' her mother said with a dismissive wave of her hand. 'Pies don't bring you love or cure cancer. Please.'

The woman was such a stick-in-the-mud that Veronica laughed. 'Well, they sure do taste good.'

'I know. I've had your pie here,' the woman said without a smile. 'Coffee please.'

Veronica poured their coffee and took their orders. Penelope was having the fruit plate. Her mother ordered the most high-maintenance plate of substitutions Veronica had ever had the displeasure of writing down on her order pad. Two eggs, one over-easy, the other sunny side up. Rye toast, extra light, but still warm, the butter on and melted. Home fries without a single charred piece of potato, which were Veronica's favourite kind, when the grill got a hold of the onions and the edges of the potatoes.

Sometimes, when she ran into people like Penelope and Buffleman — especially on the same day at the same time — she felt a small blast of that old shame. Nothing like when she was sixteen, of course, and newly pregnant with people staring at her as though she had a sign around her neck. But just a frisson of that feeling that made her . . . uncomfortable. As if her life could have gone another way entirely if only she hadn't gotten knocked up. She'd be married, maybe. With two kids. And she'd have figured out what she wanted to do with her life. Discovered her pie-baking skills a lot earlier because she'd bake for school fundraisers for her children. Maybe. Maybe not. Who the heck knew?

She glanced around at the counter, where Officer DeMarco usually sat when he came in, which was pretty often. At least he wasn't here this morning. Too bad he hadn't been here yesterday, when she could have set him upon that drunken pest Hugh Fledge who wouldn't stop asking her out. She barely remembered Nick from high school, but she knew his face, recalled he was part of Timothy's crowd. Every time she looked at Nick she felt exposed, as though he knew all sorts of things about her that weren't even true. She hated how that felt. And so she avoided him whenever she saw him at the diner or around town. But she wouldn't be able to avoid him tomorrow night at the class. She'd have to be extra polite, too, because of his daughter.

Times like this, she wondered if coming back to Boothbay Harbor was a mistake after all. If she'd ever really settle in and face anything of her past. Boothbay still didn't feel like home again, even a year later. And though she'd made some friends — Shelley, of course, right over there at table nineteen, explaining the difference between a western omelette and a country omelette — and she had lot of acquaintances, especially her clients, who seemed to rely on her as if she were a fortune teller, Veronica felt . . . lonely. Lonely for something she wasn't even sure of. Was it love? A big group of close girlfriends, something Veronica had never had except for during her seven months at Hope Home? Something was missing, that was all she knew.

'People will come and go from your life for all kinds of acceptable and crappy reasons,' her grandmother had always said in her saucy, straightforward style. 'So you've got to be your own best friend, know who you are and never let anyone tell you you're something you know you're not.'

Veronica had been thirteen when her grandmother had said all that, over a girl who'd told Veronica she couldn't be her friend any more because her mother thought Veronica looked 'too grown-up'. She'd worn a C-cup bra in eighth grade, had a thin but also curvy figure, and no matter how conservatively she'd dressed, the boys had come chasing. In ninth grade, girls – including Penelope – had started rumours about Veronica 'sleeping around' when she hadn't so much as French-kissed a boy. The few boys she'd dated had made up stories about how far they'd gone, so Veronica had broken up with them. By sixteen, when she started dating Timothy Macintosh, she'd had a reputation – when she hadn't ever even let a boy see her bra. Timothy had believed her too, said he thought she was beautiful and interesting and would never say a word about her to his friends. Girls had always kept their distance from her, so Timothy had become her first real best friend. Until a very cold April afternoon when she'd told him she was pregnant.

Bringing herself back to that day sent a fresh stab of pain to her chest. Maybe it would always hurt, even thirty years from now. Stop thinking about him, she ordered herself, calling out Penelope Von Blun's and her mother's order at the open window to the kitchen, which got an extended eye-roll from Joe, the cook. She wished she could stop. But in the first few weeks of her return to Boothbay Harbor, she'd actually seen Timothy, from a distance in the supermarket, and she'd been unable to sleep well ever since, memories waking her up. She'd been so stunned to see him that she'd jumped back behind a display of bananas. She hadn't been sure, at first, if it was really him, but then she heard his laughter as he listened to something the woman with him had said. Veronica hadn't gotten a look at her, just the back of her head and an amazing figure. Timothy's arm had been around her, and he turned to look at something, and there was that profile, the strong, straight Roman nose. Veronica had almost started hyperventilating. It had been so unexpected. She didn't think he lived in town any more; she'd looked him up just so she'd know if she had to accept that she'd run into him in town, but there was no listing for him, and she hadn't seen him before or since that one time, so perhaps he was visiting relatives.

'Oh. My. God,' Shelley said as she collected the discarded *Sunday Boothbay Regional Gazette* from one of her tables.

'What, Shel?' Veronica asked, coming over.

Shelley, a petite redhead in her late thirties like Veronica, with cat-like amber-hazel eyes, was staring at a page of the newspaper. She held up the Life & People section. 'This.'

One glance at the front page and Veronica repeated Shelley's 'Oh. My. God.' A photo of Colin Firth, looking absolutely gorgeous in a tux, next to a brief article about the movie crew that had recently set up some equipment in Boothbay Harbor, near Frog Marsh, to film scenes of a new Colin Firth comedy-drama. Below the article was a call for extras.

> Major motion picture seeks locals as extras. Apply on location at Frog Marsh between 12 and 5 Monday and Tuesday only. Bring a résumé and two photo-graphs paperclipped together, full-body and head shot, with name, phone, height, weight and clothing size written in permanent marker on the back.

So it was true. Colin Firth was coming to Boothbay Harbor — and could very well have been in the Harbour View coffee shop yesterday, despite the barista swearing on a stack of bibles that Firth had not been in the place. Perhaps he'd ducked out the back once word had gotten out that he was in there. The man had probably just wanted an iced coffee and a scone, for heaven's sake, not screaming fans bombarding him. Such as herself.

'Come by my house tonight and I'll take a bunch of pictures of you,' Shelley said, ripping out the front page, folding it up and tucking it into the pocket of Veronica's apron.

'Pictures of me? For what?'

'So you can apply to be an extra!'

Veronica laughed. 'Me? I work here. I bake a thousand

pies a week. How could I possibly drop everything to work on a film set? I once read that extras are on call all day for as long as it takes to film the scenes on location. They sit around in a tent and read or chat until the director calls them to walk by wordlessly in the background or whatever.' But still, just the thought of being an extra in a Colin Firth movie started an excitement inside her that Veronica hadn't felt in decades.

'Oh, you're applying,' Shelley said, well aware of Veronica's love of Colin Firth. At least three times a month, Veronica invited Shelley over to watch a Colin Firth film, complete with fun drinks and appetizers and pie and discussion afterwards about the film and why she adored Colin Firth so darn much. 'Didn't we just see *Love Actually* a couple of months ago?' Shelley had asked when Veronica had told her she was planning to watch it, if Shelley wanted to join her. As if you could see *Love Actually* one too many times. 'You've got money, Veronica. Your pie business will allow you to take a few weeks off, even a couple of months. You're going to miss the chance to be an extra in a Colin Firth movie in your own home town?'

No, I'm not, Veronica thought, the image of Mr Darcy walking soaking wet out of that pond coming to mind. There was no way she was missing this. She unfolded the newspaper page and stared at the photo of her heartthrob, then at the ad. She was smiling like an idiot.

Major motion picture seeks locals as extras. Good Lord, Veronica could be in the same air space as Colin Firth. She could be an extra – why not? And Shelley was right: her pie business had been doing so well that she could easily take some time off from the diner.

Veronica in same room as Colin Firth. She could look Mr Darcy in the eye!

She'd be first in line to apply.

Which meant coming up with a résumé for the first time in her life, she realized, as she eyed the kitchen window counter and saw two of her orders were up. She headed over and filled her tray. Veronica had been a waitress at busy diners since she was sixteen and left Maine for Florida. All you needed for that job was to say you had experience and then show it on the floor and you were hired. Was she supposed to list every diner she'd worked from Florida to New Mexico to Maine for the past twenty-two years? She'd think it over later as she fulfilled her pie orders. If the movie people wanted locals, they wanted real people with local jobs, everyday people, not necessarily a résumé full of accomplishments. She'd tell the truth, go to Shelley's tonight and have her picture taken, and then she'd apply with fingers crossed.

She'd make herself a Hope Pie, too. Salted-caramel cheese-cake. Just for good measure.

By 4 p.m., Veronica's house was sparkling clean for tomorrow night's pie class, she had her recipes printed to hand out, and she'd written her résumé. On her cover sheet, she briefly described leaving Boothbay Harbor just months shy of her seventeenth birthday – but not why – and making her way, alone, to Florida, where she'd gotten a job in a diner, then a few years later heading slowly west, to Louisiana, Texas and New Mexico, and back to Maine. She wrote a paragraph about working at The Best Little Diner, how she loved her regulars and enjoyed the tourists. She didn't know if that would be remotely interesting to whoever was in charge of hiring the extras. She went on Google and learned she wasn't way off base about what extras did. Lots of sitting around and waiting. Apparently, there wasn't much about what made for a good extra, what would make her be chosen over anyone else. But if they wanted 'real people', Veronica was as real as they got. According to the articles she read, the one thing an extra wasn't supposed to do or be was star-crazy, so she'd left off her enduring love of Colin Firth.

She put away her laptop, made a neat pile of her recipes and did a check of her cupboards, pantry and refrigerator to make sure she had everything she needed for tomorrow's class. Enough flour, shortening, baking soda and sugar, both white and brown. She'd have to replenish her salt supply, and pick up eggs, sticks of butter, some apples and a few pints of blueberries. She added cherries, blackberries, bananas, Key limes and dark chocolate to her list. She used her jar of molasses so infrequently that she didn't have to worry about coming up short for Leigh DeMarco's shoo-fly pie.

For the first class, she'd focus on good old apple pie –

even though it wasn't apple season – and making pie crust from scratch, but if students wanted to make special elixir pies, they would be able to; Veronica had a professional oven that could handle many pies at once, and every possible kind of filling at the ready, from fresh fruit to chocolate to coconut to custard.

Her phone rang. Hopefully it was Penelope Von Blun, dropping out of class.

'Hello, Veronica speaking.'

'I'd like to order a pie, a special pie.' The voice was raspy; thirties, Veronica thought; and there was a tinge of anger, of bitterness, but also sadness.

'Sure. What kind would you like?' From the woman's tone, Veronica had the sense she'd order Amore Pie or maybe Feel-Better pie.

'The kind of pie that would get someone off someone else's mind. Do you make that kind?'

Her boyfriend or husband was having an affair. Or in love with someone else, Veronica thought, but that didn't seem quite it. Usually Veronica could tell so much by just a voice, but there was something complicated here that Veronica couldn't put her finger on. 'Well, I'll need to clarify if you mean in a romantic sense or just someone you're trying to purge from your life.'

'Maybe both,' the woman said.

Cast-Out Pie. Veronica had made a few like that, just twice here in town and several times down in New Mexico. The first time, one of the busboys at the diner, an emotional wreck of a young man who cried while clearing the tables of any woman who had red hair like the ex who'd broken his heart, had been on the verge of getting fired for all his crying. So Veronica had stayed late and found herself using peanut butter for its stick and coconut for its grit, figuring a lighter cream-based pie that felt airy couldn't dislodge and lift, whereas the heavier peanut butter and the texture of coconut could get in there, take those feelings of gloom and doom and carry them away from the stomach, such a source of upset. She'd baked up her Cast-Out Pie, given the poor guy a slice the next morning while having a chat in the kitchen: that he was stronger than he thought, that he was in control of his own destiny, his own future, and maybe it was time to let old hurts go. Maybe it was time to focus on the new. Reel off and cast in instead.

As he ate the slice of pie – he'd had one and a half slices, Veronica remembered – he told her that he did have a bit of a crush on Jenny, the dark-haired waitress with the big blue eyes, and maybe he'd ask her out. The Cast-Out Pie had been a success and so Veronica had stuck with the peanut butter and coconut.

'I call that Cast-Out Pie,' Veronica said into the phone.

'It'll really work?' the woman asked, the voice suddenly more hopeful.

'I'll be honest – it's one of my special elixir pies that doesn't always do its job. I suppose you really, really, really have to want that person out of your heart for it to work. You have to be ready. If you're not, it doesn't seem to work. Some people are ready, they're there, but memories keep pulling them back. Others truly aren't ready to let go, even if it's self-destructive.'

'Well sometimes you don't always know what's best for you,' the woman snapped.

Veronica had a feeling this person was not ready, that the pie wouldn't work. But the pain in the woman's voice had gotten under her skin. The woman was prickly. Prickly was a very uncomfortable way to be. Veronica wanted to help her.

'I tell you what,' Veronica said. 'When you pick up the pie, don't pay me. If it works, you can come leave the money in my mailbox. Fair enough?'

She was quiet for a moment. 'All right. Tomorrow then?'

Tomorrow? She had her résumé and cover letter to go back over, the little photo shoot at Shelley's tonight, and class to prepare for tomorrow. Plus, she was working the morning shift tomorrow and had to bake two special pies for clients after work and her own salted-caramel cheesecake Hope Pie to make for herself. Tomorrow afternoon she'd need a good couple of hours to do some grocery shopping for her class and get everything set up.

And had the woman even said thank you for Veronica's offer not to take payment if the Cast-Out Pie didn't work for her?

'Please,' the woman said, and again, something in her voice seemed so desperate that Veronica couldn't say no.

She breathed out a silent sigh. 'If you come by around five p.m. tomorrow, I'll have your pie ready.'

'Thank you,' the woman said finally and hung up.

For a full minute, Veronica couldn't shake the conversation from her thoughts; there had been something unsettling in her voice, something Veronica couldn't pinpoint. She couldn't get the woman's bitter voice off her mind. Then again, that would be very helpful in making a Cast-Out Pie.

Chapter 6

Gemma

On Monday morning at ten-thirty, Gemma left the office of Dr Laura Bauer, OB/GYN, with a confirmation of pregnancy — a second positive urine test anyway — a prescription for pre-natal vitamins and a due date.

3 January. A New Year's baby.

The doctor had answered all of her questions about what foods she should avoid (deli meats, high-mercury fish, and Caesar dressing because of the raw eggs) and if she could drink just one cup of coffee a day (she could). She'd been lucky to get the appointment; June had discreetly asked Isabel for the name of her obstetrician, and thanks to a last-minute cancellation this morning, Gemma had herself an appointment. She'd get the results of the blood test in a few days, but the doc had told her that with two positive tests, she was most definitely pregnant.

She touched her stomach, still relatively flat. When would it feel real? When the baby kicked for the first time, maybe. Her wedding ring glinted in the sunshine as she walked down Main Street. I'm pregnant, she said to herself. I'm having a baby. It was real, even if it didn't feel real yet. Perhaps it was better that it didn't feel real just yet. Part of her, the part that loved her husband like crazy, wanted to call him and share it with him, but every time she reached for her phone she stopped herself. The conversation would move from him jubilantly shouting, 'I'm going to be a father!' to him talking about the move to Westchester, to The Plan — for Gemma to be a stay-at-home mother and only work part-time, if she 'insisted', at the local free weekly. The other night, June had said that sounded pretty darn good to her, and considering June had a been a twenty-one-year-old college student who hadn't been able to locate the father of her baby, Gemma understood what she had meant. Gemma was lucky. She did have a doting husband. Too doting, maybe, but she was blessed. Still, was it wrong to want the career that meant so much to her? If she had to be pregnant now, couldn't she have both? A baby and a career?

A month ago, she'd been on assignment in a Brooklyn homeless shelter, sitting on a cot next to a single mother who had nowhere to go, no skills and no way to work without leaving her two-year-old, who lay sleeping on the cot, alone. Gemma had been so touched by her story that she'd gotten the woman an interview at a daycare centre to be an aide, but the job had gone to someone else. Twenty-plus calls to daycare centres later between the two of them, the woman had gotten herself hired and a slot for her daughter. Within two weeks, she'd been able to leave the shelter for her own small apartment. Her feature story on three women at the shelter had elicited over a thousand comments on the *New York Weekly* website – some blasting her and the women for their circumstances, others full of empathy with talk of vicious cycles. This was what Gemma wanted to do – talk to people, tell their stories, some heartbreaking, some controversial, some just everyday folks going through struggles like so many. She wanted to inform, start conversations. Alexander had once said he thought Gemma's drive to be a human-interest reporter stemmed from her wanting people to be heard the way she herself hadn't felt heard as a child. Maybe so. Sometimes she thought Alexander understood her so well. Other times . . .

Perhaps she'd call him tonight and tell him the news. After her meeting with Claire Lomax at the *Boothbay Regional Gazette*. Gemma had gotten damned lucky by running into Claire this past Saturday at their mutual friend's wedding. As summer friends, the teenage Claire and Gemma would play reporter, interviewing people on the street and jotting down their answers in notebooks. Claire had always had a knack for coming up with the assignments; it was no surprise she was a big editor now at the well-read regional paper.

At the wedding reception, Claire had hugged Gemma as though they were as close as ever, and they headed over to a table with their mini-crab cakes and stilton-stuffed grapes to catch up on their lives; they'd last seen each other at June's aunt's funeral two years ago. Gemma had been honest when they caught up, which had gotten her congratulations on the pregnancy, sympathy about her issues with her husband and losing her beloved job, and an invitation to stop in this morning to discuss putting Gemma to work for the week. Claire wasn't married, but in a long-term relationship, and related to everything Gemma had told her. Claire would give her a great assignment, a story she could put together in a few days. Just having the assignment, reporting from the field, researching, Gemma would feel stronger, feel like herself again. She'd be better equipped to make her case to Alexander when he started in about how it was a blessing in disguise that she'd been laid off.

As Gemma passed a shop called the Italian Bakery, she had a sudden craving for cannoli. She peered in the window at a plate lined with the delectable pastry. Just one, she told herself. She headed in and left with four, one for now, one for June if she saw her later, one for Isabel at the inn and one for herself tonight, when she'd be longing for more cannoli. She sat down on a bench outside the shop and found her attention drawn to the passing mothers. And babies. They were everywhere suddenly. Strollers. Babies in soft carriers strapped to mothers' and fathers' chests. Or in elaborate back-pack-like contraptions. One mother wore her baby in a sling across her torso. They all had one thing in common, though.

They all looked like they'd been doing it for ever, this motherhood thing. Their faces were calm. A woman with the backpack stopped to window-shop, another pushing a stroller paused to answer her phone, then went on pushing her stroller down the street as though taking care of a baby was no big deal. Gemma had to get a grip. Clearly, you could multi-task. Clearly, she'd learn how to hold a baby and talk to someone at the same time. Mothers had been mothers since the dawn of time, for heaven's sake. She could learn. She could talk to Isabel for advice on being a working mother. Isabel had a great nanny but she'd also said June filled in for her often at the inn. Gemma's sister, older by five years, lived in California and they weren't close and never had been. Her sister ran cold, like their mother always had, and kept to herself.

She was struck with a memory of being alone in her house, having no idea where her mother was, unable to find her, her father gone as usual on a business trip. Gemma would go door to door in her house, looking for her mother, and if she came to a locked door, she knew she'd found her. Her mother had worked full-time, but she'd hired sitters to watch Gemma when she was young and then Gemma had come home to an empty house once she was old enough to be trusted with a key, her sister busy with her own life. There had to be a happy medium, but heck if Gemma knew where or what it was. She just knew she'd never had that feeling friends had spoken about — the yearning to have a baby.

Alexander often insisted it was because she was afraid, because of how she'd been raised, because she didn't have a warm and fuzzy mother. He also insisted she'd be a great mom, that she was loving and kind and full of compassion and commitment, and that was all you needed to be a great mother.

Gemma wasn't so sure about that, though. You needed something else. Something more than all that combined. You had to want to be a mother in the first place.

Out of nowhere, tears stung Gemma's eyes: it felt so awful to think such a thing, given that there was a life growing inside her. A life, a quarter-inch long, with a pipe-shaped heart just beginning to beat, according to the week-by-week pregnancy book she'd started reading Friday night. Her baby. Alexander's baby.

Gemma put her hands on her stomach, wondering if she'd feel a flutter. Still nothing. Are you a boy or a girl? she said silently to her belly. Will you have my straight light brown hair? Alexander's sandy blond? His hazel eyes? My dark blue? She wouldn't mind if the baby inherited the Hendricks' cleft chin. And, yes, their pull-you-in warmth. Complain as she did about them, Mona and Artie Hendricks would be fantastic grandparents, the kind a kid dreamed of, doting and spoiling and full of hugs and love.

A dog on a long leash came over and grabbed the cannoli out of Gemma's hand. She'd only had two bites, too. The owner was full of apologies and said she'd go right in and get Gemma another one, but Gemma smiled and opened the box and said she had extras, so no worries, that the dog had done her a favour anyway.

Thank goodness for cute, cannoli-swiping dogs to stop Gemma from thinking about her belly and how complicated her life – her head, really – seemed. She glanced at her watch. Time to head over to the *Gazette*. If she was lucky, Claire would assign her to cover the big story everyone in town was buzzing about – the film crew that had set up over by Frog Marsh this past weekend. Interviewing the wonderful Colin Firth, one of her favourite actors, perhaps over a cannoli in the Italian Bakery, would take her mind off just about everything. She'd be dying to ask him to repeat her favourite words ever uttered on screen – 'I like you. Very much. Just as you are.' But she wouldn't, of course.

And an interview with a major movie star, on her home turf – well, her summer home turf – could be her way back. The personal angle combined with a story and interview with an A-list movie star? It was the kind of story that would get her back into her old boss's good graces. It very well might get her her job back.

A weight lifted off her head, heart and shoulders, and she headed down Harbour Lane, one of her favourite side streets with its cobblestone path, where the *Gazette* offices were located, just across from Books Brothers. She smiled at the Moon Tea Emporium, a fixture on Harbour Lane, where she and the teenage June and Claire had often gone to feel more grown-up, ordering tea and tiny sandwiches. She'd also made good use of the fortune teller next door. Gemma peered in the windows, practically covered by red velvet drapes, and could see Madame Periot sitting at a round table with a woman. Maybe Gemma would stop in later. Or maybe she didn't want to know her fortune. 'You are confused and someone very close to you is getting impatient,' the middle-aged woman would say. Gemma would ask if she and Alexander would figure things out, find their happy medium, and Madame Periot would say yes, of course. She didn't need to fork over thirty-five bucks for that.

Gemma glanced at her watch. She still had fifteen minutes to kill before her interview, so she ducked into Books Brothers, where June worked as the manager. In the Local Maine Interest aisle, Gemma found her helping a man select a book about climbing Mt Katahdin.

'Crazy morning, and we've only been open since nine,' June said, giving Gemma a kiss on the cheek once her customer had gone. 'Feeling okay?'

'Something about the air up here and this town helps perk you up,' Gemma said. 'And guess where I'm headed – to see Claire at the *Gazette* about being assigned a story.'

June smiled. 'That's great!' Two customers vied for June's attention, so Gemma squeezed her hand and said she'd see her soon.

Gemma looked over the display of pretty notebooks and bought a new one to bring to her interview, then glanced at her watch. She still had ten minutes. She browsed the fiction shelves, then crossed over to non-fiction, lured by the sign that said BOOKS THAT MIGHT HELP YOU FIGURE IT OUT. Now there was a sign meant for her. There was an entire shelf devoted to marriage. Relationships. And several books on divorce. Divorce. Gemma turned away, a heaviness dogging her again, and focused on the pregnancy section. This is who you are, she reminded herself. Pregnant. Not someone who's headed for divorce. Just someone who's pregnant. And has her entire life going in a different direction. She glanced at her watch. Time to go. Time to get that life back on track.

At ten o'clock, Gemma sat across from Claire at the big, scarred desk, feeling so hopeful again. Being here in the messy office of the loud newsroom in the centre of town, the sound of keyboards clicking, of staff conversation, of editors yelling and constant knocks on the door to interrupt Claire and ask for okays or sign-offs, made Gemma feel right at home. This was her territory, even if the *Gazette* – a daily paper – offices were an eighth of the size of the *New York Weekly*'s.

Gemma pulled out her new notebook, ready to jot down her assignment. 'I thought you could assign me a piece about the movie set in town, the effect on the local economy, on morale, et cetera. I could interview Colin Firth, the other stars. I saw an ad for extras in the *Gazette* on Sunday – I could talk to the director about the hiring process, interview a few extras. There are so many interesting components.'

Claire, tall and slender with poker-straight dark hair to her shoulders and narrow dark eyes, looked exactly like the angular teenage girl Gemma remembered. Claire took a sip of her coffee, and before she could say a word someone knocked, then came in and shoved papers at her for her to sign. Claire, one of the most together women Gemma had ever known — nothing frazzled her — scanned and signed, then turned her full attention to Gemma. 'Actually, I've already got someone covering the movie set and all that, and I'll tell you, finding out when Colin Firth is actually arriving in town is proving impossible. But I asked you to come in because there is a story I'd like you to cover while you're here.'

Yes! 'Great,' Gemma said. Her pen was poised to write. She sat up straight, any vestiges of her earlier pregnancy-related tiredness gone in a flash. She was on pure adrenalin right now.

Claire regarded her for a moment and took another sip of her coffee. 'There's a home for pregnant teenagers on the outskirts of town. Hope Home's fiftieth anniversary is at the end of July, and I'd like to do a full-coverage story on the place — what the home provides, the girls there, past residents, where are they now type of thing, what it was like to be a pregnant teen fifty years ago, twenty-five years ago, and today. I want statistics on all the angles, candid quotes, townspeople's reflections, the whole shebang.'

Gemma's heart sank. A story about pregnant teenagers?

Pregnant anyones? This wasn't a subject she wanted to focus on. The skin of her arms felt . . . tight. 'Claire, I—'

Claire held up a hand. 'Gemma, the fact that you're pregnant, and — well, I'll be honest — in a state of flux, not sure of anything, is the main reason why I want you doing this story. You — questions that you'll ask, perspective that you have, or need — will bring something to the piece that none of my other reporters could right now.'

Gemma sat back. 'But—'

'Three thousand words. Front page of the Life & People section.'

Three thousand words. Front page. That was big. Hope Home. Pregnant teenagers. Would she encounter a bunch of fifteen-year-olds who were giving their babies up for adoption? Keeping them? This assignment — from their stories to Hope Home's history and past residents, the adoptive parents, the circle of it all — would be emotionally intense, to say the least. 'You know I appreciate this opportunity, Claire. It's just . . . unexpected.'

'Like most things,' her friend said.

Gemma went back to the inn and took her laptop to the parlour, where Isabel had set up a noon tea for guests. It was so cosy that Gemma could stay in this sweet room with its overstuffed couches and chairs, mohair throws and soft pillows, for ever. She helped herself to camomile tea in a pretty cup and a small slice of the best Key lime pie she had ever tasted, then got busy reading through the information on the Hope Home website.

The site was pretty basic, informative but gently written, about what the home provided – a safe haven for pregnant teenagers, room and board, counselling, a resident nurse and help with adoptive services. 'Since 1963' was written under the Hope Home logo. What had it been like to be a pregnant teenager, sent to a home, in 1963? Gemma pulled out her notebook and wrote some notes about research she needed to do today – statistics on the number of pregnant teenagers in the US in the sixties and today, what percentage of babies given up for adoption were born to teenagers versus adult women. What percentage of pregnant teens kept their babies and what percentage put them up for adoption. As she jotted down questions, she found herself writing two full pages of notes.

Did they all want to keep their babies? Did some know right away that adoption was their answer? There were some harder questions that Gemma would delve into once she'd learned the basics, questions that even she didn't want to think about.

There was a photograph of the home on the main page of the website. It sure looked nice, a sprawling white farmhouse with a wraparound porch. And a plaque – BUILT IN 1883. There were flowerpots lining the porch, and under a huge shade tree were several chaises longues in a semi-circle. Group meetings, Gemma figured. She finished her tea and craved another piece of that incredible pie, but forced herself to get off the gorgeous mahogany love seat with its soft cushion printed with glittery sea stars, like the quilt in her room.

Out on the porch, Gemma sat on the swing, pulled out her phone and pressed in the number for Hope Home. Five minutes later, she had a noon appointment with the director for an interview and a tour; Pauline Lee had said that their strict privacy policies would usually prohibit a journalist from coming by, but given the upcoming fiftieth-anniversary celebration, she would make a special exception due to the coverage of the important work they did at Hope Home and the vital services the centre provided. The director promised to talk to a few of her residents to see if they'd like to participate in the article and share their stories, and she could discuss the possibility of contact information for former residents, both recent and from decades ago, at their meeting.

As Gemma opened her notebook to jot down more questions, her phone rang. Alexander.

'I'm on my way to court so just have a few minutes, but wanted to check in,' he said. 'All that fresh Maine air and small-town niceness make you want to move to Dobbs Ferry yet?'

He was relentless.

'I haven't had a chance to look at the listing yet, Alex. I have an assignment for the *Boothbay Regional Gazette* and—'

'Gemma, you promised to look. I almost got hit by a taxi this morning. I'm sick of this city. I want out.'

'Alex, I really can't talk about this right now. I'm on assignment. And my time here is limited, so I have to do some research right now.'

'Look, Gemma, I lost out on that house I put the offer on because I underbid and then felt like I couldn't up the offer because you flipped out. I really want to move. And this is the perfect timing. You don't have a job holding you to New York City. There's no reason to live here. We've been here since we graduated from high school, eight years. Enough already.'

She sighed. 'For you, not for me.'

'So I'll just be miserable, is that what you're saying?'

'No, I'm saying that I'd be *more* miserable in Dobbs Ferry. You wanted to live in New York, it was your dream. At least you have that. But if I moved to Dobbs Ferry, I'd be miserable. I'd feel like my soul was being sucked right out of me, every day. I wouldn't know who I was there, Alex.'

New York City had stopped being his dream long ago, though, and she knew it. When they'd been married about three years, they'd been having a good-natured argument about New York, Gemma listing its wonders and Alex its many downsides, which Gemma barely ever noticed. She'd told him how, as a kid, she'd take the elevator to the roof of her parents' fancy building on the Upper West Side and go out and stare at the twinkling lights and feel lit up by possibility, by how much was out there in the world for her to dream about, to hope for. When she was upset about her family life, which was often, she'd go up to the roof and fill herself with all that wonder.

On the evening of their third wedding anniversary, he'd told her he had a surprise for her, put a makeshift blindfold around her eyes and then led her out of their apartment to the elevator. Only when he took the blindfold off did she realize they'd gone up and not down and were on the roof of their building. She'd gasped. He'd set up a table covered with a lace tablecloth, a bouquet of flowers and two covered plates, which turned out to be his one speciality, chicken parmesan over linguini. A space heater was plugged in since it was October and chilly at night, and his old boom box was playing their wedding song, 'You're My Best Friend' by Queen.

He'd done all that for her, then sat her down, told her she was stunningly beautiful and he was grateful as hell that she was his wife, that as long as he had her he would be happy anywhere. They ate and drank champagne and had one slow dance in which they barely moved, then had gone downstairs and made love more passionately, more tenderly than Gemma could ever remember.

That was just two years ago. Her dear Alex, her best friend, her husband, had created that beautiful night for her. He'd been telling her that no matter what their marriage was like at the moment, full of arguments about where to live or when to start a family, their marriage would always be her

New York City, her rock, her wonder, her possibilities. They would find a way.

Two years later, they couldn't agree on where to live.

'You've never even given the suburbs a chance, Gemma,' he said into the phone. 'You just claim to hate it because it's not New York and because you think you have an idea what it's like to live there. You have no idea.'

Gemma closed her eyes, wishing she could wave a magic wand and just fix this. That Alex would want what she wanted. That she would want what he wanted. If only they could just agree.

They could go back and forth on this for ever. Neither was wrong, but Dobbs Ferry was wrong for her – it would be the death of her. She knew that. But New York City had become the same for him. Maybe she was being as selfish as she thought he was being.

She said she had to go and heard his sigh, and pictured him on the streets of New York City, grabbing a coffee on his way to court, taxi-cabs screeching by him, crowds of people, bus exhausts blowing in his face in the humid Manhattan air. For a moment, Gemma did feel selfish. If only she could find the middle ground, the answer for both of them.

She lifted her face to the sunshine and tried to put the conversation out of her mind. June's Subaru turned into the drive, and she had Allie, Isabel's daughter, in the back seat in a rear-facing pink baby carrier. June waved and in moments had the baby in her arms, and again Gemma tried to look at the baby and feel like most people seemed to feel when they looked at babies, a squeeze of the heart, an Awww, an Oh, can I hold her, smell her sweet baby smell, the yearning to have one of her own.

But Gemma felt none of that. All she felt was fear, deep inside.

She gave June a warm smile and then escaped in her car to Harbour View Coffee to work on her interview questions. But there was a mums-and-babies kind of get-together in the back, babies everywhere she looked. Maybe the universe was trying to tell her something. Gemma just wasn't sure what.

Chapter 7
Bea

Bea could barely turn around in the narrow shower of her crummy budget motel across the bay from downtown Boothbay Harbor. But at least the water was hot, the shampoo smelled good, and on the bathroom counter was a mini-hotplate, a mug and a packet of instant coffee with non-dairy creamer and sugar. Even more importantly, the motel was cheap. Bea had gotten her last half-week's paycheck from Crazy Burger, but she'd spent a fortune on gas to drive up to Maine, and had already racked up two nights at the motel, with no idea when she'd be checking out. The motel — the cheapest she'd found in the middle of the summer in this bustling tourist town — was sixty-nine bucks a night. She could afford one more night, but even that would be pushing it. If she wanted to stick around for a week or two, get her bearings before she introduced herself to her birth mother, she'd have to get some kind of temporary job. Given that it was summer, she was sure one of the zillion restaurants needed kitchen help. After she visited the hospital, she'd look around for HELP WANTED signs or check the local paper.

Bea blow-dried her shoulder-length blonde hair with the tiny, tinny hairdryer attached to the wall, put on a little make-up — eyeliner and mascara and a quick swipe of pinky-red lip gloss — then headed back into the small room to get her bag. On the bedside table she'd put her photograph of herself and her mother at her graduation, to remind herself who she was, that this crazy deathbed secret didn't change that fact that she was Bea Crane, daughter of Cora and Keith Crane. They'd raised her, they'd loved her.

They'd lied to her.

Bea dropped down on the edge of the bed, that sick feeling hitting her in the stomach again whenever her thoughts went to that fact. Omission. And a big one. The past couple of nights, she'd lain in bed going over pieces of her childhood, instances where her parents might have told her the truth. When she'd had to do a second-grade class project, About My Family, complete with photographs and a few sentences about each one, and a classmate had said: 'You don't look anything like your mom or dad. Maybe you're a Martian.'

By the time Bea was thirteen, she was three inches taller than her father, who was five foot seven.

Maybe once the words were never said — 'We adopted you, we chose you, we picked you' — you couldn't just come out and say them when a kid was older, when it might be devastating to a seven-year-old, a twelve-year-old. Grow up with the knowledge from before your earliest memory, and it was just a part of you. Bea supposed she could understand why her parents had never told her. They'd probably wanted to over the years, but once she'd gotten beyond a certain age, they just couldn't bring themselves to shatter her world, her identity, her image of herself.

When Bea felt angry about the omission, a word she preferred over 'lie' in this case, she tried to remember that, that her parents had gotten themselves in a sticky situation they couldn't easily remedy.

Fortified by the coffee and the hot shower, she was ready to head over to Coastal General Hospital, where she'd been born. Or where she thought she had been born. Her original birth certificate listed place of birth as 'HHL', but it was signed by a doctor at Coastal General Hospital and issued from there. Perhaps HHL were the initials for which the labour and delivery ward or wing had been named. Bea grabbed her bag and headed out, and once again the brilliant blue sunshine, cotton-ball clouds and breezy mid-seventies temperature lifted her spirits. She found herself liking that she'd been born in this beautiful place, this beautiful state with its water and trees and fresh, clean air. Just two days in Boothbay Harbor, from Saturday afternoon to Monday morning, and it was already beginning to feel more familiar. But Veronica Russo loomed as alien in her mind as she had on Saturday when she'd gone to the diner. Her birth mother was a total stranger, connected to Bea in the most fundamental of ways. Bea couldn't wrap her mind around that one.

Coastal General Hospital was on the outskirts of Boothbay Harbor, a fifteen-minute drive along a stretch of rural highway. Bea had a love–hate relationship with hospitals. She'd said goodbye to her father in a hospital, though he'd been gone by the time he'd reached the ER. A heart attack – unknown heart condition – at forty-one. Bea shook her head at the thought, the memory of the look on her mother's face when Cora had gotten the call. 'My husband is dead?' she'd said into the phone, her face full of such confusion, nine-year-old Bea standing just feet away, washing an apple in the sink. That had been her first experience with hospitals, and for a long time afterwards, she couldn't pass a hospital without feeling sick to her stomach.

She'd said her final goodbye to her mother in a hospital's hospice wing, Cora barely able to move her hand in Bea's on that last day. Her mother's medical team had been top-notch and kind, and for a while the hospital had turned into a place of hope for Bea. Until there was no hope.

Bea walked up the stone path to the stately old brick building, pushed through the revolving door and asked the guy at the information desk for the labour ward. On the third floor, the elevator opened to a sign on the wall reading THE MARTHA L. JOHNSON MATERNITY WING. No

'HHL' there. Bea walked down a short hall, looking for the nurses' station, but stopped when she noticed the nursery. Beyond the glass wall were several babies wrapped in blankets with tiny caps on their heads. A nurse was picking up one red-faced baby, who settled down along the nurse's arm.

She tried to imagine herself here, as one of these babies, her birth mother standing twenty-two years ago where Bea was now. Maybe Veronica Russo hadn't stood here. Maybe when you gave up your baby for adoption, you didn't stand staring at him or her in the bassinet. Had Cora and Keith Crane stood here? Or had the adoption agency arranged the transfer internally? Did it matter, anyway? Bea's chest felt tight, and she turned to leave, grateful for the nurse walking down the hall.

'Excuse me,' Bea said to her, taking her birth certificate out of her bag and holding it up for the nurse. 'Could you tell me what this HHL means?'

The nurse glanced at Bea's birth certificate, the original stamped with NOT FOR LEGAL PURPOSES across the top. 'Well, I know that HH stands for Hope Home, but the L is throwing me. Let me go ask another nurse at the station.'

'Hope Home?' Bea repeated, following her.

The woman turned to Bea. 'It's a home not too far from here for pregnant teenagers.'

Oh, Bea thought. Veronica had gone to a home? She

wondered why she hadn't stayed at her parents' house, since they'd lived right in Boothbay Harbor. Had Veronica been sent away?

'The L stands for "lot",' another nurse explained, handing back Bea's birth certificate. 'Every now and then, a Hope Home girl will go into labour and have her baby either in the home or en route to the hospital. HHL means the baby was born in the Hope Home's parking lot.'

'I was born in a parking lot?' Bea said. Of a home for teenage mothers. Just what is your story, Veronica Russo? she wondered.

'You were likely born in an ambulance dispatched to bring your birth mother here. But you started coming before it was safe to transport.'

'I was born in a parking lot,' Bea said again, but she was thinking less about herself and more about Veronica Russo, who must have been scared out of her mind.

Hope Home was twenty minutes in the opposite direction, on the other side of the peninsula and down a long, winding road that stretched for miles. A right turn down another long road led to nothing but trees. Finally Bea found the marker, a white post that read 14 HILL CIRCLE. Another long dirt drive later, the house came into view. Bea was surprised; she'd expected an institutional-looking building. But a sign proclaiming HOPE HOME was hung off the porch of a very pretty, sprawling white farmhouse with several padded rocking chairs, and flower boxes everywhere. Big trees shaded the front yard. There was a group of empty chaises longues in a semi-circle under one shady tree. Under another was an enormously pregnant girl who looked all of thirteen, lying on a chaise and flipping through a magazine. Another very pregnant girl with beautiful long red hair was walking around the perimeter of the yard, earphones in her ears.

A few cars were parked alongside the house, stones marking spaces. Bea pulled in and wondered if she'd been born right here, in this spot.

As Bea walked around the front of the farmhouse, the pregnant girl who'd been reading *People* magazine pushed herself off the chaise and walked towards her. 'Hi, are you pregnant?'

Now that the girl was closer, Bea could see she was a bit older than she'd first thought. Sixteen, seventeen maybe. Her long, light brown hair was in a French braid. 'No. I was born here, actually.'

'Oh. So what do you want?'

'I just wanted to look around. Maybe talk to a director or something?'

'Ask for Pauline.' The girl glanced at her watch. 'She's probably right at the desk when you walk in.'

'Thanks.' Bea smiled at the girl and headed up the steps. She pulled open the screen door. Padded benches lined the entry. Further in, a woman sat at a white wooden desk with a bouquet of blue hydrangeas.

The woman looked up from the binder she'd been writing in. 'Welcome. Can I help you?'

Bea suddenly had marbles in her mouth. 'I was born here twenty-two years ago. In the parking lot, apparently. I just thought I could look around. Maybe speak to someone about the place? Get some history.'

The woman smiled. 'Sure. I'm Leslie, assistant to Pauline Lee, the director of Hope Home. Pauline's in a meeting right now, but I'm happy to answer your questions if I can.' She closed the binder and gestured at the chair facing the desk. Bea sat. 'Parking lot, huh? Sometimes our residents go into labour so fast that we can't get them to the hospital in time. You were either born on a blanket right out on the grass or perhaps in an ambulance, depending on the timing.'

Bea couldn't imagine anyone – the girl reading *People*, for instance – delivering her baby on the grass. Or in an ambulance, for that matter.

'Could you give me some information about Hope Home? I don't know a thing about it.'

'Well, we open our doors to pregnant teenagers and young women through age twenty-one. Right now we have eight girls in residence. Last month we had two more. We provide a comfortable room, meals, education – whether keeping up with classes at school or GED preparation – and counselling in all regards: emotional well-being, decision-making regarding the pregnancy, whatever that may be, and help with adoption services.'

'That's wonderful,' Bea said. 'Everything under one roof.' And the place did look homey, with its cottage décor and the flower boxes lining the windows.

Leslie nodded. 'We're non-profit and cover the costs of everything I mentioned. Medical care is not covered and is handled via arrangements made with Coastal General. All prenatal care is handled there, but we do have a nurse on staff twenty-four-seven.'

'Were you working here twenty-two years ago?' Bea asked.

'No, I joined Hope Home two years ago. Pauline's been the director for almost ten years. We do have very strict privacy policies in place, so it's unlikely anyone who was here then would be able to answer certain questions.'

Bea glanced out the window at the two pregnant girls, who were now sitting on the porch swing. Her birth mother had been one of them twenty-two years ago. There was so much Bea wanted to ask this woman, but it was really only Veronica who could answer her questions.

'I could give you a brief tour, if you'd like,' Leslie said. 'It won't be exactly as it was twenty-two years ago, but the basics are the same.'

Of course Bea wanted a tour, so she followed Leslie down the short hall to the dining room, which didn't look all that different from the dining room at the Three Captains' Inn. 'We all eat breakfast together, between seven and eight. The dining room always has healthy snacks available for cravings too.'

Next was the breathing room, then the counselling room, then exercise, a small library, then an empty bedroom, which looked quite nice. The room wasn't big, but had a white wooden bed with a stitched quilt and ruffled pillows, and a big braided blue and yellow rug was on the spotless wooden floor. On the wall next to the white bureau was a quote from Eleanor Roosevelt: 'No one can make you feel inferior without your consent.'

She wondered which room had been Veronica's. She imagined her sitting on the rocker, reading one of the books on pregnancy from the library. Or staring at the Eleanor Roosevelt quote. She was dying to know what Veronica's time here had been like.

She glanced down the hall and out the window at the two pregnant girls. The girl who'd greeted her was French-braiding the hair of the redhead. 'Leslie, I hope it's not rude to ask this, but I'm wondering something. Do most girls come here because of the stigma of being pregnant teenagers?'

Leslie glanced out at the girls. 'Yes. Sometimes it's to protect them from gossip and stress at home. Sometimes it's because we can provide round-the-clock care and education and a social factor. And sometimes, well, it's a matter of their having nowhere to go.'

Meaning that they were kicked out of their homes?

Bea pictured Veronica's parents dropping her off here and driving away, dust flying up in their wake. She wondered what the story was.

'Well, I appreciate your time,' Bea said. 'I guess I just really wanted to see the place, and I have.'

Leslie shook her hand. 'I wish you luck in finding your answers, Bea.' She smiled and sat back down at her desk, opening the binder.

When Bea stepped outside on to the porch, the redhead put down her *People* magazine, and the other girl took a bite of turkey sandwich from a plate on her lap.

'So Kim said you were born here?' the redhead said. She wore square copper earrings with the name 'Jen' imprinted.

'I was. In the parking lot, apparently.'

Her mouth dropped open. 'In the parking lot?'

Maybe Bea shouldn't have said that. Damn it.

'In an ambulance, I mean. Parked here.' At least that was what Bea assumed.

'Oh. Yesterday in prep class, the leader said that can happen, that you can go into labour fast and not make it to the hospital, but that between the resident nurse and the para-medics, everything would be fine.'

Kim took a bite of her sandwich. 'And by looking at her,' she said, 'clearly it was.' She stared at Bea. 'So you're, what – seeing where you were born?'

'Yeah. I'm thinking about connecting with my birth mother.'

'Thinking?' Kim repeated, her face falling. 'So you're not sure if you want to?'

'I didn't even know I was adopted until a few weeks ago.'

Bea rushed to explain for fear that she'd upset the girl. 'It's all been kind of a shock. So I'm just trying to figure out how I feel.'

The girls eyed each other.

'You just found out you were adopted?' Jen asked, her eyes both wide and angry. 'Your adoptive parents never told you?'

Bea shook her head. 'The longer they waited the more impossible it became, I suppose. Plus, my mother explained in a letter that she wanted to believe in her heart that she'd given birth to me. It's complicated.'

'Complicated?' Jen said. 'Try *wrong*. She totally cut your birth mother out of the picture.'

'Jen,' the other girl said, touching her arm.

'No,' Jen snapped, pulling her arm away. 'How dare she have not told you! Will the couple who adopt my baby not tell her she was adopted? Just pretend I don't exist?' She paced for a moment, and Bea felt her heart start to race. What the hell had she done? Why had she told these vulnerable girls her situation at all? They were teenagers. Pregnant teenagers. Oh, Bea, you idiot, she thought, her stomach flipping over.

'So are you going to look for your birth mother?' Kim asked, darting her eyes at her upset friend.

'Well, I'm here in town – this is where she lives. I'm not sure about meeting her. I just don't know anything.'

'God, I hate this!' Jen shouted. 'You don't even know if you want to meet the person who gave birth to you?'

'It's . . . complicated,' Bea said. She needed to apologize

to the girls for getting them upset – well, getting one of them upset – and get out of here.

'I hope my child comes looking for me one day,' Kim said. 'I mean, look at you. All pretty and healthy and nice. Who wouldn't want to know their baby turned out to be pretty and happy-looking?'

'I wouldn't,' Jen said, shooting her friend a glare. 'I mean, I think it sucks that she doesn't even want to meet her own birth mother, but I don't think I want my child to come looking for me. How the hell am I supposed to get through every day knowing one day my doorbell is going to ring?'

'Isn't that kind of a contradiction, Jen?' Kim said gently. 'Anyway, Larissa – she's the counsellor here,' she added, turning to Bea for a moment, then back to Jen. 'She said you just live your life and make it a piece of you, and if you want to be found, you can give that information to the registry, and if you don't, you don't have to.'

'I don't know what I want!' Jen yelled. 'But I don't need to know that the baby I'm giving up is going to be a real person one day, wanting to find me. So get out of here!' she screamed at Bea.

'Jesus, Jen. I do want to know,' Kim said, almost in a whisper. She turned to Bea. 'I want to know every good thing about you. I want to know that one day my baby might love me anyway, even though I'm not keeping her. I want to know she might want to know me some day.' She started crying.

'Now look what you did, idiot!' Jen said and threw her sandwich at Bea.

Bea gasped as a slice of bread hit her on the thigh and dropped to the ground, a piece of turkey and a little glob of mayonnaise sticking to her jeans. A lettuce leaf landed on her foot. She shook it off, her leg trembling.

'I'm sorry,' Bea said, her stomach twisting. 'I'm sorry. I—'

The screen door squeaked open and Leslie came out with two other women.

'Why do we have to listen to this crap?' Jen said to her, her face turning as red as her hair. 'I don't want to know. Okay? I. Don't. Want. To. Know.'

Kim started crying again and ran inside.

'I'm Pauline Lee,' a tall, dark-haired woman said to Bea. 'The director of Hope Home. I'm sorry, but I think it's best that you leave now,' she added kindly. She sat down in the rocker next to Jen and put her arm around her shoulder.

Bea stifled back the sob that was pushing its way up her throat. She ran to her car.

The other woman who'd come out with Pauline and Leslie hurried over to Bea as she was about to get in her car. 'I have tissues, if you want to wipe off that mayo,' she said, handing Bea a pocket packet of Kleenex.

Bea took the tissues, tears stinging her eyes. 'Thank you.'

'I'm Gemma Hendricks,' she said, her honey-coloured hair shining in the bright sun. 'I'm writing a story about

Hope Home and was just finishing up a meeting with the director when we overheard the conversation you and the two girls were having. Pauline said she'd keep an ear on it, and I suppose she thought it had gone as far as the girls could handle.'

'I feel horrible,' Bea said, tears streaming down her cheeks. 'I didn't mean to upset them. I didn't mean to say anything. One of the girls asked me why I was here, and I was honest, when I suppose I shouldn't have been. I should have realized they were vulnerable to what I might say.' Bea shook her head and covered her face with her hands. 'What the hell am I doing?'

Gemma touched Bea's arm. 'I'm a reporter, and as I said, I'm working on a story about Hope Home, so I don't know if I'm the worst or the best person for you to talk to, but if you need an ear, even if it has to be off record, I'm happy to listen.'

'So you were in a meeting with the director?' Bea asked.

Gemma nodded. 'Getting some history and basic information. I'm writing an article about the home's fiftieth anniversary.'

'Can you share some of the history with me?' Bea asked.

'Sure. It'll all be going in my article, so nothing I was told is confidential.'

'What I tell you about my story might be, though,' Bea said. 'Not from my perspective. I mean from my birth mother's. She doesn't even know I'm in town.'

'I'll be discreet. I won't even use your real name if that's your preference,' Gemma assured her.

Her real name. It made Bea crazy to think that if Veronica Russo hadn't given her up, she'd have a different name entirely, a different life.

Bea had nowhere on earth to be, and maybe talking this whole thing out with someone would help her hear herself think. 'OK.'

'Why don't we go have lunch?' Gemma said. 'On me.'

Twenty minutes later, Bea was sitting across from Gemma, a small black recorder on the table along with Gemma's notebook and pen, at a seafood restaurant, the events of the last three weeks pouring out of her. She told Gemma about her mother's deathbed confession, sent to her a year after her mother passed away. About calling the adoption agency. About her birth mother updating the file with every possible piece of contact information. About going to the diner to check out Veronica. Seeing her in person, a real live, walking, breathing woman. The woman who gave birth to her. Who held the answers to how she came about, who her birth father was, what Bea's history was.

'Wow,' Gemma said, sitting back and putting down her iced tea, which she hadn't even taken a sip of. 'That's some story. Can I share it in my article? What you've been through is so moving. I won't put in identifying details about your birth mother, such as where she works. Unless, of course, it works out that I have her permission too.'

'Well, how would that even come about?' Bea asked. 'I'm not even sure I want to meet her. If I'm ready, I mean. I don't know anything.'

'No worries,' Gemma said. 'I just mean if you do meet her, and if she'd like to share her story, her history. What a beautiful story of coming full circle it would be.'

'I suppose,' Bea said. 'But I have no idea if she'd be interested in making her past public. I don't know anything about her. Except that she bakes a really good pie, apparently.'

Suddenly a male voice boomed, 'Hey, folks! Colin Firth is signing autographs and taking pictures on the pier right outside!'

At least twenty people jumped out of their seats and rushed outside or crowded by the windows. A minute later, they were all back, shrugging and chatting about how he was nowhere to be seen.

'I'd know Colin Firth a mile away,' Gemma said, peering out the window. 'And I don't see him.'

'That's so weird,' Bea said. 'On Saturday, when I was at the diner, someone called out a Colin Firth sighting too.'

'Maybe he got wind of it and fled. I'd love to catch a glimpse of him, I admit,' Gemma said. 'He's one of my favourite actors. "I like you. Very much. Just as you are,"' she said in an English accent.

Bea laughed. '*Bridget Jones.* I love that movie. One of the last movies my mother and I saw together was *The King's Speech*.

She was crazy about Colin Firth. We watched it in her room in the hospital on Netflix.' Tears stung Bea's eyes. 'She loved that movie so much. She'd seen it twice already but wanted to watch it again with me.'

'Maybe not being able to say what you want to say, for whatever reason, resonated with her,' Gemma said, her dark blue eyes full of compassion.

Bea almost gasped as she understood what Gemma was saying; she envisioned Colin Firth as George VI, with his lifelong terrible stutter, thrust onto the throne and having to speak publicly to his people in order to reassure them. 'I'll bet it did. I didn't think of that.'

'Well, you've had a lot to take in over the past few weeks,' Gemma said, and Bea felt herself relax; it felt so good to talk to someone who was just plain kind. Granted, Gemma Hendricks was a reporter, and maybe all she was after here was the story, but Bea had a good feeling about Gemma. She seemed true blue.

Their lunch was served, fish and chips for Bea and the crab cakes for Gemma. When the bill came Bea offered to pay her share, even though it would hurt her wallet to do so, but Gemma insisted.

'I said it was my treat, and I meant it.'

Relief flooded through Bea. 'Actually, I really appreciate it. I'm staying at the cheapest motel in town, but I can't afford more than one more night. I'll have to find a job if I plan to stick around.' But what was she even sticking around for?

To decide if she wanted to meet her birth mother? She could do that from home.

Which was the problem. There was no home. Bea had nowhere to go, nowhere to be. She pictured the old white rental cottage on Cape Cod, the cosy living room, the small, sweet bedroom created for Bea for visits and summers. She saw her mother coming out to greet her in her cotton sundress and sandals, her hair in a loose bun, her face lit up with happiness that her girl was home for the summer. Cora Crane, her mother.

Bea glanced out the window and let out a deep breath. Suddenly, all she wanted was to really see Colin Firth out there on the pier, signing autographs and agreeing to photographs, her mother's King George VI, working so hard to be able to say what he wanted to say, what he needed to say, to his people. She wondered if her mother had tried in her own way, wishing she could come up with the words to make it less shocking — that she'd withheld the truth, that Bea had been adopted.

'Hey, you know what?' Gemma said, sipping her iced tea. 'Yesterday I overheard the manager of the inn where I'm staying telling someone she's looking for kitchen and cleaning help, that she was offering room and board. It's the Three Captains' Inn, just a couple streets up from the harbour. It's a gorgeous place. After we're done here, why don't you go back to your motel and get changed so you don't smell like turkey and mayo, and then come over? I'll introduce you to

Isabel and you two can set up a time to talk. Maybe you can just interview on the spot if she's not busy.'

Bea felt herself brighten. 'Kitchens are my thing. That would be great if it worked out. Looks like I owe you big now. For coming to my rescue at Hope Home, for lunch, for listening, and for this possible tip at the inn. You're like a fairy godmother.'

Gemma laughed. 'Now if only I could work the same magic on myself.'

Chapter 8
Veronica

Résumé and photographs in a manila envelope, Veronica headed out to Frog Marsh at three o'clock on Monday, figuring she'd be among the first in line to apply to be an extra in the Colin Firth movie. But there were at least a hundred people there already, holding their own manila envelopes. She recognized many folks from town and waved, sizing them up as her competition. Mostly everyone looked like what an extra was supposed to look like: a real person. Several women, though, were decked out and dolled up as though they were going out for New Year's Eve.

Veronica had spent an indulgent couple of hours face-deep in her closet that morning, trying to settle on the right look. She'd realized she was going to wait on a line, fill out a form and hand in her résumé and photographs, none of which required 'a look', but you never knew who might be doing the collecting and what they were jotting down on your résumé after you turned it in. Trying too hard. Too old. Too young. Too much make-up. Too dull.

She'd made herself look Everywoman-ish. The woman in the background, walking by, sitting at the next table in a restaurant, shopping at Hannaford's supermarket, cutting hair at the next station. Extras faded into the background. At five foot ten and slender, with a D-cup chest and thick, shiny auburn hair to her shoulders, Veronica had never been much of a fader, so she'd put on a pair of old jeans, a pale yellow peasant top and her comfortable clogs, swept her hair into a low ponytail and then added her Best Little Diner in Boothbay apron, as though she were heading to work afterwards. She wasn't, but how much more Everywoman could a real-life waitress be? She was an old pro at walking around wordlessly with her coffee pot in the background of The Best Little Diner. Most times, all she had to do was lift up the pot with a glance at someone, they'd nod, and that was the entire conversation. She had this extra thing in the bag.

Her confidence had disappeared and returned every few seconds on the three-minute drive to Frog Marsh. She wanted this. Bad.

The set had grown since she'd last been here. Multiple trailers instead of just one. Three vans. Barricades stacked alongside one another. A long table was set up by one of the trailers, which Veronica learned belonged to the second assistant director. She knew this because as the line grew behind her to at least two hundred people, he came out of the trailer and said, 'Peeps, listen up. My name is Patrick Ool. That's right, Ool. And yes, I've heard it all. Fool. Tool: a favourite with a certain PA — that's "production assistant" for those of you new to movie-making. I'm the second assistant director on the film, which is as yet untitled. We're filming four scenes here in Boothbay Harbor, one in The Best Little Diner in Boothbay, two on the streets and one on a cruise boat. We're looking to hire fifty to seventy-five extras . . .'

One in The Best Little Diner in Boothbay . . . Veronica glanced down at her apron and almost couldn't contain her smile. This just might be her lucky day. If Veronica could act like anything, it was like a waitress at The Best Little Diner in Boothbay. She supposed this meant the diner would be shut down for the filming days. The director or producer or whoever paid for these things must be paying Deirdre a small fortune.

'When's Colin Firth coming?' a woman near the front of the line shouted out. 'That's all I really care about,' she added on a laugh.

'You,' Patrick Ool barked, pointing at the woman who called out. 'You're banned from the set. Please leave.'

'Wait, but—' she said.

A security guard, the biggest person Veronica had ever seen, was already next to the woman, ushering her away. Veronica felt sorry for her; you could see the tears shimmering in her eyes as she kept turning back.

'Sorry, folks,' Patrick said. 'I'm not a jerk, but that was a good lesson. If you're here to get a glimpse of the stars of the film, leave now. If you're here because you think working as an extra on a major film sounds really interesting and like something you'd enjoy, please stay. Number-one rule of working as an extra is that you don't talk to the stars. You don't bother them. You don't take pictures of them. You don't tell them you've loved them since blah, blah, blah. You just don't. If we're clear on that, and you're still standing here, great.'

Well, so much for rushing Colin Firth the moment he appeared – not that he did appear; Veronica kept one eye on Patrick Ool and one eye on the trailers, hoping Colin would suddenly emerge with that dazzling smile.

She had to get hired. She had to. The more the second assistant director talked about what was required of an extra – their time, sitting around for hours, being dead quiet during filming, following directions from him – the bigger her hope grew.

Finally the line inched up, and Veronica was next to meet the three people – two men, including Patrick Ool, and a woman – seated at a long table with a stack of résumés. The woman eyed Veronica's apron, took a Polaroid of her without even giving her the heads-up to smile, jotted something down on the back, then took Veronica's manila envelope and attached the Polaroid to it with a paperclip. With a thank you and a 'We'll be in touch,' Veronica was dismissed and Patrick Ool called out, 'Next.'

It all happened so fast that Veronica hadn't even thought to ask questions, but luckily the woman in line behind her had, and Veronica overheard Patrick Ool say that selected applicants would be notified in the next few days. Tonight, if she wasn't all pie'd out after her class, she'd make herself that salted-caramel Hope Pie and have a huge slice.

The Cast-Off Pie for Veronica's newest client was all boxed up with Veronica's signature red velvet ribbon and waiting on the kitchen counter. She glanced at her watch: 5.40. The woman asked for a special rush pie and then was late picking it up? Nervy. In twenty minutes, Veronica would have a kitchen full of students for the first pie class.

Making the Cast-Off Pie had been an unexpected blessing earlier this afternoon; measuring out the thick peanut butter, mixing in the shredded coconut and chocolate chips and making the graham-cracker crust had let her take her mind off tonight, off having students like snobby former classmate Penelope Von Blun, who never let her forget who she once was – the high-school junior who'd gotten pregnant and been sent away – and Officer Nick DeMarco, who always made her feel unsettled, perhaps because he represented Timothy to her in a way and brought back how Veronica had once – and never since – felt: deeply in love. Both people would be in her kitchen, the place that had long been her refuge. While making the pie, she'd focused on what she wanted to cast off from her own heart, her own mind: feeling less than, feeling ashamed, feeling sorry that she'd gotten herself into a situation at age sixteen that had had such incredible consequences. A baby taken away. A love destroyed. A family torn apart. Veronica, alone. She found herself putting all that into the pie, those negative feelings, but instead of feeling better, her heart felt heavier.

As she'd told her client, Cast-Off Pie didn't always work. Then again, she hadn't been making the pie for herself. The recipient would make the pie her own; that was how it worked, how it had always worked.

Veronica took a final glance around her kitchen, making sure everything was ready for class. She'd set up pie stations at the big centre island, rolling-pins and labelled canisters of ingredients for six people. Two students had called this morning to drop out; one had forgotten her knitting class started this week at the library, and another was coughing so violently that she could barely get the words out that she was ill. That made six students. Tonight they'd make a traditional apple pie, working on it together, unless anyone, such as Nick DeMarco's daughter, wanted to make a special pie. Since Veronica had been teaching the class, she always handed out recipes for the special pies, as most people preferred to make them at home once they'd learned the basics of pie-making and seen that it wasn't so hard at all.

The doorbell rang. Either a very late client or an early student.

Veronica didn't recognize the woman at the door, and she

knew all her students by sight. For a moment, the woman stared at Veronica, and she realized she had seen her around town a couple of times over the past few months. She was in her mid-thirties, with shoulder-length, swirly, highlighted blonde hair and a dressy outfit, and she wore serious make-up, reminding Veronica of the way the 'Real Housewives' tended to style themselves. Veronica tried to imagine the Real Housewives of Maine running around in fleece and L.L.Bean duck boots.

'I'm here for the special pie we discussed,' the woman finally said, hostility radiating from her. 'You said it was called Cast-Off Pie.' She was dressed in such feminine, airy clothing, totally at odds with her anger — a pale lavender silky tank top with ruffles down the front, off-white pants and high-heeled mules. She wore a lot of gold jewellery too, including a wedding ring.

Her husband was having an affair? Veronica was no psychic, but she knew, somehow, that that wasn't the case.

'I have it boxed up and ready to go,' Veronica said. 'Why don't you come in and I'll go get it.' Veronica extended her hand. 'Veronica Russo.'

The woman hesitated for a split second, making Veronica curious. What was up? 'Beth,' was all she said in response.

As Veronica headed into the kitchen to get the pie, she sensed Beth staring holes into her back, shooting daggers, maybe. Her hostility didn't seem truly focused on Veronica, though; there was something complicated at work here. When she returned with the pie, Veronica said, 'Do I know you from somewhere? I think I've seen you around town a couple of times, maybe.'

'I don't think so,' Beth said, taking the pie. 'So if the pie does its job, I just leave the fee in your mailbox, right? Fifteen dollars?'

'Yes. And if it doesn't work, you don't owe me a thing.'

'Well, we'll see, then,' Beth said, offering Veronica a tight smile before turning and exiting out the door, past two women coming up the walk.

Even if Veronica wanted to think about strange Beth, her first two students had arrived. And they were a lot friendlier too. A pair of sisters in aprons, Isabel and June Nash, who owned the Three Captains' Inn, which had Veronica on standing order for two pies a week. Veronica liked both sisters, but she didn't know them well. She was several years older than Isabel, who'd called her months ago to rave about her pie at the diner and to ask her to bake for the inn. Isabel had had a baby just six months ago, but you'd never know it from her perfect figure and how elegant she looked, even in jeans and a T-shirt. Veronica was at least ten years older than June, who had the most gorgeous wild curly auburn hair, secured tonight in a bun with chopsticks. June worked in Veronica's favourite bookstore and had a very polite son called Charlie.

'I'm determined to learn how to make my own pie crust without it turning all crumbly or getting all wet,' Isabel said. 'Every time I try, it's a disaster.'

'You should have tasted the banana-cream pie I made for a bake sale for Charlie's school last year,' June said. 'I think I forgot the sugar entirely. Someone bought a slice, then came back to the table and asked for his money back!'

Veronica laughed. 'That'll never happen again, I promise.'

Next to arrive was Penelope Von Blun, who announced that her friend CeCe couldn't take the class after all because of a conflict with something. Once again, Veronica was struck that Penelope looked different. For the past few months, she seemed . . . toned down. Her shoulder-length dark hair, which was usually flat-ironed to model perfection, was natural and wavy. The make-up was minimal. And instead of her usual fashionista wardrobe, she looked kind of like everyone else, like someone who lived in Maine instead of New York City. She'd always worn gobs of jewellery, but lately Veronica had noticed she wore the same gold cross around her neck and her wedding ring. A 'make-under' instead of a makeover, really. Veronica wondered what it was about. Penelope Von Blun had had the same flashy, expensive style since middle school. But instead of pushing past Veronica and making snide comments about what Veronica was wearing or how small her house was, Penelope offered everyone a huge smile, complimented the painting of wildflowers in the hall and Veronica's earrings, then chatted up the Nash sisters and told them she'd heard 'fabulous' things about their inn. This was a new and improved Penelope.

As Isabel and June chatted with Penelope, Nick DeMarco and his daughter arrived.

Nick knew everyone, of course. Between patrolling around town and writing tickets for speeding and expired registration stickers, Nick DeMarco and the other cops in town stood out. Women usually fawned over him, since he was good-looking and widowed, but, though Isabel and June were warm and friendly, especially to Leigh, they certainly weren't fawning. Penelope was very friendly to him but not flirtatious. And Veronica, the only single woman in the house, focused her attention on his daughter's questions instead of Nick's sidelong glances. She wondered what he was thinking about her.

Just when Veronica thought Penelope couldn't possibly get any warmer or fuzzier – or less snooty – she shone her attention on young Leigh DeMarco, asking her all about her summer camp, then shook Nick's hand and told him that it was thanks to hard-working police officers like him that Boothbay Harbor was such a safe and wonderful place to live. Veronica had no idea why Penelope Von Blun had turned . . . nice, but it was a welcome change.

'So, let's head into the kitchen and get started,' Veronica said, leading the way. 'It'll be just the five of you, a perfect number for a pie class.'

'I love this kitchen,' Isabel said, glancing around the large room.

Veronica did too. The moment she'd seen the yellow

bungalow, she'd known it was the right house for her, but when she stepped into the kitchen, she couldn't believe her luck. A big country kitchen with painted white cabinets, lots of counter space and original wood floors, the room was made for baking pies. Veronica had painted the walls a very pale blue and had a professional oven installed, but otherwise she hadn't had to renovate much at all. A back door opened to a small deck overlooking a tiny yard and Veronica's container garden. She didn't have much of a green thumb, but liked to see flowers when she looked out the window.

The group gathered around the island, checking out the canisters and picking up the rolling-pins.

'Tonight, we'll make a traditional apple pie,' Veronica said. 'I know some of you might be interested in learning to make my special elixir pies. I have the most-requested recipes printed out, so if you'd like any of them, just let me know. Although we'll be making apple pie tonight, if anyone would like to make a special pie instead, you can do that too and be off on your own, asking for help as you need it.'

'Apple pie for us, right, Leigh?' Nick asked his daughter.

Leigh glanced at the floor, then at Veronica. 'Actually, I'm making a special pie. Shoo-fly pie.'

'I think I remember my great-grandmother making that when I was a kid,' Nick said, smiling at his daughter, then Veronica.

'Shoo-fly pie,' Isabel said. 'My Aunt Lolly used to love that! It's molasses, isn't it? She had such a sweet tooth.'

Veronica nodded. 'Molasses and brown-sugar crumb topping. I love it, but you don't see it made much these days.'

'What kind of elixir pie is that?' June asked, picking up a canister of baking soda and peeking in through the plastic top.

Leigh DeMarco was staring at her feet.

'It's what I call a Spirit Pie,' Veronica said. 'It can help you feel close to someone you lost.'

For a split second, it was as though everyone in the room held their breath. Nick was nodding slowly and taking his daughter's hand, and Leigh looked like she wanted to run out of the back door, but she didn't. June and Isabel glanced at each other and were silent. And Penelope's lips were pursed tight, her arms crossed against her chest. She seemed angry. But why?

'I miss my mom,' Leigh said, staring at her sneakers, but Veronica could see she was holding back tears. 'Mrs Buckman, she's our neighbour,' she added, glancing up at her dad, then around the room, 'she had one of Veronica's Spirit Pies and said she felt like her mother was right in the room with her.'

'Sometimes I feel that way at the inn,' Isabel said. 'I'll be in the foyer, putting brochures on the sideboard, and all of a sudden I'll feel the presence of my mom and dad. A few weeks ago, I was in the kitchen, whipping up an Irish breakfast for guests, and for the briefest moment it was as though my Aunt Lolly and Uncle Ted were with me, telling me I was doing a good job. Doesn't happen often enough.'

'If I could eat a slice of delicious pie that would help me feel their presence,' June said, 'I'd have a great excuse to eat the whole thing.'

Veronica smiled. 'That's the good thing about shoo-fly pie. It's so sweet you can probably only eat one slice. When I make it, and then sit with my tea and have a piece, I do feel my grandmother with me. It's the most comforting thing.'

'So why don't we all make a shoo-fly pie instead of apple pie?' Leigh said. 'We can all have a slice and we can all get to feel close to who we want.' She shuffled through the recipes on the island and pulled out the one for shoo-fly. A colour photo was attached to each recipe so that the students could see what the finished product would look like.

Penelope turned to Veronica. 'Will it work on someone who's not dead? You said it helps you feel closer to someone. Will it work if they're alive?'

'I think so,' Veronica said. 'You just think about that person while you're working on the pie, while you're having a piece, and it should help.

'Shoo-fly pie instead of apple?' she said to the class, looking at each student.

Everyone nodded, except Nick. Leigh was staring up at him. 'You can tell Mommy you're sorry, Dad,' she said.

Once again, it was as though the air stopped.

Nick took a deep breath and put his hand on his daughter's shoulder, but looked away, his dark eyes once again unreadable. Whoa. Everyone was politely looking at the canisters of ingredients again and the print-outs of recipes on the island, trying to give him – and Leigh – a little privacy.

Nick kept his gaze on the recipe that Leigh handed him.

'OK, shoo-fly pie, it is,' Veronica said quickly. 'If you didn't bring an apron, grab one from the pegs by the door, and let's get started.'

As Veronica tied her apron around her back, she glanced at Nick, who looked as though he wanted to be anywhere else but here.

Veronica held up a colour print-out of the last shoo-fly pie she'd made, a couple of weeks ago, to celebrate what would have been her grandmother's eighty-fourth birthday. Veronica's parents hadn't made a fuss over birthdays, but Renata Russo always had. 'Shoo-fly pie. It's very simple to make, but the most important ingredient will come from you, from the heart. While you're pouring or stirring or mixing or even just waiting for the pie to bake, you just think about the person you want to feel close to, and then when you're having the pie, you think about that person some more, and you'll likely feel them with you.'

'If only everything were that easy,' Penelope said with a sigh.

Veronica smiled at her. 'I didn't say it was easy. Just that it seems to work.' She turned to Leigh. 'Leigh, why don't you read out the list of ingredients while I go print out more copies of this recipe so everyone can have one.'

Leigh smiled, took the paper and began reading as Veronica

headed into her small office off the living room. 'For the crust,' Leigh was saying. 'Flour, sugar, kosher salt . . .'

Veronica came back into the kitchen and handed out the recipes. 'Thanks, Leigh. The first thing we'll do is make our dough, because we want to let it chill in the refrigerator for thirty minutes.'

The tension seemed to seep out of everyone as they all got to work, Leigh adding the flour to the bowl of the food processor, Nick pouring in the sugar and Penelope the salt. Veronica asked Leigh to pulse a few times, then had Isabel add the diced butter, and June the shortening.

'Now, some folks make their pie crusts with either just butter or just shortening,' Veronica said, 'depending on the pie, but my grandmother used both shortening and butter for her crusts, so I do too.' Veronica added a little cold water to the mix, then explained how to dust the counter so that the dough wouldn't stick and how to roll the dough into a ball. 'We want to be careful not to work the dough too much or it might get tough.'

'Everyone says making pie crust is so difficult,' Isabel said. 'But this was easy.'

Penelope wiped her flour-dusted hands on her apron. 'I'm so glad I signed up for this class. I think I'm going to bake a few pies a week for the senior citizens' centre.'

Okay, Veronica really liked this new, nice Penelope. 'Now, let's wrap the dough in cling film and let it chill for thirty minutes while we work on the filling.'

'Wait, I wasn't really thinking about my mom while I was adding the flour to the bowl,' Leigh said, her face crumpling. 'Now the pie won't work for me.'

'No worries,' Veronica said, aware of Nick's eyes on her. 'Remember, I make Spirit Pies for other people. They sit down with their pie and think about who they want to feel close to. So it works if you make the pie or if you don't. But in our case, since we're making the pie, we'll each think about who we want to feel close to as we're making the filling.'

Leigh brightened. Nick looked uncomfortable. Penelope seemed relieved. The Nash sisters were the only two that seemed to be enjoying themselves. Because they're at peace with their losses, with their grief, Veronica understood.

Veronica assigned everyone an ingredient for the filling. 'Now, as you pour your ingredient into the mixing bowl, think about the person you want to feel close to – you can just picture them, think of a memory, anything that reminds you of them, and close your eyes, then pour your ingredient in the bowl.'

Veronica watched Leigh dump in the flour as slowly as she could, her expression a combination of happiness, sorrow and determination. Nick added the brown sugar so fast Veronica almost missed it. Isabel put in the butter, and Veronica showed Leigh how to whisk it together, then June poured in the egg. Penelope stood before the bowl and as she added the baking soda, she closed her eyes for a moment as though she were praying, and Veronica couldn't help but wonder who she was thinking about. Perhaps she'd offended a friend or a relative and was hoping to be forgiven. Leigh poured the molasses and whisked it again.

'I feel her hand around mine!' Leigh yelped, glancing around. 'I feel my mom's hand!' She stood very still and started to cry, and Nick put his arm around her.

'Leigh? Are you okay?' he asked.

'I felt her hand around mine,' she said again, and even though she was crying, her face held an almost joyous wonder.

Nick squeezed her shoulder and kissed the top of her head, but he was looking out the window.

Veronica added the boiling water to smooth out the filling, startling herself for a moment because it wasn't her grandmother's sweet face that came to mind.

It was the baby girl she'd given up for adoption. Veronica had only held her for two minutes, and in those two minutes she had fantasized about breaking out of the ambulance, where it had been parked at Hope Home, and making a run for it with the baby. But as she'd looked at that beautiful little face, the three-quarter-closed eyes and wisps of blonde hair, just like Timothy's, she was reminded that she had nowhere to go and no way to provide for her child. Her parents had disowned her. Her boyfriend had insisted it wasn't his baby. And her grandmother, the only person who'd ever been her rock, was almost a year gone by then. With no help from anyone, how could Veronica hope to support a child, emotionally and financially? When the emergency medical technician gently took the baby back to tend to her, Veronica had squeezed her eyes shut and turned her face away, reminding herself over and over that the baby wasn't hers, really hers, and that she was doing the right thing, the best thing for the baby.

The right thing. How many times had she heard that phrase, over and over and over? Not from the staff at Hope Home, who knew better than to throw around platitudes that weren't necessarily true. But from strangers. Visiting parents. Anyone she told her story to. *You're doing the right thing. You did the right thing.*

I did the only thing I could do, Veronica had thought then.

Over the years, she rarely tried to imagine what her daughter looked like. At birth, the hair might have been Timothy's, but the face was Veronica's. The eyes, even just a quarter opened, were Veronica's. Same with the nose. Maybe the chin and something about the shape of the face were Timothy's. Veronica went to the sink, ostensibly to wash her hands, but really to close her eyes for a moment and let this feeling pass. But it didn't pass. The baby's face came to mind again, the feel of that tiny weight in her arms, against her chest. She felt it now, as though she were right back in that ambulance.

Since she'd come back to Boothbay Harbor last year, she'd have strange dreams about Hope Home and the night she gave birth, quite unexpectedly, in the ambulance. The baby had started coming and that was that; there was no time to get her to the hospital safely, and the EMT guy with the kind face had delivered the baby. Veronica had been having odd bits of dreams, pieces of experience, but she never let herself think too much about the baby girl or where she might be or what she really might look like. It was too painful, and she had learned at sixteen how to push those thoughts down so she didn't fall apart. Maybe these sudden thoughts about the baby while making the pie were about all those bits coming together. Maybe, subconsciously, she did always think about the baby.

'I don't know about the rest of you, but I didn't feel anything,' Penelope said, worrying her lower lip.

'I'm not sure that I felt my parents' presence,' Isabel said, 'but I did think about a memory I haven't thought about for a long time, a really good memory.'

'I did too,' June said to her sister. 'The seven of us – you and me, Mom and Dad, and Aunt Lolly and Uncle Ted and cousin Kat. Christmas at the inn when we were really little, and that stray cat Lolly took in unravelled all the garlands from the tree and then got her claws caught and brought the whole tree down.'

Leigh laughed. 'Was your aunt mad?'

'She was at first,' Isabel said. 'But our Uncle Ted was laughing so hard because the cat finally found his way out of the tree and had garland around his tail. That cat lived a good long life as the inn mascot.'

'Dad, who were you thinking about?' Leigh asked.

All eyes turned to Nick. 'My grandfather,' he said quickly,

and Veronica had a feeling he hadn't been thinking about anyone in particular. 'You would have loved Great-grandpa DeMarco.'

Leigh smiled. 'Will you show me pictures when we get home?'

Nick nodded, and she put her hand in his.

The filling for the shoo-fly pie was done, and now it was time to take the pie crust out of the refrigerator and roll it out. Everyone gathered around the island as Veronica demonstrated, and then she gave the rolling-pin to Nick, who looked as if he needed something to do. Once the pie tin was laid out and the pie filled, Veronica got them started on the crumb topping, just some brown sugar, flour, cold butter and salt.

'Can I talk to you privately?' Penelope said to Veronica as she watched over Leigh gently breaking the mixture into a crumbly texture.

'Sure,' Veronica said. 'Everyone, I'll be back in a few minutes. Leigh, just keep doing what you're doing.'

Veronica led the way to her office and shut the door behind Penelope for privacy.

'It didn't work for me,' Penelope said, a kind of panic in her blue eyes. 'What am I doing wrong?'

'Were you thinking about the person you want to feel close to?' Veronica said. 'I know you said this was a living person.'

'Yes.' She closed her eyes for a second, then opened them, frustration and anger radiating off her like the hostility Beth had had. 'I don't know. I'm not thinking about her so much as I'm thinking about what I want to happen. Does that make sense?'

'I thought you said you wanted to feel closer to this person.'

Penelope pushed a swatch of her wavy brown hair behind her ear. The diamond ring above her diamond-encrusted wedding band was the biggest one Veronica had ever seen. 'I just want this person to like me. That's all.'

OK, this was weird, and Veronica had no idea what Penelope was getting at or what she could possibly be talking about. 'Well, do you like this person?'

'I don't know, to be honest. But I need her to like me. I thought I could take your class and learn to make one of your special pies that I hear people talk about all the time. Hope Pie or whatever. But when Leigh brought up the Spirit Pie, I thought maybe it would work for this too. I don't believe in this nonsense, Veronica. But I'm not religious and, outside of a genie coming along and granting me my greatest wish, I'm stuck and will try anything.'

'Stuck wanting something, but not taking a risk because you're scared it might all go wrong?'

'Yes. Exactly.'

Veronica had no idea of the particulars, but there was true desperation in Penelope's eyes.

'I'll give you the recipe for my Hope Pie,' Veronica said. 'Maybe that'll help. Make it at home and put all the force of your wish into it. I'm planning to make one later for myself.'

Penelope glanced at her, as though surprised Veronica could want something. 'I'll try it.'

'Is this why you took the class? For the recipe?'

'Among other reasons,' Penelope said.

'Veronica,' Leigh called. 'The oven dinged. Pre-heating is done.'

'Coming!' Veronica called back.

'Let's go put the pie in the oven,' she said to Penelope. 'I'll be spending the remaining class time going over techniques, and each student will work independently on a pie crust. You can try again at the feeling you're after with this person.'

Penelope nodded and looked away. There was defeat in her face now.

'And Penelope, if you need to, you can call me. For whatever reason.'

Penelope glanced at her. 'Thank you. I appreciate that.'

A few minutes later, the brown-sugar crumb topping was over the pie and it was in the oven, and everyone was making their own pie crust as practice. The class was going well. Nick and Leigh were laughing about the dusting of flour on Nick's cheek and in Leigh's hair. June and Isabel were chatting away about family memories. And Penelope was forming her dough into a ball, much too roughly, as though she were trying to force the feeling again, forge a bond where maybe none existed. Veronica reminded her to be gentle or the dough would be too tough. And then again, out of nowhere, Veronica felt the strangest sensation of a tiny weight in her arms.

Chapter 9
Gemma

Gemma sat on the porch swing of the Three Captains' Inn with her laptop, typing up her notes from her visit to Hope Home earlier that day. She had about ten minutes left before Bea would arrive for the introduction to Isabel about the job in the kitchen. Gemma was glad she'd recorded her interview with Pauline Lee and taken notes; there was so much to take in, and each answer she got from Pauline had elicited more questions. Of the seven residents at Hope Home right now, one was keeping her baby, three were going the adoption route, including the two girls whose conversation with Bea had spiralled out of control, and three were undecided, including a very newly pregnant seventeen-year-old with a college scholarship who was considering terminating the pregnancy.

The seven girls at Hope came from all over; two were from

New York, two others from the New England states, including one from right here in Boothbay Harbor, and one came all the way from Georgia. According to Pauline Lee, none of the girls had intended to become pregnant. Two girls, caught up in the moment, had been assured when their partners said they would 'pull out', so they 'had nothing to worry about'. Another used no birth control at all, having heard that a woman could only get pregnant at a certain time of the month, and she was sure it wasn't that time for her. Two others were careless with remembering to take their birth control pills. And two others had reported that their partners had used condoms, but that they had broken.

Gemma could attest to a broken condom causing an unexpected pregnancy. But she couldn't imagine dealing with it at such a young age.

She'd lost her virginity at sixteen to her high-school boyfriend, a cute, driven fellow reporter on the school newspaper who'd unfortunately taken 'getting the story at all costs' to new heights and become very unpopular. They'd been a couple for over a year when Gemma had had enough of his relentless determination to put the story above people's feelings.

But there had been a time when she was expected to hound a woman who'd recently lost her soldier son for reaction to a controversy surrounding his death, and Gemma had refused. Another newspaper had gotten the shot of the grieving, angry woman, who'd refused to talk to reporters anyway. But Gemma's refusal to bother the woman had been noted. She'd asked her boss at *New York Weekly* if that was the real reason she'd made it onto the list of those being let go, and he'd hemmed and hawed, and said most of the time, in the types of stories she covered, people came first anyway.

There were questions she didn't want to ask for the article on Hope Home too. Questions she wouldn't ask, ones that were too personal and no one's business. There was a line, and Gemma tended to know what it was. Her high-school beau hadn't believed in it, and her admiration of him had turned to disdain.

And if she'd gotten pregnant then? If the condom had broken at sixteen instead of at twenty-nine? What would she have done?

She didn't know. But the thought that went through her mind was: There but for the grace of God go I.

Once, when Gemma was sixteen and worried that she might be pregnant because her period was almost a week late, her older sister Anna, home from college for Christmas break, had said, 'If you weren't having sex, you wouldn't have to worry about being pregnant. Don't do the thing, and you won't be the thing. It's that simple.'

Nothing was really ever so simple, Gemma thought. Absolutes, maybe. But not emotions.

Her phone rang, and she grabbed for it, hopeful that it was the director of Hope Home. Pauline had promised to ask a few of the residents if they'd be willing to speak to

Gemma to be interviewed and quoted in her article.

But it wasn't Pauline. It was Mona Hendricks, her mother-in-law. Gemma sighed and answered. She could picture fifty-six-year-old Mona, with her curly brown bob and multi-coloured reading glasses on a beaded chain around her neck, working on an elaborate recipe like boeuf bourguignon in her kitchen, which was bigger than Gemma's living room.

'Gemma, what's this I hear about you staying up in Maine for the week?' Mona asked. 'Is there trouble between you and Alex?'

Did all mothers-in-law ask such nosy, personal questions?

'I came up for a wedding, and since I lost my job, I figured I'd extend my visit with my girlfriends. I don't get to see them much.'

'Well, you won't get to see Alexander much three hundred miles away either,' she said. 'When are you coming home? I want to make an appointment with a realtor I've heard great things about. There are two new houses on the market I think would be perfect for you and Alexander. One is a colonial with—'

'Mona, I'm sorry to cut you short, but my friend just arrived, so I need to go. Talk soon. Bye.' It was a waste of Gemma's breath to remind Mona that she didn't want to leave New York City. Mona didn't hear her, didn't care how she felt. All the Hendrickses thought she was wrong and selfish for wanting to stay in the city.

Gemma might have felt guilty for practically hanging up

on her mother-in-law, but Bea had indeed pulled into the driveway. She'd changed out of her jeans and T-shirt into a pretty cotton dress and ballet pumps, her light blonde hair pulled back into a ponytail. There was something about Bea that made Gemma feel protective. Bea was all alone in the world and was dealing with an emotionally heavy situation. While Bea had been telling Gemma her story, about receiving the deathbed confession letter – a year on – from her late mother, Gemma tried to wonder how she'd feel if she'd received a letter like that. 'I didn't give birth to you. We adopted you.' But there was a big difference between Bea's mother, who Bea had described as Mother of the Year, twenty-one years strong, and Gemma's mother, who Gemma was pretty sure suffered from some kind of dissociative disorder. Gemma would read that letter, addressed to herself, and want to think, Ah, yes, now it makes sense, no wonder, she wasn't really my mother. But motherhood didn't work like that – that much Gemma was sure of. Motherhood wasn't about who gave birth to you, who adopted you, who raised you. It was about love, commitment, responsibility. It was about being there. About wanting to be there.

It's not that I don't want to be there, she directed towards her belly. It's just that . . . I don't seem to want this – motherhood – the way I want my career back. I know that's awful. Because I'm going to be a mother in seven and a half months.

You sound like Mom, she blasted herself, and again felt that icy squeeze in her heart.

'Hey,' Bea said as she came up the steps. 'I can't thank you enough for offering to introduce to me to the inn manager. I don't know if it'll work out, since I don't know how long I can promise to stay.'

'Well, let's go find Isabel. I let her know that I met someone who might be perfect for the kitchen job, and she said to just come find her when you arrived. I'll cross my fingers for you.'

They found Isabel, her baby strapped to her chest, restocking maps and brochures on the sideboard in the foyer. She extended her hand to Bea and introduced herself and baby Allie.

Gemma stared at the baby, again trying to imagine herself multi-tasking like this with a baby strapped to her chest. How did Isabel make it look so easy when it couldn't be?

Isabel shook Bea's hand. 'My interview consists of you whipping me up a traditional American breakfast, then cleaning up,' Isabel said. 'I should have told Gemma to tell you not to dress up for the interview – ratty old clothes would have done fine.'

Gemma almost laughed. Bea could have shown up in her turkey-sandwich-encrusted jeans and been properly dressed for the interview.

'Gemma,' Isabel said, 'I know this is a lot to ask, but we'll just need about a half-hour – would you mind watching Allie for me?'

Gemma froze. Watch the baby? She was shocked that Isabel

trusted her in the first place. Granted, Gemma was considered a family friend who had known the Nash sisters since they were kids, but what in the world made Isabel think Gemma knew how to hold a baby, let alone change a diaper? Maybe the baby wouldn't poop in the next half-hour.

'Won't be more than thirty minutes,' Isabel said. 'Trust me, if Bea takes half that long to make scrambled eggs and toast, she's in trouble,' she added, winking at Bea.

Gemma eyed the baby, face out to the world with her big blue eyes and chubby cheeks. She was just sitting there, looking quite curious, not crying, not making strange noises. Gemma could do this for half an hour. She should be able to do this. It would be a good practice run.

'No problem,' she said to Isabel.

'You can take her in the back yard. Her swing is out there, and her diaper bag with everything you might need is right next to it. She's been fed and changed very recently, so I think she'll be content to just be held or rock in the swing.'

'Okay,' Gemma said. I can do this. I will be doing this in seven months. I can do this.

Isabel lifted Allie out of the Baby Bjorn and handed her to Gemma. Just like that, the baby was in Gemma's arms, Gemma shifting her so that she had a good grip on her. She was so light!

I'm doing this, she thought. She'd avoided holding her own niece, Alexander's brother's daughter, until she was a year old. Gemma had finally held her when she'd been foisted, squirming

150

and fussing, in her arms when her sister-in-law had needed to use the bathroom and her husband was on grilling duty. The baby had settled down, but she'd been so uncomfortable until Mona had plucked the child from her arms.

'Good job, Gemma!' Mona had said. 'Your hideous mole and buck teeth have disappeared!'

What? Gemma had thought. She must have looked at Mona as if she'd sprouted an extra head because Mona had added, '*Nanny McPhee!* Didn't you see that film? Emma Thompson as the nanny and that handsome Colin Firth as the father of seven. Every time the naughty children learned their lesson or behaved, one of Emma Thompson's hairy moles or stomach rolls would poof, vanish! Seven children. Can you imagine?'

Gemma smiled at the memory. Colin Firth again.

And seven children? No, Gemma could not imagine.

Gemma adjusted baby Allie in her arms and nodded at Bea, who smiled at Gemma and followed Isabel into the kitchen. Just like that, Gemma was left alone with the baby. She glanced down at Allie's profile, her tiny nose, the big cheeks. She was so pretty. Gemma walked down the short hall to another small sitting room and library, where sliding glass doors led to the back yard, fenced on all sides. The yard was big and went back far, with huge trees shading it and a small boulder at the far end. On the patio were chaises longues and umbrellas, and Allie's swing was next to one of the chairs. Gemma sat down, the baby sitting on her lap, and Gemma gave her a little bounce.

This was going okay. This wasn't so bad.

Gemma glanced along the windows until she found the kitchen and saw Bea at work at the counter, Isabel sitting at the table, talking.

'I'm going to have a baby,' Gemma whispered to Allie. 'In January, I'll have a baby just like you.'

Fear gripped her again. It was one thing to watch a baby for a half-hour and give her back. It was another to be responsible for a baby for the next eighteen years. For the rest of her life, Gemma amended.

Allie began . . . fussing seemed the right word. Gemma stood and shifted her in her arms, rocking back and forth a bit the way she'd seen her sister-in-law do. Allie calmed down, but then got fidgety.

'Maybe you want to be in your swing,' Gemma said, setting Allie down in it. Yes, that seemed to do the trick. Gemma pushed the on switch, and the pale yellow and white swing gently moved back and forth.

Gemma's phone rang again, and she wasn't sure she should answer it, since she was babysitting, but she saw mothers and caregivers talking on the phone all the time as she passed them on the streets and playgrounds, and Allie was safely ensconced in the swing.

Gemma pulled her phone from her pocket. Pauline Lee.

'One of our residents has expressed interest in talking to you for the article,' Pauline said. 'Chloe Martin. She's seventeen, five months pregnant, and planning to keep her baby.'

Seventeen and keeping her baby. At seventeen, Gemma's biggest worry was about getting into the college of her choice. Chloe Martin's life would be completely different.

'Is there a particular time that works best for me to come interview her?' Gemma asked.

'If you're free tomorrow at noon, that works for her.'

'That's perfect,' Gemma said.

It was Monday, barely seven o'clock, and time-wise, for the article, Gemma was right on track. She had the information Pauline had given her, the pictures she'd taken with her phone camera, Bea's story, and now a resident's. Hopefully tomorrow and Wednesday she'd be able to interview past residents and perhaps an adoptive mother. She could have the piece written and sent to Claire at the *Gazette* by Friday morning, when Alexander expected her to head home to New York.

She did miss her husband. And granted, it was only Monday. But Gemma was not looking forward to leaving Boothbay Harbor. She felt so . . . herself here. Safe. Far, far away from her husband's opinions and so in tune with her own. He wasn't hounding her the way she thought he might; he texted instead of calling, letting her have this time to herself. She leaned back on a chaise longue, one eye on Allie, and let herself relax, the late-June sunshine still abundant in the sky at seven o'clock.

Allie began fussing in the swing. Gemma pushed the off button and scooped Allie up, but she was starting to cry. Oh no. Now what? Gemma bounced her, but she started crying harder, and her face was turning red. Nanny McPhee, I need you, Gemma thought. Emma Thompson would have Allie cooing in no time.

The baby was squirming and crying hard. A couple who'd come out on to the patio were staring at Gemma.

How long had it been since she'd come out? Twenty minutes? Maybe she'd peek in and see if Isabel and Bea were finishing up? She didn't want to interrupt the interview, especially an 'interactive' one.

The baby screamed louder. Isabel's face appeared at the window, and in moments she was coming towards Gemma. Gemma felt like an incompetent moron. She couldn't handle a crying baby? She couldn't do this for thirty minutes.

She'd confirmed what she already knew. She wasn't cut out for this.

'What's wrong, sweet cheeks?' Isabel said to Allie, taking her from Gemma. The baby continued to cry, which, Gemma had to admit, made her feel a little better. 'Gas in the tummy? Teething? Let's go try your favourite teething ring.' She smiled at Gemma. 'Thanks for watching her. I forgot to mention she's teething up a storm right now. Oh, and by the way, your friend Bea knows her way around a stove. Her scrambled eggs rivalled my Aunt Lolly's, and that's saying something. I was called to the front door to sign for a package, came back, and she'd even cleaned everything up in the time I was gone. I'll check her references, but I'll tell you, I owe you, Gemma.'

The baby was just teething. Gemma wasn't the worst carer on earth. And Isabel wasn't annoyed at her for not being able to handle Allie. Add Bea getting the job — if her references checked out — and Gemma would say today had gone from crazy to pretty darn okay.

At noon the next day, Gemma arrived at Hope Home for her interview with seventeen-year-old Chloe Martin. She recognized Jen and Kim, the girls Bea had been talking to yesterday. They were lying on the chaises under a tree, each reading a book on pregnancy. Another girl, who wasn't yet showing, was doing some yoga moves. Gemma headed in and found Pauline at the front desk.

Pauline stood up. 'Hi, Gemma, Chloe is waiting for you in her room. I'll introduce you.'

The director led Chloe to an open door down the hall. A girl who looked to be around five months pregnant sat on one of the two beds in the room. There were at least ten posters above her bed. Pink sticking out her tongue. Adele with her beehive. The band Fun. Vincent Van Gogh's 'Starry Night'. Chloe was pretty, with silky brown hair to her shoulders, and hazel eyes.

'You can sit there if you want,' Chloe said, pointing at the chair of the desk near her bed. An identical desk was across the room near the other bed.

'Thanks for letting me interview you for my article. If you don't want me to use your name, I can change it to protect your identity. If there's anything you tell me, and you realize now or later that you don't want me to write about it, you just say, okay? And I'll take it out.'

'Okay,' Chloe said. 'That sounds good.'

'Is it all right if I record our interview?' Gemma asked.

Chloe leaned against the wall, her legs straight out in front of her. She held a throw pillow to her stomach, embroidered with *I love you.* 'Sure.'

Gemma put her recorder on the desk and pressed Play, then got out her notebook and pen. 'Pauline told me you're keeping your baby. Can you tell me about making that decision?'

Chloe put her hand on her belly. 'I always knew I'd keep him – I don't know if it's a boy or a girl, but something just tells me it's a boy. I'm going to name him Finn.'

'Finn, I like that name.' Gemma hadn't considered names yet. The thought hadn't even occurred to her. Because the baby doesn't feel real yet, she reminded herself. Because you haven't accepted reality.

Chloe smiled. 'Me too. It's not after anyone.'

'Can you tell me about the father of the baby?'

Her face lit up. 'Dylan. He's my boyfriend. He's stood by me when no one else has. My parents think I'm ruining my life. My mom said she'd be a good grandmother and she'd babysit on occasion but that if I was making this choice, it would have to be whole hog, that I couldn't rely on her to raise this baby for me.'

Gemma couldn't stop focusing on how young Chloe was. Seventeen. And about to be a mother in four months. 'Where will you live after you give birth?'

'I've already got a job lined up. An elderly lady who lives around the corner from us down in Massachusetts and needs a live-in caregiver hired me. There's a small studio apartment attached to her house, and I'll get room and board and a small salary. My boyfriend and I will get married when I turn eighteen, and then Vivian said he can move in too. He's finishing high school and I'm getting my GED.'

Gemma hoped with all her heart that this would all happen. 'Why did you come to Hope Home, Chloe?'

Chloe glanced away for a moment and gripped the pillow tighter. 'My mother made it clear that if I was insisting on having the baby, I'd have to do this on my own, she wasn't going to make this easy on me. She researched homes for pregnant teenagers and there was a spot open, so here I am.'

'Do you think what they were doing was tough love?'

Chloe shrugged. 'I'm getting through it, is all I know. I'd rather be home than here, especially because Dylan can only visit me on weekends for like a whole Saturday. It's OK here, though.'

The home did seem like a warm, inviting place for these girls. 'How did you feel when you found out you were pregnant?'

'Scared. But I love Dylan, and I can't imagine giving our baby up. I know most of the girls here are, but I just can't.'

That had to be a big topic of conversation among the residents. 'Does that affect your relationship with them?'

Chloe shrugged again. 'Some think I'm making a huge mistake, that at seventeen I won't know how to be a good mother, that I'm not giving my baby his best possible shot at life. But I think I'll be a good mother. Everyone says I'm kidding myself, that I don't know anything about what I'll be facing.'

'Do you feel ready to be a mother?'

'I know I'll take care of him. I'm not some irresponsible loser. I've been reading some of the books on baby care. But you know what? The reason I'm not really scared?'

Gemma leaned close.

'I love the little guy like crazy already,' Chloe said.

Gemma sat back. She talked to her stomach sometimes, in an attempt to feel part of what was happening to her body, but the baby still didn't feel real. Maybe once it did, Gemma would feel a bit like Chloe felt.

'Do you have kids?' Chloe asked, looking at Gemma's wedding ring.

'No, but I'll tell you a secret. I'm pregnant. Just seven weeks.'

Gemma sucked in a breath. Why had she blurted that out? Because it's bursting inside you, she knew. She *wanted* to talk about it. And this girl, this seventeen-year-old girl, was so sure of herself that Gemma had forgotten for a moment that Chloe *was* just a girl. A girl in a very different situation from Gemma's.

'I haven't told anyone but a girlfriend yet,' Gemma rushed to say. 'Even my husband doesn't know. I'm waiting for the blood test confirmation.'

Her doctor had told her the test results would be in by tomorrow or Thursday at the latest. She'd get the positive results, and there would be no excuse for her not to pick up the phone and tell Alexander. It would be wrong not to tell him.

She'd get the results and then she'd tell him. She'd go over her plan before she called, lay it out for him how she saw their future. But he'd steamroll her, she knew it.

'You're so lucky,' Chloe said. 'You're married, you've lived life, you have a career. It must feel like a real blessing. God, I wish I were in your position. I'm so jealous.'

Gemma sat back on the chair, the breath knocked out of her for a moment.

Chapter 10
Bea

On Wednesday morning, Bea woke up in her little room at the Three Captains' Inn, her bed much more comfortable than at the super-budget motel. On the second floor, a large former utility closet had been transformed into a cosy room with a small arched window out of a fairy tale, pale cabbage-rose wallpaper and a full-sized bed with a beautiful carved wooden headboard and a soft old quilt embroidered with seashells. There was also a small dresser with a round mirror above it, a soft rug and a painting of a distant light-house. Bea could live without a private bathroom; there was a large bathroom right across the hall that no one used because the other three second-floor rooms had private baths. And Gemma's room was just upstairs on the third floor, a tiny one like Bea's, across from the honeymoon suite, which was now taken over by three very serious Colin Firth fans.

Bea had moved in late last night, just a day after the interview with Isabel. Her boss at the Writing Centre and her first boss at Crazy Burger — not Crazy Barbara — had apparently given her glowing references. She was starting work this morning, which was perfect because she had very little money left. She was responsible for cooking the guests' breakfasts, leaving the order-taking and schmoozing to Isabel. After breakfast, she'd clean up the dining room and kitchen, tidy up the common rooms and patio and keep a running list of what grocery items the inn was running short on. Her work day began at six and ended at eleven, and for that she received a room, free breakfast, use of the kitchen for all other meals, and a small salary. The inn was beautiful and cosy and so close to downtown. After what had happened on Monday afternoon at Hope Home, Bea had felt so adrift, so unsure of what the hell she was doing here, but thanks to Gemma, she now had some grounding. Even better, Isabel said she was okay with Bea's inability to commit to the entire summer. The Fourth of July was booked solid, the week before and after, and Isabel had said as long as Bea could promise to stay until mid-July, she could have the job.

And now that she felt more grounded, she also felt a bit more ready to contact her birth mother. Maybe today was the day. She could call her, they could meet for lunch or something like that, and since Bea was staying in town for a few weeks, they could have coffee now and again, so that Veronica wouldn't have to feel obliged to spill out her entire life story in one hour-long first meeting. Unless she wanted to, of course.

At least, that was how Bea envisioned it would go. They'd meet for lunch and talk. Bea would ask about Veronica's life, about her family. She'd ask who her biological father was and if Veronica thought he'd be open to contact. Then their lunch would be over and they'd go their separate ways. But now that she was here, with a place to stay and a job, she could meet with Veronica a few more times, and perhaps they could get to know each other a little.

Not that Bea had any idea how their first meeting would go. If she'd even *want* to get together with Veronica a second time. She flipped over on her back and reached for her mother's cross-stitched pillow, hugging it to her chest. Everything in her life was so unfamiliar and strange that the pillow, with its blue and green and orange tree of life, was as effective a soother as the stuffed Winnie the Pooh she'd had as a child.

The sun was just starting to rise. Bea got out of bed and moved over to the narrow chair wedged by the beautiful little window and looked out at the breaking dawn over the huge oak trees. She loved this room. On the small dresser, she'd put her two favourite family photographs next to the collection of pretty seashells that were here when she'd arrived. She moved to the dresser and picked up the photo of herself as a four-year-old with her parents. 'You are my parents, no matter what,' Bea whispered, setting the picture down and picking up a seashell, which reminded her of her father. Keith Crane had loved the ocean, and had told Bea when she was very small that if she had a question she couldn't figure out the answer to, all she had to do was find a seashell, big or small, hold it up to her ear and listen.

'Do I ask it the question?' seven-year-old Bea had asked.

'Nope. No need,' her dad had said. 'The question is already inside you. You just have to hold the shell to your ear and listen. Really listen.'

She remembered beach trips over the years when she'd find a shell and hold it to her ear, silently asking her burning questions. Will I make friends in my class? Does he like me back? Does my dad watch over me? She'd listen hard, and the shell itself never said anything, but as she pressed it against her ear, hearing the whoosh, she'd know the answers to her questions. Much later, Bea would learn the answer depended on what she believed deep down. Sometimes shells had no answer for her. Sometimes they confirmed the worst. Sometimes, they offered hope. But Bea had been asking her burning questions to seashells for as long as she could remember.

Bea held the shell to her ear. 'Should I call Veronica Russo after my shift today and introduce myself?' she asked.

Bea thought it was time. She'd arrived in Boothbay Harbor on Friday and now the weekend had passed. She'd struck gold on seeing Veronica in the diner the day she'd arrived, but she hadn't been back to The Best Little Diner in Boothbay again;

the thought of returning had made her feel both oddly exposed and like some kind of a stalker.

She listened. There was a whoosh. And then the answer, coming from inside her. Yes.

There were five guest rooms at the Three Captain's Inn. The three on the second floor, and two on the third floor. Breakfast was served between seven o'clock and eight-thirty for the current twelve guests. At seven on the dot, Bea's first orders came in for the Osprey and Seashell Rooms – four various egg dishes, including a bacon and Swiss omelette, which was exactly what she'd made herself before her shift had started, a bagel with cream cheese, two bowls of cereal and a plate of sausage links for the kids, and two fruit plates. By seven-forty-five the dining room was in full swing, guests leaving, guests arriving, and Bea was in dynamo mode, scrambling eggs and flipping pancakes like an old pro. As Isabel had come into the kitchen with the orders, she'd commented more than once how impressed she was at Bea's cooking skills and shared the compliments to the chef she'd gotten from her guests. After having her burgers measured and her pay docked for every slight infraction at Crazy Burger, Bea was thrilled.

At eight-thirty, she made crêpes for the newlywed stragglers in the Bluebird Room, a couple in their late twenties who took their plates out to the back yard and fed each other bites. Bea watched them through the window as she began rinsing dishes for the dishwasher, smiling at how lovey-dovey they were.

Gemma came down in the nick of time for a hot break-fast, and when Isabel brought in her order, Bea made sure her omelette was perfection. Gemma had done her a huge favour. She was a little curious about the woman. Gemma had a warm, pretty face, and when she smiled her entire face lit up, but something seemed to be troubling her just under the surface. Or maybe Bea was imagining it. Bea had noticed Gemma twisting her wedding ring a couple of times, and when she'd come into the dining room to clear the final tables, she found Gemma sipping her herbal tea and staring out the window a bit forlornly, and again she wondered what Gemma's story was. Gemma's husband wasn't with her at the inn, unless Bea just hadn't seen him. But then Gemma had gone off on an interview, the lovebirds had cleared out of the parlour and, just like that, the breakfast rush was over.

After the dishes were cleaned, dried and put away and the kitchen left spotless, Bea cleaned the dining-room tables and swept and mopped the floor, then headed out to the patio to straighten the chaises and collect coffee mugs. She grabbed messy newspapers and neatened them, adding them to the basket just inside the door. In the parlour, she refilled coffee cups and sliced up lemons for iced tea for a few guests, collected more mugs and teacups, picked up the pie, bagels and muffins that Isabel had laid out for morning stragglers, and put everything away.

By ten o'clock the inn's common rooms were spotless, so Bea just hung around, making herself useful as needed. Straightening the maps and brochures on the table in the foyer. Cleaning up a trail of sand from the kids. She went through the refrigerator and pantry, making a list of what Isabel would need to restock. Eleven a.m. Quitting time. Bea liked her duties. She wasn't cooped up in the kitchen the entire time; she got to mingle among the guests in the parlour and back yard, chatting about where they were from. And she'd surprised herself a few times by being able to answer questions about where certain landmarks were. A few days of walking around Boothbay Harbor, trying to get this place – in which she'd been born – inside her, and she'd learned more than she realized.

She had a phone call to make. Up in her room, she got out her notebook and her phone, sucked in a deep breath and pushed in Veronica's number. Hi, my name is Bea Crane, she practised in her head. I was born on 12 October, twenty-two years ago. I'd like to meet you, if you're interested. You can reach me at this number. I'm staying at the Three Captains' Inn.

Answering machine. 'Hello, you've reached Veronica Russo. I'm unable to answer your call right now, but if you leave a message, I'll return your call as soon as possible.' Beep.

Damn. Bea hung up, her heart beating a mile a minute.

She could call back, leave a message. That would give Veronica a moment too, instead of being bombarded with the call and Bea at the other end all at once.

But when she picked up the phone, she found herself unable to press in the numbers. She needed to do this in person. She needed to go see her, to not draw this out any more. Bea changed out of her work clothes and back into her interview dress, which was just a pale yellow cotton dress with cap sleeves, a little something more than just jeans and a T-shirt, but nothing fancy. She put on her sandals and headed out, her heart beating too fast again.

Bea walked the half-mile to Veronica Russo's house. She'd driven past it at least ten times since she'd been in town, and at the sight of it, a cute lemon-yellow cottage with glossy white shutters and flower boxes on the windowsills, her heart starting going crazy again.

But there wasn't a car in the driveway, and the house didn't have a garage. Veronica was likely at work, and Bea had a feeling she'd gone to her house as a stalling tactic. She would never be ready for this, it would never feel right, so she might as well get it over with now.

Just in case Veronica was home, Bea walked up the path to the front door. She rang the bell and waited, but she knew Veronica wasn't here, that the door wouldn't open.

She could go to the diner. She could introduce herself, then tell Veronica that perhaps they could chat on Veronica's break. She wants to meet you, Bea reminded herself. She drove back to the inn and parked there, then walked down the long, winding two streets to Main Street and over to the diner.

She glanced in the big front windows and didn't see Veronica, but maybe she was in the back. It was in between breakfast and lunch, not very crowded. Bea pulled open the door, her heart beating, her hope rising.

This was it.

She'd sit in Veronica's section, and when she came to hand her a menu or ask her if she could get her something to drink, Bea would come right out with it.

My name is Bea Crane. I'm sorry for just showing up like this, but I don't really know how to do this, and I felt funny leaving a message. I was born on 12 October, twenty-two years ago.

It would be a start.

Bea glanced around for Veronica to determine what section was hers, but she didn't see her. Maybe her shift started later? She'd ask a waitress if Veronica was working today.

She went to the counter. The young waitress who'd served her the day she'd arrived a week ago was refilling a woman's coffee. Bea waited until she came over.

'Menu?' she asked.

'Actually, I just want to know if Veronica Russo is working today.'

'Lucky stiff got hired as an extra on the Colin Firth movie

— made first cut too. Instead of delivering eggs and burgers all day, she'll be hobnobbing with the stars.'

An extra on the Colin Firth movie? That was unexpected.

Now what? Maybe she could find out where they were filming today. Equipment was still out by Frog Marsh. She'd start there. A friend of Bea's from college had been an extra on a romantic comedy once, and she'd said the extras mainly sat around for hours until they were called. Perhaps Veronica was just sitting on a blanket, reading a book or staring into space.

She'd head over and decide what to do when she got there. Her MO lately.

Three huge beige tents, trailers, lights, cameras, and barricades were being set up by the pond now. There were barricades in front of the third tent and a guard sitting beside it, a bagel on a plate on his lap. The guy she'd met the night she arrived came out of a trailer beside the first tent, eyes on his clipboard.

'Filming today?' she asked him from the other side of the barricade. It was the grumpy production assistant. Tyler Echols. The girl reading *To Kill a Mockingbird* wasn't around this time.

He didn't look up from his clipboard. 'I'm not at liberty to discuss.'

So officious. 'Can you tell me where the extras are?'

This time he did look at her. With irritation in his dark blue eyes. 'Are you an extra?'

'No, but I know someone who is, and—'

He went back to his clipboard. 'You'll need to stay behind that barricade, then.'

'Can you just tell me where the—' Bea began.

'Look, I'm just doing my job, okay?' Tyler said, walking away and disappearing into the crew coming and going. Who needs you, anyway? she shot at him silently, then wove her way through the crowd watching from behind the long barricades, straining their necks to spot anyone famous, eyeing signs on the tents for the word 'Extras'. Bingo. The one at the far right. Ten minutes later, as she crossed the barrier to peer inside it, Tyler Echols was back, pointing beyond it, then at the big guy sitting in a chair and devouring his bagel, which he paid more attention to than anything else.

She moved behind the barricade. The grump grimaced at her and went back to his clipboard. She turned to the woman beside her. 'I guess they're filming today?'

'Test footage, apparently,' she said. 'For lighting and whatnot.'

Bea strained to look at the group of people lining up at a table on the far side of the extras tent. Food. Bagels and tubs of cream cheese, cold cuts, cookies. She looked for Veronica, but there were so many people milling inside the tent. Bea saw the grump with the clipboard chewing out some guy who looked like he wanted to punch him, and she headed around the other side, where two new trailers were now, surrounded by barricades and guarded by a large man balancing a plate of scrambled eggs and home fries on his lap.

She waited until he was looking down at his plate, then leaped over the barricade. If she could just get to the other side, where the tent flap was wide, she could peer in. Maybe she'd catch Veronica just sitting or eating breakfast, and ask to speak to her.

'You don't give up, do you? I assure you, Colin Firth is not here.'

Bea whirled around and there was Tyler Echols. 'I'm not here to stalk Colin Firth! Someone I know is an extra, and—'

'Ah, so you're stalking an ex. I get it. But if you don't stay behind that barricade I'll have to alert Security. I take stalkers seriously when it comes to my actors – and my extras. On another movie, some lunatic woman threw a cup of orange juice at Hugh Grant just to recreate that *Notting Hill* scene. Another fan rushed him and grabbed his balls.'

Okay, fine, she got it. He had a job to do. But he was so dismissive. She glanced at his badge. TYLER ECHOLS, PA – production assistant? 'Look, I'm not interested in Hugh Grant. I have zero interest in the movie stars. I—'

He pulled out his phone. 'You're going to get me fired. So if you don't stay where you're supposed to, I'll call the police.'

The guy was impossible! 'I'm here because my birth mother is an extra on this film and I'm just hoping to watch and decide if I want to introduce myself and—'

God, what the hell was wrong with her? Did she just

blurt all that out? She let out a deep breath and stared at her feet.

Tyler made a sound that sounded like a snort, but tucked his phone back in his pocket. 'You're lucky, then. I can save you the trouble.'

'The trouble of what?'

He glanced at his clipboard and checked something off. 'My sister is adopted – she's sixteen and was obsessed with finding her birth mother, thought it would solve all her problems with grades and the jerk boys she goes for.'

'Wait, she's adopted but you're not?' Bea asked, wondering about the family dynamics.

He looked at her, and for a moment she saw actual warmth in those sharp blue eyes of his. 'My parents had me, then couldn't conceive again. The adoption process took years, which is why Maddy is seven years younger than I am. She was always open with me about how she felt as the adopted kid, so I spent months trying to track down her birth mother for her. I finally get her name and location – which wasn't cheap, by the way – and if I could do it all over again, I'd save myself the money.'

'Sorry, Tyler, but you seem incredibly easy to disappoint,' she said without thinking. It was nice of him to go to all that trouble of finding his sister's birth mother. 'You don't know my situation,' she added.

He ignored that. 'Yeah, well, the lady wasn't interested in meeting my sister. In the end, all she wanted was money.

Maddy – my sister – is still screwed up over the whole thing. So, really, I'm doing you a favour.' He pointed to the barricades. 'Either stay on the other side, or I'll call that guy.' He pointed to the big man in the chair.

'Yeah, he's really paying attention,' she said as the guard popped a bunch of home fries into his mouth. But at least she'd been downgraded from the local police. 'And anyway, my situation is very different.'

'I'm just saying you should proceed with caution. Reality and fantasy are two very different things.'

Bea's stomach twisted.

A man in his late twenties, with messy dark brown hair and gorgeous blue eyes, came up behind Tyler. 'Problem here?' he asked Bea. His badge said SAD PATRICK OOL. 'This brute bothering you?'

'He's just incredibly bossy,' Bea said. 'I know one of the extras and wanted to watch her work, that's all. I'm not here to bother the stars, I swear.'

'What's your name?' Patrick asked.

'Bea Crane.'

Patrick smiled at her. 'Well, Bea Crane, you can watch all you want.' He put a badge around her neck with GUEST written on it in black letters. 'I'm the second assistant director on this film, and if this guy bothers you, you tell me.' His cell rang. 'Be right there. Don't touch anything,' he barked into the phone, then pocketed it and sighed. 'Fire after fire,' he said to Bea. 'Hope we run into each other again,' he added, holding her gaze.

Bea watched him rush away, then shot Tyler something of a triumphant smile.

Tyler rolled his eyes. 'He's a notorious womanizer, by the way.'

'That you being realistic again?' she asked.

'Do what you want.'

He stalked off, and Bea shook her head, wondering what the heck his problem was. But she wasn't about to give Tyler Echols, PA, too much thought; she was free to be here with her guest pass, and walked right past the guard with a wave, which he returned. From this side of the tent, she could see inside more clearly. At least fifty people were sitting down with plates and foam cups, some congregating over by the food table.

Then she saw her.

Veronica was sitting on a folding chair, a muffin on a little round plastic plate on her lap, talking to the woman next to her, her expression animated. She seemed lit up, glowing from within.

She was right there. Bea's birth mother.

She could walk right in. Introduce herself.

Except maybe she'd come off as a little bit nuts for 'stalking' Veronica on the film set. Working as an extra was obviously something special to Veronica, given how happy she looked, and Bea would just throw a huge monkey wrench into it.

'Oh hi, I know you're working on the movie here in town, but here I am suddenly – the daughter you gave up for adoption!'

Bea's stomach turned over. Crap. How many times was she going flip-flop about this? Call, don't call. Approach, don't approach.

Argh! This was so frustrating! *Nothing* felt right. Including winging it.

Bea would just call her tonight. She'd call, giving them both space – Bea to put the phone down and calm her beating heart; Veronica a chance to digest the fact that her birth daughter had made contact. If Bea got the machine, she'd leave a message.

She was about to leave when Patrick Ool walked up to her.

'Sorry about Tyler giving you a hard time,' Patrick said. 'I appreciate how seriously he takes his job, but sometimes he takes it a bit too seriously. Anyway, I'm just going to say this outright, Bea. I met you ten minutes ago, and I can't stop thinking of your face.'

Bea blushed. The guy wasn't traditionally good-looking, but there was something about him, something . . . sexy, and he was staring at Bea as though she were drop-dead beautiful. She had to admit, it did nice things for her ego.

'Has that ever happened to you,' he said, 'where you meet someone and you just wish you could go off on a walk with them or sit across a table with a cup of coffee and just talk?'

She smiled. 'It's happening now.' He'd actually managed to distract her from her flip-flopping brain. That was good.

He smiled back at her. He had one dimple, she realized. And those gorgeous blue eyes. 'Can I take you to dinner tomorrow night? It'll have to be early, since we're wrapping for dinner at five, and I'll need to be back to check the dailies at seven. But a good start, I think.'

'Agreed,' Bea said.

'Tomorrow at five, then. Where should I pick you up?'

Guys were the farthest thing from her mind, but a date with an interesting, cute movie dude? She could use a little distraction right about now. And yeah, someone to talk to.

Chapter 11
Veronica

Veronica loved being on the set, loved sitting in this big tent marked EXTRAS HOLDING PEN. Even if yesterday and most of today she and her fellow extras had done a lot of sitting around and waiting for . . . not much of anything. She'd spent most of her time chatting with the people sitting near her — whispering over mutual admiration of Colin Firth — thinking up new pie recipes and wondering how her students had fared with making their own shoo-fly pies. Since Monday night, two days now, she'd thought about calling each student to ask if they'd made the shoo-fly pie at home with the recipe she'd handed out. But that had felt intrusive with this particular bunch, with the uncomfortable Nick DeMarco, who his daughter thought might want to say sorry to her mother. And ten-year-old Leigh, who'd lost her mom so young, with so much hope in her sweet face. Veronica couldn't imagine calling the formerly snooty Penelope, of the cryptic trouble, though she wouldn't be surprised if she got a call from Penelope. And Veronica didn't know Isabel, who felt like a client first and a student second, or June well enough to get personal, so she'd just decided to wait until next Monday night for the answers to her questions.

She still couldn't believe the universe had cut her this lucky break of being chosen to be an extra. Late Monday night, long after her students had gone home and she'd cleaned up the kitchen, her cell phone had rung with The Call. An excitement, a feeling she hadn't experienced since she was a young teenager, had burst inside her; she felt, in her toes, along her spine and the nape of her neck, a firecracker going off inside her and catching her by surprise. She'd wanted to be an extra on the Colin Firth movie, yes. But she hadn't realized how much she wanted it. Perhaps she hadn't let herself want something that badly in a long time. It was a bit of an escape. A chance to lay eyes on Colin Firth – to have a crush on an actor felt luxurious to Veronica, a self-indulgence she'd allow herself, and then some.

Just like that, she was an extra, something that had been a twinkle in Shelley's eye at the diner just days ago. Her boss was thrilled for Veronica and told her to come back to work whenever the fairy-tale experience was over. It did feel a bit like a fairy tale, watching all these productive-looking people rushing around with their clipboards and iPhones, hauling equipment and calling for meetings. The extras had been instructed to come in regular clothes they'd wear on a routine morning, so Veronica had opted for her uniform, which got a 'Fabulous!' from the wardrobe manager, who'd checked over every single extra and sent many to the small tent next door to change. In the big white tent with her yesterday and today were around twenty-five people, several of whom were reading books with titles such as *Break into Acting!* and *How to Make It in Hollywood*. She and another extra had made a list of every Colin Firth film they could think of. Veronica planned to watch a movie a night. A Colin Firth marathon sounded heavenly after a long day of dreaming about seeing him in the flesh. But if he was here in town, he wasn't on the set. She kept an eagle eye out and so did several other women sitting near her, who made sure to keep their Colinmania on the down-low in case Patrick Ool was walking around with his intolerance for star-stalkers.

Yesterday, she and around thirty others had arrived at eight o'clock in the morning for some lighting work, and then filming was expected to begin today, but an actress had hurt her knee early this afternoon, and filming had been pushed back again and then again.

Now it was nearing four o'clock, and finally Patrick Ool came into the tent and informed them shooting was a go. Yes! The extras around Veronica sat up with excitement. Patrick explained the scene again: the female star, a beautiful actress whose name Veronica kept forgetting, was standing in the nearby pasture of wildflowers with her selfish mother, who was trying to talk her out of her misgivings about her upcoming wedding to her supposedly perfect man, who was not Colin Firth. The mother was played by a popular British actress whom Veronica adored, and for a moment she couldn't take her eyes off the arresting woman, then snapped to attention. Patrick had gone over the rules – no ogling the stars, no talking to the stars. No talking, period. And no photographs.

Veronica and the twenty-five or so extras walked out to the barricade labelled EXTRAS WAIT HERE. Patrick placed about ten of them around the scene, some on the path between the pond and the pasture, some in the pasture sitting down to a picnic, two walking dogs. Veronica was to walk by when the mother said her first line and look nowhere in particular, checking her watch once. The woman behind her was to carry a brown-paper grocery bag. A man was to wave at someone in the distance. Most others were to just walk by at normal pace.

Patrick called, 'Get ready, people,' and again that burst of excitement lit up in Veronica. She was so close to the two actresses, standing just inside the pasture, that she could see the worry lines on the mother's forehead and see how exquisitely beautiful the younger actress truly was.

The director called, 'Action!' and Veronica waited until the mother said her first line before walking by, looking nowhere in particular as instructed. But just as she had passed, the mother pointed her finger in the younger woman's face with such disdain, such anger in her expression, it shook loose a memory that made Veronica's hands tremble. She walked as naturally as she could, checked her watch as she'd been told, then ambled off to the side, out of camera range, and realized she was actually shaking. Good God. What was wrong with her? One finger-point and she was a mess?

She rarely let herself think about her parents, her mother's cruelty. But as she stood on the other side of the barricade, suddenly feeling so alone amid so many people milling about and watching the scene being shot, she felt lost in the memory, of her own mother sticking her finger in sixteen-year-old Veronica's face, in much the same jabbing way, after Veronica had blurted out that she was pregnant.

She wouldn't let herself remember that conversation. Not here, not now, especially. Being here on the set, being a part of this magic, felt a little bit like Christmas. But the truth was that, twenty-two years after that finger-jabbing, those cruel words, the pain of that memory was as vivid as ever.

She closed her eyes tight against it, but so many different words, sentences she'd never forget, from her mother, from Timothy, jumbled in her mind. Focus on the scene, she told herself. A movie is being filmed in front of your eyes. You could see Colin Firth tomorrow for all you know! But she couldn't stop seeing her mother's face, the anger, the shame. This was the new normal, now that she was back home. Hadn't she come here to face her past? But how would remembering how cruelly her parents had treated her help? How could those thoughts do anything but sting, remind her that, except for her friends, she had no family?

She'd have to learn to deal with her memories, somehow. She was back home now, and memories were everywhere. She was grateful when Patrick called out to the extras, 'Great job, people,' and let them know they were dismissed for the day and expected back at eight o'clock the next morning to reshoot that scene two different ways.

Two different ways. Countless takes, perhaps. She'd have to get over that finger jab fast if she wanted to be part of this movie.

As she left the tent and slipped on her cardigan against the breeze, she heard footsteps behind her.

'Va-va-voomica,' a man's voice said, then chuckled as though his nickname for her was adorable. 'I came down here to check out the film set and saw you in that big tent. How about we go for a drink? You can fill me in on the life of an extra.'

Ugh. The pest, Hugh Fledge. Just pretend you didn't hear him and dash away, she told herself. And from the slight slurring of his words, he'd clearly already had that drink. She quickened her pace.

'You won't be able to resist my charm and good looks for long,' he called out on a laugh just as she rounded the corner.

For ever wouldn't be long enough. Would he ever stop bugging her?

Hugh Fledge wasn't much of a distraction from her thoughts, though. She avoided walking past the pier where she and Timothy Macintosh had kissed many times, but her memories trailed her all the way home.

Veronica tended not to think about anything but pie and its mission when she was baking, so when she got home she set to work on an Amore Pie for her neighbour's friend, thinking only of Colin Firth as Mr Darcy telling Elizabeth Bennet that he loved her and couldn't pinpoint when she'd captured his heart: 'I was in the middle before I knew that I had begun.' Oh, Mr Darcy, she thought as she finished forming the dough into a ball, not surprised that she could recall so many lines from the movie. Tonight she'd watch *Love Actually* for perhaps the tenth time, even if it was a Christmas movie. It was exactly the kind of film she needed.

The phone rang and Veronica grabbed it, a dusting of flour on the receiver.

It was Beth, the client who'd ordered the Cast-Out Pie.

'It didn't work,' Beth said. 'I should have known it was just bullshit.'

Whoa. The woman's voice was so angry, but Veronica heard something else inside it: pain.

Give her a little slack, Veronica told herself. 'Did you think about casting this person from your heart while you were eating the pie?'

'Jesus Christ, I'm not the one who's casting someone out.

It's *him* who has to get someone else out of his goddamned head.'

There it was. Perhaps her husband was having an affair. Veronica had never been married, but she could certainly understand the pain that would cause. 'Ah.'

'I just wanted you to know it's bullshit,' Beth said, her anger rising. 'I'm not paying.'

'That was the deal, so that's fine. I'm sorry it didn't work for you.'

'Yeah, you're sorry.' Beth slammed the phone down.

God. What the hell was that about?

She was in no mood to make Amore Pie with that woman's anger and frustration still so heavy in her mind. She'd give herself the thirty minutes for the dough to chill, let the tension ease out of her, then conjure up Colin Firth walking out of that pond, his white shirt dripping wet. Hear him tell Elizabeth Bennet how he felt about her. 'My feelings will not be repressed. You must allow me to tell you how ardently I admire and love you.'

She'd put the dough in the refrigerator and was just adding the chocolate to a mixing bowl when her doorbell rang. She glanced at the clock on the wall. Six o'clock. Had she forgotten a client was picking up a pie? She doubted it. She had nothing but time to think the past two days in the extras tent. Her Amore Pie client – the shy gal who worked part-time behind the circulation desk at the library – wasn't due to pick up the pie from her neighbour until tomorrow morning.

184

Veronica wiped her hands on her apron, checked off 'choco-late' on her recipe so that she'd remember where she was up to, then went to her front door.

Nick DeMarco.

Once again, she froze for a split second, the way she always did when she saw him. Whether up close and personal – standing a foot in front of her, like now, like two nights ago in her kitchen – or around town as he patrolled the streets on foot or in his police car, she froze for the slightest moment. He was a constant reminder of her past. When she'd been hired at the diner a year ago, Nick would come in, as he sometimes did, for breakfast or lunch, and said his hellos, that it was nice to see her again, and then he seemed to keep a distance. Or maybe she was imagining it. She hadn't been sure if he knew who she was because he made it his busi-ness to know who was in town, or because he remembered her as the junior who'd gotten knocked up by his friend – or said she had – and then mysteriously disappeared. Unlike some other patrons at the diner, he wasn't a flirt, didn't stare at her, and she couldn't read him at all. Which made her even more aware of him.

'I'm sorry to just barge in on you like this,' he said. 'I wanted to let you know that Leigh and I won't be taking your class any more.'

She looked at him, hoping to read something in his expres-sion, but he had his usual poker face. Cop face. If this was a time or schedule conflict, he would have called. But he'd come to the door, which meant there was something else going on here.

'Was the shoo-fly pie just too upsetting for Leigh?' Veronica asked. 'I know she's only ten and perhaps I over-step—'

'It's not—' he began, then leaned his head back and sucked in a breath. He shook his head slightly.

There went the poker face. She opened the door wide. 'Come in. I'm working on a pie – Amore – right now. We can talk in the kitchen.'

He was in uniform, and took off his police hat, which she set on the counter next to her bowl of apples. He brushed back his dark brown wavy hair with his hand. Despite how big her kitchen was, how tall she herself was, Nick was six foot two, maybe three, and muscular, and he overwhelmed the space. Overwhelmed her.

She moved to the island counter and added the eggs, brown sugar and corn flour, whisking them together. She glanced at Nick, standing on the opposite side of the counter. He looked uncomfortable, so she thought it best not to rush him.

'The pie is working too well for her, actually,' he said. 'She's had three slices of the pie since Monday's class, and she says every time she even forks a piece, she feels her mother with her, can smell her perfume, feels the wool of her favourite red sweater.'

She stopped whisking. 'Well, then that's good, isn't it?'

'Her grandparents – her mother's parents – think it's some

kind of voodoo nonsense and don't like it. They don't like me, really.'

Veronica looked at him then, and he glanced away, out the window.

'I assume it's not voodoo nonsense,' he said. 'Just power of suggestion. Just pie, actually.'

She smiled. 'Yes. It is just pie. With some prayers and wishes and hopes baked in. The elixir pies seem to work for people because of the spark of hope in their name – Feel-Better Pie, Amore Pie, Spirit Pie.'

He leaned back against the refrigerator, letting his head drop back. 'Got a pie to make sure you don't lose your kid?' he said, his voice breaking a bit. He turned around and faced the window, jamming his hands into his pockets.

'Nick? What's going on?'

He turned back to her, looking between her and the floor. 'Leigh's grandparents think she might be better off with them. If she lived with them, they say, she wouldn't have to go to an aftercare programme at school. She'd come home off the school bus to a waiting, loving grandmother instead of a single father with unpredictable hours, an unpredictable job. They think she needs a maternal influence, specifically her grandmother's. The thought of my marrying again makes them sick. Any time I have so much as a date they seem to know about it.' He turned towards her. 'What the hell am I doing? I came here to tell you we wouldn't be back to your class and now I'm blurting out my life story. Jesus.'

'I'm glad you explained,' she said. 'Leigh is such a sweet girl, and the shoo-fly pie really seemed to comfort her. That's all it is. Comfort.'

'I know. What's crazy is that when she asked if we could take the class, I thought, Perfect, her grandparents will like this – good, clean fun for a father and daughter to do together. How wholesome.' He rolled his eyes. 'Instead, my former mother-in-law called me at work today, screaming up a storm about "this voodoo pie nonsense" Leigh's been talking about, and again said she was thinking of filing for custody.'

'That's serious,' Veronica said. 'Is she just upset or do you think she really will?'

He shrugged. 'Maybe she just needs reassurance. Or maybe she'll really file the papers.' He shook his head and let out a harsh breath. 'I'm going out of my mind – obviously, since I'm telling you all this. But I wanted to explain why we won't be back Monday. I can't give the woman ammunition.'

'Understood,' she said. 'I feel bad that this caused a problem. The pie is really just about comfort. That's all.'

He crossed the kitchen, leaning against the counter and looking out the window again. 'I was in the process of filing for divorce when the accident happened. Our marriage was falling apart and things weren't good between us. My wife – she was having an affair. I found out and it was the last straw. But then she died, and my former in-laws, who didn't know about the affair, have hated me ever since. I'm sure they think I initiated the divorce because I was the one sleeping around.'

'Oh, Nick, I'm so sorry.'

'Leigh's staying at their house tonight. This has got me so worked up I don't even want to go home. Just makes me think of what it'll be like if they try to take her away from me.'

'You can help me make this pie,' Veronica said, gesturing at her mixing bowl. She'd give up on the Amore Pie for the moment; worry and stress and the threat of custody battles didn't make for a good love pie for a hopeful client. 'Just a plain chocolate pudding Happiness Pie for you to take home. No voodoo nonsense.'

He nodded, offering something of a smile.

'You can grab the dough from the refrigerator,' she told him, wondering if he even remembered her. He never brought up high school. Maybe he recognized her as someone who'd gone to his school and that was it. Maybe he didn't even know she was the girl who'd been Timothy's girlfriend, the girl who'd 'accused' him of getting her pregnant. She'd bet anything he did know, though. 'It's been chilling long enough.'

He seemed grateful to have something to do. He got out the dough and spread some flour on the surface, then began rolling it.

'You were paying attention in class, I see,' she said.

'I always pay attention. Job requirement.'

Yes, indeed, he knew exactly who she was. 'I'll bet. How about some coffee?'

'I could use a strong cup,' he said, continuing to roll the dough.

Veronica stepped away to the coffee maker, glad to turn her back to him for a moment. God. This was unexpected. She added an extra half-scoop of Sumatra to the filter, noticing that her hands felt trembly, not like during the movie shoot, more shaky, as though she wasn't on solid ground.

'You clearly love your daughter,' she said. She hadn't meant to say that out loud; she'd been thinking it, but it just came out.

He nodded. 'I do. More than anything. But her grandparents are right about some stuff. I can't be there when she gets home from school. I do have a job that puts my life in danger when I'm her only living parent. I do suck at cooking.'

'You know how to roll out a pie crust,' she said.

He smiled. 'Thanks to you, I do.'

The pie crust was ready to be filled, but a few minutes later, after he'd drunk half his coffee, he said he should be going.

'I need to go for a long walk and process all this, think,' he said. 'Maybe I can take a rain check on a slice of the chocolate pie.'

'Sure,' she said.

Just like that, he was gone.

Veronica couldn't stop thinking about Nick. She felt for him, obviously. But there was something else going on here, something unexpected, an attraction to Nick DeMarco that she wouldn't quite let rise to the surface. She felt it, though. Because he'd opened up to her about his marriage and family issues? Because he'd stood so close that she could smell his soap? Because, as much as he reminded her of who she'd once been, he was a part of *her* history?

There was no doubt he was very attractive. And lately, when she'd be alone in her house, watching a film such as *Love Actually* or *Mamma Mia!*, she'd be filled with wistful longing to feel like the characters did: in love.

Yeah, because they *are* characters, Veronica realized. There was safety in fantasy. Nick, on the other hand? Reality.

She sat on the window seat in her kitchen, looking out at the back yard and sipping the coffee she'd made for them. His half-finished cup was still on the island counter, where he'd left it before he'd gone, in quite a hurry, as though he couldn't wait to get away. He probably felt as though he'd said too much.

It was just past eight, and dusk was finally beginning to fall. No matter how she tried to move her thoughts away from Nick, to the pie she still had to bake, to packing her bag for tomorrow's long day in the extras' holding pen, for going over her schedule to make sure she knew what pies she'd need to bake tomorrow night, she couldn't get Nick off her mind. Had he always been so attractive? He was tall and well built, yes, with that dark, wavy hair and deep brown eyes, and he had a great jawline, but she'd never paid much attention to him as a man before; he'd always represented something else to her: her very distant past. Timothy. A life she barely felt connected to yet couldn't get away from this past year. Her own doing.

Her doorbell rang, and she started at the sight of his police hat on the counter next to the bowl of apples. She hadn't even noticed he'd left it behind. Veronica usually noticed everything.

She assumed it was him and went to the door with the hat in her hand to save him from having to come up and wait for her to get it; he clearly needed some time and space, and she'd give it to him.

She opened the door and there he stood.

'I usually don't go around leaving my hat in people's kitchens,' he said with a brief smile.

'I—'

The phone rang, and Veronica ignored it, letting her answering machine pick it up. She was about to offer Nick the other half of his coffee in a travel cup when a woman's voice began leaving a message.

'Hello, Veronica?' the melodic voice said into her machine. 'My name is Bea Crane. I was born on 12 October 1991 in Boothbay Harbor, Maine. I'm here in Boothbay Harbor, staying at the Three Captains' Inn. I'd like to meet you, if you're open to that. You can reach me on my cell at 207 5551656. Bye for now.' Click.

Veronica went still, heard herself let out a strange sound,

and dropped the hat on the floor. She stood there, in some kind of daze, aware that Nick was kneeling at her feet, picking up the hat and staring at her. Then he was leading her to a chair in her living room and helping her sit down.

'Veronica? Are you all right?'

Her hand flew to her mouth. The baby. Her baby. The daughter she'd given up for adoption.

She'd called.

Veronica started crying, stood up, then sat down, then stood up.

Nick stood beside her. 'Veronica?'

'I—' she began, but words wouldn't come. She stood there, sobbing, and then felt arms, strong arms, around her. She let herself slump into them and cried, unable to stop, unable to speak. Finally, she began sucking in air and calming down. 'It's – it's . . .'

'The baby you placed for adoption?' He sat in the chair next to hers. 'What she said, and the birth date . . . I just put two and two together.'

She closed her eyes and nodded. She hadn't been wrong that he remembered. 'I've always updated the file at the adoption agency so she'd be able to find me when and if she wanted. I've been waiting for this day since she turned eighteen. She's twenty-two now. I can't believe it.'

'I should go, give you some privacy to call her back.'

'Actually, I think I'm glad I'm not alone right now. It's such a shock. I guess I'd lost hope that I'd ever hear from her.' Bea Crane. Her baby was named Bea Crane. Her voice was lovely. She sounded so polite and kind. Tears started stinging the backs of Veronica's eyes again.

Nick went into the kitchen and returned with the box of tissues she kept on the counter. He handed her one and sat back down. 'Can I get you a glass of water? Anything?'

She shook her head. 'You and . . . Timothy were friends back then, right?' she blurted out. She sucked in a breath. She hadn't even meant to ask.

He nodded. 'He is the father?'

'Yes. I know he told everyone he wasn't. But he definitely was. There was no one but him. I had quite a reputation for a virgin.' She shook her head. 'All in the past.'

'To tell you the truth, I feel a bit like that now with my in-laws. They think I'm this terrible jerk when it couldn't be further from the truth. And now I'm letting them push me around? Over pie?'

He was giving her an out, to change the subject, to tell him to go. But she was glad he was here, strangely enough. The connection to her past, to Timothy even, seemed more of a comfort than anything else. She'd always been so alone with thoughts of that very lonely, confusing time when she'd been sixteen. When she'd had the baby, alone in an ambulance with the kindly EMT. She'd been alone with the memory of handing that baby over and never laying eyes on her again. Twenty-two years was a long time to be alone with those thoughts.

'At sixteen I let everyone push me around, I guess,' she said. 'I didn't know how to stand up for myself, how to make people believe me.'

'I try hard to teach my daughter that she has to believe in herself, that that's how it works. You believe in yourself, and to hell with what anyone thinks.'

She nodded. 'You're a good father, Nick. Her grandparents must know that.'

'Sometimes people see what they want to see.'

That was terribly true, Veronica thought.

'For the past twenty-two-years – actually, from the day I was sent away to Hope Home – I kind of shut my eyes to everything. I tried so hard not to think about what I'd left behind. My parents who wanted nothing to do with me. The boyfriend I'd lost, like that,' she said, with a snap of her fingers. 'The future I envisioned for myself. Back then, I couldn't imagine what it would be like to have something so vital in the back of my mind, always there, something that had changed my life yet wasn't a part of it going forward. I had to tamp everything down so it wouldn't feel real.'

'Did it work?'

'Too well,' she said. 'I've spent so much time trying not to feel anything.'

He looked at her for a long moment. 'But now here your daughter is, very real, asking to meet you.'

'It feels wrong to think of her as my daughter. I didn't raise her. I wasn't her family.'

195

He squeezed her hand.

Veronica bit her lip. 'I could pick up the phone right now and in a second I'll be talking to her. To Bea Crane. I can't believe it. I wonder who she is, what she's like, what she looks like.'

'Are you going to call her back tonight?'

Suddenly she didn't know. She couldn't imagine just picking up the phone and calling Bea back. She wasn't sure she could handle it. 'I just want to sit with it for a bit. It's more shocking than I thought it would be.'

He stood up. 'I'll let you have your privacy then. I need to get going, return the squad car. Maybe Leigh and I will be here Monday for the pie class. I don't know. I don't know what the hell I'm supposed to do.'

'Do what feels right,' she said. 'Actually,' she added, 'do what you need to do.'

'You too,' he said, and then was gone again.

Two hours later, Veronica sat at the kitchen table, looking from the landline phone to anywhere else. She wasn't ready to make this call. At first she'd planned to call Bea from her bedroom, thinking she'd feel safe and comfortable reclining on her bed against the array of soft pillows, seeing all her familiar things and keepsakes, but she'd realized she needed to be in her kitchen, among her pie plates and the faint smell of chocolate and caramel. A fresh mug of coffee sat untouched in front of her, next to the phone.

Bea Crane. Here, in Boothbay Harbor.

She'd known Bea Crane for nine months and two minutes, and now here she was, no longer that six-pound weight she'd held against her chest, but a grown woman of twenty-two. She tried to envision Bea. Did she look like Veronica? Like Timothy? A combination of both? She had no doubt Bea was tall; Veronica was five foot ten, and Timothy was over six foot. She wondered if Bea had gotten Timothy's thick, light blond hair, that beautiful fine-spun hair all the Macintoshes had had.

She was going to ask about him, too, Veronica knew. Was she supposed to tell Bea the truth about everything? How she'd been treated by her family? By Bea's biological father? That she had no idea where Timothy Macintosh or his family were now? Veronica could give her own brief history, of course, but she couldn't imagine telling a curious twenty-two-year-old the more painful circumstances of her birth. She would tell Bea that she'd been sixteen and she'd placed her for adoption to give her the best possible life. That was true, after all, and that was what she'd tell her. Veronica didn't have to tell her what her mother had said, what her mother had called her. Or how Timothy had screamed at her and walked away. She wouldn't tell Bea any of that.

She stared at the phone.

They would talk. A bit of small-talk. They would meet for coffee or lunch or dinner. They'd talk about their lives. Bea would probably want to know her medical history, and

Veronica could provide that, what she knew, of course. But then what? What would they talk about? They would be like strangers but with the most fundamental thing connecting them.

Just call her back already, Veronica told herself, picking up the receiver, but her hand started trembling and she waited. She found herself wishing Nick hadn't left; he'd encourage her to press in the numbers, top off her coffee, tell her to go ahead.

She'd memorized the phone number. She pressed it in, slowly.

Two sets of chimes rang. Then: 'Veronica?'

She sucked in a breath and went still, grateful that Caller ID had saved them both from awkward introductions. 'Yes. Hello.'

Silence for a second, and then, 'Hello.'

Okay, this would be awkward regardless; they were both nervous. 'I'm glad you called,' Veronica said. 'I was hoping you'd call.'

'The adoption agency said you updated the file every time you moved, so I thought you must want me to, one day.' Bea's voice, the cadence, was so different from Veronica's. 'I'm glad you're glad.' Silence. 'Oh God, I sound like an idiot already.'

Veronica laughed. 'No. Not at all. I'm as nervous as you are.'

Silence.

'I've been waiting for this day for a very long time,' Veronica said. 'Hoping to meet you again, know that you were okay.'

I wasn't supposed to think about you. I told myself not to. My friends at Hope Home told me not to, that it was the only way to get through. But as much I locked down memories of you, I've thought about you every day. If you were happy. If your parents were loving.

On your birthday, every year, sometimes I'd be unable to get out of bed, but then I'd think of you blowing out the candles on your birthday cake, and I'd feel better . . .

'I am okay.'

'Good,' Veronica said. 'That's what I wanted to know most of all.'

'Should we meet?' Bea asked.

Veronica felt her heart swell, and tears pricked the backs of her eyes. 'I'd like that.'

'I'm just not sure how this is supposed to go,' Bea said, 'how it's supposed to feel. I don't know anything,' she added, and her voice sounded so strained.

Given how nervous Bea sounded, perhaps she would feel more comfortable coming over to Veronica's house, getting an outward glimpse of who she was, instead of sitting in a neutral coffee shop or restaurant and aware of people at nearby tables listening to their conversation. Veronica could set up a nice tea for the two of them, and bake a pie, a Happiness Pie.

'I'd much rather come to your house,' Bea said when Veronica gave her the choice.

Again, Veronica tried to picture Bea. Would she look like a younger version of herself? Would she share some of Veronica's traits? Her likes and dislikes? She didn't know all that much about ways of nature versus nurture, but she figured that at the least Bea would look something like her. Veronica had been a waitress more than half of her life; except for her pie-baking skills, she didn't even know what she might excel at, what she wasn't much good at. She couldn't hit a tennis ball, and she was no maths wiz, but she read a lot, could spend every night watching a movie, and she did like to travel. God, she'd bore Bea to death tomorrow with who she was.

'Tomorrow, evening? I won't be home until around six or seven o'clock. I could make dinner, or if you'll have already eaten, I can make a pie.'

Bea was silent for a few seconds. 'I have early dinner plans, but I figure I could be over by eight, if that works.'

'Eight o'clock tomorrow night it is.'

And just like that, the baby girl she'd held against her chest for less than two minutes on an October night would be knocking on her door tomorrow.

Chapter 12

Gemma

The knock on her door at the Three Captains' startled Gemma. She glanced up from her laptop on the small desk by the sun-filled window to the clock: it was just past nine in the morning. She got up reluctantly; she'd been working from the moment she'd woken two hours ago and hadn't even been down to breakfast, but was on a good roll. The first few paragraphs of her article on Hope Home — its history, some statistics then and now — were done, opening up to the long middle of the piece, which would focus on human interest: past residents, current residents. True stories.

Gemma stretched her arms above her head on the way to the door. When she opened it, Bea Crane stood there, looking like she might burst.

'I did it,' Bea said. 'I called my birth mother last night.

We're meeting tonight at her house.' She lifted her hands in front of her. 'I'm shaking.'

Gemma squeezed Bea's hand. With her blonde hair pulled into a ponytail, her pretty face free of make-up, Bea looked so young. 'What was the call like? Oh, gosh – I must sound like the nosy reporter here. I'm asking as a friend. Remember to just say, "This is off the record," and everything you tell me will be private.'

'I trust you to be discreet. Well, discreet enough,' Bea said. 'The situation – my situation – is so intensely personal, but I can't be the only person who didn't know she was adopted. If someone like me reads your article and it helps her decide what to do . . .' She glanced at Gemma. 'Maybe Veronica will be interested in talking to you and giving her perspective.'

'That would be so great if she would,' Gemma said. 'Of course, I don't expect you to show up at her house and say, "Nice to meet you. Want to repeat all of this to a reporter writing an article on Hope Home?"'

Bea smiled. 'Definitely not. But I will bring it up. She should know I'm talking to a reporter about her, even if her name isn't used.'

Gemma hoped Bea's birth mother would be open to talking to her for the article. The dual perspective of a birth mother from Hope Home and the daughter she placed for adoption making contact – it would add so much to the article. But Bea and her birth mother were meeting for the first time tomorrow; Gemma wouldn't expect to talk to Veronica – if at all – for days. It all depended on what kind of person Veronica was, how open to sharing her story she was.

'If you need someone to talk to, as a friend, just knock or call, okay? Even if you just need a little reassurance before you head over to her house tonight.'

'I appreciate that,' Bea said. 'I'd better get back to work – the kids from the Osprey Room had a little oatmeal-flinging war in the dining room.' She smiled and then dashed down the stairs.

Gemma closed the door, her thoughts whirling about the meeting Bea and Veronica would have, the emotion that would be in that room tonight. Bea's story was so heart-tugging. Deciding to find her birth mother and learning that the woman had updated the file at the adoption agency and left every possible piece of contact info. Driving up to Maine and getting to know the place she'd been born. Having the conversation with the two pregnant girls at Hope and how it had spiralled out of control for everyone. Making contact with her birth mother; a first meeting. If Gemma could get the birth mother's side for the article . . .

Gemma grabbed her phone, called Claire at the *Boothbay Regional Gazette* and explained that she might have the opportunity to talk with a birth mother and her daughter who were reuniting, get both their perspectives, and maybe she should take an extra couple of weeks for the article since Claire didn't officially need it until mid-July.

'No problem on the time,' Claire said. 'I really don't need it until 18 July, to run the Sunday before the fiftieth anniversary, which is the end of July. So take your time. I'd rather have a really full, knock-out piece, and perspectives like the ones you're getting are exactly what I had in mind.'

Perfect, Gemma thought, sentences of her article forming themselves in her mind. She'd really have the time now to develop her story, go deep, write the heck out of it.

She was supposed to go home tomorrow, but she'd just given herself an extra couple of weeks here, she realized. *Because I don't want to go home.*

She'd gotten herself in even deeper now; she'd have to call Alexander and explain that she'd be staying a bit longer – without saying why. She bit her lower lip, glancing at the photo she'd put on the bedside table of the two of them sitting on a bench in Central Park, their arms entwined, their smiles so genuine. He deserved to know, but how could she tell him just yet? A blast of sour squeezed into her throat; she would have to Google whether she could take antacids while pregnant.

Keeping the secret was too much. This morning she'd woken up in a cold sweat, unable to remember details of her unsettling dream; all she'd known was that she felt guilty about something. Duplicity. She thought about how, just weeks ago, she and Alexander had vowed to spend an evening in together – *not* talking about moving or not moving, not talking about job-hunting, not talking about how Alexander had to close the windows on the Manhattan traffic so that they could actually *hear* the movie he'd selected. They'd ordered in Mexican food, Gemma had whipped up frozen mango smoothies, and they'd spent a relaxing evening on the couch, riveted to the film *Tinker Tailor Soldier Spy*. Colin Firth himself, so typically moral and upstanding, playing a double agent in the British secret service.

Colin Firth, keeping secrets. Lying.

Her heart clenched. She would have to tell him. And soon.

She stood before the mirror hanging outside her closet door and put her hand on her stomach, turning to the side to see if it looked even a bit rounder. Not yet. But she was definitely pregnant; her doctor had called this morning with the news that her blood test was positive.

She took in her slightly pale complexion, the bit of shadow under her dark blue eyes, which might be from working so intensely the past few days. Her light brown hair, falling straight to her shoulders, seemed thicker, though, unless she was imagining it. More luxuriant, somehow. And her nails were longer. Her nails were never this long.

You're so lucky, she heard seventeen-year-old Chloe Martin echo in her head.

It had been just over a week since she'd seen that plus sign on the pregnancy test. A week that she'd kept the news a secret from Alexander. But she still wasn't ready to tell him. Another couple of weeks to finish the article, turn it in, and then she'd be ready to go home. Already, after just a few days at being in full-on reporter mode, conducting interviews, doing research and writing, she felt more like her old self – and she was a bit more used to the idea of being pregnant. In two more weeks she'd be much more confident, have stronger legs to stand on when she told Alexander the news.

She picked up the phone and pressed in the number of his cell phone. She wouldn't mention the pregnancy yet, but she did have to tell him she wouldn't be coming home tomorrow after all.

'Two more weeks?' he repeated after a deadly silence. 'What the hell is going on, Gemma?'

'I just want to go more in-depth with the article. I might have a chance to interview the birth mother of one of my sources. It'll round—'

'Gemma, you were going to Maine for a weekend. Then it turned into a week. Now it's three weeks.'

'I'm just—'

'Are you saying you need a break from us? If that's what this is, Gemma, just goddamned say so. Don't make it about an article for some small-town paper.'

I need a break from you, she said silently, closing her eyes.

'Neither the article nor the newspaper is small to me, Alex. Why can't you understand how important my career is to me?'

Silence for a moment. 'Gemma, you lost your job. It's gone, you need to face it. You're chasing a one-off piece that can't go anywhere, not in the way you want. If you're leaving me, just say so.'

She winced at that; she hated hurting him this way. She paced around the small room, her heart beating too fast. Calm down, Gemma, she told herself. Look at this from his perspective. He wants what he wants just as much as you want what you want. 'Alex, I'm just trying to . . .' find my way through this new normal, she finished silently, one hand on her stomach again. Find myself in this.

'Just trying to what?' he barked. 'What the hell are you trying to do besides screw things up between us?'

'I'm pregnant!' she shouted, then started to cry.

Oh God.

There was silence for a moment. 'What? Gemma – what?'

'I'm pregnant, Alex.' She could barely believe she'd said the words aloud to him.

'Are you sure?' he asked, the tone of his voice changing – dramatically. Instead of anger, there was . . . wonder.

'Two positive pregnancy tests and positive blood test results today.'

'Oh my God, Gemma. This is amazing! We're going to have a baby! Wait a minute,' he said, the voice changing again, growing hesitant. 'How long have you known?'

'I took the first pregnancy test last Wednesday. It was positive. I was so shocked – as you can imagine. I thought maybe my cycle was off because of the stress of losing my job. I only took the test to rule out the craziest reason why my period would be late. We'd used a back-up plan when I was on those antibiotics.' She closed her eyes and sat down on the edge of her bed. 'But there it was, a pink plus sign.'

He was quiet again for a long few seconds. 'Gemma, you've known you were pregnant for a week and didn't tell me? You left for Maine and didn't tell me?'

'It's a loaded topic, Alex.'

'Loaded?' he repeated, his voice full of disdain. 'So you're not happy about it? Is that what this is all about?'

'I don't know.'

'You don't know,' he repeated flatly. 'And were you going to tell me during this call if it hadn't just come out?'

'I don't know that either. I don't know anything except that I don't want to move to Dobbs Ferry and live next door to your parents. I don't want a part-time job at the local paper if I *insist* – as you put it – on working. I don't want this life you're trying so damned hard to force me into.'

'Well, guess what, Gemma, you're pregnant. It's not about you any more.'

'Who the hell is it about?'

'The baby. Me. Us. Our marriage, our family.'

She suddenly felt very, very tired. 'I don't know how I feel about any of this, Alex. I need time to . . .' She needed to hang up. She needed time to process this, that she'd told him. 'I'm going now, Alex. I need to go.'

Click.

She dropped her head in her hands and cried.

Gemma checked the address of the woman she was due to interview in three minutes. Caitlin Aureman, 33 Banyon Road. The small white cape house halfway down the street with the scooter and the Big Wheels tricycle out front was the place.

Gemma had been walking along Main Street, needing to be 'alone in a crowd'. The conversation with Alexander had drained her, and she couldn't stay cooped up in her small room. She'd gotten a herbal iced tea and a bagel with cream cheese and sat on a bench, trying to calm herself down and eat a few bites, when Pauline Lee had called with the news that a woman who'd lived at Hope Home fifteen years ago as a fifteen-year-old, and had placed her baby for adoption, was interested in speaking with Gemma for the article, but only had a two-hour window. Gemma had been grateful for somewhere to go, something to focus on besides her marriage.

She pressed the doorbell, and a woman who could only be described as weary opened the door. She looked like she hadn't slept well – or perhaps in days. There was a baby swing in the living room, and lots of kid paraphernalia around the room.

'You must be Gemma Hendricks,' she said. 'I'm Caitlin Aureman. I forgot to mention to the Hope Home lady that I have to insist on anonymity – that you won't use my name in the article. Hope Home was good to me, and I have only positive things to say about it, but if I'm going to be truthful about how my life has been since, I don't want my real name used.'

'I can assure you I won't use your name. I'll make up a name and throw off the details a bit to protect your identity. I appreciate your willingness to sit down with me.'

Caitlin led Gemma across the living room and they sat down on the sofa. Gemma pulled out her recorder and her notebook, and the woman started talking before Gemma could even get out her pen and ask a question.

'Everyone said, "You'll ruin your life if you have a baby at fifteen,"' Caitlin said. '"You have your whole life in front of you. Put the baby up for adoption. It's the right thing. For both of you." On and on. I even agreed to go live at Hope Home so that no one in town would know I was pregnant, so that it would stay a family secret. Well, here I am, thirty years old, and I did everything everybody told me to do. I went to college. I went to law school. I got all the "See, you listened to us, and now look at you." Well, fifteen years later I have three kids under five, I can forget about my career, and I can't even hear myself think ninety per cent of the time. I'm not saying I could have achieved everything I did with a baby at fifteen — who knows, maybe I could have. I just know that it all added up to me sitting at home with three kids, a husband who's never home and a career that's basically over. Why the hell did I work so hard? To be treated like the invisible woman at my husband's business functions? I'm suddenly a stay-at-home mother so I have nothing of value to say? I hate this.'

This will be me, Gemma thought, her head spinning for a few seconds. I don't want this to be me. Focus on the interview, she reminded herself. 'Can I ask a personal question?'

Caitlin let out a harsh laugh. 'I think I've made it clear you can.'

'Did you plan to get pregnant with your first child from your marriage?'

Caitlin shook her head. 'It was an accident. Twins. I wasn't really ready, but I was excited. I thought I could do it all, be Superwoman, even though everyone said it was impossible. I thought I could work full-time and be a great mom and take cooking classes and learn to speak Italian and take yoga. Boy, was I in for a rude awakening.'

'So you had a plan, but life didn't go accordingly?' Gemma didn't want to hear the answer. Clearly Caitlin had had a plan, big plans for herself.

'Exactly. One of the twins was sick a lot with ear infections, and the other would wake up every couple of hours, and my husband would argue with me endlessly about quitting the firm and staying home with the boys. I know it sounds awful, but I didn't want to. I loved my job, loved the office environment, getting all dressed up every day. I didn't want to stay home with the twins all day, as much as I loved them.'

'But then both worlds started suffering,' Gemma said, more statement than question.

'Exactly. Home and work. My marriage was a wreck. I blamed my husband for not helping more; he blamed me for being selfish and not agreeing to quit when we could swing it financially if we were careful. The pressure won and I quit, and suddenly I had three kids and had been out of the game so long I couldn't see myself ever finding my way back to who I used to be.'

Who I used to be. That was exactly what Gemma was afraid of: waking up one day and wondering what had happened to the person she used to be.

'I know I'm not that woman,' Caitlin said. 'I'm not twenty-five and childless and a rising young associate. But sometimes I hate who I am now. That my life feels like it's not my own. That's how I felt at fifteen and pregnant. Like my life wasn't my own. It wasn't.' She shook her head. 'Maybe it's just me, though. I know two other attorneys at my old firm who have kids and manage to put in their hours and be great moms. They make it work. I couldn't.'

Gemma too could think of several working mothers who seemed to have great balance — exactly what she was hoping to achieve. 'I really appreciate your being so open and honest. I think many women will be able to relate to how you feel.' Not Gemma's sister-in-law, who'd had a very similar experience to Caitlin's, minus the teen pregnancy. Lisa Hendricks

Johnson gave up a high-powered job to stay home with her baby and loved her life, every moment of it. 'I was meant to be a mother,' Lisa said all the time. 'My whole life has been leading me to this,' she'd say, wiping her toddler's runny nose while patting her seven-months-pregnant belly.

'Do you have kids?' Caitlin asked Gemma.

'Not yet.'

Caitlin nodded. 'I didn't think so. You don't look exhausted enough.'

Gemma smiled, but she wanted to cry.

'You remind me so much of who I used to be,' Caitlin said. 'Here you are, conducting an interview, writing for the paper. Living your life, the one you probably imagined when you were a teenager.'

The sound of a car pulling into the driveway had Caitlin leaping up to peer out the window. 'It's my mother with the baby.' She glanced at her watch. 'She's a half-hour early coming back. Lana must be fussing up a storm.'

Gemma stood up. 'I won't keep you then. Thank you so much for your time, Caitlin. And I just want to say – I hope you can find a happy medium for yourself.'

The front door opened and an older woman came in, carrying a beautiful baby, who was indeed fussing up a storm. 'She's been crying non-stop.'

Caitlin took the baby and bounced her a bit. 'Right,' she said to Gemma with a roll of her eyes. 'A happy medium.'

Gemma thought she might ask Caitlin's mother a few questions about what it was like fifteen years ago when her daughter had been a teenage resident of Hope Home, but the woman was already rushing out the door, calling over her shoulder that she'd phone Caitlin later.

'I can't even sit down to a half-hour interview,' Caitlin said, shaking her head. 'There is no happy medium.'

Gemma wished she knew what to say to make the woman's resentment, the way she looked at her life, abate some. But what she'd said hit so close to home that all Gemma could do was wish Caitlin well. She'd send her a little something tomorrow, maybe a gift certificate to a restaurant in town where she and her husband could go if her mother or a sitter would watch the kids. Something to take her away from her life for a little bit.

Why was it this way for some women and not others? she wondered, thinking of herself and Caitlin in one dreary category, and women like her sister-in-law and her neighbour Lydia Bessell in the other. Mindset? You chose this or that because of this or that, though sometimes, of course, you had no choice whatsoever, and then there you were, in your life. There was another category, though. Mothers with full-time jobs who made their lives work — because they had to, because they wanted to. Gemma would be in that category. She would, she assured herself. Despite how much Caitlin had wanted her life to work. Everyone was different.

Gemma didn't even have a job. Or a baby in her arms, just

yet. She had no idea what she was talking about, how anything would be. And that might be the scariest part of all.

After a long day of research and two more interviews — one with a current resident of Hope Home and another with a woman who'd adopted a baby from a Hope resident five years ago — Gemma arrived back at the inn at around five o'clock, desperate for a hot bubble bath and her book: *Your Pregnancy This Week.*

A man sat on the porch swing, and from the distance of the dark driveway he looked so much like Alexander that for a moment her heart swelled with such longing for her husband that she had to draw in breath. Despite everything happening between them right now, she missed him. She wished she could turn to him with all her fears, her worries, the way she'd always been able to. But she couldn't in this case.

I do love you, Alexander, she thought. I do. So much. I just wish—

The man on the porch stood up. It was Alexander.

Gemma gasped as he came towards her without a word and wrapped his arms around her. She fell against him, holding him tight, so relieved to have him standing right here. Just let everything fall away and let your husband hold you, she told herself.

'I should have known you'd fly up here,' she said. 'My head is in so many different places that I didn't think of it.'

'No kidding.' He offered a half-smile and put his arm

about her shoulders and they walked up the short stone path to the steps.

'We're having a baby,' he whispered.

'I'm scared to death.'

'I'm not,' he said.

She led him into the inn, quiet on a sunny late afternoon. They headed up the stairs to the third floor, and Gemma unlocked her door.

The two of them barely fitted in the room together. She drank in the sight of him; with all their arguing, she'd forgotten how attracted she was to Alex, how easily his face, his body, could overwhelm her. In her frame of mind, exhausted, she'd have to be careful around him. She needed a hot bath and her husband's strong arms – but she couldn't let him strong-arm her.

She closed the door behind him. 'I can learn how to be a mother, I know that. But I can't learn how to want what you want. I don't want to move to the suburbs and be a stay-at-home mom. It's wonderful for those who do want that, and yes, I get that it's a blessing that we can afford it in the first place. But I want to be a reporter. I want to work on exactly the kind of stories I'm working on now. Tonight, a birth mother is meeting the daughter she gave up for adoption twenty-two years ago.'

He put his hand on her stomach. 'I don't see why you can't do this from Westchester, then. You'll work part-time at the local paper. If you're assigned this story here, why not there?'

I'm not moving to Westchester to live next door to your family, damn it! 'I don't want to leave the city.' The local newspaper might not hire her anyway, she knew full well.

He shook his head and sat down on the edge of the bed. 'Well, I do, Gem. And I'm not raising this baby in the city. I won't.'

'Well I won't move to Westchester.'

He dropped his head back and let out a frustrated breath. 'How are we going to work this out?'

She sat down beside him and took his hand, and he closed it tight around hers. 'I don't know. I just know that I want to stay here for the next couple of weeks and work on this story. I want to get used to being pregnant, come to terms with it. It's completely unexpected.'

'Come to terms with it?' He shook his head. 'Do you know how lucky we are?'

She closed her eyes for a moment, wishing he could understand.

'Fine, come to terms with it, if that's what you have to do. If that's what it takes to make you see that moving to Dobbs Ferry is in all our best interests. We'll have my family right there for support, babysitting, family community. The neighbourhoods I'm interested in are full of young families like us. We'll fit right in.'

'But I won't.'

He closed his eyes in frustration. 'I don't know how you can stand this tiny room. Why not get a bigger room?'

'June gave me the dear-old-friend discount on this single,' she said. 'The regular rooms go for almost two hundred a night, and I didn't want to take a room away from a full-paying guest. And I like this room. It's cosy. Isabel, June's older sister, manages the inn and she's been great to me.'

He came towards her and reached out his hand, his expression tender. 'I miss you, Gem.'

Tears filled her eyes. 'I miss you too.'

He sat on the bed, leaned against the headboard and pulled her back against his chest, wrapping his arms around her. 'We'll figure it out.'

How, though? Gemma wondered, Caitlin Aureman's weary face flashing into her mind.

Chapter 13
Bea

In a romantic little Mexican restaurant on a pier, Bea sat across from Patrick, the tall, dark and intelligent second assistant director on the Colin Firth film, listening to him tell a hilarious story about an A-list movie star he'd once worked with, without mentioning names. She liked that he didn't name-drop or talk behind the actors' backs. She liked that he'd said some of the biggest movie stars were among the nicest people he'd ever met. She liked the way he listened intently to her, the warmth in his expression. She liked him. He was twenty-eight, from Seattle, and his dream was to produce interesting documentaries. He'd been around the world on various film shoots, but he wasn't full of himself at all. And the more Bea looked at him, the hotter he got. He was exactly her height – Bea rarely wore heels or she'd tower over most people – with narrow blue eyes, freckles and sexy dark, wavy hair. He'd picked her up at the inn right on time, and they'd walked to the colourful restaurant, where he'd made a reservation, though at five o'clock it hadn't been necessary.

After the waiter left with their orders, he asked her to tell him all about herself, and she wanted to blurt out that in less than three hours she'd be meeting her birth mother for the first time ever, but instead she found herself telling him about her mother's death and losing sight of her own dreams to be a teacher, and that maybe getting fired from her crutch job at Crazy Burger had been a blessing in disguise.

'What brought you to Boothbay Harbor, Maine?' he asked, swiping a tortilla chip through the excellent dish of salsa between them.

She explained about the letter from her mother. The weeks she'd spent walking around Boston going back and forth about looking up her birth mother. And then finally deciding to drive up to Maine to check her out. 'I won't name names, either, but the reason I've been hanging around the film set is because my birth mother – who I'm meeting for the first time later tonight – is one of the extras. I found out she was working on the film and just wanted to look around.'

He raised his margarita glass to her. 'I admire what you're doing, Bea. That takes guts. All of it. Especially after getting hit with such a whopper of a letter like that. Have you gotten a little more used to it all?'

'I guess. Sometimes it feels like it can't possibly be true, but then I take out my mom's letter and re-read it, and I know it is true.'

'I'm doubly sorry that Tyler was giving you a hard time yesterday. But then again, if he hadn't been, I might not have overheard you guys arguing and I might not have seen you at all. I'm pretty glad I did.'

She smiled. 'Me too.'

When their entrées arrived — *enchiladas suizas* for Bea and steak fajitas for Patrick — they talked about everything and anything, from movies they both liked and hated, to books, to places they'd travelled — he had Bea beaten there — and the weirdest foods they'd tried. Bea told him about having to measure her Mt Vesuvius burgers to make sure they were exactly one foot tall, and he told her about filming on location near the volcano in Italy. They talked so easily, so naturally, and Bea found herself laughing for what felt like the first time in a month. Maybe several months.

After dinner they had coffee and split a basket of cinnamon *churros*, then headed out to the back deck overlooking the bay, where they both tried to pick up the crab from the touch tank, but were bested by an eight-year-old who picked it up without getting pinched.

As they were leaving, Bea told him she'd walk him back to the set, since her birth mother's house was nearby and she was due over there soon. 'I can't believe I'll be face to face with her, talking to her, in less than an hour.'

'I'd love to hear how it goes,' Patrick said. 'Tomorrow is

nuts, all day, but maybe you can come by my trailer around one o'clock for a quick lunch on the set. I can impress you with the craft services table – that's the catering.'

Bea smiled. 'I'd like that.'

He smiled back and took her hand, the comfort of it, the warmth, startling her. Yup, she liked this guy.

As they approached the trailers, which had grown much busier since yesterday with people milling about and rushing around, a man's voice called out, 'Hey, people, Colin Firth is signing autographs in front of O'Donald's Pub!'

A swarm of people ran towards the little pub, but the only person standing in front of it was an elderly woman who was feeding two seagulls from her bakery bag. She let out a yelp at the crowd racing towards her, and a man came out of the pub – also not Colin Firth – and jumped in between her and the storming mass. 'Watch it, people,' he shouted. 'Don't run the lady down.'

'Is Colin Firth in there?' a woman asked.

'The only Colin in O'Donald's Pub is my drunk uncle visiting from Scotland,' the man said. 'What's this nonsense?'

Bea looked back at the guy who'd called out the Colin Firth sighting. Tall and very skinny and quite possibly a little bit drunk, the fortysomething man, who had a huge smile on his face, looked like the one who'd asked out Veronica at the diner. 'Is he just yelling out random Colin Firth appearances to make people run around like crazy?'

Patrick glanced at him. 'He must be, because Colin Firth

isn't even in the country. He's not due here on set for at least a few days.'

Bea barely had time to thank Patrick for dinner before three different staffers rushed him with various emergencies.

'Until tomorrow, then,' he said, giving her a very quick and sweet kiss on the lips.

She smiled. 'Until tomorrow.' She watched him hurry towards the field of wildflowers, where a group of people were crowding around one of the cameras.

Bea heard a loud snort, and then a familiar voice said, 'Don't say I didn't warn you.'

She turned around to find Tyler sitting on a director's chair next to his sister, who had *To Kill a Mockingbird* open on her lap again but was looking everywhere but at the book.

'I don't even know you,' Bea said. What was with this guy?

'Oh hey, you're the one who knows everything about this book, right?' Maddy said to Bea, holding up *To Kill a Mockingbird*. 'Do you know who this Boo guy is?'

Bea smiled at her. 'Boo Radley. He's the town recluse in Maycomb. Because no one ever sees him, but everyone knows he's been holed up in his family house from childhood, they come to all sorts of conclusions about him. Wrong conclusions. Boo ends up saving the day for the kids. His characterization has a lot to say about the harm of gossip, the harm of assumptions.'

Maddy sat up. 'Really? I hate gossip. A few months ago, someone started a rumour about this girl at my school and she never came back after spring break. Maybe I'll read a little more, to get to the parts about him.'

Bea smiled. 'It's a great book. Honestly. The whole thing.'

'Oh my God, is that Christopher Cade over there?' Maddy said, staring at the tall, handsome actor on the field, surrounded by people with headsets and clipboards.

'More reading, less staring,' Tyler told his sister, pushing his wire-rimmed glasses up on the bridge of his nose.

Maddy rolled her eyes at him. 'I already have his autograph anyway.' She went back to the book, but stole glances towards the very good-looking actor every few moments.

Tyler had gone back to pretending Bea wasn't standing a foot in front of him, so she glanced at her watch. She might as well start walking over to Veronica's.

'Good luck with the book,' she said to Maddy, ignored Tyler and headed towards the harbour, her heart fluttering in her chest.

Bea stood on Veronica Russo's little porch, staring at the red front door, at the doorbell, which she still hadn't rung.

She glanced up at the sky and closed her eyes, thinking of her mother. She wondered how Cora Crane would feel about her standing at her birth mother's door, about to ring the bell, about to meet the woman whom Cora had spent so many years hiding via omission. She must have realized Bea would seek out her birth mother; she couldn't suddenly have this truth sprung on her at age twenty-two and not do anything

with it. She'd have gone crazy otherwise, wondering, speculating, imagining, turning the truth over and over in her mind.
It was right that she was here. Yes, Cora Crane had kept that
truth a secret, but in the end, she wanted Bea to know. Where
it took Bea was up to Bea. She knew her mother had accepted
that while she wrote the letter. Cora had needed peace. She
touched the tiny gold heart locket necklace her mother had
given her, and now it felt as though her mother was here with
her.

I love you, Mama, she said silently up to the sky, dusk
just beginning to darken the blue.

She pressed the doorbell and held her breath.

The door opened and there was Veronica Russo, who
gasped and covered her mouth with her hand.

Veronica looked at Bea for the longest time. 'Oh my goodness, oh my goodness,' she said, tears coming to her eyes.
'It's so nice to meet you, Bea. I don't think I've ever meant
that phrase more in my entire life.'

Bea smiled. 'I'm glad to meet you too.'

Bea tried not to stare, but she couldn't help herself. She
wasn't a carbon copy of Veronica, but she saw enough of
herself in her face, in her height, that she began looking for
the details – the straight, almost pointy nose, the slightly too
big mouth, the texture of the almost straight hair with its
wave, if not the colour. Veronica was beautiful. She wore a
lavender shirt embroidered with silver along the neck and a
white skirt with a flouncy hem, and low-heeled sandals. A

few gold bangles were on one wrist, a bracelet watch on the other.

Bea had spent a good half-hour pawing through the makeshift closet in her room, trying to decide what was appropriate to wear for a first date *and* to meet your birth mother for the first time. She'd gone with her white skinny jeans and a silky tank top in her favourite colour, yellow.

Veronica ushered Bea into the living room, where a big square tray was set up on the coffee table, holding a pie, an ornate teapot and cups. 'Why don't we sit on the sofa?' she said, gesturing for Bea to sit.

They sat on opposite edges, clasping and unclasping their hands. Bea put her hands underneath her thighs and glanced around the room. Cosy, homey. The sofa was plush velvet ecru with lots of colourful throw pillows, a matching love seat perpendicular to it. A crowded bookcase took up one wall, and a stone fireplace another. It was easier for Bea to look around than to stare at Veronica, which was what she wanted to do. Stare.

'I'll be honest,' Bea said. 'I'm at an advantage here because the adoption agency, where I got your contact information, told me where you worked. So I went to The Best Little Diner last week, when I first arrived in town. I just wanted to see you from a distance, if that makes sense.'

Veronica seemed startled, but she said, 'It does. I'm sure I would have done the same thing.' She picked up the pot. 'Tea?'

Bea nodded, and Veronica poured, and Bea noticed that Veronica's hands were a bit shaky. Bea added a little milk and a sugar cube, and lifted the pretty cup to her lips just to have something to do with her own shaky hands. The smell of the Earl Grey was soothing.

When Bea looked up, Veronica was staring at her, but then she glanced away. 'You can look,' Bea said. 'I got to stare at you when I went to the diner. You're just about more familiar to me than I am to you. Except you've known about me all my life. And I just discovered you existed a month ago.'

'You have my eyes,' Veronica said. 'And height, of course.'

'The hair is my father's?'

Veronica seemed to stiffen, unless Bea was reading too much into it. 'Yes,' she said, glancing away.

No elaboration. Did she not want to talk about him? Had their relationship ended back when Veronica was pregnant? Had he stayed by her side through the pregnancy but stress tore them apart? Bea was so curious, but she sensed she should stick to Veronica herself right now, especially for their first meeting.

Bea took a sip of tea. 'There's so much I want to ask you, I hardly know where to begin. Can you tell me how old you were when I was born?'

'Sixteen. I turned seventeen just a month later.' Veronica set out two small plates on the coffee table. 'Pie? It's chocolate fudge.'

She doesn't want to talk about herself, Bea realized. Bea

sensed that Veronica would answer her questions, but her body language, the stiffness of her shoulders, her tight expression, made it obvious that talking about this wasn't easy.

'I'd love some pie,' Bea said. 'I had your chocolate fudge pie at the diner the day I was there. That's how I found out which waitress was Veronica Russo. One of the waitresses called to you by name and said your pies were to die for.'

Veronica smiled. 'I'm kind of known for my pies in town.'

'I can understand why,' Bea said, taking a bite. 'Delicious.'

Okay, I don't want to make small-talk about pies, Bea thought. I want to know who you are. Who you were. Where I came from — and why.

'Is "Russo" Italian?' Bea asked, figuring she'd stick to the reasonably neutral to start.

'Yes. My father's family came from northern Italy, Verona, *à la* Romeo and Juliet. My mother's family was Scottish.'

'And my biological father's family?' she asked.

'Scottish too,' Veronica said. 'I remember that because it was something we had in common. We were partnered on an ancestry project in high school. That's how we started seeing each other.'

Italian and Scottish. Not a drop of Irish, as she'd always thought, like both Cranes. With her light blond hair, pale brown eyes and pale complexion, Bea was often thought to be Scandinavian.

'How long were you dating?' Bea asked.

Veronica picked up her tea and took a sip. 'Not long. Six months.'

'Were you in love?'

'I thought so,' Veronica said. 'I was, anyway.'

Bea waited for her to elaborate, but Veronica gave Bea a tight smile and took another sip of tea.

Bea took another bite of her pie, then put her fork down. 'How did your parents take the news? About your pregnancy, I mean.'

'Well, it wasn't ideal,' Veronica said. 'So they reacted the way many parents might.'

'They were upset?'

She nodded. 'I was sixteen and my life as a typical high-school junior was suddenly interrupted. They had a hard time with that. My parents had expectations for me, that I'd make them proud, go to college, build a career, get married, have children − in that order.'

'And my birth father,' Bea said, unable to stop herself from trying again. 'Was he upset too?'

Veronica topped off her tea, even though her cup was practically full. She was stalling for time. 'He was pretty shocked,' she finally said.

'Do you have a photograph of him?' Bea asked.

Veronica put down her teacup so quickly that Bea figured if she hadn't, she might have dropped it. 'I do. Just one. I kept it in a keepsake box, and there was one time during the pregnancy that I took out the picture and looked at it. And then I turned it over and put it on the bottom of the box and never touched it again.'

Bea bit her lip. She wouldn't ask to see it right now. 'He must have hurt you pretty bad, then.'

'Well, that's in the past,' she said, too brightly.

'Veronica, can I ask you something?' She seemed to brace herself. 'Are you not saying too much about what life was like for you back then because it's painful to talk about? Or to protect me, maybe? To spare my feelings?'

'Maybe a little of both, but mostly the latter. This is your history, after all. And you've come all the way here to learn about it, where you come from. I'd like to give you the basics without the unnecessary gritty details.'

The gritty details were truth, though. And Bea wanted truth. Not sidestepping, not omission. Not any more.

'I can handle it,' Bea said. She'd buried both her parents. She'd discovered – at twenty-two – that she'd been adopted. She could handle just about anything.

Veronica nodded. 'It's not easy for me to talk about my past, mainly because I don't talk about it ever. I kind of had to put a lock and key on the subject twenty-two years ago or else I'd have gone crazy.'

'Because it was so painful?'

'My parents didn't handle the news well. Your biological father didn't either. And I was sent to a home for pregnant teenagers, where I didn't have a single visitor in the seven and a half months I was there. Even that is a bit hard for me to say — I guess because I hate the idea of you having this in your head. That these blood relations of yours weren't exactly . . . supportive.'

'You didn't have anyone?'

Veronica shook her head. 'I had an amazing grandmother — my father's mother, Renata Russo. But she passed away a few months before I found out I was pregnant. She would have saved my life back then.'

'Would you have kept me, do you think, if your grandmother had been alive?'

Veronica took a deep breath. 'Maybe. I really don't know for sure.'

'It's crazy for me to think that I might have had a completely different life, a completely different childhood. A different mother.'

Veronica seemed relieved that the focus had switched from herself to Bea. She shifted her body slightly more towards Bea. 'Did you used to think about that a lot as you were growing up?'

'Actually, I didn't know I was adopted until a month ago. My parents never told me. My father died when I was nine, and my mother died last year. She told me the truth in a letter she'd arranged to have sent a year later.'

Veronica was staring at her. 'Wow. That must have been some shock.'

'It was,' Bea said.

'What was your mom like?' Veronica asked.

'The best. The absolute best.'

Veronica smiled. 'Good.' Tears shimmered in her eyes. 'That's what I always hoped, all these years. That you were somewhere safe and wonderful with loving parents.'

Bea's parents' faces flashed into her mind. Yes, she had been somewhere safe and wonderful with loving parents all those years.

She stood up suddenly, wanting to leave. This was crazy, all of it. What was she doing here with this . . . stranger? And Veronica Russo *was* a stranger. A total stranger.

Cora Crane was my mother. Keith Crane was my father. That's all I need to know.

Why couldn't her mother have left well enough alone? Bea wondered, that hollow pressure forming in her chest again. Bea would have gone on not knowing, blissfully ignorant that she was a different person entirely. That she was Italian and Scottish and not a bit Irish. That she'd come into this world because of the woman sitting a foot in front of her.

She needed fresh air. A break. She needed to digest all this privately, not that she'd learned all that much. She just knew that her skin felt . . . tight.

Veronica stood up too. 'Are you all right?'

'I should get going,' she said.

'I hope I didn't scare you away. Say too much. Or too little. I want to answer your questions. I just don't want to overwhelm you.'

'With the truth?' Bea asked.

'Yes.'

'That way of thinking kept me from knowing I'd been adopted in the first place,' Bea said — too harshly, she realized. 'Maybe if I'd always known, this would be a little easier. I would have had my entire life to lead me here one day.' She had no idea what she thought. What she felt. She just knew she needed air. She needed to leave.

'I understand, Bea.'

Bea hated the concern in her eyes. 'You're a stranger!' Bea wanted to shout. A total stranger.

'When you're ready,' Veronica said, 'if you want, I'd like to meet again. I'd love to learn more about you.'

Bea tried to smile but she felt so jumpy and uncomfortable. 'I'll call.' She sounded like one of those non-committal guys after a so-so date. 'Thank you for the pie,' she added, grabbed her bag and headed towards the door. Veronica opened it for her and she hurried out, aware that Veronica was staring after her.

Oh, darn, she thought as she was about to say goodbye and then flee. She'd forgotten to tell Veronica about Gemma's article. 'I almost forgot. I found out about Hope Home from my original birth certificate, and when I went for a visit a few days ago, I met a reporter who's writing a big article about the home's fiftieth anniversary. I told her my story — I didn't give your name, of course. But I wanted you to know that I did talk to her. She's staying at the same inn I am too. She got me a temporary job there, and it comes with a room.'

Veronica's eyes widened. 'So you'll be staying in town for a while, then?'

'For a couple of weeks,' Bea said. Was Veronica happy about that? Worried?

'I appreciate that you didn't give the reporter my name. I'm pretty well known in town because I work at such a popular diner and because of my pie business too, but I'm a pretty private person. I'm not sure I'd want my personal history in the paper.'

Bea froze. 'Are you upset that I let her interview me?' She kicked herself for not considering that Veronica might be prickly about the article.

'No, not at all,' Veronica said, and Bea studied her to gauge whether she was telling the truth, but Veronica turned away for a moment.

'I think she's especially interested in the here and now where we're concerned,' Bea rushed to say. 'I know she'd love to talk to you too. But I know she'll understand if you're not interested.'

Veronica offered a tight smile. 'I don't think I am.'

Bea's stomach clenched. This was all intense enough, without bringing a newspaper article into it. 'I can understand that. Well, goodbye then.'

'Goodbye,' Veronica said, and Bea could see tears shimmering in her eyes again that she was trying hard not to show.

Chapter 14
Veronica

Veronica shut the door behind Bea, half wanting to go running after her and hug her tight and ask her to come back, half wanting never to have to answer another of Bea's questions again.

Bea looked so much like herself and Timothy. She had Timothy's blond hair, and there was something about the shape of her face and the general expression that were all Timothy Macintosh, but the features were Veronica's. The round, pale brown eyes. The straight, pointy nose. The wide mouth. She had a squarish chin, like Timothy. She was tall, like both of them. Fine-boned, like Veronica.

You have my nose, Veronica had thought over and over while she'd been sitting so close to Bea, trying not to stare. And my mouth. I see myself in your face.

Every time Bea smiled, which hadn't been often, she saw

her own smile, with Timothy's long, even, white teeth.

She sat back down on the sofa, staring at Bea's teacup, the faintest bit of berry-coloured lip gloss on the rim.

The phone rang, and Veronica would have ignored it, but it might be Bea.

It was Nick DeMarco. Relief unwound the tight muscles of her shoulders.

'Just checking in,' he said. 'I know you were meeting with your birth daughter tonight.'

Veronica burst into tears. She couldn't stop. She sat there, clutching the phone and crying, unable to speak.

'Veronica, I'm coming over. Just hang on.'

She hung up the phone and buried her face in her hands. You're just overwhelmed, is all, she told herself.

She went into the bathroom for a tissue and dabbed under her eyes, but when she looked in the mirror, all she could think about was how much Bea looked like her, that the young woman who'd been sitting on her sofa fifteen minutes ago was the same six-pound weight she had held against her chest in the ambulance twenty-two years ago.

The doorbell rang, and the sight of Nick, in jeans and a dark green Henley T-shirt, almost obliterated all other thoughts. The look in his eyes — concern, curiosity . . . interest, Veronica thought — was everything she needed right now. She did have friends, and she did open up to Shelley often, but she mostly kept to herself and never talked about the baby she'd given up for adoption or her travels the past twenty-two years. But Nick knew; he knew her from high school. He knew Bea had called her. He knew they'd met for the first time tonight. And here he was, standing on her doorstep, strong shoulders and all.

She couldn't remember the last time she'd had strong shoulders to lean on, and she was overtaken by the need for him to pull her into his arms and just hold her. He wouldn't, of course, that would be crazy, but she wanted him to – and that scared her. She'd learned to rely on no one.

Veronica was so used to movies – and movie love – transporting her, standing in for her fantasies of love. But now, it wasn't Colin Firth as Mr Darcy who she wanted to hold her. It was Nick. The real thing.

'The two of you got together tonight?' he asked.

She nodded, and stepped aside for him to come in. 'I could use some coffee. Maybe a glass of wine.'

'I'll have whatever you're having,' he said. 'Leigh's on a sleepover tonight at her friend's and will be going to school straight from their house, so I don't have to rush back.'

'How are things with her grandparents?' she asked as she led the way into the kitchen.

'They call Leigh every day – sometimes I think more to check up on me than because they want to hear that she has double-digit-multiplication homework. God forbid she didn't have eggs for breakfast one day – I never hear the end of it. And when she told them she was going on a sleepover tonight after having stayed at their house last night? They assumed

I pushed her into the sleepover so I could have "women over".'

'Oh, Nick, I'm so sorry you have to deal with all that pressure. I figure it's hard enough to raise a girl on your own.'

'Tell you the truth, it's not that hard. Mostly because Leigh's a great kid, but things are good at home. We have a routine, we have a strong relationship. I give her what she needs, I'm there for her. But because I'm not her mother, because of the trouble between us when her mother died, I've been her grandparents' enemy for two years, and now they're keeping a list of my infractions.'

'Because of a Pop-tart for breakfast? Or whatever wasn't eggs?'

'She had a bowl of Cheerios and a glass of orange juice, and that was too skimpy for them.'

Veronica found a bottle of wine that Shelley had given her last Christmas. She wasn't much of a drinker, but she could use a glass of nice red wine right now. 'I think we could both use some of this.'

He sat down at the round table by the window, and for a moment Veronica was struck by how the moonlight filtering through the curtains rested on his dark hair, on his green shirt. 'Anyway, forget my crazy life. Tell me about meeting your daughter.'

'She's exquisite,' Veronica said, handing him his glass of wine as she sat down across from him. 'Lovely. She seems very intelligent, polite, kind. She had no idea she was adopted until just a month ago. She found out in a letter sent after her mother's passing.'

He raised his eyebrows. 'And are both her parents gone?'

She nodded. 'I can't imagine how shocking that letter must have been. She must have started questioning everything she knew about herself.'

'She must have had a lot of questions for you.'

'I had no idea how hard it would be to answer those questions, though. I don't want to tell her how awful it was back then, how my parents treated me, how her father treated me, how completely alone I was.'

He took a slug of the wine and looked down at the table for a moment, then up at her. This time, she could read his expression: compassion. 'Sixteen years old. You must have been so scared.'

She also took a sip of wine. 'I was. Sometimes, when I look back on that time, I don't know how I got through it.'

He shook his head and was quiet for a moment. 'I remember Timothy telling us – a group of his friends – that his girl-friend was saying he'd gotten her pregnant and that there was no way it was true. I wasn't sure what to think then.'

She felt that old familiar stirring of shame, of embar-rassment, in her gut. 'Because of my reputation?'

'Because Timothy was my friend and I didn't know you at all. He never brought you around us.'

Veronica nodded. 'He used to tell me he didn't want me to hang out with his friends because he hated what they thought they knew about me, he hated my reputation. He said he was never able to change it. They wouldn't think he was seeing me because he really liked me, but because 'I'd "go all the way".'

'I wasn't all that close with him; I was more a friend of a few of his close friends, but I remember how everyone would talk crap to him about getting lucky. God, I'm sorry, Veronica.'

'Well, then I got pregnant and confirmed everyone's opinion of me. The slut got knocked up. I thought he'd stand by me, tell everyone that he was the only guy I'd ever been with, but I think he was so shocked, scared maybe, that he wanted to believe the worst so he could walk away, pretend it didn't involve him.'

'So he told everyone he wasn't the father, that he used condoms, that it couldn't be his.'

Veronica nodded. 'I never saw or heard from him again. Not a word. The day after I told him I was pregnant, I was sent away, to Hope Home, you know, the residence for pregnant teenagers on the outskirts. My parents washed their hands of me – they even filed emancipation papers on my behalf so I'd be legally independent. And then after I had the baby, I left the state. How can I tell Bea all this?'

'The truth is the truth, isn't it?'

Veronica shrugged and looked away. 'When she was sitting right next to me, all I could think of was that she'd been that baby girl I got to hold for two minutes. Completely innocent, having nothing to do with how she was brought into the world. I don't want her to know the truth. Even if she says she wants it.'

'You're a good person, Veronica,' he said, reaching for her hand and holding it. 'I'm sorry I didn't know you back in high school. I'm sorry I wasn't your friend.'

She started to cry again, and he was beside her in seconds, lifting her out of the chair and wrapping his arms around her after all.

He held her for barely fifteen seconds, but it felt like for ever – in a good way. She could smell his soap, the faint scent of laundry detergent, and the feel of his arms around her was better than anything she could have imagined.

She backed away, afraid that he'd kiss her when she couldn't handle it; the idea of it scared her so much that she moved across the room and turned her back to him. Thirty-eight years old and unable to act normal in front of a man. God.

'Should I go?' he asked, leaning against the counter, his hands in his pockets.

She turned around. 'No. I'm just . . .'

'Overwhelmed?'

She nodded. 'Exactly that, yes.'

'Meeting your daughter is monumental, Veronica.'

Yes. And so is being in your arms like that.

'My head feels like it's going to explode,' she said.

'If you're all talked out, we can just watch a movie.'

He'd surprised her. 'That's exactly what I am. All talked out.'

'That's two out of two on reading you,' he said.

He didn't seem to be flirting; there was gravitas in his expression. Compassion again. She hadn't been able to read him before, and it was unnerving that he was so good at reading her.

'A movie sounds perfect. Take us both out of our lives for a couple of hours.' She thought about the film she had on deck for tonight. 'Have you ever seen *A Single Man*? It's about a British professor grieving over the loss of his partner in the early 1960s. I missed it when it first came out, but now that I'm an extra on the Colin Firth movie shooting here, I plan to watch every one of his films. He was nominated for an Oscar for this role.'

'I had no idea you were an extra for the movie. That's great. What's it like?'

She told him about mostly sitting around for two days, and how yesterday, they'd started filming a scene in the meadow. 'My job was to walk and check my watch at the same time, and I almost messed that up.' She didn't have to mention the finger-jabbing. She was glad to be finished with heavy conversation and memories.

'Well, let's celebrate your new gig by watching *A Single Man*, then. I haven't seen it.'

And so, fifteen minutes later, they were sitting in the living room, watching the opening credits of *A Single Man*, a slice of blackberry pie on a plate in front of him and two cups of coffee on the table. If anyone had told her a few weeks ago that one night in late June she'd meet her daughter, tell Nick DeMarco her life story down to the last detail, then watch a movie with him, his feet up on the ottoman, his arm stretched out across the back of her sofa, his fingers brushing her own shoulder, she would have laughed. Now here they were.

'This pie is insanely good,' he said, his fork cutting through another chunk. 'Is this one of your special kinds?'

'It's just plain old Happiness Pie.'

'Nothing plain or old about happiness.'

She smiled at him, a weight lifting off her shoulders – why, she wasn't sure. She just knew that she never wanted him to leave this room. As long as he didn't touch her or try to kiss her, that was. Yet, anyway.

A half-hour after he'd gone, Veronica still sat on the couch, wondering what the heck had happened to her. She had a full-blown crush on Nick DeMarco and was fretting over whether or not he'd kiss her as though she really were still back in high school.

What she needed right now was another movie, something else starring her fantasy man, who never made her so nervous that her legs trembled and her heart clenched and her palms got sweaty. Colin Firth made her knees weak in a completely different way. A safe way. A TV screen as barrier.

Fever Pitch, Veronica realized. That was the movie she needed right now. She could seriously identify with poor Ruth Gemmell, a tightly wound high-school English teacher in love with a guy whose very nature made her want to run kicking and screaming away from him. Colin Firth played a crazed British football fan who spoke of his beloved team twenty-four-seven, when Ruth wanted to talk about life and literature – and their impossible future. Not that Nick was a rabid fan of any sports team, but what he represented to Veronica scared her to pieces.

She slid the DVD of *Fever Pitch* into the VCR, and just the sight of her dear Colin, back in 1997, with his wild hair and tender eyes, so very different from his proud, smouldering Mr Darcy, took her away to England, her own matters of the heart soon forgotten.

Chapter 15
Gemma

The morning light streaming in through the filmy curtains woke Gemma, and she was surprised to find Alex in bed beside her. A full week away from him, and she'd gotten used to hogging the centre of the bed and the blanket. She'd gotten used to him not being there. And lately, yes, his not being there was a good thing. But the sight of him – sleeping soundly, facing away from her, his broad, tanned back, the way his thick sandy-blond hair curled behind his ear – was still familiar and comforting.

They'd argued all night long, getting nowhere. They'd gone out to dinner, for Chinese food since she was craving sesame chicken and fried dumplings, and she'd laid out her plan to him. She would find a great new job as a reporter, despite disclosing her pregnancy. She would work until the last minute, then take maternity leave. During her leave, they would line up a loving nanny with impeccable references, then she would return to work on schedule. They would alternate taking time off for when the baby was sick or had an appointment with the paediatrician. Both of them would take time off for parent-teacher conferences, concerts and various holiday celebrations. She would not, under any circumstances, become like Caitlin Aureman, she'd added to herself.

'Absolutely not,' he'd said after a long, hard stare.

'Yet my plan is exactly what you're planning to do, isn't it? Except you won't be taking maternity leave – no need, right? And I'll be your nanny, won't I? I'll be the one staying home with the baby. I'll be the one taking the baby to doctor's appointments.'

'For God's sake, Gemma, you're not going to be the nanny. You're going to be the mother. And a damned good one.'

Intellectually, she was beginning to realize she *could* be a good mother. She was an investigative reporter, for heaven's sake. She'd read and research every step of the way to know what to do and how to do it. Supporting the newborn's neck. Breastfeeding. Burping the little one with a pat on the back.

It was the emotional aspect that worried her. That she didn't have the *instincts*. But saying that would just make Alexander refute it.

'You're so lucky that your life won't change at all. You don't have anything to consider,' she said.

'What? Of course I do. I'll be solely responsible for taking financial care of our family. I'll be a father. My entire life is going to change. How can you say it won't?'

'You're not giving up a job you love. Why can't you see this?'

'Gemma, I'd give up my job in a heartbeat if that scenario were possible. Sweetheart, I wish you could see that the timing couldn't be more perfect.'

She'd known he would say exactly this.

'So if the roles were reversed,' she said, 'if it were you who'd lost your job, you'd be fine with staying home with the baby, being a stay-at-home dad, your entire life revolving around the baby instead of prosecuting criminals, pursuing justice, making a difference in the world?'

'I'd be making a difference in my own home, in my own family. So yeah, I'd be more than fine with it.' He reached for her hand. 'Gemma, you're pregnant. You don't have a job. You've sent out a bunch of résumés and haven't gotten a call back. How easily do you think you'd get your dream job when you have to disclose at an interview that you're pregnant?'

'Can we just eat?' she said, stabbing her fork in a dumpling. She was surprised she didn't lose her appetite.

'Gem, I love you. We're going to have a baby. Aren't you happy about that at all? We're having a baby.'

She put her fork down, tears stinging the back of her eyes. 'I'm not going to be a good mother anyway,' she whispered. 'I don't have a maternal bone in my body.'

He took both her hands. 'You do so. You're incredibly

loving and kind and generous. You have a huge heart, Gem. You're going to be a great mother.'

'I don't know where you get that faith from,' she said, but as usual his faith buoyed her up some, made her feel better. 'Do you really think I'd be a good mother?'

'You will be a great mother. No doubt.'

Now, the memory of how relieved she'd been to hear him say it, to hear in his voice how much he believed it, made her spoon against him in bed, her cheek against his warm shoulder. She wondered if he could be right, if she could work at it, develop maternal instincts. Maybe once you had the baby, hormones and biological impulses took over. She would love her baby, that much she knew. Maybe love was three-quarters of the battle, the big motivator.

He turned around to face her, lying on his side, and the streaming sunlight lit his hair. 'How are you feeling, Gem? Tired?'

'Actually, I feel pretty good. I'm really looking forward to today's plans. I've got three interviews scheduled. One with a teenager who's giving her baby up for adoption, and two with residents of Boothbay Harbor who have strong opinions on Hope Home and the effect they feel the place has on the town. One woman thinks that a home for pregnant teenagers encourages teenagers to get pregnant, gives them a false sense of security. Another feels there should be a centre in every county in the state.'

'I see you're in full reporter mode,' Alex said. 'But I meant how you're feeling physically. Don't you have anything to say about being pregnant? How it feels; whether you think it's a boy or a girl; names you've been thinking about? You've had a whole week to think, remember?'

'I've spent the week getting used to the idea of being pregnant at all. Not thinking of names.'

He leaned up on one elbow. 'I'm thinking Alexander Junior if it's a boy. Gemma Junior if it's a girl.'

She raised an eyebrow. 'Really? Gemma Junior?'

He trailed a finger down her cheek. 'I'd love a mini-Gemma. With your beautiful face and that whip-smart mind.'

She almost started to cry. 'Why do you love me so much, Alex?'

'Because I do. And we're going to work through this. Somehow.'

Somehow. Somehow they'd have to.

She kissed him, hard, and felt his hands travel under the blanket on to her stomach, then up slowly to her breasts.

'They're bigger,' he said, wriggling his eyebrows at her.

'Oh, that's romantic.'

He laughed and pulled the blanket over their heads, shifting himself on top of her, and Gemma forgot all about interviews and baby names and the word 'somehow'.

After a fabulous breakfast of country omelettes that Bea whipped up for them, Gemma walked Alex to his rental car in the driveway. She'd been dying to sneak into the kitchen to ask Bea how it had gone last night, but the dining room was packed with guests, and she knew Bea would be crazed in the kitchen. She'd find her after Alex left.

He lifted his face to the beautiful late-June sunshine. 'The air up here is amazing. So fresh and clean. I'm not thrilled we're living three hundred miles apart, especially now that you're pregnant, but at least you're in a picture-postcard town. And maybe this place really will help you see things my way a little bit. Suburban life, slower pace, no killer taxis, everyone knows your name, playgrounds everywhere you look, pre-school fees that cost less than a house.'

'You're not supposed to be telling me your evil plan to get me to embrace moving to Westchester, Alex.'

He smiled. 'I just want us both to be happy. I don't know how we're going to work that out. But it's what I want.'

'Me too.'

He hugged her and kissed her goodbye, reminded her to take her prenatal vitamins, and then he was gone, the silver car turning on to Main and disappearing out of sight.

By five o'clock, Gemma was exhausted and wanted to crawl right back into her comfortable bed at the inn, but she remembered Alex wouldn't be there to give her a massage — neither back nor foot. Suddenly she didn't care about having the bed to herself and avoiding talk of suburbs and pre-schools. She'd forgotten how wonderful he could be, how much she could count on him, how good he could make her feel. But she had no idea how they could find a happy medium. Without her moving to Dobbs Ferry. Next door to Mona Hendricks.

She sat on the porch swing, resting her head against the rim and staring up at the beautiful puffs of cloud in the blue sky.

'Ready to go?'

Gemma sat up, glad to see June standing in front of her car in the driveway, and her adorable nine-year-old son, Charlie, waving to Gemma from the back seat. Gemma grinned at him and waved back. They were headed to a birthday party for June's husband, Henry, at the bookstore they owned. A night off from working on the article, from thinking about her life, was just what she needed, and then later it would be Movie Night again at the inn.

Books Brothers was tucked away at the end of Harbour Lane. Gemma loved the shop, with its handle in the shape of a red mini-canoe on the door. The moment you opened the door, you left the world behind. Low jazz played, and the rows of gleaming walnut bookshelves, the overstuffed chairs and sofas, and the interesting artefacts and old books on shelves high up on the walls, made you want to stay and explore all day. By the check-out desk there were café tables, and a coffee station always held coffee canisters, milk and sugar, plus a plate of sample goodies. Now, for the party, that table held various bottles of wine, champagne and juices, and a gorgeous buffet of appetizers. Gemma was about to grab two tiny pigs in blankets when she remembered

Alex saying hot dogs were full of nitrates and off-limits for the pregnancy. She went for the mini-quiche Lorraine instead.

The party was crowded; Henry Books was a beloved fixture in town, even if he was on the quiet side and left managing the store to June, who loved her job. Gemma adored their story: almost ten years ago, Henry had employed June as a twenty-one-year-old who'd dropped out of college when she discovered she was pregnant — the father, a guy she'd had a whirlwind two-day love affair with, unable to be located. Apparently Henry, ten years June's senior, had loved her from afar for years, but two years ago, after finally learning that her son's father had passed away long ago, June was ready to say goodbye to the past she'd held on to and open her heart to Henry. They lived on a big houseboat docked behind the store.

Gemma watched them now, her dear old friend with the long, curly auburn hair that Gemma had always coveted, speaking to her son with such love, such tenderness in her expression, as Charlie told a funny story about something that had happened at day camp. Henry was belly-laughing, and then scooped up Charlie and swung him around, accidentally bumping Isabel in the butt. Isabel whirled around and started tickling Charlie all over. They made family look so . . . inviting, reminding her of how she'd felt about the Hendricks clan before their warmth turned into suffocation. The Nash sisters weren't overbearing in the slightest, though.

Gemma tried to picture herself and Alexander walking with their toddler holding their hands, and swinging him up with an 'Upsy-daisy!' But she couldn't see it, couldn't see any of it. Any time she tried to imagine herself with a baby, she felt a heavy pressure on her chest.

'Stop being so demanding!' her mother would snap at her if she tried to tell her about something that had happened at school, or if she'd asked why her mother hadn't come to a chorus concert. 'I have a full-time job, Gemma. You'll understand when you're an adult.'

What she understood, now that she was an adult, was that she was just like her mother, no matter what Alexander said about her supposed big heart. If she had such a big heart, why would her job – a job she no longer had – come first? Why was her career more important to her than starting a family? Why wasn't she rejoicing in being pregnant, talking to her baby as she lay in bed at night?

Why wasn't she thinking of baby names?

Because you're scared. Scared of everything. Losing who you are. Not being able to do both – be a reporter and a mother. Snapping at your little child for asking a question, for wanting more of you.

Gemma's chest began to constrict and she turned away, pouring herself a glass of cranberry juice and trying to stop her brain from going places she didn't want it to go. Focus on the party, she told herself. Look around for Claire.

But Gemma's attention focused itself on six-month-old

Allie, Isabel's daughter, in the arms of her dad, Griffin. Theirs had also been a relationship that had taken compromise, and the two of them had made it work. Griffin, a veterinarian, had been divorced when he and Isabel had met two years ago, when he and his daughters had been guests at the inn, the sixteen-year-old daughter angry at the world, Isabel dealing with the end of her own marriage. Isabel too hadn't thought she had what it took to be a mother, but she still wanted a family, wanted a baby. She'd embraced stepmotherhood from the get-go, and now, with her own baby, Isabel seemed like the perfect mother, the kind Gemma wished she could be. She watched Allie stretch out her arms for her mama, saw Isabel's eyes light up, watched how she took the baby with such joy, cuddling her against her pretty blue dress. Griffin put his arm around Isabel, and they both stared in happy wonder at their daughter.

This was how it was supposed to be. Maybe it really did just happen; maybe you could have no maternal instincts, no baby fever, no interest in motherhood, at the moment, anyway, but you had a baby, you looked at your baby's face, and you fell in love. Maybe that was how it was. Gemma sure hoped so. Because right now, she still didn't even feel pregnant. No flutter. Certainly no kicking yet: her doctor and *Your Pregnancy This Week* had said that would come later on, in the second trimester. It was helpful to Gemma to know that Isabel managed to work full-time at the inn, though, granted, she had her baby at work most of that time. Gemma couldn't exactly bring her infant to a busy newsroom, tending to him or her with one hand while typing with the other.

We're going to work through this. Somehow . . .

There was a big commotion, and Gemma saw that June and Isabel's cousin, Kat, who'd been living in France and working as a pastry chef for the past couple of years, had arrived with her long-term boyfriend. According to June, they'd gotten engaged a couple of years ago, but Kat had broken it off to follow her dreams to leave her home town and study baking in Paris. Kat and Oliver were holding hands and clearly very much in love. Kat, tall and blonde and pretty, looked a lot like Oliver, also tall and blond. They kissed, and Gemma caught the lingering look they gave each other.

Kat and Oliver had managed to make it work too, Gemma thought, swiping a mini-potato and cheese dumpling from the buffet. She'd wanted one thing, he'd wanted another, and they'd made it work. Kat had left the country and broken off their engagement, but they were together now.

Gemma had left the state. And there would be no breaking of anything – especially not vows. She and Alexander loved each other – that was not in question. And they both wanted the other to be happy – while being happy themselves. They both wanted this to work, and it would.

Gemma had trained to be a reporter. She had close to

eight months to train to become a mother. A good one. The kind of mother a baby deserved.

At the thought, the tightness in her shoulders unwound. I *will* be a good mother, she told herself, a hand on her belly. And that is a promise, little one.

Chapter 16
Bea

A few minutes before nine o'clock on Friday, Bea headed into the parlour of the Three Captains' Inn for Movie Night. Her boss Isabel was there, and Isabel's sister, June, and there was Gemma, sitting on the love seat and waving her over to the empty spot next to her. Bea hurried over before one of the members of the Colin Firth fan club could beat her to it. Bea had never been so glad for a familiar, friendly face. She'd spent last night tossing and turning for hours after her meeting with Veronica, and all day today she'd wandered around aimlessly, trying to figure out what she was uptight about.

What seemed to be bothering her the most was that she didn't know what she was supposed to do with Veronica Russo, now the first meeting was over. Who was she to Bea? Last night, at Veronica's house, she was overcome with the notion that Veronica was a stranger. But she was hardly a stranger. For God's sake, she'd given birth to Bea. But now what? She'd get her father's contact information from Veronica, if she had it — or at least a place to start, since there were a few Macintoshes listed in the Boothbay Harbor phone book — and then what? Were she and Veronica supposed to be friends?

'Did you turn your phone off or something? I tried to call you a few times,' Gemma said. 'How was last night?'

'It went . . . okay,' Bea whispered back. 'She's very nice. But it was a little strained for both of us. I told her that you were writing an article on Hope Home and would love to interview her, but she said she wasn't up for that.'

'That's okay,' Gemma said. 'And thanks for asking her.' She leaned closer. 'Another reason I called is because Isabel mentioned that the Colin Firth movie we're watching is *Then She Found Me*. It's about a birth mother trying to connect with the daughter she gave up for adoption. I wanted to prepare you in advance. I saw it when it first came out in theatres, and it's a wonderful movie. But it might hit close to home.'

'Maybe I'll learn something useful,' Bea said, touched that Gemma had tried to call her.

Isabel and June, handing out popcorn around the room, introduced their cousin Kat, who was visiting for the weekend. Kat was holding two bowls of popcorn, one with her arm against her chest, and Bea jumped up to help.

'Perfect — that one's for you guys on the love seat,' Kat

said. 'Everyone have popcorn?' she asked, glancing around the room.

The Colin Firth fan club, three best friends from Rhode Island who were wearing their HAPPINESS IS COLIN FIRTH T-shirts again, had taken over the big white sofa; three other guests, one of whom had the pickiest breakfast order that Bea had ever seen — hold the this, add the that — were in overstuffed chairs; and Isabel, June and Kat, and Isabel's sweet elderly helper Pearl, were on the padded folding chairs. Bea offered her seat to Pearl, but she said the chair was better for her back.

'I love that you're doing Movie Night again,' Kat said to Isabel. 'I feel like my mom is watching with us.'

Isabel had told Bea that her Aunt Lolly, Kat's mother, had left the three of them the inn when she'd died two years ago. Movie Night had been an inn tradition for years, and when Lolly had passed away it had been Meryl Streep month, in honour of Lolly's favourite actress. Lolly had raised Isabel, June and Kat after the death of her husband and the Nash sisters' parents in a terrible New Year's Eve car accident that had taken all their lives seventeen years ago. Movie Night and Lolly were synonymous to the women.

June squeezed Kat's hand.

'I'll bet she is,' Isabel said, standing up with the DVD and heading over to the console table. 'Okay, everyone, get ready for *Then She Found Me*, starring our Colin Firth, who has yet to make an appearance in town, unfortunately, and the wonderful Helen Hunt, Bette Midler and Matthew Broderick.'

Isabel shut off the lights, and Bea took a handful of popcorn. So much for leaving her thoughts behind and being swept away by a movie, but, as she'd said to Gemma, maybe she would learn something, get some perspective.

Bea watched as Helen Hunt, who played a thirty-nine-year-old teacher in New York City, sees her husband, Matthew Broderick, walk out of the door the day before her mother dies. Then Helen's biological mother, played by a pushy Bette Midler, appears in her life, insistent on getting to know her, and Helen is resistant. She'd had a mother. Bette is a bit on the obnoxious side and makes up crazy stories about her father being Steve McQueen. When Helen gets involved with a student's father, played by Colin Firth, she starts to calm down, finding herself actually feeling happy. But then she realizes she's pregnant, a long-time dream, from a one-night stand with her own estranged husband, and she has to figure out all the pieces of her life.

'You okay?' Gemma whispered.

'Yeah,' Bea whispered back. 'Veronica's not pushy like Bette Midler at all. I told her I needed some time to process everything, and she hasn't called. Bette would have been at my door this morning. She'd be here now, pushing you out of the way.'

Gemma smiled.

Bea wondered if Veronica felt like Bette did, if she wanted

Bea in her life, wanted to be close. Maybe she, too, needed some distance from Bea's questions about her biological father, about Veronica's own parents.

Bea loved the scene in which Colin Firth attends a party for Bette Midler with Helen Hunt. She loved how protective he is of Helen, how clearly enamoured with her he is. She was glad she had a date with Patrick tomorrow afternoon. Just a little something fun and sweet and romantic for her to have to herself.

But the more she watched, the more she realized that Veronica and Bette had something very much in common. The same hopeful look in their eyes.

Another night of tossing and turning. Bea's alarm went off at five-thirty on Saturday morning, and she felt like hell. She'd been unable to stop thinking of Bette Midler, on her knees, begging for a chance, promising to do whatever Helen Hunt wanted. Maybe Bea had rushed out of Veronica's house too soon.

She trudged into the shower, which helped, then got dressed and slogged down the stairs to the kitchen, where she made omelettes and waffles and today's special, blueberry pancakes. Afterwards, she cleaned the dining-room tables, then swept and mopped the floor, imagining Veronica waiting by the phone, wondering if Bea would call back. With that hopeful expression.

They'd met on Thursday night. It was now Saturday.

She was so tired, she just wanted to fling herself into bed for a good hour's nap, but before she could, she grabbed her phone and called Veronica.

'Veronica, it's Bea.'

Veronica was silent for just a moment. 'I'm so glad you called,' she said, her voice catching. She cleared her throat, and Bea realized that Veronica had probably been in knots over whether Bea would get in touch again.

Bea had done the right thing. 'I thought maybe we could get together again. Dinner tomorrow night, if you're free?'

'I'd love to get together, Bea. But rather than have dinner, I'd like to take you on a tour.'

'A tour? You mean of Boothbay Harbor?' Bea had already seen all the sights. She'd even take a whale cruise around the bay. She didn't want to ooh and ahh over lighthouses. She wanted to know the where, what, why and how of her birth.

'A tour of my life when I was sixteen,' Veronica said, clearing her throat again. 'We'll start at the high school and end at the Greyhound bus station.'

Bea's heart skipped a beat.

Two hours later, Bea sat inside the empty crew trailer on the movie set, still parked by Frog March, waiting for Patrick. The door burst open.

'I'm not going back, so don't waste your breath,' Maddy Echols snapped to someone behind her.

Tyler, her brother.

He stared at Bea. 'What are you doing in here?'

'Meeting Patrick for lunch.'

He rolled his eyes, then turned to his sister, who'd stormed in and sat down on a narrow bench. 'Maddy, you are going back. You want to take sophomore English when you're a junior?'

She pushed her long hair behind her shoulders. 'Leave me alone. I can't understand a word of the stupid book. I'm not reading it.'

'I bought you the CliffsNotes to help you.'

'So now I have to read that too?' she shouted.

He threw up his hands. 'Fine, fail the class. Fail high school. Drop out.'

Bea realized she was watching them as though she were at a tennis match. Both spoke in the same rapid-fire way. They looked nothing alike, of course: Maddy was petite with wavy dark brown hair and huge hazel-green eyes, and Tyler was tall and angular, with that mop of sandy blond hair. She'd put Tyler at twenty-three, maybe twenty-four. He had a dimple in his left cheek, which she probably hadn't noticed before because he never smiled. But the chewing on the inside of his cheek brought it out. He worried about his sister, that was obvious.

'I don't mean to eavesdrop,' Bea said, 'but since I'm sitting right here . . . I assume you're talking about *To Kill a Mockingbird* again?'

Maddy turned to her. 'You mean *To Kill a Loser Bird*.'

That got her Tyler's trademark eye-roll. 'It's a great book,' he told his sister. 'One of my favourites.'

'Like we're so similar,' Maddy muttered.

'Maddy, I graduated from college – Beardsley – last year with an English degree,' Bea said. 'I'm planning to be an English teacher. Middle school or high school. I've read *To Kill a Mockingbird* at least five times since I was a sophomore in high school, and like I said, I wrote my senior thesis on it. I could help you, talk you through the themes of the book or whatever's giving you trouble.'

Tyler was watching her, she knew.

'You're in summer school, I presume,' Bea said to Maddy.

'And if she doesn't pass the class by reading the book and writing an essay with a grade of B minus or better,' Tyler said, staring hard at his sister, 'she fails and will have to take sophomore English again when she's a junior in the fall. Then she'll end up short of English credits to graduate.'

'So what?' Maddy said. 'It's not like I'm necessarily going to college. I don't need to read *To Kill a Stupid Bird* in order to backpack around Italy.'

'I backpacked around Italy the summer I graduated from high school,' Bea said. 'I had the most amazing time.'

Maddy's face lit up. 'Really? I'm obsessed with Rome. I want to see the Coliseum, throw coins in the Trevi Fountain. See the angels. And the Sistine Chapel.'

'If you pass this class, I'll take you,' Tyler said, gritting his teeth.

The girl stared at him. 'Seriously?'

'Seriously. You pass the class and I'll take you to Italy. You'll see the Sistine Chapel.'

She wanted that trip, Bea could see. Bad. Bad enough to pass the class.

'You can help me?' Maddy said to Bea.

'We don't even know her,' Tyler said quietly, his eyes on Bea. He was clearly mimicking Bea from the other day, but his expression was serious. He cared about Maddy, that much Bea was sure of.

'I'm staying in town for the next few weeks. At the Three Captains' Inn. I tutor at Beardsley during the school year, so I'm experienced. Here's my ID from the Writing Centre.' She took it from her wallet and handed it to Tyler.

He studied it, then handed it back to her. 'Maddy, can you wait for me outside for a second?'

Now that Italy was on the table, Maddy jumped at his request.

When the door closed behind her, he said, 'How much do you charge?'

'If I wasn't broke, I'd offer to do it for free,' she said. 'But I'm working for my room and minimum wage at the inn, so I really could use some extra cash. Fifty bucks an hour.'

'Fifty bucks? Jesus.' He moved aside the little curtain at a window and peered out at Maddy, who had her compact out and was reapplying her gooey lip gloss. He let the curtain drop. 'Fine. But I want you to work with her in the library

— not our mom's house or here. I want her to take this seriously.'

'Okay. The library it is.'

He pushed his wire-rimmed glasses up on his nose. 'The class ends in three weeks. I'm thinking once a week for two hours should be fine.'

'So you're from Boothbay Harbor?' she asked.

'Two towns over,' he said as though giving personal information was a hardship for him. 'The high school's regional.'

The door pounded. 'Hello, I'm sweating out here,' Maddy shouted.

'One sec,' he called out. 'When can you start?'

'Whenever you want.'

'How's Wednesday? I take her out to dinner every Wednesday night so I know it works for both our schedules.'

A hundred bucks would buy a nice outfit and decent shoes for the dinner cruise Patrick told her he wanted to take her on sometime soon.

'Meet her at the Boothbay Harbor library at five,' Tyler said. 'Will that work?'

She nodded, and he stepped towards the door, then turned back to her.

'Don't bring up the birth-mother thing,' he said. 'She'll get angry and distracted.'

'Okay.'

He headed for the door again, then turned back once more. 'Did you meet yours yet?'

'I don't really want to talk about it,' she said.

He stared at her, then shrugged and went down the step.

Patrick only had time for a twenty-minute lunch, but Bea didn't mind. It was fun to eat in the air-conditioned trailer, watch the occasional assistant come in then dart out when it was clear this was a private lunch. Over Italian subs, he told her about production schedules and call sheets, which listed where and when the actors had to show up. He explained he was something of a backstage manager, making sure everything was as it should be for filming the scene.

Bea liked him. A lot. He was good-looking and smart and responsible for quite a bit on this film. He asked right away how meeting her biological mother had been, and when she told Patrick she'd rather talk about him, he still tried to keep the conversation about her. Bea told him more about losing her way last year, after her mother's death, and that she planned to apply to a hundred schools until she got a job as an English teacher. Patrick said he thought it was noble, that teachers should make more money. She liked the way he looked at her, his intelligent blue eyes full of interest, respect . . . desire.

He was called away to douse yet another fire, as he put it, but not before he kissed her. 'The next few days are going to be crazy, but maybe you could come by my hotel Tuesday night. For a late dinner around eight? I won't be back till right before then, and I have to get up at the crack of dawn, but I'd love to sit on my balcony with you and have some great room-service fancy dinner and just talk. And I mean that – just talk. This isn't some ploy to get you in bed. Not that I don't think you're incredibly beautiful, Bea.'

She smiled, and he kissed her goodbye, again a sweet kiss on the lips. This was perfect. Now she'd have something exciting to look forward to, especially if Veronica's 'tour' was too much, too hard to take in. And Bea was sure that it would be.

Chapter 17
Veronica

Veronica sat in her car in the driveway of the Three Captains' Inn at noon on Sunday, reminding herself that she was here as much to deliver three pies as she was to pick up Bea for the tour of her life. She got the pies out of her trunk, her monthly invoice in an envelope taped to the top box. The box labelled BLUEBERRY reminded her of Nick; he'd mentioned that Leigh had caught a bad cold on Friday, and Veronica had baked a special Feel-Better Pie and brought it over Friday evening. Nick's house was a white clapboard cottage not too far from downtown. Leigh had been propped up on the sofa watching *How to Train Your Dragon*, and she'd invited Veronica to come watch with them, but Nick hadn't seconded the invitation. Veronica hadn't been sure if two movies in two nights with her would be one too many, or if maybe their evening together on Thursday had been a bit too unexpected. He'd left soon after *A Single Man* had ended, giving her a squeeze of the hand when she'd expected a kiss. Not that she'd been ready for a kiss from Nick DeMarco – talk about loaded – but since then, the thought of kissing him had managed to lull her to sleep at night. Fantasy versus reality again. In any case, the truth was that she did want to feel his lips on hers. She wanted him to want her.

Because he represented her past? Because she hadn't been accepted back then? Because the one guy who had accepted her – someone Nick had been friends with – had turned around and betrayed her? Or maybe it was much scarier than any of those reasons. Maybe she just . . . liked Nick.

Boxes in hand, she headed up the pretty stone path to the porch of the inn. For almost a year now she'd been making weekly deliveries of her pies to the Three Captains', and the beautiful Victorian building was as familiar as her own house, only now her birth daughter was inside. Waiting for her in the parlour to go on a tour of Veronica's life at age sixteen.

This was your idea, she reminded herself, placing the pies on the table inside the foyer, where she always left them for Isabel. She went into the parlour, but Bea wasn't there yet. The inn smelled wonderful, the hint of bacon and warm bread in the air. From where she sat on the love seat, she saw Bea appear at the landing of the stairwell, in a pale pink top and skinny jeans, and stood up as Bea walked into the room.

'So you're responsible for how good it smells right now?'

Veronica asked as they headed towards the front door. She was surprised she could make small-talk.

'If I do say so myself — yes. And the dining room has been closed since ten o'clock too — brunch hours for Sunday. Everyone wanted bacon this morning — I must have fried up five pounds. If you smell bread it's Isabel's doing — she's taking lessons from the owner of the Italian bakery. Hot crusty Italian bread with butter? Nothing better.'

'She's taking my pie class too,' Veronica said as she opened the passenger door of her car for Bea. 'With all her new skills, she may put me out of business.'

'Your pies are a big hit at the inn, especially at teatime. Isabel says no one could ever come close to touching your pies. I wanted to tell her that Veronica Russo, pie maven, is my biological mother, but I know you probably want to keep that private.'

Veronica hated how tight her expression must seem. Why did she want to keep it a secret? A holdover from how her parents had made her feel? From how her one trip into town, at seven months pregnant, had made her feel? Ashamed. Dirty. Damaged. The whispers and stares of people she knew, of strangers too, had been unbearable.

Bea buckled her seat belt. 'Are you sure you really want to take me on this tour? If it's too much for you, I'll understand.'

'It will be too much for me,' Veronica said. 'And that's probably a good thing. I came back to Boothbay Harbor to

271

face my past, to stop running from it. But being here alone hasn't been enough – I've kept a year of my life balled up inside me, locked up tight. I need to . . . let myself remember.'

Veronica drove the short distance to Boothbay Region High School, which was located on Main Street. She passed it all the time, but rarely let herself look at the building. She'd hated who she'd been there, how she'd felt in those halls and classrooms. Only for five brief months, when she'd been Timothy Macintosh's girlfriend, had none of that mattered. She'd walked the halls with her head high and, for the first time, she'd felt as though nothing could touch her, hurt her.

She pulled into the parking lot and stared up at the school. 'When I look back on it now, it seems crazy that I was in love with him after just a few months of dating, but you know how it is when you're sixteen. The weight of a day feels like a month, everything happens so fast and with such intensity.'

Bea nodded. 'I'm embarrassed to say it's still like that for me.'

'You have his smile,' Veronica said. 'My mouth, but his smile. I loved his face so much I could just stare at him for hours. He had light blond hair, exactly like yours, and the most beautiful hazel eyes. He was a bit of a rebel, but not a trouble-maker. He wore a beaten-up black leather jacket that smelled like his soap, and if it was remotely chilly, he'd give it to me. I used to love wearing that jacket.'

'His name was Timothy Macintosh, you said?'

She nodded. 'We met in history class when we were paired on an ancestry project. Everyone was always so surprised by the quiet guy in the leather jacket with his head down suddenly raising his hand to ask intelligent questions or give right answers. I had such a crush on him, but when he asked me out, I said no at first. I was so used to being asked out because of my reputation – because of the lies spread about me, first by a group of mean girls who didn't like the way the popular boys were following me around, and then by the boys who made up stories about sleeping with me. And I told him so. I told him off, actually – it was the first time I'd ever done that, stood up like that. But he insisted he liked me for me and that he wouldn't even try to kiss me for a month if I went out with him.'

'Did you hold him to that?'

'I sure did. And he didn't try. We spent so much time together that first month, too. He didn't try once.'

Bea smiled. 'I love that.'

'Me too,' she said, lost in the sweet memory for a moment. 'We had such honest conversations – about how we felt, about school, our teachers, our parents, the world, government, everything. He came from a rougher background than I did, and I cared so much about him that I wanted to take him away from all that by just loving him with all my might.'

'Did you?'

'For five months, I did. And then I found out I was pregnant.' She started the car and drove the three miles to the house she'd grown up in, pulling over across the street. 'See that blue house, number forty-nine? That's where I grew up. My period was late, over a week, and I was shaking when I took the pregnancy test. I was so scared when that plus sign appeared. I told myself it couldn't be true – we'd used condoms. But I took another one later in the day, and it was positive too. It took me a week to work up the nerve to tell my mother. I was so afraid to say the words out loud. But then while my parents and I were having pancakes one morning, I just blurted it out.'

Bea was staring from the house to Veronica. 'And they didn't take it very well.'

'Understatement of the year. I'll never forget the expression on my mother's face,' Veronica said, the memory so vivid that as she repeated her mother's words, verbatim, to Bea, it was as if she were reliving it right now.

'Your grandmother is rolling over in her grave,' her mother had screamed, her father just shaking his head and muttering, 'How could you be stupid, so careless?' Over and over.

Veronica had wished with everything inside her that her grandmother was still there, that she could tell her everything. She knew her grandmother would have wrapped her arms around her, told her everything would be okay, that they'd get through this, that they were Russos, and Russos were strong.

All she had was her mother, pointing her finger in Veronica's face and saying, 'This makes you trash. No better than Maura's trashy daughter who got pregnant and now has a toddler at seventeen. And I won't stand for it.'

Veronica had stood there, shocked.

'Just what the goddamned hell is everyone going to think?' her mother had said, shaking her head. 'God damn it.' And she reached out and slapped Veronica across the face.

Veronica winced as though her mother had slapped her all over again.

'Oh, Veronica,' Bea said.

Veronica's mother was strictly pro-life; she'd made that clear every time the news came on, so there was no discussion of options. Veronica believed in choice, but had her mother felt different and insisted she terminate the pregnancy, Veronica would have fought her. The moment she'd discovered she was pregnant, her mind instantly went to having the baby – and keeping it. With that so firmly in her heart, adoption was the only answer for Veronica. It just so happened to coincide with her mother's plans.

She sucked in a deep breath. 'I ran – to the one place that felt safe: our "spot".' Veronica started the car and drove back to Main Street, not too far from the high school, and parked across the street from Seagull Lane, a brick alleyway leading to the bay. The place where she and Timothy had kissed, finally, for the first time. Their meeting spot.

The place where she'd told him she was pregnant.

'I found a payphone and called him,' Veronica said. 'Barely able to speak for the sobs coming from so deep inside me.

He'd rushed to meet me – right there,' she added, pointing to the alleyway. 'And I was so scared to tell him. Despite how close we were, all we'd talked about, the plans we'd made to run away together after high school, I was afraid to say the words. His mother had gotten pregnant at sixteen, and she had a hard life because of it, and I knew he'd be very upset at the news.'

'What did he say?' Bea asked.

'He didn't say anything for the longest moment. Then he told me it couldn't possibly be his baby. He said a lot of other things.' She closed her eyes for a second. 'But it was his. Couldn't possibly be anyone else's. I was so shocked, so hurt, then I went back home in a daze, and my mother told me to pack my bags, that there was a spot for me at Hope Home. I was gone the next day.'

'The next day,' Bea repeated. 'I can't believe how fast it all happened. I can't imagine what you were going through.'

Veronica drove the five miles to Hope Home, along the long dirt driveway to the pretty white farmhouse with its porch swing, still so familiar. There had still been some snow on the ground when she'd arrived as a sixteen-year-old in early April. 'This was actually a bright spot. I lived here for seven and a half months.'

Veronica told Bea what it was like back then at Hope Home, how some girls had been sent away because their families were embarrassed to have a pregnant teenage daughter, but that most parents visited every week with care packages full of treats and L.L.Bean sweaters and books about pregnancy and what was happening in your body, even though the Hope Home library was full of those. And those girls had gone back home after their babies were born and adopted, stories made up about two semesters away as foreign-exchange students.

She explained how no one had visited her in the almost eight months she'd been there. How her mother had called twice — once, her voice strained, to see if she needed anything, and another time to let her know the family dog had died. Even after that, when her mother had clearly wanted Veronica to feel worse than she already did, Veronica had hoped she'd call again; but she hadn't. And any time Veronica called home and left a message, no one returned her calls. So she'd eventually stopped phoning.

'Oh God,' Bea said, and Veronica was aware that Bea was trying to catch her eye. 'You must have been so lonely.'

Veronica kept her gaze on the white farmhouse, on the swing. 'Well, to tell you the truth, my parents always made me feel lonely, even before I got pregnant. They were always on the cold side, difficult to get to know, very proper, impersonal. My mother found someone just like herself in my father. They even brought up the idea for me to get emancipated so that they wouldn't be held liable in any way.'

Bea shook her head. 'But you had friends at Hope Home?'

Veronica nodded. 'Some of the girls didn't get along all the time, but generally we did. The staff were wonderful.'

'Good,' Bea said. 'I'm very glad to hear that. You went into labour at Hope Home but I started coming while you were in the ambulance?'

'I was screaming my head off – in so much pain, scared out of my mind – but the EMT guy who delivered you was great to me. He said there wouldn't be time to get to the hospital, and he coached me through the whole thing. Then suddenly, there you were. I got to hold you for two minutes, and then he took you to clean you up. You were just a foot away in a plastic bassinet, but it felt awful.'

'What about on the way to the hospital?' Bea asked. 'Were you able to hold me again?'

'The social worker who accompanied us said safety regulations prohibited it, and besides, it wouldn't be a good idea.'

'So you wanted to?'

Veronica sucked in a breath. 'Yeah.'

Bea was quiet for a moment. 'Did you ever consider keeping me?'

Veronica didn't answer; she drove off again, this time to Coastal General Hospital. She parked in the main lot, and they both glanced up the stately brick building. 'I had fantasies about it. Of running away with you. But I was sixteen and had nowhere to go, no family, nothing. And the social workers reassured me that I was doing the best thing for you, that I was being selfless and not selfish. I was desperate to hear that over and over.'

'So what happened after I was born? Did you ever get to see me again?'

Veronica glanced away. She didn't like these questions. 'Just once. On my way out of the hospital. Even though I was told I shouldn't look, that it might be too painful, for my last memory to be of leaving you. And that nurse was right. Even thinking about how I'd held you those two minutes in the ambulance were enough to do me in. So I learned to close it all off. After a while, I had trouble even conjuring it up at all.'

Bea was quiet for a moment. 'So after you left the hospital, then what?'

'I went back to Hope to pack my things. I'd decided to go to Florida. And before I left, I called the adoption agency and left my name for the file and said I'd call to update when I found a place to live. I felt like if I didn't leave my name, one day it would feel like it never happened at all, that I didn't give birth to a baby girl. But on the way to Florida, I ended up working damned hard to make myself feel exactly that way – like it didn't happen.'

'I can understand that,' Bea said. 'After all you'd gone through. How did you make it on your own in Florida? How did you get there? You weren't even seventeen.'

This was easier to talk about. She started the car again, driving to the Greyhound bus station in Wiscasset. 'I was an emancipated minor at that point, thanks to my parents preparing the paperwork for me. I had around six hundred dollars saved from my part-time job, so I asked for a ride to here and bought a one-way ticket to Miami.'

'Why Florida?'

Veronica explained that Florida was an old dream of her grandmother's, where there were no blizzards and lots of orange groves. Even though Veronica loved winter, loved snow, she'd always thought the hot and sunny orange-filled dream sounded magical. Once there, she lied about her age, got a waitressing job, something familiar, and found a nice female roommate in an apartment complex with palm trees and a pool. She'd stayed in Florida for a year, had a boyfriend or two – no one she'd loved, and certainly no one she'd tell her story to. When one of her boyfriends accused her of cheating on him, something Veronica had never done in her life, it had reminded her of Timothy and she packed up again. By then she was almost eighteen and wouldn't have to lie about her age. Things would get easier. She'd headed west, crossing the South, staying for months at a time in various towns until she'd hear about someplace new and pack up. She'd stayed in New Mexico the longest, but then her former beau had ditched her in Las Vegas when she wouldn't marry him, and she'd known she had to come back home if she ever hoped to fix herself.

'I half expect you to drive us to Florida right now,' Bea said, smiling.

Veronica smiled back.

'Did you talk to your mom again?'

'I tried over the years, calling on her birthday, my father's birthday. Christmas. But the conversations were stilted. No matter how many years passed, they couldn't forgive me, couldn't move on.' Veronica drove the fifteen minutes back to her house, parking in front of it. 'Then I moved here.'

Just before she'd moved to Boothbay Harbor she'd called her mother in California to let her know she was moving back home, that she was hoping to put her past to rest, even though they'd be living three thousand miles apart. Her plan had been to finally do what she should have done long ago: give up on her mother the way her mother had given up on her. Of course, the moment she'd heard her mother's voice, she still longed for her, for something to change. But it hadn't. In twenty-two years, Veronica had come to understand something about limitations, that sometimes, even when you needed them most, the people you loved couldn't rise to the occasion. Not wouldn't. Couldn't. Her mother's response to her call: 'I think too much time has gone by, Veronica, but I wish you well,' and Veronica had hung up, the breath knocked out of her. Good Lord, it was no wonder she was the way she was. With a heart that didn't work right.

'I'll drop you back at the inn,' Veronica said. She was spent. Even more so than she thought she'd be.

When they pulled up to the Three Captains', Bea said, 'Thank you for all that. I wanted to know, and though some of it wasn't easy to hear, I'm glad I know the truth. Are you all right?'

'I'll be fine. How about you?'

Bea nodded. 'I'll be okay. I just need to digest it all. I have a date, so that'll help. I guess I should mention that I'm dating someone who works on the film. Patrick Ool? He seems like a great guy. We've only gone out once.'

The two worlds entwining seemed strange. 'Oh yes, I know Patrick. He's in charge of the extras. I mean, I don't really *know* him, but he treats us very well, makes sure we know what we're doing and that we're comfortable.'

'I haven't told him that you're my birth mother,' Bea said. 'I mean, I've told him that meeting my birth mother is the whole reason I'm in town and that she's an extra on the movie, but I didn't mention your name. I'll absolutely keep your privacy.'

Veronica nodded. 'Thanks,' she said, unable to look at Bea for a moment. She kept her gaze out of the windshield, suddenly feeling so . . . exposed. 'I don't know if it matters, but like I said, I haven't shared the fact that I gave up a baby for adoption with many people, so I do like the idea of keeping that private.'

She was so exhausted. Why didn't she feel better? Why didn't facing her past this way, going back over everything, make her suddenly open up inside?

She glanced at Bea, whose expression had changed. Did it bother Bea that Veronica wanted to keep it private? Veronica had spent so long keeping her past to herself, not talking about it, keeping it locked up tight. 'Bea? Did I say something to upset you?'

'I'm just thinking about my mother. About all the times she might have told me – when I was four, five, six years old. She wanted to wipe all that away, pretend the adoption never happened. She made it so for herself – and for me.'

Veronica wanted to say something, about how love and hope and need could sometimes make you do – or not do – what you knew you should. Sometimes to protect others, sometimes to protect yourself. But she didn't dare say anything about Bea's mother, the woman who'd raised her. And all she really knew about Cora Crane was that she'd done a beautiful job as a mother, raising the wonderful young woman who'd just been on a tour of Veronica's sixteenth year.

'Now what?' Bea said. 'I mean, I'm not even sure what we're supposed to be, who we are to each other.'

'We're a part of each other's history.'

'I guess that doesn't necessarily have anything to do with the future, though.' It was a statement and not a question, Veronica noticed, her heart constricting. Bea bit her lip and got out of the car. 'Thank you for today, Veronica,' she said through the open passenger window. 'I know it had to be very hard on you.'

Doesn't necessarily have anything to do with the future . . . So was that it? Would she never hear from Bea again? 'It was worth it.'

283

Bea sucked in a breath. 'I just don't know how I'm supposed to feel about you. I'd better get going. Thank you again for today,' she said, then hurried into the inn.

I know how I feel about *you*, Veronica thought, watching Bea disappear through the front door. How I've always felt about you, since the moment you were placed on my chest as a newborn.

Veronica loved Bea, always had. And she knew then that that was what she'd been unable to face all these years.

After half a day on set on Monday, Patrick, whom Veronica could not look at without thinking of Bea, dismissed the extras because of a lighting issue. She was glad to leave: she felt a bit claustrophobic in the tent with the crowd and her thoughts closing in on her. On the way home she stopped at the farmers' market for peaches for tonight's pie class, and stocked up on strawberries and Key limes for special pies she needed to make this week.

At home, she placed the peaches she'd bought in two big bowls on the island counter, but even the beautiful, fresh fruit, one of her summer favourites, couldn't shake the unsettled feeling lodged in her chest, in her heart.

I'm not even sure what we're supposed to be . . . how I'm supposed to feel about you.

It was complicated. And not.

Would she never hear from Bea again? Had Bea found what she'd come for — answers to her questions, a person to put to the reality of 'birth mother' – and would she now leave, no interest in forging a relationship?

She understood Bea's problem; she wasn't sure what they were supposed to be to each other either. They were not mother and daughter. They were not . . . friends. They were connected, though, in a biological, fundamental way. Perhaps Bea would decide biology did not a relationship make. But for Veronica, Bea had never been about biology and birth. She'd always been about the future. Veronica had given Bea up so that she could have a future. She hadn't expected to be part of that future, not until Bea reached adulthood. And now that she was an adult . . .

The doorbell rang, and Veronica hoped it would be Nick and Leigh. He hadn't called to say if he was coming or not, and with a kitchen full of students, she wouldn't be able to talk to him about her personal life anyway, but the sight of him would help. She wished that was only because he was so attractive to her, but it went further than that. What she was beginning to feel for Nick DeMarco felt a lot like need.

When she opened the door, Nick and Leigh stood on the porch, Leigh carrying a pie wrapped in plastic. Thank you, Veronica whispered silently to the universe.

'I made you a chocolate pudding pie,' Leigh said, holding out both hands. 'It doesn't do anything. It's just good. Or, at least I hope it is. I made one yesterday too but I forgot the vanilla, I think. I remembered everything this time.'

Veronica smiled and took the pie. 'I love chocolate pudding pie, and I'm touched you made this for me. Thank you.'

She was aware of Nick watching her, and his face, his body, his presence, had their usual effect. She felt a combination of relief, happiness and something fluttery in her stomach, like butterflies or good nerves.

'Leigh, if you want to head into the kitchen and choose your apron and start reading over the recipe on the island counter, go right ahead. We're making peach pie tonight. I'm putting you in charge of measuring out the dry *and* wet ingredients.'

'I love peaches!' Leigh said, disappearing into the kitchen.

Veronica closed the door behind Nick. 'I'm glad you two are here.'

'I thought about not coming,' he said. 'But then I remembered that when you let people try to control you, to dictate how you should live, you've given up. I might be a little afraid of Leigh's grandparents, I admit it, but I'm not afraid of pie.'

She smiled and wanted to hug him. Luckily, the phone rang, keeping her from making possibly unwanted displays of affection, and she went into the kitchen to answer it. It was Isabel, reporting that neither she and June could make it to class; June, Henry and Charlie all had bad colds, and Isabel was playing nursemaid at their houseboat.

The doorbell rang, and there was Penelope, still looking very toned down. The mass of expensive jewellery was still absent, and she wore a simple gold cross around her neck. Also once again, Penelope was as friendly as could be, complimenting Leigh on her T-shirt and hair, telling Nick he was doing a fine job as a single father, and thanking Veronica for offering 'such a fun and informative pie class'.

With her three remaining students around the centre island, they set to work on the peach pie, Nick and Penelope on slicing, and Leigh on measuring out the ingredients. Unless she was imagining things, Penelope kept staring at her. Whenever Veronica glanced over, Penelope would smile fast, then shift her eyes away. Veronica had long ago given up on wondering what was going on in Penelope Von Blun's mind. Back in high school, Penelope had ignored her completely; she hadn't been mean to her, she simply pretended Veronica didn't exist. But over the past year, if Veronica saw her around town, or in the diner, like the other day, Penelope would stare at Veronica, or whisper to her mother. Maybe those days were over.

'Mmm, this smells so good,' Leigh said, closing her eyes and inhaling over her mixing bowl, the smell of peaches, nutmeg, vanilla and brown sugar fragrant in the air.

Penelope poured the filling into the pastry case, and Nick laid the top crust over the pie and pressed the edges together. When the pie went into the oven, Veronica spent fifteen minutes talking about pastry again, how technique was the most important part of making the crust, the not-overworking, the not-kneading, and then they practised making lattice tops because Leigh wanted to, even though their peach pie didn't have a lattice.

'So, did your shoo-fly pie work?' Leigh asked Penelope, dipping her finger against the sides of the bowl and licking the bit remaining. 'Mine did. But I'm not supposed to talk about it. Oops,' she said, putting her hand over her mouth.

'You can talk about whatever you want,' Nick said. 'I'm glad the pie works for you. I'm glad for whatever makes you feel close to your mother.'

'Grandma thinks it's voodoo nonsense, though,' Leigh said. 'I told her what we put in the pie, every ingredient, and even though there's nothing black-magicky about anything in the pie, she still said it was the idea, not the ingredients.'

'I think it's like prayer,' Penelope said suddenly. She'd been a bit quiet for the past forty-five minutes. 'It's just about comfort, that's all.'

'Did it work for you?' Leigh asked her again.

'I don't know,' Penelope said, and she looked very sad for a second.

The timer pinged, and Veronica had Nick pull out the oven rack so that Penelope could make three slashes in the top of the pie. Then they turned down the temperature of the oven and the pie went back in for another thirty minutes.

'What about you, Veronica?' Leigh said. 'Did having the shoo-fly pie help you feel closer to your grandmother?'

'It always does,' Veronica said. 'Even just looking at shoo-fly pie, that crumbly brown-sugar topping, makes me think of Renata Russo. I can smell her Shalimar perfume as though she's right next to me. I can hear her voice, stories she used to tell me about when she was a girl and learned to bake pies. I can feel her with me, and it's like Penelope said – it's pure comfort.'

'That's how I felt every time I ate my shoo-fly pie,' Leigh said. 'Like my mom was right there with me. Sometimes it just felt like she was in me, though. That's just as good.'

'It sure is,' Nick said, running his hand down his daughter's pretty brown hair.

A half-hour later, the pie came out and they waited as long as they could for it to cool, and then Nick served a slice to everyone. They all declared it delicious, and Veronica divided the leftovers between the DeMarcos and Penelope. At eight-thirty the class was over, and Nick said he'd better get his little pastry chef home to bed, that she had camp the next morning. Veronica didn't want them to leave. She liked having Nick in her house, in her kitchen, and she adored Leigh.

'Talk to you soon,' Nick said, his gaze lingering on her for a moment.

As she stood by the open door, watching Nick and Leigh walk to his car, Veronica realized that Penelope wasn't behind them.

Veronica found her in the kitchen, sweeping the floor. 'Oh, Penelope, that's thoughtful, but I'll do that.'

Penelope put the broom back in its wedge of space by the back door, then went to the sink, wet a paper towel and began wiping down the island counter. 'You lived at Hope Home back when you were in high school, right?'

If Penelope Von Blun was cleaning, ostensibly even, this wasn't about bringing up Veronica's past as a pregnant sixteen-year-old. This was about Penelope. Veronica sensed this conversation called for tea, and she added water to the kettle and set it to boil. 'Yes, for almost eight months.'

'Did . . . any of you girls talk about the kind of parents you wanted to adopt your babies?'

Ah. Now Veronica had an idea what this was about.

'Most of us had closed adoptions, so it's not like we could pick and choose, but we talked about it, of course.'

Penelope scrubbed at a clean expanse of counter. 'And what was it that all of you seemed to want in adoptive parents?'

'Well, we wanted the parents to be loving and kind. Lacking in bad tempers, not like some of our fathers.'

'What else?' There was desperation in Penelope's voice.

Veronica shut off the burner and poured the water over Earl Grey leaves in the teapot. 'That's it, really. "Loving" seemed to be the key word.'

Penelope stopped scrubbing. 'But how would you know if someone was loving? I mean, you'd have to really get to know them, right? It's not something you can just tell from a few brief meetings.'

'You can generally tell someone's disposition right away, though, don't you agree?'

Penelope looked like she was about to cry. She flung the balled-up paper towel on the counter. 'My husband and I have tried for years to get pregnant. And now I'm thirty-eight and my chances are slimmer and slimmer. So we decided to look into adoption, and I know there are so many couples hoping for a baby – we were told it could take a long time. But then a girl from Hope Home chose us. I can't tell you how happy I was, maybe happier than I've been in my entire life. But now she might be unchoosing us. She likes my husband, but says she's not sure I'm the right mother for her baby after all.' She turned away and covered her face with her hands.

Oh dear. 'Why did she choose you and your husband in the first place?'

Penelope looked up at Veronica. 'To be honest? Because we're wealthy. The girl comes from the wrong side of the tracks, had a rough, impoverished childhood – she's still a child – and it's very important to her that her baby be raised with wealth, that he or she never want for anything, whether breakfast or an iPhone. It's important to her, and she wants a wealthy, Catholic family from Boothbay Harbor only. So we finally fitted the bill for a birth mother. But then she met us, and I tried to be what she wanted, but the more time we spent with her, the more dissatisfied with me she seemed to get.'

Veronica poured two cups of tea, and gestured for Penelope to sit. 'What do you think her issue is?'

'My husband says I'm coming across as forced, that I need to be myself. But I know what kind of image I project – snobby. I'm trying to change that.'

I noticed, Veronica thought. But it can't be faked.

Penelope added milk and a sugar cube to her tea. 'I know I'm not the friendliest person there ever was. And maybe I have a reputation of being snobby. But I'd love this baby with all my heart – and my heart is big, Veronica. I might not show it to everyone, but my husband knows it. And my mother. My sister too – I'd do anything for my family. And this baby, this precious angel I want to love and raise and share my life with – I'll be the most loving mother. I know that more than I've ever known anything.'

'You need to tell her this, Penelope. You need to say it just like you said it here. You need to tell her from here,' Veronica said, touching her chest. 'It needs to be more than words She needs to hear you mean it.'

'I've tried – three times. She doesn't like me.' Tears shimmered in Penelope's eyes.

'I think you should go see her. Just you. The real you, not this toned-down, false you. You in all your real Penelope Von Blun glory. Tell her, from the heart, what this baby means to you. How you want to raise her. Tell her why you'll raise her baby better than anyone else could. Tell her everything you think about every night before you fall asleep. That's usually where the truth is.'

Penelope nodded, then reached over and grabbed Veronica into a hug. 'Maybe I should take home a recipe for your Hope Pie.'

Veronica went over to her pie binder and took out a recipe for salted-caramel cheesecake pie. 'I don't think you'll even need an elixir pie, Penelope. I feel your hope in waves.'

Close to eleven o'clock that night, Veronica was sitting on the edge of her bed, rubbing lilac-scented lotion into her dry elbows, when her phone rang. Nick? Penelope, maybe?

'Hello?'

Bea. Veronica was so surprised to hear her voice that she almost dropped the receiver. After brief hellos and some talk about today's unusually hot weather and how it wasn't great for pie-baking, Bea said, 'I've been thinking, and I would like to contact Timothy Macintosh.'

'I expected you'd want to.' Veronica wondered what would happen when Bea did call him. How he'd respond.

'Do you have a place for me to start? I did a search for "Macintosh" in the area, and there are quite a few. No Timothy Macintosh, though.'

'I know someone who might have his current address. I'll call you right back.' Veronica hung up, a strange pressure on her chest. She called Nick, and he did have Timothy's address.

He lived in Wiscasset, just fifteen minutes away, in the same town where Veronica and Bea had been yesterday during their brief stop at the bus station. Nick had run into him last Christmas while shopping in Best Buy, and Timothy had handed him his card. He was a boat mechanic.

A boat mechanic. Living just fifteen minutes away.

Veronica sucked in a breath, called Bea back and told her what Nick knew. Her stomach churned.

'Thank you, Veronica,' Bea said, and Veronica couldn't get off the phone fast enough.

She went upstairs to her closet, to the back, where her hope chest was. She'd kept the things she'd brought with her to Hope Home, and things she'd saved, move after move, over the past twenty-two years. She reached into the bottom and dug out the picture of Timothy Macintosh and looked at it. Sixteen-year-old Timothy was standing in their spot, wearing that leather jacket, his hands in his jeans pockets, a sweet smile on his face.

It didn't hurt like Veronica thought it always would, perhaps because of all the opening up she'd done recently. God, he looked a lot like Bea. She was walking proof that she was his daughter.

Veronica put the photograph in a small manila envelope and wrote Bea's name on it, then added a note: *Thought you might want to have this. Timothy Macintosh, March 1991.*

She'd walk it over to the inn in the morning and leave it in the mailbox. That settled, she headed upstairs to her bedroom, put *The Importance of Being Earnest* into the DVD player and slipped into bed, ready for a fun Colin Firth movie that would make her laugh. She had a feeling she'd sleep pretty well tonight.

Chapter 18
Gemma

After another long day of research and interviews, including a heart-tugging lunch with a woman who'd given her baby up for adoption back in 1963, the year Hope Home opened, and a poignant hour spent with a pregnant fifteen-year-old who would only let her baby be adopted by a wealthy, local couple, yet was having trouble finding a loving enough set of 'filthy rich' prospective parents, Gemma stopped by the movie set, hoping to catch a glimpse of Colin Firth and talk her way into an interview. Claire at the *Gazette* had said that she'd assigned a reporter to cover the movie being shot in town, but that didn't mean Gemma couldn't try to score an interview with the actor herself. Now that she was almost done with her research, she'd be ready to write the long middle section of her article over the next couple of days, and then she'd be done. She'd have to give up the

ID card that Claire had made up for her. She'd have to go back to being unemployed.

She'd have to go home and face her future: to be the kind of mother she wished she'd had, to be the mother her baby deserved.

But an interview with Colin Firth could be her ticket to a job. A one-on-one with an A-list movie star. An Oscar winner. A handsome English actor whom everyone respected. It would add a bit of cachet to her clippings – and just might get her her dream job. Maybe even her old job at *New York Weekly*. And once she was employed again as a reporter, Alex would have to accept her plan to stay in the city.

Except he hated the city now. And making him stay wasn't fair to him.

'Hey, everyone! Colin Firth is signing autographs in The Best Little Diner!' a man called out, and a big crowd rushed towards the harbour and up to Main Street. Gemma was embarrassed by how quickly she took off for the diner; she cut through a brick alleyway that she remembered from her teenage days and raced into the diner, out of breath, a crowd hot on her heels. The diner was crowded even at ten in the morning, and Gemma glanced all around, hoping to spot him and get to him before anyone else could. 'Excuse me, Mr Firth,' she'd say, 'I'd love to treat you to dessert, perhaps a slice of that delicious-looking blackberry pie on the counter, if I might ask you a few questions for the *Boothbay Regional Gazette*.' But there was no sign of him in the diner. Not in the booths, not at the counter, not flattened against the wall trying to escape detection while he awaited his dinner.

'Well, where is he?' a woman shouted, pushing past Gemma.

A waitress was refilling the little sugar bowl at the next table. 'Where's who?'

'Colin Firth. Someone said he was in here, signing autographs.'

The waitress, a short redhead in her early forties, raised an eyebrow. 'This again? If Colin Firth were in here, do you think I'd be arranging packets of fake sugar? Or would I be a puddle on the floor?'

'She's just saying that,' another woman yelled, racing around to look in the bathrooms – including the men's. 'He's probably hiding in the kitchen!'

'I'm not, I swear,' the waitress called out. 'If you're not here to eat, beat it.'

Maybe Gemma could catch him coming or going from the set, she thought as she left the diner with a large herbal iced tea. She'd watched two of his films at the inn, *Bridget Jones's Diary* and *Then She Found Me*, and she'd seen a few others over the past few years – *The King's Speech*, *Love Actually* and *Mamma Mia!*. After she worked on her Hope Home article tonight, she'd watch one of his more recent films and sketch out ideas for how to frame the story. Oscar winner arrives in small-town Maine. Mr Darcy comes to town. An Englishman in Boothbay Harbor. Perhaps he'd share what sights he'd taken in while in Maine, if he had, and Gemma could frame it as a bit of a travel piece too. And by a fan, of course. She adored Colin Firth and had no doubt she'd be that puddle on the floor herself while standing just inches from him, listening to him talk in that beautiful accent. Her mind was whirling as she neared Frog Marsh, where the number of trailers had quadrupled. Gemma's phone rang just as she pulled out her little notebook to jot down ideas. Her mother-in-law's name flashed across her screen. Oh no.

'Gemma, just what on God's green earth do you think you're doing?' Mona Hendricks asked, her voice full of judgemental anger.

Gemma rolled her eyes. Had Alex told her she was pregnant? Granted, they hadn't talked about telling or not telling people at this early stage, but the later Mona knew, the better. 'I don't know what you mean, Mona.'

'You know perfectly well what I mean. You're pregnant and running around Maine for three weeks? You're giving Alexander a hard time about moving to Dobbs Ferry?'

Jesus. Had he set his mother on her?

'Oh, he tried to make out like it didn't matter to him. He said you two might end up staying in the city because you feel so strongly. Just how goddamned selfish can you be?'

'Excuse me, Mona, but why isn't Alexander selfish for wanting to move to Westchester when I want to stay in the city?'

'Don't be daft. You know perfectly well why. You're

pregnant. You're bringing a life into this world. It's not about you.'

Like son, like mother. Alexander had said that same thing.

'Mona, this is between me and Alexander.' *Don't let loose on her. Just get her off the phone. Don't add to your problems.*

'This is a family issue. We're all here in Dobbs Ferry. And now that you're expecting, the three of you belong here too. Think of the baby, if your own husband doesn't matter to you.'

'I have to go, Mona,' she said. 'Goodbye.'

Anger bubbled in Gemma's stomach. How dare she! *Think of the baby, if your own husband doesn't matter to you.*

She had to get an interview with Colin Firth. She had to.

After an hour of fruitless calls to find out when Colin Firth was due to arrive in town — even the guy Bea was dating, the assistant director on the film, wasn't sure because of scheduling conflicts, according to Bea — Gemma got to work on her article about Hope Home. She couldn't stop thinking about Lizzie Donner, the fifteen-year-old resident who was insistent that her baby be adopted by a wealthy family from Boothbay Harbor, where she herself had been raised in poverty. Gemma's heart had gone out to the girl as she'd shared her story. Lizzie had thought she'd found the perfect prospective adoptive parents — very wealthy, Catholic like herself, living in Boothbay Harbor in a mansion on the water — but every time she met with the couple, she found she didn't like the wife. 'I want my baby to have everything she'll ever dream of,' Lizzie had said. 'I thought that was the most important thing. But the wife is so phoney and fake — how could she be a good mother to my baby?' Gemma left out that last line as her hands flew over the keyboard of her laptop. She'd promised Lizzie she'd only write the gist of what was important to Lizzie and not disparage anyone, especially since Lizzie hadn't written off that couple just yet. Gemma thought about her own mother — not fake, but cold. Her parents were very well off, but money and vacations and expensive summer camps certainly hadn't made anyone happy.

Gemma moved on to the paragraph about Lindsey Tate, a New Hampshire woman who'd adopted a baby whose birth mother had been a Hope Home resident fifteen years ago. She was looking back at her notes about Lindsey when a strange pain began in her stomach, like menstrual cramps. She put her hand to her belly and stood up, thinking she'd been hunched over her laptop too much. But the pain intensified. Gemma walked around her room, as much as the small space would allow, and the pain got so bad she doubled over.

What was this? Was she losing the baby?

She opened her door and braced herself against the jamb, the pain getting worse in her abdomen. 'Isabel?' she called out, startled by the desperate wail in her voice. Please be here.

'Gemma?' Bea called from upstairs. 'Are you all right?'

'I'm having really bad pains in my stomach,' Gemma said, barely able to get the words out.

Bea rushed down the stairs, and in moments she was back with Isabel.

'I'm pregnant,' Gemma said. 'Just nine weeks. The pain is really intense.'

Isabel's eyes widened. 'I'm taking you over to Coastal General. Bea, can you cover the inn?'

'Of course. Anything you need.'

Gemma could barely stand straight up as Isabel helped her down the stairs. What was happening? She walked, doubled over, to Isabel's car, the cramping pain unrelenting.

'Honey, listen. I don't want you to worry about anything,' Isabel said as she backed out of the driveway. 'When I was in the early stages of pregnancy, I also had some severe abdominal pain, and it turned out to be nothing. The ER will likely do an ultrasound and just check you over. Don't worry.'

But Gemma was worrying. She'd never felt cramps this bad. 'Am I losing the baby?'

Isabel sped up, her knuckles white on the steering wheel for the duration of the fifteen-minute drive. Gemma doubled over, rocking a bit up and down.

'We're here.' She pulled up to the emergency entrance and called out, 'My friend is nine weeks pregnant and having severe stomach pains!'

In moments, Gemma was in a wheelchair and being pushed through the automatic doors into the ER. Before she knew it, she was lying on a cot, two nurses hovering to take her vitals and insert an IV of fluids. Breathe, she told herself. The pain began to lessen some. A doctor came over and introduced himself as the OB attending and explained that he was going to spread some cold jelly-like substance on her belly for the ultrasound.

'Okay, there's the heartbeat,' he said, and Gemma glanced up at the screen, her hand over her mouth. 'I'm not quite sure what caused the pain, but you've told me it has abated, and the baby is fine.'

Gemma couldn't stop staring at the flashing heartbeat, at the foetus right there on the monitor. A part of her, a part of Alexander. For the first time, she felt connected to the life growing inside her. She was really going to have a baby.

A baby she would have been devastated to lose, especially without having had the chance to feel something – and she didn't mean a flutter. She meant connection. The stirrings of love.

A nurse helped wipe off the jelly from her stomach, and then told her to lie and rest there for thirty minutes before she'd come and discharge her. She stared up at the ceiling, overtaken by something that felt a lot like wonder.

Gemma had been instructed to take it easy for the evening, but a walk didn't seem like much exertion. She found herself drawn to the playground on Main Street, always full of children climbing over the fairy-tale-character structures and being pushed on the swings. She was hoping that after the scare her perspective would be different, that she'd suddenly have all these warm and fuzzy feelings, that the elusive maternal instinct would suddenly settle into her bones, her bloodstream, and she'd be a different person altogether.

But as she watched two toddlers packing sand in buckets in the sandbox, she felt . . . nothing much at all. No rush of Oh, how adorable, I wish I had one of those.

There was only the same cold fear. That she wasn't up to the task, that she'd fail as a stay-at-home mother even with all day to practise at her new life.

She pulled out her phone, about to call Alexander and tell him about the scare she'd had, that everything was fine, the baby was fine – but she'd just worry him and he'd insist she come home this minute, and Gemma couldn't do that. She closed her eyes for a moment and let out a deep breath. Right now, she could use his strong arms around her, a tight hug, and maybe just the sound of his voice would comfort her some. But she wouldn't call him. And it wasn't just because he'd book her plane tickets home on the spot. It was because she needed to deal with her fear, that icy clawing in her chest, *herself*.

For reasons she wasn't even clear on, Gemma found herself pressing in her mother's telephone number.

'Gemma, it's lovely to hear from you.'

How formal. 'Mom, I wanted to ask you a question. Did you plan your pregnancy with Anna or was she an accident?'

'What kind of question is that?'

'I'm just curious. I know your career is very important to you, so I wondered if you planned getting pregnant or not.'

'I did plan it. And five years later, I was ready for a second baby – you. What's this all about?'

She hadn't expected that. She'd always figured both pregnancies had been surprises. But her mother had planned the 'interruption' to her life and career. 'I'm pregnant. I'm due in January. I guess I'm just thinking about how I'm going to handle everything.'

'There's no need to be all dramatic about it, Gemma. You'll hire a well-vetted nanny and you'll do what you need to do. I'm surprised at the news, though. I thought you wanted to focus on your career for a few more years yet. You're not even thirty. I was thirty-four when Anna was born. Thirty-nine with you.'

God, is this what she sounded like to Alexander? Probably. Where were the congratulations? Where was the 'I'm going to be a grandmother!'? What did you expect? she reminded herself. Your mother suddenly being all maternal when you can't even manage it?

Except Gemma was different now – if just a little.

'Well, I'm pregnant now.'

'Yes, indeed!' her mother said, finally injecting a note of excitement in her voice. 'And congratulations. If you're thinking of names already, you can consider Frederick, after my father.'

'Actually, Alex likes Alexander Junior or Gemma Junior.'

Silence. 'Are you kidding? I never know when you're kidding.'

'I'm not sure,' Gemma said, smiling to herself. She was amazed that the sweetness of the memory of Alexander trailing a finger over her cheek while suggesting Gemma Junior as a name, telling her she was beautiful and whip-smart, overrode her mother's flat, cold demeanour. 'Well, I just wanted you to know the news. I'd better get going.'

When she hung up, it wasn't with the usual hole in her heart, wishing that her mother was different — though, yes, it would be nice. Her mother was who she was. Gemma was who she was. Alexander was who he was. All she knew was that she felt a little fuller where there used to be empty space, and not anywhere near her belly, either. Was it the pregnancy? Not wanting it, then almost losing it and realizing that she did feel something for the little burst of life inside her? Maybe it was these past weeks, working on a story about women, about family, about pregnancy, about interruption, about hope, about despair, about dreams — a story that had ensnared her, heart, soul and mind.

Chapter 19
Bea

'I can understand how you feel,' Patrick said as he sat down across from Bea at the little round table on the balcony of his hotel. Even the view of the lit-up harbour, the incredible dinner he'd ordered from room service, and her very attractive date couldn't get Bea's mind off all Veronica had told her, shown her.

Bea sipped her wine, her appetite for her grilled salmon gone. 'But was it mean of me to say it to her? That I don't know what she's supposed to mean to me?'

She was so damned confused. Last night, when she'd called for Timothy's contact information, Veronica had sounded so strained. But this morning, she found an envelope with her name on it slipped under her door. Inside there was a photograph and note. Her biological father. *Thought you might want to have this. Timothy Macintosh, March 1991.*

Bea had stared at the picture for a long time. She looked a lot like the teenage boy standing there in the leather jacket. But despite how long she looked at it, she felt no connection to the person in the picture at all. Probably because of all Veronica had told her. Timothy Macintosh had never felt any connection to her. But Veronica had.

Bea hadn't done anything with that contact information. The piece of paper on which she'd jotted down his name and address and telephone number lay under one of the seashells on the dresser in her room at the inn. Last night, when she'd hung up with Veronica, she'd picked up a shell and asked it her burning question: Should I call Timothy Macintosh?

There was the usual whoosh, but nothing else. No yes. No no. Just . . . nothing. She'd wait a couple of days and let it all settle inside her – that she had his address and phone number, that she could contact him when she was ready.

'This relationship is new to both of you,' Patrick said, taking the last bite of his swordfish. 'It's okay to have some speed bumps. To figure things out, how you feel, what you're comfortable with. For both of you.'

Bea nodded. That made sense. There was no rush, and she couldn't feel something out of nothing. She would have to feel her way with Veronica. Just as Veronica would need to do the same with her.

Patrick stood up and moved behind her, and she felt warm, strong hands massaging her shoulders.

'Thank you for talking me through it,' she said. 'And thank you for dinner. It was great. The whole evening was great.'

'You're welcome. And I had a great time too.' He sat back down and scooched his chair closer to hers. 'Tomorrow's insanely busy at the set, and we're going to be setting up shop at a diner in town for a few days, but maybe you could come by around five, to say hi? I don't want the whole day to go by without seeing you.'

'I'd love to, but I've got a tutoring gig at five. With Tyler's sister, Maddy.'

'Tyler Echols, the PA?' he asked, frowning. Was that concern on his face?

Bea nodded. 'He's paying me fifty bucks an hour. I can definitely use it.'

'I probably shouldn't say anything,' Patrick said. 'But given what you're going through with your own birth mother . . .'

Bea stared at him. 'What are you talking about?'

Patrick seemed to be weighing whether or not he should tell her. 'Look, I don't know Tyler too well and maybe I misheard him, but I don't think so. About a month ago when we were filming in New York, I overheard him talking to another PA buddy of his about how his sister was adopted and that he found her birth mother for her — and shook her up for money. He was just out of college and broke and figured she'd feel guilty and give him whatever he wanted to arrange a meeting between them. To his credit, he did seem to have real interest in helping his sister, but I got the sense he figured he'd kill two birds with one stone, you know? Set up contact — and line his pockets.'

'God,' Bea said. 'That's vile.'

'If he wasn't so good at his job, I'd fire him. And who knows — maybe he was just talking smack. I don't know. But I just figured I'd tell you in case he tries to get out of paying you for tutoring his sister.'

She'd be on red alert. 'I appreciate it. Duly warned. So did he get money out of the birth mother?' She remembered Tyler saying the experience was disappointing, so clearly not. And no wonder Tyler had said not to bring up the subject with his sister. Maybe they were both grifters. Or maybe Maddy didn't know what Tyler had tried to do.

'I don't know,' Patrick said. 'Just make sure he pays you fair and square, okay?'

A warmth enveloped her and she smiled. 'Okay.' She missed that, someone looking out for her.

She'd give the tutoring one session and get a feel for Maddy. If she seemed shady, Bea would quit. But she wouldn't spite Maddy just because her brother was a class-A jerk.

'I love this view,' Patrick said, and this time, his face and the lights and the boats worked their magic. They sipped their wine, and then he took her glass and put it down and kissed her.

All thoughts of birth mothers and birth fathers and shady production assistants went out of her head; she could only think about Patrick's lips, the beautiful sensations running up and down her spine. How long had it been since she'd been kissed? Almost a year. Too long.

His hand went to the zipper of her jeans.

She covered his hand. 'I really like you, Patrick. But let's take this a little slower, okay? In fact, I should get going. But thank you for tonight.'

'You sure I can't convince you to stay?' he asked, running a hand down her back.

'I should go,' she said reluctantly. Who knew what five more minutes together would bring, and she wasn't ready to add sex to their very new relationship. 'See you soon?'

'Can't be soon enough,' he said and gave her a kiss goodbye to remember.

Maddy Echols was ten minutes late for her first tutoring session. Bea would give her another ten, then leave. She sat at a square table in the 'Quiet Room' of the Boothbay Harbor library, trying not to think about what she'd learned about Tyler – and possibly Maddy. Shaking up Maddy's biological mother for money? Could it be true? Tyler did seem to care about Maddy, but he'd also shown himself to be a jerk who couldn't be bothered to be civil.

A minute later, Maddy poked her head in, and Bea could see she was annoyed that Bea was there.

'You were hoping I'd given up on you, huh?' Bea asked.

Maddy smiled. 'Kinda.'

'Well, I need the money. And you need to pass this class. So sit your tush down and let's talk *To Kill a Mockingbird*.'

Maddy sighed noisily, dropped her backpack on the table and sat.

'You have to write an essay?' Bea asked.

Maddy nodded. 'I have to pick one of four quotations from the book that supposedly means something to me and write a five-page typed essay on what the quote means, using more quotes from the book, at least five.' She started writing her name in pen on her palm.

Bea halted the pen. 'Let's see the four quotes.'

'I already picked one, actually. That was the easy part.'

'That's great. Read it to me.' If she'd chosen a quote, Bea's job wouldn't be as difficult as she'd feared. Often the students she tutored at the Writing Centre didn't look at the assignment until they were forced to.

Maddy pulled a sheet of paper from her binder. 'This is from Atticus Finch. I think he's the father of the kid who narrates the book? Okay, here it is: "I wanted you to see what real courage is, instead of getting the idea that courage is a man with a gun in his hand. It's when you know you're licked before you begin, but you begin anyway and see it through no matter what." It's the longest quote of the four and I totally get it.'

Bea was encouraged. 'Tell me what it means to you, since that's part of the assignment – to choose a quote that means something to you.'

'Well, when I first read all the quotes, I was like, boring, boring, bor-ing. And then I got to this one, and it reminded me of something that happened last year.'

'Can you tell me about it?' Bea asked.

Maddy bit her lip and looked away, glancing at Bea every now and then. 'I'm adopted, and my brother helped me look up my birth mother, but she wrote back that she didn't want contact and that it was her right and please not to contact her again. But I wrote her another letter anyway, telling her I just wanted to maybe see her once and see if I looked like her.' Maddy's eyes started getting watery. 'So when I read that quote, that's what I thought of. I was totally licked before I began, but I wrote her again anyway because I had to.'

It took everything in Bea not to reach out and hug this girl.

'She wrote back again to say sorry, she didn't want contact and that was final,' Maddy said, 'but she enclosed a picture of herself. Want to see it?'

'Sure,' Bea said, trying to imagine herself – at sixteen, no less – getting that kind of response from Veronica. How disappointing – crushing – that must have been for Maddy.

Maddy handed her the picture. The woman looked rough around the edges.

'I was adopted too,' Bea said. 'In fact, the whole reason I'm in Boothbay Harbor is because I came to meet my own biological mother.'

Maddy's jaw almost dropped open. 'Seriously? What happened?'

'Well, she seems like a wonderful person, but I just don't know who she's supposed to be in my life. We got together twice, she answered all my burning questions – and then some – and now I just don't know where we go from here. I've backed away, I guess.'

'I can't relate at all. I can't imagine not wanting my birth mother in my life, especially if she's nice. You're so lucky.'

Bea reached over and squeezed Maddy's hand.

'Since you're still here, though,' Maddy said, 'maybe the quote applies to you too.'

'What do you mean?'

'Well, you're the one who kind of got licked by your own self. You wouldn't still be here if you didn't want a relationship with her. But you said you backed away even though she's wonderful. My brother's always saying people can be their own worst enemies.'

Huh. Bea smiled. 'I think you might be on to something there. A plus,' she added, and Maddy beamed at her. But she wasn't about to earn Tyler's hundred bucks by talking about her own state of confusion. 'Have you read more of the book? What that quote – which you understand very well – means in the book is really, really interesting. Heartbreaking, but interesting.'

'I can't get past the second page. Like I care about the details of the town? It's so boring.'

'Well, those details help explain what life was like then, when the book takes place. It would be like you explaining your life here in Maine to someone a hundred years from now.'

'What was it like then?'

Bea gave Maddy a quick lesson on the 1930s and the Depression, on what race relations were like in the South. 'Then comes Atticus Finch, a very honest, honourable lawyer, a widower with two young kids, whose job it is to defend an African American man accused of raping a white woman. No one thinks the black man deserves a trial to begin with. They just think he's guilty and should hang. Atticus knows a jury won't believe his word over hers.'

'So . . . that's what the quote means – the lawyer knows he's going to lose but he defends the guy anyway?'

Bea nodded. 'And against a lot of ill-will in town too. He ends up opening a lot of people's eyes. But foremost, he teaches his children something very, very important.'

'What?'

'I want you to find out for yourself,' Bea said. 'You know, since we're alone in here, I'm gonna shut the door and read the first chapter to you. When you go home tonight, you read the next two chapters. Then the next two the following night. Keep doing that, two chapters a night, and we'll discuss where you're up to at our next session.'

'Okay,' Maddy said, and Bea knew she had her. The girl's ears were open.

*

Tyler was right on time to pick up Maddy two hours later. He looked different without his clipboard and production-company ID hanging around his neck. Less . . . jerkish.

'I'm going to ace this class,' she said to her brother, then put her earphones in and dropped down on a stately leather chair in the main room with *To Kill a Mockingbir*d.

'I can see this went well,' he said. 'I'm surprised.' He pulled out two twenties and a ten and handed the bills to her. 'Thanks.'

Well, at least he didn't try to get out of paying, as Patrick had warned he might.

'We're headed to Harbour Heaven, Maddy's favourite restaurant, for dinner. You could come, if you're free. She seems to like you.'

Bea wasn't a cynical person in general, but she couldn't help thinking that Tyler had only invited her so he could steer the conversation back to *To Kill a Mockingbird* and get Maddy an extra hour of free tutoring. 'I have a date with Patrick, but thanks.'

He made his trademark move of rolling his eyes. 'I hope you're not pinning your hopes on him. I'm telling you, he's notorious.'

'He seems great to me.'

'Right. He probably promised your biological mother a speaking role, right?'

'He doesn't even know which extra is my biological mother.'

'You know why? Because he doesn't care. You're just some pretty young thing to him. Just be careful. That's all I'm saying.'

Now it was Bea's turn to roll her eyes. Patrick had spent a lot of time showing Bea he did care, by listening. 'Thanks for the unsolicited advice.' She walked over to Maddy and tapped on her shoulder. Maddy removed one ear plug. 'Remember, read two chapters every night this week. We'll meet again next Wednesday. Promise you'll do the reading?'

'I promise, I promise. The Trevi Fountain is waiting for me.'

Bea liked Maddy Echols, and there was no way she'd let her fail the class. She hoped like hell that Tyler's bribe of Italy and the Trevi Fountain wasn't all hot air and that he'd actually take her.

When she got back to her room at the inn, Bea slid the shell aside and picked up the piece of paper with Timothy Macintosh's contact information, and stared at it.

Maddy's words came back to her. *I can't imagine not wanting my birth mother in my life, especially if she's nice. You're so lucky.*

Bea didn't know how lucky she'd be when it came to her birth father. He'd denied being her father twenty-two years ago. He'd walked away from Veronica completely. Veronica had never heard from him the entire time she'd been at Hope Home, or afterwards.

Maybe he'd really believed what he'd told Veronica. That

he wasn't the father, that he couldn't be. Maybe he wasn't a bad guy.

Bea picked up the shell and put it to her ear. Should I call him? Right now?

The whoosh in her ear told her nothing. It was like a Magic 8-Ball saying: Ask again later.

She could pick up the phone right now and call, just as she'd done with Veronica. But she'd had the advantage of knowing Veronica wanted to be contacted. Timothy Macintosh truly was a stranger. And given the way he had walked away from Veronica, he likely would not be open to hearing from Bea at all.

She stared out the window, at the stars, at the treetops illuminated by the moon. This was something she had to do, had to finish.

She took a sheet of Three Captains' Inn stationery and wrote:

Dear Mr Macintosh,
I hope you won't find this letter terribly intrusive. My name is
Bea Crane, and I'm the biological daughter of Veronica Russo,
who has named you as my biological father. I was born on 12
October 1991 in Boothbay Harbor. I understand from Veronica
that you denied being the father of her baby, and I understand
that you might not be my biological father. I am writing because
I'm here in Boothbay Harbor, and have recently met Veronica for
the first time, after having found out, only very recently, that I

was adopted. I'm interested in meeting you, if you're open to it, and would be open to taking a DNA test, if you'd like to go down that route. I'd love to know about my biological father's family background. That's all I'm interested in, by the way — I just want to assure you of that.

    Thank you

    Bea Crane

She addressed the envelope and headed out to the mailbox on the corner of Main Street, watching it disappear down the chute.

Chapter 20
Veronica

Veronica spent Saturday in her kitchen, surrounded by flour, butter, sugar and baskets of fruit. She was on her twelfth client pie of the day, this last one a Key lime Confidence Pie for her neighbour, Frieda, who was nervous about applying to nursing programmes for a second career. As Veronica grated lime zest into her mixing bowl atop the condensed milk, egg yolks and Key lime juice, she tried to summon up her own confidence – to call Bea. To call Nick. She hadn't heard from him since Monday night. Not a word since he and his daughter had left her house after the pie class. She'd been so sure he'd stop by or call – something – but he hadn't. Maybe she'd been reading more into their blossoming . . . friendship than was really there. Or perhaps there was some fall-out from his taking Leigh to her class when her grandparents were up in arms about it. She couldn't stop thinking about him, though, which had had her Amore and Hope Pies come out perfectly the past several days.

Her phone rang, and she wiped her sticky fingers and grabbed the receiver, her fingers crossed that it was Bea. She hadn't heard from Bea since Monday night either, when she had called to ask for Timothy's contact information. Five days. Had she called Timothy? Had he denied being her father? Or was she sitting across a table from him in a restaurant right now?

'Hello, Veronica speaking.'

Silence for a moment. And then, 'Veronica, it's Timothy. Macintosh.'

Veronica dropped the receiver and grabbed for it. Jesus Christ. Her heart was pounding, and her lips felt dry.

'Veronica?' he said. 'Are you there?'

She took a deep breath. 'I'm here.' She didn't have to wonder how he'd tracked her down; her number and address were listed in the telephone directory.

'I received a letter yesterday from someone named Bea Crane. Is it true? Am I the father? And I mean without a shadow of a doubt?'

She sat down at the table, trying to get over the shock of hearing his voice. But the moment she spoke, her own voice rang strong and clear in her ears, the way it hadn't twenty-two years ago. 'I was a virgin when I started dating you, Timothy,' she said matter-of-factly, surprised at the lack of anger or blame. 'You were the only guy I slept with until I was nineteen.' It was the truth, just as it had been all along. She no longer cared if he believed her.

She froze at how true that was. She no longer cared. Something shifted inside her and a space opened, but it wasn't a hole.

She heard his own intake of breath. 'You're sure. You're absolutely sure.'

'I'm sure. As sure now as I was then.'

He was quiet for a few seconds. 'She wrote me a letter. She said she'd be willing to take a DNA test if I wanted her to. I suppose I should, just for legal purposes.'

Veronica could hear the worry in his voice, the fear. It was much the same voice it had been at sixteen, if a bit deeper. Still only thinking of himself. Well, she was thinking of Bea, and since Bea wanted to meet him, Veronica wanted to ease the way for that to happen. 'She's twenty-two years old and was legally adopted as a newborn. You have no legal obligation to her, Timothy, if that's your concern.'

He seemed to take that in for a bit. 'This is just so crazy, so sudden. She says she wants to meet me, to know about her biological father's family and medical history.'

'She's a lovely person, Timothy. I can assure you of that.'

'I just don't know,' he said. 'I've kept track of the time. When . . . the baby would turn eighteen. I wondered if I'd get a call.'

Veronica stood up and paced as much as the phone cord would allow. 'So you did wonder if you were the father?' You might have said something then, she thought, rolling her eyes. But she knew that fear had held him back. Just as it would now with Bea.

'Well, I've always known it was possible. To be honest, I've been thinking about it a lot lately. My wife says it's haunting me. Especially because I saw you recently, about six months ago. My wife and I were visiting friends of hers, and as we walked past a diner I saw you. I don't come to Boothbay much since my parents moved out a long time ago. I almost passed out when I saw you – it was just so unexpected. I'd heard you moved down south.'

'I moved back to town a year ago.'

'My wife thinks I should have settled the answer of whether or not I really fathered your baby a long time ago. For the last few years, she's been telling me to call you and ask you straight out. But every time I picked up the phone, I put it down. Not even a month ago, Beth handed me the phone and begged me to call you and just find out once and for all instead of letting it eat at me like this.'

Veronica froze.

Beth. Her client who'd ordered the Cast-Out Pie.

The kind of pie that would get someone off someone else's mind . . .

The question. That was what Beth wanted to cast out of his heart.

Jesus Christ, I'm not the one who's casting someone out. It's him who has to get someone else out of his goddamned head.

Beth, who never did pay her, was Timothy's wife.

'I *have* always been kind of haunted about it,' Timothy said. 'Not knowing if it was true, if I treated you terribly. I've never known the truth. I never wanted to know. I was scared out of my mind back then, Veronica. When you told me you were pregnant, I freaked. All I saw was you ending up like my mom: a baby at sixteen, dreams smashed, washed up within five years. Life nothing but drudgery and working shit jobs.'

She was silent, unable to believe the guy she'd thought was her soulmate, her kindred spirit, could have felt so differently about something so vital. She hadn't looked at the situation the way he had, hadn't thought about dashed dreams and being trapped. To sixteen-year-old Veronica, the pregnancy, though accidental, had flashed an escape signal from her dreary life with her parents. Equally immature – more so, she knew. Regardless, though, he'd betrayed her.

'I'm sorry, Veronica,' he said, his voice breaking. 'I'm sorry for how I treated you, what I put you through. You had to go through everything alone.'

She found she didn't have to block the image of him, standing there in the brick alleyway the last time she'd seen him. His expression, the anger as she'd told him, shaking and crying, that she was pregnant. The memory had lost its power. She lifted her chin. 'I think when you see Bea, if you agree to meet with her, you'll know once and for all that she's your daughter. She has your hair, your smile. There's just something in her expression that's all you.'

'God,' Timothy said. 'I'm sorry, Veronica. I'm so sorry.'

He started sobbing, and then there seemed to be someone in the background, talking to him, and then he said he had to go and he hung up.

Veronica sat in her kitchen for over an hour, the call from Timothy echoing in her head. She glanced at the unfinished pie. She'd lost track of what ingredients she'd added. She'd have to throw it away and start over, not that she could tonight. Confidence was something Veronica was lacking in right now, about Bea. About how this would go between her and Timothy.

She picked up the phone, pressed in Nick's number and told him about the phone call.

'Come over,' he said. 'Leigh's been asleep since eight-forty-five. Bring your pie ingredients if you want. I'll help you bake.'

Twenty minutes later, she sat at Nick's kitchen table, sipping a glass of wine as he stood a foot away, making a Confidence Pie. The sight of him, barefoot and in a blue T-shirt and jeans, separating egg yolks, grating the lime zest, made her want to stand up and kiss him.

'You okay?' he asked, whisking the ingredients.

'I'll *be* okay. It was just so . . . strange talking to Timothy.'

'I'll bet. Sounds like he finally accepted the truth, though.'

'Thanks for inviting me over,' she said. 'I needed this.'

He sat down beside her and took her hand and held it.

When he looked at her, she wondered if he was going to kiss her — and then he did.

She was about to wrap her arms around his neck and kiss him back with everything inside her, but the doorbell rang.

'Talk about bad timing,' he said. 'Hold that thought.'

When he went to the door, she heard the voices of a man and a woman, the woman saying something about Leigh's watch, which she'd left at their house, then, 'What's that I smell? Lime juice? Are you drinking?'

'I'm making a pie,' Nick said, his voice weary. 'Thanks for bringing back Leigh's watch. I'll tell her you brought it over.'

Instead of the sound of the door closing, a woman in her early sixties, with a silver-blonde bob, burst into the kitchen. She stared at Veronica. 'It's you, isn't it? That pie lady. Leigh described you to a T,' she added with disdain. She turned to Nick, furious. 'And now you have women over on a week-night? When Leigh's asleep in her room?'

'Gertie, first of all, Veronica and I are baking a pie, not having sex in the living room.'

A tall, thin man, also in his early sixties, came into the kitchen. 'Don't be crude, Nick.'

'You two listen right now,' Nick said forcefully. 'I'm not going to live this way. Not a moment longer. I love Leigh with all my heart — you know that. I'm doing my best — and yes, my best *is* good enough. I'm sorry that Vanessa died. Things might not have been working out between us, but I loved her, I cared about her. And now you're fighting me on

326

being a parent to Leigh when I'm the only one she has left? Be her grandparents – I've never taken that away from you. Have I ever tried to limit the time she spends with you?' He turned around, his hand shaking even while gripping the counter.

'I'll go,' Veronica said. 'I think the three of you need to talk.'

She slipped out the kitchen door.

Veronica stayed up as long as she could, hoping Nick would phone and tell her how he and Leigh's grandparents had left things, but by one o'clock he hadn't called, and she must have fallen asleep soon after. She could still feel the imprint of his lips on hers, feel that beautiful urge to kiss him back. She wondered what would have happened had his in-laws not burst into the kitchen.

Nick was the past and present in one, and she had a serious thing for him. She couldn't help smiling when, for the third time in twelve hours, she whisked together egg yolks, condensed milk, Key lime juice and zest for Frieda's Confidence Pie. She felt it, felt the little opening inside her heart. She liked Nick DeMarco and, from that one kiss last night, she knew he liked her too. A lightness that she hadn't felt in years settled around her, inside her.

My heart is open to Bea. My heart is open to Nick.

This time, she got the pie in the oven.

Just as she closed the oven door, the phone rang.

Penelope Von Blun.

'I wanted you to know I did what you said,' Penelope said. 'I prayed over three salted-caramel cheesecake Hope Pies that our prospective birth mother would listen, that she'd believe everything I was saying, and then I called her and asked if I could talk to her, just me and her, and she said yes. I told her that I'd been trying to impress her, to be what she wanted, so I toned down my style and tried to look more church-going or something. I told her what I thought about before I'd drift off to sleep, sometimes thinking so much, wishing so hard, that I couldn't get to sleep at all. I told what her baby would mean to me, why I thought I would be a good mother. I told her everything. And I think she started to like me.'

'I'm very glad to hear that, Penelope.' Veronica was starting to like her too.

They hung up, and Veronica flashed to an image of herself at sixteen, pregnant, at Hope Home, at group counselling, in private therapy with the very nice social worker who came once a week to meet with each girl. When she'd first arrived at Hope, she'd refused to say much at all, but slowly, week by week, she began opening up. She thought of those girls there today, thought of all they were going through, all they needed to say. Maybe, with her experience, she could be a help to them.

An hour later, Veronica delivered her pie to Frieda, wished her well with the nursing-school applications, then drove to Hope Home before she could change her mind.

*

328

Veronica pulled open the screen door and smiled at the woman at the front desk, in the same place it was decades ago. 'My name is Veronica Russo. I lived here twenty-two years ago when I was sixteen and pregnant. Hope Home did me a world of good, and I'd like to volunteer here in whatever capacity you might need.'

The woman smiled, stood up and extended her hand. 'We can use all the experienced help we can get. Let's sit down and you can tell me about yourself and fill out some forms. We'll have to check your background and references, of course. When would you be able to start? A volunteer flaked out on me and I was counting on her help at our free-talk period this weekend.'

Veronica sat. 'I'd like to start as soon as I can.'

As Veronica sat on a chair in the extras holding tent late Monday afternoon, her thoughts once again went to Nick, who still hadn't called. All day she'd tried to put it out of her mind. He was probably dealing with Leigh's grandparents. Perhaps they'd spent the weekend together, as a family, and were ironing things out.

One kiss doesn't obligate him to you, she reminded herself as she headed home and prepared her island counter for her students, once again having no idea if two of those students would be coming or not.

At a few minutes before six, June and Isabel arrived with Charlie, and then Penelope, looking like her old self – a good thing. The jewellery was back. The make-up. The real Penelope. And likewise, her smile was very real. 'Things are good,' Penelope said. 'I'm hopeful again.'

Veronica barely had time to talk to Penelope because the doorbell rang, and a shot of pure happiness burst inside her. She opened the door – but Nick and Leigh weren't alone. Leigh's grandmother was there too. Nick introduced them officially.

As Nick and Leigh stepped in and chatted with the other students, Leigh's grandmother said, 'I wanted to apologize for how I acted the other night. That wasn't fair of me.'

That was a turnaround. 'Stay for class?' Veronica asked.

The woman seemed pleased by the invitation. 'None of those strange pies? I'm not a fan of that mumbo-jumbo.'

'Just good old strawberry-rhubarb tonight,' Veronica said. 'Then I'd love to stay.'

As Leigh led her grandmother into the kitchen, Nick whispered in Veronica's ear, 'Took me the last two days, but I got through.'

Veronica smiled. She felt like something was getting through to her too.

On Tuesday morning, Veronica heard from Patrick Ool's assistant that the extras for the diner scene wouldn't be needed until 2 p.m., so she called Pauline Lee and asked if she could come earlier. A group session was set for ten, and Veronica offered a pie-baking lesson. She gathered the ingredients she'd need and drove out to Hope Home, turning on to the road with its canopy of trees. When the white farmhouse with its hanging sign and porch swing came into view, Veronica saw herself sitting on that swing, scared, worried, fearful for how she'd feel after she had the baby and gave her up, and she remembered the counsellor, a lovely woman named Annie, sitting down beside her and just holding her, letting her cry. That was exactly what Veronica wanted to do for the girls here. Listen. Be a shoulder.

She parked in the lot, near the very spot where she had given birth in an ambulance. She sat there and watched the few girls who were walking around the yard. They looked so young and vulnerable, though one or two had a tough edge to their expressions, to their make-up. Just before ten o'clock she headed up the three steps and pulled open the screen door. A woman she didn't recognize sat at the desk.

'You must be Veronica,' she said, standing up. 'I'm Larissa Dennis, head counsellor here at Hope Home. You're just in time to join Group.'

The director appeared, welcomed Veronica and sat down at the desk, and Veronica followed Larissa into the large room that faced the back yard. There were ten huge purple bean-bags in a circle, and some rocking chairs. The room itself was just as it had been twenty-two years ago, painted a very pale blue with inspirational posters on the walls.

As the clock struck ten, girls began coming in and sitting

down on the beanbags and chairs. One very pregnant girl chose the recliner. Many of them had anxiety balls in their hands.

'Morning, girls,' Larissa said. 'We have a new volunteer joining us for Group every week. Veronica Russo lived here at Hope Home twenty-two years ago as a sixteen-year-old. She'll be helping guide discussions and just generally being of support and service. Turns out Veronica is a master pie baker, so she'll be in the kitchen when she's not needed. Anyone who wants to learn to make a few different kinds of pie, meet in the kitchen after this Group.'

There were a bunch of 'Me!'s, which made Veronica smile.

'I'm craving pumpkin pie so bad,' a red-haired girl on a beanbag said.

'Key lime.'

'Chocolate cream.'

'Anything but apple pie. Too boring.'

Veronica smiled. 'How about one of each?'

The girls cheered. Pie had a way of making people happy. Even — especially, maybe — pregnant teenagers.

'Any consensus on topic today?' Larissa asked the group.

'Since someone is here who used to live here, can we just ask her questions?'

Larissa looked at Veronica. 'Okay with an impromptu Q&A?'

'Ask away,' Veronica told the girls. 'Just say your name first so I can get to know who's who.' She glanced around, glad she didn't know the name of the girl Penelope had her hopes pinned on.

'I'm Allison. Did you regret giving up your baby?' a girl with poker-straight blonde hair asked.

No easy pitches here, Veronica realized. 'To be very honest, no, Allison. I had a total lack of support. From my family, from the baby's father. I was alone. And very scared. Giving up the baby felt like the right thing to do.'

'Did the kid ever try to find you?' another girl asked. 'Oh, I'm Kim.'

'Yes,' Veronica said. 'Very recently, too. I'd left my contact information with the adoption agency and the Maine State Adoption Reunion Registry.'

'It must be weird when the kid you think you'll never see again suddenly comes back into your life,' another girl said.

'It brings up a lot of old memories, that's for sure.'

'Remember that blonde chick who came by a couple of weeks ago? She was trying to decide if she wanted to contact her birth mother,' Kim said to another girl who had serious attitude in her blue eyes. She looked angry and conflicted, and Veronica made a mental note to be available to talk to her during the pie-tasting. Some girls needed to ease into asking the questions they most wanted answers to. 'The one who said she was born here in the parking lot?'

Veronica froze. They were talking about Bea. No doubt about it. Bea had said she'd come here.

'I felt bad for her,' Allison said.

'Oh my God, Jen, remember how you threw your turkey sandwich at her for making Kim cry?'

'Not my proudest moment, but I was so pissed at her for not knowing how she felt. How could you not know how you feel? She shouldn't have come here.'

It killed Veronica to think of Bea, who seemed not to have a mean bone in her body, getting yelled at it, getting a sandwich thrown at her. Bea must have felt awful.

'Everything is a learning opportunity,' Larissa said.

'I'm going to be very, very honest,' Veronica said. 'I think that girl you're talking about is my birth daughter. Long blonde hair? Brown eyes? Tall?'

'Oh my God, yes,' Jen said.

Veronica nodded. 'We did finally meet, and I'm so glad.'

'I like knowing that someday my baby will try to find me,' Kim said. 'I know you don't, Jen, but twenty years from now you might feel totally differently.'

'Doubt it,' Jen said. She turned to Veronica. 'So what now? You're suddenly all mother—daughter?'

'We're working on just getting to know each other.'

Jen glanced around at the other girls, then back at Veronica. 'Can I ask you questions about your family? My mother hates my guts for embarrassing her. Apparently, everyone knows and she had to quit her country club.'

'My family wasn't supportive. Some families are. I had friends here whose mother and fathers would visit them a few times a week. It made me feel awful, but it made me want to find my own happiness, you know?'

'So what did you do?'

'I decided what I wanted for myself. To travel, see the country.'

'I want to move to California. The second I'm eighteen, I'm out of Maine,' Jen said.

'What about the father?' Allison asked. 'Is he still in the picture?'

'No,' Veronica said. 'He told me it couldn't possibly be his baby. And I never saw him again. I think he was scared to death and used his fear to turn on me.'

'God,' Kim said, glancing at a girl with long brown hair who looked to be around five or six months pregnant. 'That's like Jordan, Lizzie.'

'Thanks for reminding me,' Lizzie said. 'I'm trying to totally forget he ever existed.'

'Did you?' Jen asked Veronica. 'Forget he existed?'

'No. But I tried also.' She glanced at Lizzie. 'It got better, though. I pushed a lot of it out my mind, willed myself to forget. But I'll tell you something. It's important to deal with your feelings, let them out, cry if you feel like crying, ask questions if you have them. If I could go back and change something, you know what it would be?'

They all stared at her.

'I would have opened up more to people. Told them what I'd been through. Talked about it. I wouldn't have hidden it.

I wouldn't have thought it was something to be ashamed of. I would have talked about how scary it all was.'

'Well Jen never shuts up,' Kim said, 'so she won't have that problem.'

Jen threw her squeezy ball at Kim, and everyone laughed.

The girls continued to ask questions and Veronica was as honest as she could be without instilling any real fear or worry. She liked being here, liked listening, liked talking to them.

'You were wonderful,' Larissa said as she walked Veronica to the kitchen, where she would bake three pies and give a lesson to whomever wanted to learn the fine art of pie crusts.

'Thank you. I used to be one of them. So it was easy.' As she was about to go into the kitchen, she turned back. 'Oh, Larissa. I heard there was a reporter writing an article on Hope Home. If you have her contact info, I'd like to talk to her.'

I would have opened up more to people. Told them what I'd been through. Talked about it. I wouldn't have hidden it.

Now she'd take her own advice.

The moment Veronica arrived home, she called the reporter, Gemma Hendricks, who wanted to talk to her right away. They'd be meeting at her house in a few hours. Veronica headed into her living room to tidy up for the interview, picking up the newspaper she'd dropped on the coffee table this morning. She hadn't gotten to it yet, and now she saw there was a long article about the movie set on the front page and how, thanks to the crew, business was booming in town, from the inns and hotels to the restaurants and shops. A photo of Colin Firth in a tux appeared with the caption: *Everyone's waiting for the English actor to make an appearance!*

Huh. Not too long ago, Veronica would have tossed off a 'Yeah, especially me!' at that caption. But her fantasy man had changed. He wasn't a movie star, playing roles that made her yearn for what she missed so terribly. Like Colin Firth himself, her fantasy man was someone very real, flesh and blood, capable of hurting her.

A risk she'd take.

She took a last look at Colin Firth's gorgeous face, those intelligent, warm brown eyes, the tousle of dark hair, but another gorgeous face nudged him out of her mind. Nick's.

Suddenly, out of nowhere, she though of cherries. Cherries, with their beautiful deep red colour, their burst of sweet and tart flavour, the way they'd always reminded her of tiny hearts, especially when there were two on a stem.

And even though she'd made quite a few pies at Hope Home this morning, she longed to go to the farmers' market for a pound of the fruit and spend some time in the kitchen making a cherry pie.

Henceforth to be known as a Colin Firth Pie.

All this time, she couldn't make herself a Colin Firth Pie because her heart had been blocked. By fear. Fear of letting herself love. And if you feared love, all the Amore Pies in the world wouldn't help bring love into your life. First, you'd have to make yourself a Colin Firth Pie. And to make a Colin Firth Pie, you'd need a clear head and a warm, willing heart.

Veronica could check both of those off her list of ingredients.

Chapter 21
Gemma

Late Tuesday night, close to midnight, Gemma left Veronica Russo's house with a bag containing two boxed pies, one fudge and one Key lime. The streets were still teeming with Fourth of July tourists even though the Fourth had come and gone, the decks of restaurants jutting out on piers still lit up and full of people. She couldn't wait to get back to the inn and finish her article. Veronica's story, all she'd shared, had moved Gemma to the point of tears more than once. Now, her article would come a beautiful full circle.

She crept into the inn, worried about waking anyone up, but the newlyweds in the Osprey Room were right behind her, waving an unopened bottle of champagne and asking Gemma if she thought Isabel would mind if they raided the refrigerator for some of that incredible pie she always seemed to have. The couple were clueless, but sweet, so Gemma gave them the fudge pie Veronica had sent her home with, keeping the Key lime Confidence Pie for herself.

As she headed upstairs and passed Bea's door, she was so tempted to knock and tell Bea everything Veronica had said, but of course, she wouldn't. *All these years, twenty-two years, I thought I was running away from my past. I thought I'd come back to Boothbay Harbor to face that past. But it turns out my past — the pregnancy, reactions from my family, from the baby's father — all that paled in comparison to what I was really running from: how much I loved that baby girl I held for two minutes against my chest. How much I love her now, even though I barely know her. You can love someone without knowing them much, did you know that? I fought against it all these years. But not any more. Regardless of whether my daughter wants me in her life or not, I'll always love her.*

Maybe that was what maternal instincts were all about, Gemma thought, unsettled (in a good way) by all Veronica had told her. She slipped on her noise-cancelling headphones to block out the laughter coming from the newlyweds' room and got to work, her fingers flying over the keyboard of her laptop as she worked on the long middle of her article, the personal stories. A birth mother reuniting with the daughter she'd given up for adoption. A teenage girl determined her baby be raised by a wealthy couple, only to discover that money alone wouldn't satisfy her — only a loving heart. A birth mother, now married with children, who'd never told her husband of the baby she'd given up for adoption seventeen years earlier. Gemma wrote until her eyes started to water.

At just after two in the morning, the article was done. She sat back, expecting to feel sad, bereft that it was over, but all she felt was proud — she had never been so sure that she was doing what she was born to do.

One of the women she'd interviewed, a prospective adoptive mother, had used exactly that phrase. *I feel like I was born to be a mother, but I'm not sure it'll ever happen . . .*

You're so lucky, she remembered another interviewee, fifteen-year-old Hope Home resident Chloe Martin, saying to her when Gemma had revealed that she was pregnant.

I am lucky, she knew. She was having a baby. And when she arrived home, she'd surprise Alexander by suggesting they go check out cribs and strollers and lullaby-playing mobiles. She'd throw herself into learning to become a mother the way she'd thrown herself into researching her article for Hope Home. Then she'd rework her résumé and send it out to a fresh batch of news organizations. She'd find a job eventually. And together, she and Alexander would make it all work.

She'd be the mother she wanted to be.

In the morning, with the sun shining bright into her window, Gemma woke up from a strange dream in which she couldn't get her baby out of a sling on her chest, but the baby wasn't an infant; she had a woman's face and looked scarily like

Gemma's mother. She sat up, trying to shake the remnants of the dream from her memory. That wasn't one she wanted to look up in the dream dictionary.

Gemma supposed it meant she still worried she'd be like her mother. Or that she was carrying her worries about being a good mom and it was all tied in to her own feelings about her own childhood. Maybe a lot of both, she knew.

She lifted up her pyjama top and put her hands on her belly, only slightly beginning to round. 'Hey, little one,' she said, tears stinging her eyes. 'If you're listening, I want you to know that I will love you. The minute I meet you, I'll love you. How could I not? That is not even a question. I think I'll feel like Veronica Russo does – that I always loved you. Even if I didn't know it.'

A note was slipped under her door, and Gemma got out of bed to pick it up.

Today's breakfast special is crêpes – chocolate and/or strawberry! xo Bea

Bea was such a sweetheart. Right now, she knew Bea was unsure how much more she'd get to know Veronica, what she and her birth mother were to each other, how – and whether – to forge a relationship in the future. But with Bea's big heart and how she'd lost her other family, and Veronica's strength of hope, Gemma had a good feeling they'd work it out.

She reached over to her dresser for her laptop and proofread her article, just under three thousand words, then proofed it again, then sent it by email to Claire at the *Boothbay Regional Gazette.*

You're done, your last hurrah. And I'm damned proud of you.

She wasn't in the mood to eat breakfast with her noisy fellow guests, so she skipped the crêpes and headed out to the Harbour View coffee shop for a decaf iced mocha and a scone, then took a long walk around the pretty side streets of the harbour. She'd miss this place. She'd have to go home by week's end; but that didn't mean she couldn't spend her remaining time hunting down when Colin Firth would arrive and securing an interview. There was talk that he was coming to town on Saturday to film his scenes, but there'd been rumours before and not a sign of him. Now, with the article finished, Gemma could put all her investigative energy into scoring that interview.

As she walked down Meadow Lane, she watched a father push his toddler on a tyre swing hung on an old oak tree in the front yard of their house, and she smiled at them, imagining Alexander doing the same thing. This was Alexander's dream, she realized, to be doing exactly that.

Her head and heart a bit more settled, Gemma was about to turn back to the inn to call Alexander and let him know she'd sent in her article when she noticed the cutest house a few doors down, a yellow 'craftsman' cottage with a narrow deck running the length of the second storey and a quaint porch with a rocking chair, and between the sweet scene with the tyre swing and that rocking chair, Gemma could almost see herself sitting on that porch, rocking her baby back and forth. Becoming someone new, someone she didn't know but could grow into.

She touched her hands to her belly. Exactly a week ago, she'd been on a hospital cot, wondering if it was over before it had begun for her, before her baby had had a chance to begin.

She took a picture of the house, making sure to get in the deck and the porch, and texted it to Alexander: *Maybe you could find something like this for the three of us in Dobbs Ferry. A porch with a swing is a must. xxG*

In a few minutes he texted back: *I'm thrilled, but are you telling me that my meddling mother actually changed your mind? Sorry she got on to you. She told me about it, and I told her she had to back off.*

Wasn't your mother. It was me. I want to do the right thing for us, for the three of us. I love you, G.

'And I love you too, sweet pea,' she whispered to her belly.

At 11 p.m., Gemma dragged herself back to the inn. She'd talked to at least twenty-five crew members at the film set, some saying Colin Firth would arrive Saturday but had a packed schedule and couldn't talk to the press, others saying he wasn't due till early next week — and wouldn't be talking to the press. She'd made at least a hundred phone calls — to his talent agency, to the movie studio — consulting everyone from assistants to executives to get information. She'd even gotten as far as his manager's assistant's assistant, who'd said something non-committal about schedule changes and she was so sorry but she really couldn't pin down a date for his arrival in Boothbay Harbor.

Grrr. Gemma sat on her bed, tapping her pencil on her notebook. This is so frustrating, she thought, and—

Her stomach rumbled, and for a second Gemma froze, pressing her hand to her belly. Was that her first flutter? Was that the baby? She grabbed her *Your Pregnancy This Week* book, but a quick scan of a sidebar said not to expect to feel the baby move until the eighteenth to twentieth week.

Guess that wasn't you, sweet pea, she told her belly.

Her stomach rumbled again, and Gemma realized she was starving. She'd been so busy stalking the film crew for news of Colin Firth and making fruitless phone calls that she'd forgotten to eat dinner. Luckily she still had lots of Veronica Russo's pie left.

'Let's go get some Key lime,' she said to her stomach, as though it were perfectly normal to chat away with your belly.

Maybe it was.

By ten o'clock the next morning, Gemma still hadn't called Alexander to tell him she'd finished the article, that she was coming home . . . soon. She lay on her bed, her hands on her stomach. She'd had breakfast with June, and let it all come out, and even June had said that, for all she knew,

Gemma could love suburban life. After all, she loved Boothbay Harbor, a tiny town.

But Boothbay Harbor was different. Boothbay Harbor had always been a saving grace, a harbour in itself to Gemma, the place her father had taken her for a month every summer after her parents' divorce. She'd always been happy in Boothbay, the vibrant coastal town a constant ray of sunshine. She had friends here, wonderful memories. And she loved the old wooden piers and boats in the bay, the cobblestone and brick streets lined with one-of-a-kind shops and every imaginable cuisine. She'd talk to Alexander about vacationing here next summer. Maybe every summer.

Her email pinged, and Gemma grabbed it, hoping it was Claire to say she loved the article and had another story for her — not that Gemma would do that to Alexander, as much as she'd want to.

It *was* Claire. *Gemma, your piece was beyond fabulous! My boss loved it. He wants you on staff — that's how impressed he was. I'm prepared to offer you a full-time job as a senior reporter covering human interest, plus your own column, with full understanding that you will take maternity beginning late December . . .*

Gemma burst into tears. A job offer. One she couldn't accept.

She imagined herself living here in this sweet small town she adored, working on stories like Hope Home, having her own Sunday column. Spending time with old summer friends who'd blossom into everyday friends. Making new friends, good friends, like Bea. Watching her belly grow, month by month, and spending weekends decorating the nursery in a house like that old yellow craftsman, a house she could live in, breathe in, become a mother in. Coming home after work to Alexander, where they'd learn to be parents together.

Living three hundred miles away from her mother-in-law. For all that, she'd leave New York City in a heartbeat.

The offer was almost cruel, considering she couldn't call Claire and scream, 'YES!' at the top of her lungs, which was what she wanted to do. So instead she called Alexander. 'Claire – knowing I'm pregnant – offered me a full-time job as a senior reporter with my own Sunday column. At a decent salary too – well, not by New York standards, of course. I wish I could take the job. Why can't any of the New York City papers I sent my résumé and clips to see in me what she sees?'

'Gemma, you're a great reporter and a great writer. Between the economy and newspapers shutting down, you're caught in the crossfire. But you had a great last assignment, and now you'll come home and embrace your new life.'

'I know, I know,' she said. 'Hey, how about you quit your job, and we move here to Boothbay Harbor and I take the job at the *Gazette*?' She couldn't even believe she'd said it aloud.

Silence. 'Honey . . .' he said, his voice gentle. 'I make three times the salary they're offering you.'

'I know.' Still, it was nice to fantasize about.

'And listen, Gem, I've been thinking. If it's Dobbs Ferry

in particular that bothers you, we don't have to move so close to my family.'

That was something, at least. 'I guess that would help.' But she knew he was thinking one town over, not a county away. 'I'll drive down Saturday morning, okay?' she said, unable to keep the tears out of her voice. 'I have some great people to say goodbye to up here.'

'I'll see you Saturday night, then. Listen sweetheart, you're going to love your new life. It's our next step.'

Gemma didn't quite believe it just now, but she was determined to try.

Chapter 22
Bea

Bea stood in front of 26 Birch Lane in Wiscasset, a fifteen-minute drive from Boothbay Harbor, her finger poised to ring the doorbell. In moments she would meet Timothy Macintosh, her biological father. She closed her eyes for a second and summoned up the advice Patrick had given her today at lunch – to remember that Timothy had called her back, invited her to his home. Timothy had sounded like a kind enough person on the phone, if a bit hesitant. He'd explained that half of him truly had believed he wasn't the father of Veronica Russo's baby, while the other half had worried all these years that he was. That had been weighing on him a long, long time, and he wanted to face the truth once and for all. He'd been terrible to Veronica, and really, had Timothy reacted differently, Veronica might have kept

Bea. Married Timothy. Bea might have been raised right here in town with her biological parents.

She touched the gold locket at her neck, picturing her mother's sweet face, her father's crooked smile. Life had happened as it had. And she was ready to take the future as it came.

She rang the bell.

There was a simultaneous gasp when the door opened. He was twenty-two years older than the boy in the photograph, but he looked so much like her. Very tall, with thick, wavy blond hair. His eyes were hazel, not brown like hers, but there was something so similar about their faces. The shape maybe. Something in the expression, the way they smiled.

'I don't think you'll need that DNA test after all,' the blonde woman standing slightly behind him said, her voice full of wonder.

Timothy had his hand over his mouth. 'It's very nice to meet you,' he finally said, holding the door open for her to step in. He squeezed his eyes shut and shook his head as though he couldn't believe what he was seeing. 'I need to get myself together here,' he said. He cleared his throat and attempted to smile. 'This is my wife, Beth. Our daughter is out with friends, but maybe you can meet her another time, after we've sat down with her to tell her about you, of course.'

Bea smiled at him, this man who looked so much like her. Her stomach flipped over – in a good way. A half-sister. I have a sister, she thought, a burst of joy fluttering in her heart. 'I'd like that,' she told him.

Bea had to leave the Macintoshes at four, since she had to meet Maddy for their tutoring appointment at five. Yesterday Tyler had called to switch tutoring days from Wednesday to Thursday, since their grandparents had come to visit, but keeping the first meeting with Timothy to an hour and a half seemed about right anyway. Not too much too soon. Both Timothy and Beth were very formal and awkward with Bea, but she'd chalked that up to nerves. They were kind, bending over backwards to share stories about Timothy's family, whose ancestors came from Scotland, with Beth filling in titbits that Timothy couldn't remember. Bea jotted down what Timothy had said about his family's medical history, an uncle with agoraphobia, a grandmother who'd died of lung cancer, a bit of depression here and there, but overall strong, hearty folk. Timothy's mother had been a nurse, and his father in construction, like Bea's own father, and both Macintoshes seemed to love hearing about Bea's childhood. Timothy and Beth had been married for seventeen years, and given how they'd sat with their arms entwined the majority of their afternoon with Bea, it appeared they were very close, that Beth was something of a rock for him. They were planning to tell their daughter about Bea that night, and Timothy promised he'd call about getting together again in the future.

She left Wiscasset with a lightened heart and drove back to Boothbay Harbor, but once again Maddy was late for their tutoring session. Bea was right on time at five o'clock, but the crew trailer, where they'd arranged to meet this time instead of the library, was empty. The plan had been to meet up there and then go find a quiet spot a good distance away, under a shady tree, and talk more about the essay question for *To Kill a Mockingbird*. Bea had re-read the first half of the novel since last week and found so many beautiful lines and passages that reminded her of the quote Maddy had chosen to write about. The reading, the tutoring – all of it made Bea surer than ever that she was meant to be a teacher.

There weren't too many people hanging out by the crew trailers; a crowd was lined up by the craft-services tent. Maddy, though, was nowhere to be found. After their terrific session the other day, Bea was sure she wouldn't try to ditch her tutoring.

Bea went outside and glanced around. No sign of Maddy.

Ah, wait. A flash of her long dark hair and unmistakable laughter came from in front of one of the trailers, where it was parked by a fence. What was she doing squished over there? Bea headed over and heard more giggling. Maddy was with a boy, clearly. And her make-out session was about to be interrupted for her tutoring session.

'Maddy, you're—'

She wasn't with a boy. She was with a man.

Patrick Ool.

'What the—' Bea began, almost unable to believe what she was seeing.

Patrick's face turned red. He jumped away from Maddy, and his expression changed as though he'd already formed the lie he was about to spew.

'She's sixteen,' Bea screamed at him.

He looked *faux*-shocked. 'What? She told me she was nineteen.'

'It's true, I did,' Maddy said.

Bea felt sick to her stomach. She shot him a look of disgust, then turned to Maddy. 'Maddy, it's time for our session. Let's go. Now. And you,' she said to Patrick, 'you can go to hell.'

'I thought she was nineteen!' he said. 'And sorry, Bea, but maybe if you weren't such a prude. I mean, how many times have we gone out now?'

Bea stopped, turned around and punched Patrick Ool in the stomach as hard as she could.

She heard Maddy gasp and Patrick mutter, 'Crazy bitch' before she grabbed Maddy's hand and marched her away.

'That "prude" comment, does that mean you guys were seeing each other?' Maddy asked, glancing sheepishly at Bea as they headed past the barricades to a quiet area that Bea had picked out.

'*Were*, yeah.'

'Sorry,' she said. 'I didn't know.'

Bea shook her head in disgust. 'You told him you're nine-teen?'

'He asked how old I was, so I lied. He said, "Yeah right," though. I'm really sorry, Bea.'

Bea could almost feel steam coming out of her ears. She stopped and turned away from Maddy, giving herself a minute to calm down. Even if Patrick the prick had believed she was nineteen, he knew she was Tyler's sister. And he obviously had it in for the guy. She kicked at a rock, then resumed walking. 'And he started making out with you anyway. Scum. Maddy, you have to be careful of men like that. Especially on film sets. Stick to boys your own age, okay? Please?'

'Okay, okay,' she said with a shy smile, and Bea knew Maddy truly felt bad about what had happened with Patrick. 'My brother lectures me about that all the time. I actually wish I'd listened to him for once.'

Bea yanked the ends of Maddy's hair playfully. 'Your brother seems to care about you a lot, Maddy. Appreciate it. I have no one.'

'Why not?'

'Because sometimes I'm an idiot about who I choose to spend my time with. Your brother told me Patrick was a womanizing jerk, and I didn't believe him.'

'Tyler never lies. It's pathological. I could have told you that.'

Bea had a feeling that Tyler Echols hadn't hit up Maddy's birth mother for money. Patrick must have lied about that to make sure Bea didn't listen to Tyler's assessment of him. Patrick had gone out of his way to undermine Tyler – probably because Tyler *wasn't* a jerk.

Bea stopped under a shady tree and spread out the blanket she'd brought in her tote bag. 'Sit,' she said to Maddy. 'Let's get cracking. We'll forget about bad men and focus on good men. Like Atticus Finch.'

While Maddy took for ever to get out her book and notebook, all Bea could think about was how blind she'd been. Granted, Tyler hadn't always been easy to like – or listen to. But she'd been wrong about him. And she was glad for it.

The second tutoring session went as well as the first. Maddy had read the chapters, and was able to discuss the text and relate two passages back to the essay quote on her own. With Bea's nudging, she had found three more in the first six chapters alone. Bea loved this – prompting Maddy with careful questions that would lead her to make connections, and watching her face light up. Maddy had progressed from calling the book *To Kill a Boring Bird* to proudly explaining what she thought the real title meant.

'Hey.'

Maddy couldn't close her book fast enough at the sight of her brother. Bea was hoping that by their next session Maddy would be so into the book she'd want to keep talking about it.

'Can we talk privately for a minute?' Bea asked him.

'Don't tell me you're quitting,' Tyler said. 'She talked non-stop on the way over earlier about Scout and Jem and Atticus and Boo.'

Bea smiled. 'Nope, not quitting.' As Maddy's earphones went in, Bea led Tyler several feet away and relayed the sorry story about coming upon Patrick kissing Maddy, and that he'd sworn up and down that Maddy had told him she was nineteen.

Tyler's cheeks turned bright red and he let out a string of muttered swear words.

'I owe you an apology, Tyler. He's pure scum and I didn't see it. How are people such effortless liars?'

'Years of being around certain kinds of actors have rubbed off on the jerk. I was an idiot for bringing Maddy here. But it's not often we're filming in her back yard, so I wanted to do something for her to cheer her up.'

'Because of how upset she's been over what happened with her birth mother?'

He nodded.

'I owe you another apology. Patrick told me I should be wary of you because you'd hit up your sister's birth mother for money. He said he overheard you talking to another PA.'

'What an ass,' he said, shaking his head. 'It was the other way around. Her birth mother tapped *me* for money. I said I didn't have any to give, which was true. Maddy wrote to her again six months ago, but the letter came back marked "return to sender", no one there. Maybe that's for the best, for Maddy.'

'Yeah, it probably is. I'm glad she has you. I wish I had an older brother looking out for me.'

'*I've* been looking out for you,' Tyler said, his expression a mixture of serious, tender and full of . . . *liking*. 'You just didn't know it.'

She smiled. 'Guess so.'

'Can you keep an eye on Maddy for a few minutes? I'm going to go have a talk with Patrick. And by talk, I mean I'm going to punch his lights out.'

'Before you get yourself fired, rest assured I already punched him in the stomach.'

'I'll make sure to aim higher, then. His nose maybe. Or much lower, perhaps, with a solid kick.'

Bea laughed, and for a second they were both silent.

'So maybe you'll have dinner with us tonight?' he asked.

'I thought you didn't like me.'

'Well you thought wrong, again.' He smiled at her, maybe for the first time since she'd known him.

For a minute there, over sesame chicken and fried dumplings, Bea thought Maddy might bolt out of the restaurant.

'You know what happens when you mess with men like Patrick Tool?' Tyler had said, pointing a chopstick at his sister. 'When you go too far with any guy? You can end up pregnant, Maddy. And then you'll have some very unfun choices to make.'

'Not listening,' Maddy said, covering her ears.

He pulled her hands away. 'I'm dead serious,' he said. 'Denise was fifteen when you were born.'

'Okay,' she snapped. 'I get it. It was just *kissing*.'

'And you were surrounded by trailers and inns. Very easy access to closed doors.'

'Can I eat my dumplings before they get cold?' Maddy shouted.

'When I know you're listening,' he said. 'Really listening.'

'God, I am. I hear you.'

Bea sent Tyler a smile across the booth. She didn't know Maddy very well, but Bea would put money on the odds that she was listening.

They tried to split the last dumpling in three, which sent it flying off the table and made Maddy laugh. By the time they were cracking open their fortune cookies, Bea wished they'd just sat down, so that she could spend another hour with these two. Tyler was smart and funny and serious and kind, and Maddy was on the immature side, but had a lovable centre.

Bea read her fortune: 'You can never be certain of success, but you can be certain of failure if you never try.'

Wasn't that the truth? Bea slipped it in her pocket.

'What did you get?' she asked Maddy.

'"A smile is your personal welcome mat."' Maddy rolled

her eyes and grinned like a maniac. 'How's that?' She took a nibble of her cookie. 'What's yours say, Tyler?'

Tyler cracked his open and pulled out the fortune. '"An inch of time is an inch of gold."' He raised an eyebrow, then popped half the cookie in his mouth.

'Let's ask for new fortunes,' Maddy said. 'Only Bea got a good one.'

'You get what you get and you don't get upset,' Tyler sing-songed, tapping Maddy's hand with her unused chopstick. 'Remember how Dad always used to say that?'

The famous eye-roll was back. 'He still does. And anyway, doesn't that totally contradict Bea's good fortune? If what you get sucks, you should get upset.'

Bea laughed. With a little more age and wisdom, Maddy would be just fine.

When they had walked back to Main Street, where Tyler's car was parked, Maddy got in and put in her earphones.

'Can I drop you home?' he asked.

'Nah, the inn's just up the hill.'

He glanced up the twisty road, then back at Bea. 'So maybe we could do something sometime?'

'Definitely.'

He smiled. 'I'll call you tomorrow then.'

He squeezed her hand and looked at her, then got in. As Bea headed up Harbour Hill Road, she glanced back, watching until the tail lights were out of view. She had no idea where she'd be living in a couple of weeks. And Tyler would be travelling the world, working on films. But that didn't mean they couldn't be friends. At least, just to start with.

On her way to the inn, Bea pulled out her phone and called Veronica.

'Would you like to get together soon? This past week, I was thinking that I wasn't sure I had anything left to ask you, anything more to tell you, but I was . . . running a bit scared, I think. Overwhelmed. And it turns out I have a lot to tell you.'

'Oh, I know all about that,' Veronica said. 'And I have a lot to tell you too. How about tomorrow night at seven at my house? I'll make you lasagne and you can help me bake a pie.'

'I'll be there,' Bea said, thinking that Cora Crane would like Veronica Russo a lot.

Chapter 23
Veronica

It was so strange to be holding her order pad, wearing her typical uniform of jeans, white button-down shirt and Best Little Diner in Boothbay apron, when there were three large cameras, microphones and huge lights in every direction inside the diner. So many people stood on the sidelines. Veronica glanced out the window at the crowd of people behind a barricade across the street and was startled to see that pain in the neck Hugh Fledge, waving his arms at her over his head like a lunatic and blowing a kiss at her with a huge goofy smile. She hoped he was as harmless as he seemed — a pest who wouldn't give up but didn't seem . . . unhinged. She'd talk to Nick about what she could do to get Fledge off her back.

For this scene, Veronica was the counter waitress. The new second assistant director, Joe Something (apparently Patrick

Ool had been reassigned to Equipment and wouldn't be working with the extras; rumour had it he'd been caught canoodling with a minor), told her she had wisdom, kindness and Maine in her face, and he wanted her front and centre.

Veronica wondered about the rumours about Patrick and worried for Bea, but perhaps it was part of all that Bea wanted to tell her. That and how her meeting with Timothy had gone.

I could never stop caring about her, no matter how deep I buried my feelings, Veronica realized as Joe Something went over the blocking — where actors stood for the scene — with one of the actresses.

The assistant director blew a whistle that he wore around his neck, which was his annoying way of getting everyone's attention. Good, time to shoot — not that Colin Firth was filming today. Rumour had it that he was coming to town tomorrow, but if Veronica had a penny for every time . . . And besides, the fact that she wanted to get this scene over with so she could go to Gray's Grocery and buy the ingredients for lasagne told her that her heart wasn't so much in being an extra any more. Bea was coming to dinner tonight; her heart was in that.

Each table in the diner was full of extras, and the counter was half full; Veronica got a good chuckle at the 'typical Maine diner customer'. There was the crusty old man reading a newspaper and having the fried haddock and chips. Three teenage girls who looked like they stepped out of an L.L.Bean catalogue. The reserved middle-aged woman in twinset and pearls, whose instructions were to dab her lips twice while eating her apple pie – one of Veronica's. A dad and his young son, with an adult- and a child-size fishing pole leaning against the wall next to them. Two twentysomething hipster types with a map of Maine spread out in front of them. And Veronica behind the counter with her coffee pot.

All her counter needed was Colin Firth. She got her fix of seeing his handsome face by watching his films; over the past two weeks, she'd seen three more of his movies – and had watched *Love Actually* twice more since it made her so damned happy.

And so damned sappy. Veronica Russo, sappy. That was a wonder.

But forget Mr Darcy. He was a character, an idea. A good idea, but still an idea. And Colin Firth, despite how much Veronica loved him, was an actor. Nick DeMarco, on the other hand, was six feet and two inches of reality, and she was ready for him. When she'd made her Colin Firth Pie the other night, it wasn't Mr Darcy she'd been thinking about as she stirred her cherries and sugar and vanilla. And it wasn't Colin Firth she'd imagined as she'd eaten every last bite of the first slice. She'd only thought of Nick.

The actors got into place, and Veronica gave the set her full attention. In this scene, the female lead and her fiancé were having an argument that involved her dumping a lobster roll on his head and storming out. They'd rehearsed the scene with an empty plate four times, and had shot it twice today with the real thing, which meant hour-long breaks to wash the lobster bits out of Christopher Cade's hair and change his shirt. Apparently, Wardrobe had thirty of the same blue dress shirt at the ready.

As they waited for the sound guy to attend to whatever was causing the problem, Veronica relaxed behind the counter and decided that after dinner tonight she'd teach Bea how to make one of her Happiness Pies. One of her own favourites: fudge.

Veronica had the lasagne in the oven and was mincing garlic for the Italian bread when her phone rang. Please don't be Bea cancelling, she prayed.

'I'm so bursting with happiness I can hardly speak,' Penelope said. 'Lizzie – the girl I told you about, our prospective birth mother – said yes to us! Thank you for all you did for me, Veronica. I won't ever forget it.'

'I'm so happy for you, Penelope,' she said, her own heart even fuller at the thought of Penelope and Lizzie each finding what she needed in the other.

When the phone rang again a few minutes later, Veronica worried that she'd gotten lucky with the last call, which meant this call would be bad news.

But it was Beth Macintosh. 'I wanted to apologize to you for how I acted,' she said. 'Timothy had always been torn up about whether or not he'd fathered your child, but ever since he saw you through the diner window several months ago, it's all he'd talk about. Did I? Was I? What if? It got to the point where our marriage was strained. Then one day, friends of mine in town mentioned your name — not even knowing your connection to Timothy — and your elixir pies, and I thought I'd kill two birds with one stone, as they say.'

'So maybe the pie worked in a roundabout way, after all,' Veronica said.

Beth was quiet for a second, but then laughed. 'I guess I owe you fifteen bucks.'

'That one's on me.'

'Thank you,' Beth said. 'Goodbye — for now, anyway,' she added.

Veronica smiled.

Over Veronica's delicious — if she did say so herself — lasagne, garlic bread and a crisp green salad, Bea told Veronica about meeting Timothy and Beth.

'It was a bit awkward,' Bea said, lifting up a gooey forkful of lasagne. 'I think he's still uncomfortable with the whole thing, but Beth said they'd tell their daughter about me and they'd like to get together again.'

'I'm glad you found him. You've settled something, and given him an answer to a question he couldn't let go of.'

Bea lifted her glass of iced tea and clinked Veronica's.

As they ate, Veronica told Bea that she'd sat down to an interview with Gemma Hendricks and poured out her life story, and Bea told Veronica all about Patrick Ool and why he'd gotten reassigned to Equipment.

'Good Lord,' Veronica said, shocked to hear the news. 'You just can't tell with some people. I never would have pegged him for a creep.'

Bea smiled and reached for a piece of garlic bread. 'That makes me feel better, because neither did I.'

'So . . . are you and Tyler dating now, if I can ask?'

'Of course you can ask. But I'm over dating for the moment. I suddenly like him, that's all I know. Considering I hated his guts a week ago, I think I'll just take this one super-slow. The cast and crew are heading to London to shoot for a week. And sometime soon, I guess I'll be heading back to Boston to look for teaching jobs.'

Oh. Veronica should have known she'd be heading back to Boston. But she'd figured Bea would stick around for the summer at least. 'You have family there?'

'There's no one, actually. Just me.'

Spit it out, Veronica told herself. Just say it. 'And me,' she finally dared to say.

Bea looked at her, her head tilted to one side with a shy smile. 'And you.'

Maybe that was too much for Veronica to have said. She changed the subject. 'You're so lucky you know what you want to do. I never really knew. Sometimes I think about opening up my own little pie diner. But it's just that – a dream.'

'A diner of pies? That sounds incredible. And since your pie is the best anyone's ever had, you should open your own place. Who wouldn't swarm a pie diner all day?'

Veronica did have a lot of money socked away. Maybe she'd look into it. Huh – Veronica Russo, business owner. Owning her own place instead of serving. Staking her claim. She liked the sound of that.

Bea took a bite of lasagne. 'I thought maybe you wanted to be an actress or involved with films. Because you became an extra.'

'Oh, I only did that to get a glimpse of Mr Darcy in the flesh. Colin Firth. He's my secret heartthrob.'

Bea gasped. 'He was my mother's favourite actor too!' She looked at Veronica for a long moment, as if absorbing that. 'She loved his accent. I do too.' She did an imitation of him that Veronica recognized from *Bridget Jones's Diary*. 'You know what's funny? Tyler ended up being a bit like Mr Darcy. I thought he was the biggest jerk. Turns out he's pretty wonderful.'

'I think I might have a Mr Darcy too,' Veronica said, unable to hide her smile. 'He was never a jerk, though – he's just all the good things about Darcy. Honest and honourable, trustworthy, a man of conviction. And drop-dead gorgeous. And you know what, Bea? I'm ready to get back to my life. I'll make tomorrow my last day as an extra and spend tomorrow night scouting out possible sites in town for a pie diner. There's a place on Main I noticed the other day. It needs work, but just standing there, I could see my blackboard of ten different kinds of pies, ordinaries and elixirs. I have quite a bit of research to do into what it takes to open up shop, but I can't wait to dive in.'

My last day as an extra. Was she really going to make Friday her last day, when Colin Firth was supposed to show up on Saturday? Yes. Because, as much as she wanted to see him in the flesh, she'd already found what she'd been looking for all along: her heart to blast wide open, finally. And it had.

Bea smiled. 'I'll be first in line at that pie diner.'

'So . . . maybe you could apply for teaching jobs up here in Maine,' Veronica said.

From the smile Bea gave her, the open invitation to Veronica's life had been received. 'You mean just stay in Maine?'

'Sure. You have a place to live. A job in the mean time. And you know that my door is always open.'

Bea came around the table and hugged Veronica, who hugged her back. They lingered that way, neither wanting to pull away too fast. 'Maybe I will stay, then.'

'Yoo hoo, everyone,' a man's sing-song voice called from outside, 'Colin Firth just passed me on the street!'

'What the heck?' Veronica said, peering out the window. There was someone out there, in the driveway. A tall, skinny man holding a can stood at the far end of the driveway. She headed to the living-room window for a closer look and saw it was Hugh Fledge.

He'd been behind all the fake Colin Firth sightings? Sending people racing around hoping to get a glimpse of the actor? What a pest!

He shook the can in his hand and aimed it at the far end of her driveway. Oh, no. That wasn't beer. It was spray paint. She was about to run out and confront him, then realized she could bring in the heavy hitters, a.k.a. the police. She grabbed her phone and called Nick.

'That drunken fool who keeps asking me out – Hugh Fledge – is waving a can of what looks like spray paint on my driveway.'

'I'll be right there,' Nick said. 'I'm patrolling near by. Wait for me – don't confront him.'

But Fledge was now spraying on her driveway – with black paint. He'd gotten as far as B I. No big wonder what letter was next.

She opened the front door and shouted at him. 'I've called the police. You'd better stop. Now.'

'Go out with me and I will, Va-va-voomica,' he said, shaking his hips at her and continuing with the T.

'This is harassment,' she said. 'You're going to get arrested.'

He was wiggling his finger at her in a 'come get me' sickening way. She'd march over and try some tae kwon do that she'd once learned, but she had no idea what he was capable of, and Bea could get mixed up in it all. Just as he was about to spray again, she ran over and knocked the can out of his hand. He was wobbling, she realized. Drunken fool.

Nick arrived in his squad car and rushed over to Fledge. 'Veronica, you should have waited for me,' he said as he hand-cuffed Fledge, who kicked Nick in the shin, earning himself even more jail time. Nick secured him in the back of the squad car. Good riddance.

'I didn't want him to finish,' she said.

He smiled, then glanced over at Bea in the doorway. 'I'm glad to see you have company.'

'We're baking a chocolate-fudge Happiness Pie later.'

'Maybe you could teach me, Saturday night. After dinner at Grill 207?'

Now it was her turn to smile. Saturday. Colin Firth day. Correction: Nick and Veronica day. 'I'd like that.' She had a very good feeling that Saturday night would be the start of something wonderful between them.

He looked at Veronica, his dark eyes full of so many things. 'Pick you up at seven.' He gave her hand a brief squeeze, then got in the car and drove off.

'We could scrub that B I away while the coffee perks,' Bea said.

As Veronica worked on the B, and Bea on the I, the ridicu-lousness of them kneeling on the driveway and scrubbing off the drunken pest's graffiti made them giggle. All Veronica could think about was that she had met Bea in the driveway for the first time, and now here they were, together again for a new beginning.

Chapter 24

Gemma

The parlour was crowded for Friday's Movie Night at the Three Captains' Inn. The Colin Firth fan club, wearing their HAPPINESS IS COLIN FIRTH T-shirts, had checked back into the inn since the town was buzzing that the actor was due to arrive in town tomorrow to shoot a scene at The Best Little Diner in Boothbay. The guests from the Seashell and Bluebird Rooms were scattered around the parlour, including two husbands – according to Isabel, men rarely came to Movie Night since shoot-'em-ups were rare on the marquee. June was handing out cute bags of popcorn that her son had decorated for the event, and Isabel was handing out slices of Veronica Russo's pies.

Bea and Veronica were waiting on the big sofa and had saved Gemma a seat. Veronica had brought over three pies for the occasion, and Gemma helped herself to a slice of chocolate-fudge pie, since she'd missed out on the one she'd given the newlyweds the other night. The sweet couple were snuggled up on a beanbag, feeding each other the Key lime, their arms entwined. Gemma remembered when she and Alexander used to do sickeningly lovey-dovey stuff like that, and she smiled. She missed Alexander. If she had to go home and face her future, at least she was going home to him.

'Everyone ready for *Girl With a Pearl Earring*?' Isabel asked.

Girl With a Pearl Earring. Gemma flashed back to one of her earliest dates with Alexander, at the Metropolitan Museum of Art, when they were twenty-three and didn't have much money, and they'd looked through postcards of art for their bulletin boards at work. Alex had bought her two Vermeers, 'A Maid Asleep' and 'Girl With a Pearl Earring', and she'd always loved both, but especially the 'girl's' haunting face, her eyes, that one beautiful pearl earring. She still had those postcards, but now they were in her big box of stuff from when she'd had to clean out her desk at *New York Weekly*. Suddenly she wished Alexander were here, sitting next to her, holding her hand.

Tomorrow, she thought, the warring feelings settling down some.

The lights went off and the movie began, and Gemma was transported to the seventeenth-century Dutch Republic, as a poor teenage maid named Griet, played by Scarlett Johansson, slowly dares to assist and model for the master of the house, the reclusive painter Johannes Vermeer, who has a very jealous pregnant wife.

Between the exquisite period detail and the intensity of Colin Firth's performance, Gemma was riveted to the screen, as was everyone else.

'The longing between them!' June said as the lights were turned back on. 'Aside from how beautiful the movie was, the photography, the absolute longing that was captured between Griet and Vermeer almost made me uncomfortable.'

'Because it couldn't be, and because their connection was so special,' Bea said.

'Did Colin Firth look incredibly hot with that longish hair or what?' one of the members of the fan club said. 'All those smouldering gazes!' She fanned herself.

There was general agreement on that.

The discussion continued for a while, some saying the movie didn't have enough action, but Gemma thought it was beautiful – and very sad – as it was. The newlyweds left for their room, giving each other exaggerated haunting gazes *à la* Griet and Vermeer, and Gemma had to laugh. The fan club insisted that Colin Firth would be here tomorrow; someone who knew someone who knew someone had gotten word to one of them that he was arriving in the morning to film scenes in the diner, but Veronica, beset by the fan club for details and information, swore on a stack of imaginary bibles that even she – and the assistant director – couldn't say for sure if he'd be there.

Gemma smiled at how important she'd thought an interview with him would be. And it would be important to editors who'd relish a story on him, especially from the perspective she had in mind, of a travel piece. But now all she wanted was to go home and see her husband, feel his arms around her, and slowly morph into the new Gemma – mother-to-be, a role that she would put her heart and soul into, whether it was incredibly difficult for her or not. She was ready to go home, wherever that home turned out to be. She'd make her new life work for her, somehow, some way.

Slowly the room began clearing out. Bea and Veronica left for Harbour View Coffee, and Gemma helped Isabel and June clean up the pie crumbs and pieces of popcorn from between sofa cushions and the floor. And then it was time to go, up to her room, for her last night of sleep as the old Gemma, intrepid reporter, city dweller.

Someone knocked on the front door of the inn, and Isabel wondered out loud if she'd missed getting ready for a late arrival, but when she returned, there was Alexander.

Gemma stared at him. 'Alex? What on earth?'

'You think I'd let my beloved pregnant wife drive seven hours hunched over the wheel of our little Miata?' he said. 'I flew up to drive you home tomorrow morning.'

He was wonderful that way. 'Thank you.' She hugged him, breathing in the scent of him, the security of him. Sometimes it felt very, very good.

She couldn't believe he was really here, standing a foot in

front of her, looking a bit tired, his sandy blond hair mussed, but otherwise absolutely wonderful.

'Let's go for a walk,' he said. 'Show me that yellow house you texted me a picture of. I want to see what you have in mind. I want you to be happy.'

She knew he did. Holding hands, they walked out into the warm July night, a beautiful breeze lifting the ends of Gemma's hair. They walked down to Townsend, then turned on to Meadow Lane. 'That's it,' she said, pointing to the craftsman she loved, with the widow's walk and porch swing.

He looked at it, then turned back to her. 'I've been doing a lot of thinking the past couple of days. I think you *should* accept the job offer from the *Boothbay Regional Gazette*, Gemma.'

She stared at him, her stomach dropping. 'Are you saying you want to split up?'

'Are you nuts?' he asked. 'Of course not.'

'Well, Dobbs Ferry, New York, is a long commute to Boothbay Harbor, Maine.'

'True, but this isn't,' he said, pointing at the yellow house.

'What?'

'I told you that somehow we'd find a way to make this work for both of us,' he said. 'And here's what I came up with: your idea the other night. I'll quit, we'll move up here, and you'll be the breadwinner, supporting us with your full-time job as a reporter.'

Gemma's mouth dropped open. 'But like you said, you make three times what the *Gazette* offered me.'

He cupped her face between his hands. 'We have a lot of money socked away. I can take off a few years if we're careful.'

Her head was spinning – half with joy, half with disbelief that this was really happening. 'You're going to be a stay-at-home father?'

'Why not? I could use an extended break from my job with all its stress. When Gemma Junior starts pre-school, I'll go back to work. But for these three years, we'll cut expenses. We'll get three times for our apartment what I'll pay for a house here. My parents won't be thrilled we're moving so far away, but it's an hour-and-a-half plane ride from New York. You'll be a working mother, and I'll be the stay-at-home dad. We'll both change diapers.'

Gemma's eyes filled with tears. 'I am the luckiest person on earth.'

'We're both lucky.'

Epilogue

In the morning, Bea, Gemma and Veronica were invited to the movie set, thanks to Tyler, and the special passes around their necks helped them navigate through the crowds behind the barricades lining Main Street. But when they arrived at The Best Little Diner, they learned the shoot was delayed for three hours — and no one was confirming if Colin Firth was on set or not.

Veronica led Bea and Gemma out the back door to the coffee table that had been set up behind the diner, along with trailers and equipment she wouldn't have thought could possibly fit back here.

'Hey, everyone, it's Colin Firth!' a man's voice called out.

Gemma rolled her eyes. 'I love how no one's even bothering to look. We've all had enough of the loser who called wolf.'

'Loser who called hunk, you mean,' Bea said.

Veronica stopped short. 'Wait a minute. The guy who kept shouting out fake Colin Firth sightings is in jail.' She shook her head. 'Oh, whatever. Colin Firth is still my favourite actor and always will be, but I'm ready to—'

Ooof. She bumped right into someone's shoulder.

'Pardon,' said a very familiar male voice with a British accent.

She gasped as Colin Firth himself, wearing jeans and green wellingtons, briefly smiled at her with that irresistible smile she'd seen a thousand times in movies and on TV, and then quickly disappeared into a huge trailer parked in a wide alleyway a few feet from where they stood.

'Oh my God,' Bea said. 'Was that *him?*'

Gemma laughed. 'I've been looking for Colin Firth for weeks and he walks right past me the day I'm going home. Figures.'

'I know what you mean,' Veronica said, barely able to contain her grin. 'I said I'd live if I didn't see him, but to be honest, those five seconds were worth everything. First of all, I will never wash this shirt again. Second, he spoke to me!'

'And smiled at you,' Bea said, wiggling her eyebrows.

Veronica's knees *had* gone more than a little weak. 'And what a smile. Still, all I really want right now? To go scouting out locations for my pie diner with Bea.'

Gemma nodded. 'A few days ago, I'd have been busting down that trailer door to get an interview with him. But now all I want to do is go house-hunting with my husband, right here in Boothbay Harbor.'

'I still can't believe you're moving here,' Bea said. 'I'll see you at Movie Night at the inn some Fridays, at least?'

Gemma slung an arm around her. 'Definitely. And Veronica, hurry up and open that pie diner because I'll be craving your fudge pie throughout this pregnancy.'

'Bea and I made you a fudge pie last night, after we left the inn,' Veronica said with a smile. 'It's in the fridge at the inn, with your name on it. It's for everything you've done for Hope Home and for us. I can't wait to read your article.'

Gemma gave Veronica a quick hug, but they were bumped apart by some women jockeying to see inside the diner.

Bea glanced at the trailer Colin Firth had darted into, now surrounded by a huge crowd of people as police officers tried to keep some order. I saw him for you, Mama, she said silently up to the sky.

Then the three women headed away from the set as more shouts rang out that it really was him this time.

A Note About
Veronica's Elixir Pies

I wish there were room to include all of Veronica's special elixir pies, but there's only space for one, and how could I not choose her Colin Firth Pie?

As for the others, just remember that the elixir part of Veronica's pies, whether her chocolate-caramel-cream Amore Pie or her Key lime Confidence Pie, is about you – not the ingredients. Use any recipe you'd like, e.g. for peanut-butter coconut pie or blueberry pie, and while you're gently rolling out the pastry or mixing your sugar and butter and chocolate, think of what you wish for. Then think some more while you're savouring the finished pie. Or, if you're pressed for time, just go buy a pie from your favourite bakery, and wish away while you're enjoying every last bite of a slice. Your wishes just might come true.

> *Amore Pie:* chocolate-caramel-cream pie
> *Spirit Pie:* shoo-fly pie
> *Feel-Better Pie:* blueberry pie
> *Confidence Pie:* Key lime pie
> *Cast-out Pie:* peanut-butter coconut pie
> *Hope Pie:* salted-caramel cheesecake pie
> *Happiness Pie:* your favourite kind
> *Colin Firth Pie:* cherry pie

Veronica's Colin Firth (Cherry) Pie

This recipe was handed down to me from my dear great-grandfather Abraham, an Englishman who learned to make pie from his own father, a baker, so that he could impress the young lady he'd been courting (my great-grandmother). Impress her, he did! Whenever I make this wonderful old-fashioned pie, I always think of love and gallantry. It was no surprise to me that Veronica chose it as her Colin Firth pie.

Ingredients

300g flour
150g chilled unsalted butter, cubed
150g margarine

150g caster sugar

pinch of salt

1 egg yolk

2 tbsp cornflour

1 tsp cinnamon

1 tsp vanilla extract

¼ tsp almond extract

4–5 tbsp cold water

500g sour cherries, pitted

1 tbsp milk (for brushing top of pie)

2 tbsp granulated sugar

Method

1. **Pie crust:** mix flour, butter, shortening, 1 tbsp caster sugar, and pinch of salt in food processor until crumb-like. Add egg yolk and 4–5 tbsp cold water. Pulse to form a ball. (You can do this all by hand with a pastry blender and spatula as my great-grandfather did, too, but I always over-handle so prefer the processor!) Chill for 30 minutes in refrigerator.

2. **Filling:** In large bowl, mix the cornflour, remaining caster sugar, cinnamon, vanilla and almond extract, then stir in cherries.

3. Preheat oven to 180°C/fan160°C/gas mark 4

4. Roll out half the pie crust on a floured surface and line greased pie dish. Trim the edges, pour in cherry filling.

Add a few tbsps of water on filling. Roll out remaining pie crust and cover the cherry filling (you can cut out lattice strips to make a pretty flower/star-like design in the centre by making slits. Press the edges to seal.

5. Brush the top of the pie with milk and sprinkle with the granulated sugar. Bake for 40 minutes.

6. Before taking out pie to cool, think of Colin Firth, perhaps emerging from the lake in that white shirt, or telling Bridget Jones that he likes her, very much, just as she is.

7. While enjoying your Colin Firth cherry pie, picture Colin Firth from *Love Actually*, mangling his Portuguese proposal to his beautiful Aurelia. It's the very earnest *trying* and that's what I've always loved most about our beloved Colin Firth, the ultimate gentleman.

Acknowledgements

Huge thanks to Alexis Hurley, Kate McLennan, Karen Kosztolnyik, Caroline Hogg, Ali Blackburn, and everyone at Simon & Schuster's Gallery Books and Pan Macmillan. A huge thank you to every writer's secret weapon — an amazing writer friend: Lee Nichols Naftali.

I will never forget watching the BBC mini-series of *Pride and Prejudice* back in the mid-nineties and saying to myself, *Who IS that?* when Colin Firth appeared on screen. I've been captivated by him ever since. Thank you, Mr Firth, for your fifty plus roles, for making us swoon, for making us believe and care, for transporting us — the joy of movies.

extracts reading groups
competitions books new
discounts extracts
competitions
books new events
events
books
extracts reading groups
interviews events
events extracts
discounts
new books events
events new
discounts extracts discounts

www.panmacmillan.com

extracts events reading groups
competitions books extracts new

Pirates Galore

Sid Fleischman

Illustrated by John Hendrix

For Julian

CATNIP BOOKS
Published by Catnip Publishing Ltd.
Islington Business Centre
3-5 Islington High Street
London N1 9LQ

This edition published 2007
1 3 5 7 9 10 8 6 4 2

First published in USA under the title *The Giant Rat of Sumatra or Pirates Galore*

Text copyright © 1985 by Sid Fleischman, Inc.

The moral right of the author has been asserted

A CIP catalogue record for this book is available from the British Library

ISBN 978-1-84647-021-9

Printed in Poland

www.catnippublishing.co.uk

Contents

Chapter 1   *1*
The Giant Rat of Sumatra pokes its nose off the
coast of California, and things begin to happen

Chapter 2   *10*
Of piranha fish and a room full of villains

Chapter 3   *16*
In which One-Arm Ginger tips his hand, and I
get an earful

Chapter 4   *22*
Desperate events aboard The Giant Rat, and a
bucket of whale oil

Chapter 5   *27*
Regarding the fate of The Giant Rat and other
important matters

Chapter 6   *34*
Containing one surprise after another

Chapter 7   *41*
In which a pile of rubble bursts apart, and what
jumps out

Chapter 8   *48*
And then what happened

Chapter 9   **55**
Containing various matters, including an unpleasant stowaway

Chapter 10   **63**
In which appears the lady in velvet, and Captain Gallows loses his boots

Chapter 11   **74**
In which the tall Mexican talks more than necessary

Chapter 12   **77**
Containing an excess of villains and a kick in the dirt

Chapter 13   **81**
In which I keep my eyes peeled, and the judge gives a hopeless shrug

Chapter 14   **84**
In which Sam'l Spoons returns, and a dead man rises from the deep

Chapter 15   **89**
A whaling ship blunders in, and I peel off my jacket

Chapter 16   **93**
Containing a full account of the notorious duel and how it ended

Chapter 17   **100**
Containing a sprinkle of rain and news of Candalaria

Chapter 18   *104*
Enter the man with fleas in his beard

Chapter 19   *108*
In which news arrives and I leave

Chapter 20   *111*
In which villains spring forth and amazements
abound

Chapter 21   *116*
Being full of derring-do and daring don't

Chapter 22   *120*
How the bold Giant Rat of Sumatra met her
fate, and history was made

Chapter 23   *125*
Containing all manner of things, including the
secret of Don Simplicio

Chapter 24   *131*
In which Candalaria returns, and surprises lurk
about

Chapter 25   *138*
Being full of emeralds and punishments and a
scruffy ship homeward bound

Author's Note   *145*
In which the ink-stained writer confesses, and a
trilogy is revealed before your eyes

San Francisco

Los Angeles

San Diego

Mexico
1846

Pacific
Ocean

Chapter 1

The Giant Rat of Sumatra pokes its nose off the coast of California, and things begin to happen

My story begins on the night an owl blundered into the belfry and rang the church bells. The town awoke with a sense of doom. It was an omen. Something evil was in the air.

Through drifts of fog, an exhausted sailing ship came creaking into the harbour. After a long voyage, it was down to its last puff of wind and its last cask of fresh water.

Under its needle nose of a bowsprit clung a dreadful figurehead—a giant rat. The creature, painted mustard yellow, had been carved out of a mahogany log felled in the jungles of Sumatra. The rat, big as a tiger, had once glared at the world through bold and cunning emerald eyes. But the gems had been pried out by thieves, leaving the giant rat to wander the seas like a blind man. The ivory teeth had yellowed, but remained bared and sharp as crooked nails—a rat eager to sink its jaws into the throat of the unwary.

The ship had come halfway across the world to this sleepy bay on the Mexican coast of California. What was she doing in San Diego? *The Giant Rat of Sumatra* was a pirate ship, a bold outlaw accustomed to plying her trade from Sumatra to the China Sea.

Standing calmly at the ship's rail, I sniffed the air for some dry scent of the earth out there in the dark. It seemed an eternity since I had set foot on land. I'd already had enough of the sea to last me until my voice finally changed. I was twelve years and ten months old and the ship's cabin boy.

I turned to catch sight of the ship's master as he came sliding down the ratlines. The man took a leap like a tall, big-boned acrobat to the bowsprit. There he peered through the rags of fog and shouted orders in midair. "Steersman! An inch to starboard, if you'll be so kind! This channel is tight as a priest's collar! Aye, that's better, shipmates! Steady!"

He was a large man, but I had noticed how light on his feet he was. Drenched by hours bareheaded in the fog, his coarse black hair glistened like needles. He was as apt to be lending a hand pumping water in the bilge as at his sextant fixing the course. He regarded no job aboard ship as beneath him.

It was clear to me that the ship's master was no stranger to this strange port of call. He knew that a vast bed of seaweed lay near the entrance: He skirted it. He appeared as familiar with the bottom of the bay as with the deep creases in his own hands, weathered under foreign suns.

"God bless my eyesight!" he exclaimed with immense pleasure. The captain had a loud, hearty laugh when he felt like laughing, as he did now. "We've brought our pigs to a fine market, sahibs!" It was a Hindi term of respect he was fond of tossing about the decks. "That's San Diego itself hidin' in the fog dead ahead and about to welcome Captain Gallows back. Aye, I've come home after all these years!" He made a sharp chopping motion with his hand. "Drop the hook!"

With a rattling of its rusty chain, the anchor dropped and found the bottom. The ship swung around like a dog pulled tight on its leash.

As I watched him, I could tell that it amused Captain

Gallows to sail under such a foreboding name. He flung out orders in a grab bag of languages while he strode toward his quarters. "Jimmy Pukapuka, be so kind as to fetch up a bucket of whale oil and refill the warning lights. In the fog, we shall want to glow like a ghost, amigo!"

"Aye, Cap'n."

"Calcutta, open our last keg of water. And run up our flag!"

"What flag, Cap'n?" replied the second officer, as broadly muscled as a bull.

"Anything but the skull and crossbones. Mr. Ginger! Post a man on watch! Everyone else turn in. Sleep well, shipmates, for tomorrow you will become gentlemen! Cabin boy! We do have a cabin boy, don't we? I recall fishing one out of the sea months ago. Where is that shipwrecked cabin boy?"

"Here, sir."

"Polish my English boots! I don't intend going ashore tomorrow looking like a beggar."

The deck had almost cleared when I sat myself against a deckhouse to polish the boots. Jimmy Pukapuka, a burly Pacific Islander with swirling tattoos on his cheeks, had carried up a full bucket of whale oil. He was soon finished refilling the port and starboard lanterns, with oil left over in the bucket.

"Catch a wink, Shipwreck, boy," he remarked, hanging up the oil bucket and vanishing below decks to his bunk.

It was almost inevitable that the crewmen would call

me Shipwreck. I had, after all, been dredged up out of the sea. Boston born, I had been taken aboard a smelly whaling ship by my stepfather, an angry man and a harsh ship's officer. He told me that eleven years was quite old enough to earn my own keep. And a sea voyage would toughen me up for a short-tempered world.

After more'n a year and a half, a short-tempered storm off the Philippines had blown the ship into matchsticks. I had found myself clinging like a barnacle to a splintered oak beam. At the other end, cursing to the skies, hung the one-armed chief mate.

The two of us were plucked from the sea by a fast, nimble ship with the figurehead of a great carved rat. Spouting seawater and sputtering, I remember looking around for my stepfather.

"There is no one alive left floating in this storm," the ship's young captain had told me and briskly turned away as one accustomed to death at sea. I recall raising myself to an elbow, as if to check the raging storm for my relative, and then I fell back, exhausted.

It was days later that I fully grasped my situation. I was alive, but just barely, with nothing of my own but the shirt and breeches that had dried to my salt-crusted skin. What would happen to me? My stepfather, with his disapproving grey eyes, was forever gone. I relieved my grief with a dutiful shrug from time to time. As the weeks passed I realized that I no longer truly missed the man. I felt unburdened.

But what would happen to me, now grown to twelve years and ten months? I'd find that out, day by day. The world was full of surprises, I was discovering, for hadn't I already landed on my feet? The young captain had put me quickly to work running errands as ship's cabin boy. The turbaned second officer, whom everyone called Calcutta, had found me a blue coat with brass buttons that fitted except for the sleeves.

"Made in London, that coat was!" he had exclaimed with a certain pride in the quality of the ship's appointments. I had rolled up the cuffs and gone about my duties.

The other survivor, the one-armed man, was all battered face and thundering voice and four-cornered oaths. An experienced mariner, he was pressed into service when the former chief mate vanished one night off the Sandwich Islands. Whether the officer had slipped into the sea or was given an unfriendly kick was a subject of below decks gossip.

When I first discovered that I owed my life to a band of murderous pirates, of common sea scum, I was wary and tried to keep a safe distance. But as I came to know the crew, cut-throat by cut-throat, my forebodings diminished. While the men struck me as profoundly ignorant, except for knowing the points of the compass and the direction of the wind, they showed no more greed than I'd seen about the streets of Boston. I wondered if more than two or three of them would qualify as genuine cut-throats.

For their part, the pirates were bedazzled that a twelve-year-old cabin boy could read and write as cunningly as the captain himself. To them, I was a wonder! On occasions I wrote a letter home for Chop Chop, the top-sailman, big as a water buffalo. Or for Trot, the wispy-haired sailmaker. I sensed that the man hadn't a soul to write to, but the pretence had brought a sparkle to his watery eyes. "Look ye, address it to Miss Emilie Trot in Cardiff!" he had insisted in a loud, boasting voice. He was beginning to believe his own lie, it seemed to me, but there was no harm in it and I had scribbled away.

I put away these thoughts and finished polishing the maroon boots. What long legs the captain walked on! The man had the carefree air of a gypsy. All he lacked was a gold ring dangling from his ear.

He'd earned some fame, Calcutta told me, by his sharp nose for the richest cargoes afloat in the Far East—other pirate ships. Maybe it eased his conscience to prey almost entirely on his own kind, I thought—though he seemed prepared to make exceptions.

Now, like a homing pigeon, he had brought his ship to Mexican waters. What would he do tomorrow? Step ashore like a conqueror returning home in maroon English boots?

Finally I left his footgear standing and crossed to the open rail. Peering through the drifting fog, I again hoped to glimpse a treetop or a headland. Maybe San Diego would be the port to find another ship, one bound for

New England, thousands of miles away. All I wanted now was to find some way home.

I reached into my pocket for a sea biscuit, months stale and hard as a bone. I began to gnaw on it. Was this what my stepfather had meant by toughening me up? A near drowning and now sea biscuits! I felt toughened up more than necessary.

Out of a swirl of fog, a heavy hand landed on my shoulder and dug in like a claw.

"What you gazin' at, Shipwreck?"

I looked up sharply. I knew the voice well enough, now set at a whisper at my ear. This was the man who had survived the sinking with me—One-Arm Ginger. Now a ship's officer, Mr. Ginger might not be next to God aboard *The Giant Rat of Sumatra,* but he was next to the captain himself.

"Scurry aft," he commanded. "Lower the flyboat. Not a sound, mind you. It's private business."

"The flyboat? It's hardly big enough for two, sir."

"How am I to row ashore with one arm, I ask ye? Fetch the oars!"

"I've the captain's boots to finish shining."

"You can polish later. Step along before the fog lifts."

I jammed the biscuit in my coat pocket. What strange errand was the chief mate up to, sneaking ashore in the fog?

With the sleeve of his blue coat hanging loose and empty as a gutted fish, the man seated himself opposite

8

me in the nutshell of a boat. I began to row.

"Land's sittin' that way, me lad," the barrel-chested mate said, poking a thick finger through the fog. "Can't you smell the hide houses? It's La Playa, around the bend from the town, stinking just the same as I remember it. It must be five years ago I jumped ship." He cackled softly. "Too lawless for San Diego, is La Playa. Smell it! Aye, it's the stink of cowhides our clever captain can't get out of his high and mighty nose, if you ask me. He's got a score to settle here, from the smoulder I seen in his eyes. Row, Row, lad."

Chapter 2

Of piranha fish and a room full of villains

I could hear thin sounds of laughter and revelry ashore. I steered toward the distant noise as if it were a compass setting. Soon a lighted window came glowing through the fog, now beginning to fray into black lace.

"Look there!" said One-Arm Ginger with a happy

flutter of his eyebrows. "That's me old drink house, matey! The Red Dolphin! And sounds like Sam'l Spoons himself still leadin' the seafarin' choir! I'd know that cacklin' voice if I was stone deaf!"

We pulled up on a wet sandy beach and trudged the few steps to a seaman's tavern with its red wooden sign dripping the night's fog like blood. Flinging the door open, One-Arm Ginger burst through the doorway. For an instant laughter was sucked out of the room. Who was this wild-eyed figure in the middle of the night? The devil himself in brass buttons?

"Don't you know me, lads? It's Ginger himself, about to make each seagoing man of you rich as a king! Is that you, Sam'l Spoons, you old thief? Don't you remember yur old shipmate?"

The bar-keeper, wearing an apron so dirty he might have been cleaning fish, lifted a lantern for a closer look.

"Ginger! Ain't you been hung once or twice yet? What happened to your arm?"

"Eaten off by piranha fish!"

"Gnawed? Naw!"

Ginger waved his empty sleeve. "Ain't that proof enough?"

"Must have felt a tad unpleasant, matey!" exclaimed the bar-keeper, crossing himself.

"I was so soaked in black rum I felt hardly a nibble. I woke up the next morning with me arm dangling in the Amazon River, gnawed to the bone, and I been One-Arm Ginger ever since."

In the shadows of the earthen floor, an otter hunter with long, greasy hair raised his voice. "If that story's true, I'm stupid, mate!"

Ginger raised a tangled eyebrow. "Then you're stupid, lad! The bottom truth is I'm looking to employ a crew of able-bodied men who won't fret if I make 'em ugly rich. I'll stuff so much gold in yur pockets, both knees'll bend like barrel staves. How about you gents, all three? You there, with your harpoon, is it sharp? Can you strike a barracuda with it?"

"A minnow, sir!" said a short seaman wearing a black neckerchief. "And dance a jig at the same time, can Ozzie Twitch. Not that it's any business of yours!" he added, topping off his reply with a laugh. Then, with his bare feet on the sandy floor, he jumped into a sailor's jig. I saw dead flies stuck to the fresh tar of his seaman's pigtail.

"You'll do," said One-Arm Ginger, his eyes shooting about. "And the rest of you brave lads, you ain't afraid of the hangman's rope, are ye? For we may be sailin' outside the law. If there be an ounce of pesky honesty in your bones, there's the door of the Red Dolphin and it's wide open."

No one stirred. I was uneasy standing there. I didn't like the chief mate's mangy shadow falling across me. What riches was he promising this riffraff? The ship's biscuits? It crossed my mind that my stepfather had drowned with a psalm on his lips while this rogue was plucked from the sea with curses on his. Where was the sense in the senselessness of it?

One-Arm Ginger was grinning. "No one streakin' for the door, I see. You with me, too, Sam'l Spoons?"

"I'm too old for that brand of mischief, brother. This whitewashed adobe is treasure enough for old Sam'l, now I've joined the Mexican nation and become an upstanding Californio."

"You got come over with holiness?" asked One-Arm Ginger contemptuously. "I seen you crossin' yourself every time I pause for breath. I thought you was flea-bit."

"Aye, to own me own land I had to take on a full cargo of the king's own religion. Folks kick you out if you ain't been baptized. Everyone in this bilgewater port goes to Mass except the sea lions and the coyotes." He crossed himself again. "And think how it impresses the natives with me purity, Ginger! You go right ahead with your bloody business and don't mind me. I see you won the loyalty of me guests. As full of greed as their hide'll hold, the lot of 'em."

"Drinks for the house!" commanded One-Arm Ginger with a generous sweep of his hand. "I've found me as fine a set of villains as ever crossed salt water!"

The bar-keeper shifted his glance to me. "A small portion for the lad? I'll only charge you half."

It was as if the chief mate had forgotten me standing behind him. He turned and his cheeks puffed up. "Who told you to stick to me like a pilot fish, cabin boy?" he asked. "Return to the ship, and when you see Captain Alejandro Gallows himself, give him a salute from me and a respectful thumb of the nose." He burst out a laugh. "Sam'l, give this shipwrecked boy a candlestick to light his way through the fog."

I shook my head. "The fog's lifting. I don't need a candle to find *The Giant Rat*."

"Take the blasted light! Do as you're told!"

An empty bottle with a limp candle plugged into the neck was stuck into my hand. Only then did the man's cleverness flash through my mind. As he watched the candle flame recede in the night, One-Arm Ginger could be assured that I wasn't close by and listening at the window.

I closed the door behind me and hurried through the sand to the flyboat. I looked back and hesitated only a moment. Then I planted the candlestick upright on the wooden seat and pushed the flyboat into the bay. I hardly paused to wonder how I would get back to the ship without it. As the flyboat drifted away I watched the flame glittering like a toe dancer in the night.

Peering back at the Red Dolphin, I wasn't surprised to see the face of One-Arm Ginger pressed against the window. The man's eyes peered into the night: watching the candle flame grow smaller.

Keeping myself low, I crept back to the tavern wall. Once the chief mate's broad face was gone from the window, I raised myself close enough to listen. What bloody venture was One-Arm Ginger hatching inside the tavern? I pressed my ear closer, afraid of what I might hear.

Chapter 3

In which One-Arm Ginger tips his hand, and I get an earful

"There's treasure sitting at anchor out in the harbour, lads," said One-Arm Ginger. "Gold coins from India and jewels from China so bright they'll blind yur eyes."

"I'll risk lookin' at a feast like that!" piped up the otter hunter. I caught sight of his face glowing up like a lantern with sudden greed.

"Treasure talk is cheap in these waters," said Ozzie Twitch, the harpooner. "Treasure to the touch is another thing."

"It's there in the captain's own sea chest," replied One-Arm Ginger with a snort. "Didn't I see it with me own eyes? Ain't he been hoarding like a miser through the years? Aye, so he could return here where he was born poor as dirt. Like a fish to his spawning ground, you see, but risen in the world! He'll be taking the longboat ashore at first light to buy himself a hilltop or two. He told me so himself! Aye, quitting the sea, the tall Mexican is, to set himself up like a duke of the realm!"

My breath caught. Was this how the chief mate was going to repay Captain Gallows for fishing him out of the sea? With robbery? With bloody murder?

The harpooner clamped a suspicious eye on One-Arm Ginger. "Why you cutting us in, mate? Born generous, were you? Why split the treasure with sea worms like us?"

One-Arm Ginger flung his fist in the air, almost touching the low ceiling, and pounded it on the bar. "Will you tell me how I can tote that heavy sea chest with one hand? I'll tell you. I'll need the tentacles of an octopus!"

"Then lead the way!" exclaimed the otter hunter. "Tomorrow soon enough?"

"Tonight!" replied One-Arm Ginger sharply. "I posted no man on watch. Tonight we'll steal aboard, silent as mice, and relieve the captain of the burden. A sharp harpoon at his throat ought to tame him."

"Not a pretty way to show your loyalty," remarked the harpooner.

"Treasure is treasure," answered One-Arm Ginger.

At that point, I dropped down from the window. I needed to scurry back to the ship and wake the captain.

I turned to run, and ploughed into the arms of the bar-keeper in his smelly apron.

"I thought I saw white eyes at the window!" Sam'l Spoons declared. "I reckon you got an earful. Don't you know me old shipmate'll wring the breath out of you? Like water from a sponge. Touchy as a marlin spike, is he."

I said nothing. I felt myself wriggling like a caught fish.

"Well, I don't want murder on me doorstep," said the bar-keeper. "Not good for trade. Come along, quiet now, sonny!"

The bar-keeper dragged me to a rough wooden door at the back of the tavern. He flung me inside and locked the door.

"I'll let you out before you're full grown, I promise you. Can't let you run off and get your neck wrung, can I?"

I put my back to the wall while a dog began to growl across the pitch dark room. I stiffened. My heart thundered, not in terror for myself so much as in fear for Captain Gallows, about to be croaked in his sleep.

The dog's growling ventured closer. I couldn't pick out the beast, but he could sense my body heat approaching him in the mouldy, damp-smelling room. Moving slowly, I fished the half-gnawed biscuit out of my pocket.

"Dog," I whispered. "Here's some grub for you. A first-rate sea biscuit. Hard as a bone. You got yourself a name? You bite? Smell this."

I waited, frozen. Then I could feel the dog's breath on my hand.

"Be quick about it, dog," I muttered earnestly. "Grub it down and let me find a way out of here."

The dog carried off the biscuit, and a moment later I could hear his teeth grinding away.

"Now, dog, how can I get out of here?"

I felt around in the heavy dark. There seemed nothing in the storeroom but barrels and bottles, an anchor chain, and an oar or two smelling of the sea. I found the door and tried it again. It was locked tight.

As I moved away, I heard the animal scratching away at the earthen floor. Was he burying the bone-hard biscuit? Near the door?

Following the sound, I bumped into the dog. The growling had stopped. I put out a hand to risk petting the animal's back. Woolly as a sheep.

"Easy, mate. Dig if you want to. Maybe you can dig us both out of here."

Only as the words left my mouth did I realize what I'd said. Smart dog!

Like a blind man, arms stretched before me in the dark, I found my way back to the oars.

I chose one, feeling the edge of the paddle. It wasn't a shovel, but it would do.

I felt my way back to the door. "Stand aside, dog."

I dug away as if I were paddling a canoe—for my very life. The hole grew slowly larger. I kept digging away as my mind drifted to the tall captain and the gossip I'd heard in my fo'c'sle bunk.

The crew believed he'd fallen into the trade of piracy by accident. While hardly older than me, he'd served aboard a ship in the China trade. He had been taken prisoner aboard *The Giant Rat of Sumatra* and put to work bailing out the bilge. Before he was twenty, with a commanding boldness and a quick wit, he had raised himself to the position of second and then chief mate. When the ship's master had the carelessness to get himself hung from a Hong Kong gallows, the young chief mate was elected captain and assumed a new name. Captain Gallows! "Aye," Calcutta had remarked, "the name honoured our old master, left hanging aloft as a perch for the bewildered Hong Kong harbour seagulls!"

I kept measuring the enlarging hole with the blade of the oar. Moments later I could no longer hear the dog grinding away on the biscuit. Had he slipped out?

He had!

I fell to my stomach. I pulled myself into the hole, arms out, and squeezed myself into the night.

I jumped around to the window, hoping to glimpse One-Arm Ginger still there, flailing his hand in the air and scheming. But too much time had passed. The tavern had fallen silent.

The assassins were already afoot.

I turned and ran for the waterline.

Chapter 4

Desperate events aboard The Giant Rat, and a bucket of whale oil

I could see the foggy glow of the port lantern on *The Giant Rat of Sumatra* at anchor in the bay. And I thought I could make out a longboat slipping like a ghost through the darkness.

I wished now I hadn't sent the flyboat floating on the

tide. How was I going to sound the alarm? I cast my eyes about but saw no sign of a flickering stub of a candle. Perhaps it had burned itself out.

I heard a voice thundering within myself. Captain Gallows is asleep in his bunk! Can't you swim to the ship? That far?

I remembered the oar left behind in the storeroom. If Sam'l Spoons owned oars, he must own a boat. Would that be a boat making soft lapping sounds on the tide? Farther around the shore?

I followed my ears. Tucked behind a shallow bend I found a rowboat tethered like a goat to an iron stake in the earth. The oarlocks stood empty. Of course, I thought! The bar-keeper kept the oars from being stolen.

I tried not to lose any more time than I had to. I rushed with sandy shoes back to the rear of the tavern. I crawled back under the door and was quick to discover one oar and then the other.

I worked them under the door and out. Soon I had them in the boat's oarlocks and shoved off into the bay.

As I scraped the hull of *The Giant Rat of Sumatra,* its side lanterns lit, I knew I was too late. An oaken longboat was already tied to the jack ladder. It waited quietly for the attackers to return and flee.

I untied the longboat and shoved it away to drift free. I climbed hand over hand up the jack ladder, not sure now what I could do except to wake the crew. How calculating of the chief mate to have posted no man on watch!

But once I reached the deck, the hatch doors flew open and out backed One-Arm Ginger himself, a knife flashing in his hand. Beside him came the harpooner, the long handle of his weapon broken off.

I acted on instinct. My attention was quickly drawn to the bucket of whale oil Jimmy Pukapuka had left hooked to the deckhouse.

I grabbed the bucket. It was still heavy and, mercifully, half full. That would do! I splashed the whale oil on deck. It landed in a great puddle near the feet of the villains as they came backing out of the hatch, flailing away with their weapons.

"Fools! Dolts! Chaff and bran!" came the captain's booming voice. "Sea worms! I'll send you headlong into eternity!" He appeared now, a tall, grinning Mexican with a jungle knife in his fist and bookish words flying from his lips. The blade, as broad as a bed slat, flashed like lightning, backing the men out of the hatch.

I saw with a rush of relief that the captain was very much alive and on his feet. He seemed to be enjoying himself hugely.

But quickly the captain was forced to back away. The three ruffians advanced on him, knives and harpoon whipping the air. The fight disappeared into the hatch. I froze, my heart pounding.

Moments later, the doors of the hatch again flew open, but now it was Captain Gallows backing into the night. The assassins were driving him out on deck.

"You've trifled with my good nature and the laws of mutiny, Mr. Ginger!" shouted the captain defiantly. "I'll be obliged to hoist you and your fellows from the yardarms! I shall hang you up like soiled laundry!"

"Blast yur eyes, sir!" shouted One-Arm Ginger.

"Fight on, *cucarachas*! I have stepped on more menacing cockroaches!"

To my horror, I saw the captain take a long backward step. As he slipped on the oiled deck, his legs flew from under him. He ripped out oaths in several languages.

The scoundrels were quick to rush on the fallen captain with their blades hoisted in the air.

But their legs, too, went spinning.

The ship rolled in the tide, and the four men went slithering toward the open railing. Setting my feet firmly against a deck cleat, I caught the captain's bare brown arm and held tight.

One-Arm Ginger, now as oily as a sardine, slipped over the side. He flopped into the sea with hardly a splash and only a gasp of surprise. Clinging to him, the harpooner followed, and then the otter hunter, his long hair flying.

"Who in thunder spilled oil on deck!" the captain shouted, clinging to me as if I were a solid post. He carefully steadied himself on his slippery feet.

"I thought they were going to finish you off, sir," I answered. "I meant only to tangle their feet with whale oil."

The captain cocked a black eyebrow. "Did you,

Shipwreck? That was lively thinking." And then with a shout, "Where in blazes is the man on watch? Who let that sea scum aboard?"

"Mr. Ginger didn't post a watchman, sir. I heard him say so."

"Sly rascal."

"Yes, sir."

"Must I call you Shipwreck, cabin boy? Do you have a proper name?"

"Shipwreck'll do."

"Shipwreck, I'm obliged to you."

I felt a glow of pride in myself. I was glad to please this man who had plucked me from the high seas.

The scuffling on deck was bringing a few sleepy seamen on deck.

Said the captain, "You, Jimmy Pukapuka, stick your head over the side and see if any of those sea vultures can swim, which is unlikely. The rest of you, dredge up buckets of seawater and wash down the deck, before we all follow the nitwits over the side."

Jimmy Pukapuka gazed over the side and finally announced, "Nothing down there, Cap'n. Only a sea lion enjoyin' his guests."

Captain Gallows waved in his crew. "Lower your chins, shipmates. Anyone want to say a few solemn words for these muckworms and murderers? No? Padre, have mercy on their souls, but lock up your silver candlesticks. Amen."

Chapter 5

Regarding the fate of The Giant Rat and other important matters

At the break of dawn, Captain Gallows sent the remaining longboat ashore for fresh water and galley supplies from among the hide houses. Now that it was light, I could see what appeared to be an abandoned fort at the headland. Closer in stood the ramshackle warehouses of La Playa, with stiff cowhides folded and piled like the weathered pages of old books. Around the bend, San Diego seemed to be keeping the scruffy place at arm's length.

The second officer, Calcutta, who had seen the world several times over, told me the hides would be shipped to Boston and return as leather shoes and boots for the Californios. Other hides would be traded in China and India for silks and ivory and perfumes and porcelain dishes.

"See San Diego, around the bay?" said Calcutta, pointing a stubby finger. "You could put that dusty town itself in a bird's nest, but don't be fooled, lad. San Diego is captain of the hide trade. Important as London town, if you're a cow!" And the second officer laughed.

As soon as I could, I rowed ashore, finding Sam'l Spoons asleep on the counter and snoring thunderbolts.

"Thanks for the borrow of your boat," I muttered, being careful not to disturb the bar-keeper.

The dog was off in a corner, asleep, too.

But *The Giant Rat's* flyboat was floating like driftwood on the incoming tide. Soon I was able to wade out knee-deep in the water to reclaim it and row to the ship. That's when the longboat came in sight again, this time with Captain Gallows standing at the stern, one polished maroon boot resting on a sea chest. His eyes surveyed the few adobe buildings farther around the bay that called themselves San Diego.

Now that the pirates had reached their destination, I realized that I was finished with *The Giant Rat of Sumatra*. I could see three ships at anchor in the bay. By thunder, one of them might be setting its course for the long voyage around South America to New England. And I'd be home, at last!

It was now more than twenty-one months since I had left my actress mother standing under her orange parasol on India Wharf in Boston. Had word trickled back that my stepfather had drowned? How could she guess that I had survived, shipwrecked but floating? It seemed a lifetime ago that I was an eleven-year-old with my head buried in the collar of my new coat while my stepfather dragged me aboard the doomed whaler. I couldn't get my mother's festive orange parasol out of my mind. Shouldn't it have been a sad black for the occasion? Falling asleep night after night in my fo'c'sle bunk, I would wonder why she hadn't balked at letting me be carried off to sea. I recalled being homesick before the ship left the wharf. Was she glad to get me out from underfoot? The parasol was all smiles. I wasn't sure that she had liked having a child to look after. Well, I didn't need looking after anymore.

It was hours before Captain Gallows returned to the ship. From the way the boat crew lifted it, the captain's sea chest was now light as a gourd.

"Amigos!" he called out. "On deck! You company of scoundrels! I said I would make gentlemen of you, and I shall!"

The bewildered pirates gathered around the mainmast. As I had never come to feel that I belonged to their company, I climbed a rope ladder apart from the others to listen.

"Look you, mates," the captain said, stroking his jaw. "You have served this voyage well. Did you grumble to leave our pirate waters? Shall I remind you that five nations were seeking to hang you together like a bunch of grapes from the nearest gallows? Amigos! These waters are safe. Go ashore. If you dab your faces with fresh water, you might even be seen to be human."

"The last time I washed me face, Cap'n, it shocked me out of a year's growth!" said Bajo, the cook, laughing. "I didn't know I was that no-account ugly!"

The captain grinned. "When we shared out our accounts off Sumatra, you spent every copper the day we docked in Singapore. When we shared out again, you lavished your spoils on Hong Kong. In Manila, your purses were full and lumpy, but I have kept you aboard to preserve you from yourselves. The time has come to cock an eye at our profession. We are at the end of our sea road, shipmates! We have been all but swept off the oceans of the world. Our hunting grounds have shrunk to a few trifling seas in the Far East! Gentlemen, we are as out-of-date as the longbow!"

"God preserve us all!" exclaimed Jimmy Pukapuka.

Said Calcutta, "Don't talk like my mossy old bones are ready for the boneyard, Cap'n."

"And me not yet twenty!" chimed in Jimmy Pukapuka. "Finished, says you?"

The captain took a breath. "You lads have brought *The Giant Rat of Sumatra* to our last port of call. Her eyes have been gouged out. The sails hang in rags. Her ship's bottom is crawling with sea worms. The time has come to gather up your trinkets and abandon ship."

"Upon my conscience," muttered Trot, the barefooted sailmaker. "Can't we patch her up?"

"The patches already have patches," said Captain Gallows.

"But only six or eight times over," remarked Calcutta. "There's still life in this seagoing old rodent, Cap'n."

Captain Gallows shook his head. "You may linger aboard until you find another berth. There is a hide ship loading nearby where I have found you honest employment—if you are tempted by the novelty of that brand of work. Or you may join me ashore. I have already arranged to buy a great rancho and a thousand head of cattle."

"Turning your back on the sea?" exclaimed Trot in open-eyed amazement. "Strike me dead! What are you going to do with all them cows?"

"I shall become a hidalgo."

"What in tarnation is that?"

The captain answered with a snort and a laugh. "A title reserved for a full-rigged gentleman—whether he is one or not."

"I declare," said Trot, wiping his neck with a rag.

"And I declare that you seagoing men can fling a rope like a vaquero on horseback," the captain continued. "You are welcome to join me and put earth between your toes."

A few of the buccaneers, including Jimmy Pukapuka and Trot and Calcutta, volunteered to stick with the captain and become gentlemen of sorts.

I found myself peering at the ship loading up nearer shore. Like a trail of ants, men were carrying aboard cowhides dried and folded over poles. Was the ship bound for Atlantic waters? There might be room aboard for a cabin boy.

The voyage home would take months. I could hardly expect my mother to know me as I came bursting through the door. The sun had roasted me brown as a coconut, and my hair had bleached like so much straw. I must have grown two or three inches.

The captain was talking again. "They tell me ashore that there is trouble in Mexico. I must warn any of you men who wish to jump ship here and go your own way—foreigners are viewed with suspicion. Especially Americans. Mercifully, none of you are Americans, eh?"

I stiffened a little. What did Mexico have against Americans? I waited for the captain to pause for breath, and called out, "That hide ship, sir. Heading out for New England, if I'm lucky?"

"Bound for Canton."

I gave a disappointed sigh. China. I sat on a yardarm,

my legs dangling free, I'd have to turn up another passage home. How long would that take? Again, there flashed across my mind that picture of my mother with her garden-party orange parasol seeing me off in Boston for a dangerous life at sea. How could she have been sure I'd be back?

"Shipwreck!"

"Aye?"

"Pack up your things," said Captain Gallows.

"Everything I own is in my pockets, sir. All my old life drowned."

Had the captain forgotten that he had dredged me out of the sea?

"I will confer with you in my quarters," said Captain Gallows.

Chapter 6

Containing one surprise after another

The captain's cabin stretched the width of the ship, with aft windows set at a slant and overlooking the water. I stood at the door and cleared my throat.

"I forgot," the captain said, not bothering to notice me. "You said you were an American. Come in."

I stepped through the doorway. A breeze was blowing through the cabin, and it smelled of seaweed.

"So what shall I do with you, American? Are you homesick?"

"A little."

"Only a little? I was never homesick."

"Yes, sir."

"I was once a cabin boy."

I said nothing.

"Amazed, eh? Every proud and noisy frog was once a tadpole. San Diego has always had the hide trade, ships coming and going, so it was easy for me to run away to sea. I was only a little older than you. My first voyages were to China. Then to England. It was a hen ship."

I had heard about hen ships. It meant the captain had kept his wife aboard.

"That grand lady saw a spark in me and decided to teach me to read and write. When we got to London, she put me in school. Don't I talk like Shakespeare himself?"

The captain burst out laughing. I found it difficult to look up. I couldn't imagine why the ship's master was telling me all this. Or how the man had gone from Shakespeare to piracy.

As if reading my mind, Captain Gallows leaned forward and lowered his voice. "Don't wonder what I am doing aboard *The Giant Rat of Sumatra*. I will tell you. It is difficult to be a poor Mexican. So I became a rich Mexican."

I didn't know whether to smile or let the remark go by me. Was the captain so exalted that he didn't have anyone aboard he could talk to? Was that the way it was with ships' masters, who held the power of gods? Talking to a cabin boy was talking to thin air, wasn't it? Did he really care what I thought of him?

"I detected a spark in you," continued the tall Mexican. "It appears that you are going to find yourself beached in this sleepy pueblo for a while. Leave that to me. If I were to have you taught to read and write—just imagine! You might grow up to be another Captain Gallows."

"I can already read and write, sir."

"Blimey, is there nothing left remarkable beneath the visiting moon?" he exclaimed. It struck me as something he'd got out of a book. Was that what Shakespeare sounded like? "But you still have the misfortune to be an American."

Captain Gallows began pacing the cabin, ducking his head to avoid the lantern hung from the ceiling. "The news ashore is that Mexico is at war."

I stood unmoved, looking up at the captain. I was sorry that there was a war, but what had that to do with me? Soon I'd find a passage home.

"We are at war with the United States," the captain added.

My gaze faltered. *With the United States*. Did that mean at war with me, Edmund Amos Peters? And how near was the war? There were certainly no cannons booming over this quiet San Diego bay.

"News travels slowly," remarked Captain Gallows. "Fighting began weeks ago. It has not yet reached here."

"Why would Mexico attack the United States?"

"Spoken like a patriot! But it is the United States that has invaded Mexico." The captain turned and bent to stare out the stern windows. "You won't see any ships out there flying your flag. This is a Mexican port. Trade with Boston has stopped. As the devil would have it, Shipwreck, you are not going to find a passage home."

My heart tightened. My plans were turning to ashes. I could think of nothing to do but stare at my feet. How long was I going to be stuck in this confounded Mexican village?

"You may be regarded as an enemy foreigner," said the captain. "War is bound to breed suspicion and craziness. I am told that a militia is forming to battle the Americans. I think you'd better stick close to me, eh, amigo?"

Enemy foreigner? I was too dumbfounded to speak. I felt a little frightened. Couldn't I escape somehow to the United States? How far was it? A thousand miles? Two? Where was it? Beyond Texas somewhere? Too far to walk!

"Meanwhile, you can do me a service," said the captain. "Ashore they tell me that the law has broken down. Around every bend in the road there is another bandit or cut-throat. My rancho lies almost half a day's ride north of here. I am going to trust you with a great secret. I will be travelling with something of amazing value. Look."

Suddenly, as if he had plucked them out of thin air, the captain held large green stones between the fingers of each hand. They flashed and glowed like cold stars.

"Shipwreck! Do you know what these are?"

I stared at the stones. I knew nothing about gems, except that they were bright and flashing. "Green rocks."

"Trashy rocks, eh? Ah, but what trash! These are emeralds! Two of them, fat as walnuts! Gaze at them, cabin boy. Can you guess where they came from?"

"I think so."

"Tell me."

"The eyes of the giant rat."

"Exactly!" the captain exclaimed. "How cunning of the captain before me! He told everyone they were mere bits of glass. What safer way to protect them from thieves, yes? But no sparkling stones could fool the eyes of a waterfront thief in Hong Kong, who gouged them out. Behold, lad, you are indeed gazing at the stolen eyes of *The Giant Rat of Sumatra!*"

I looked at them again. They seemed to flash lights of their own in the cabin shadows, like the lightning bugs I remembered in Boston.

A smile flickered across the captain's face. "I had hardly been the ship's master a year when word reached me that a Malay thief was trying to sell a pair of great emeralds across the water in Macao. We set sail, and I found him. I might have strangled the scoundrel on the spot, but he had a wife and three children with him.

What could I do? So I bought the gems, fair and square, with gold from my private account, and they became mine, no? It's these green treasures, worth a ship's cargo, that our one-armed friend Mr. Ginger, got wind of and came after. Whether others in my crew have similar schemes, I cannot guess. But these green eyes are no longer safe in a pouch around my neck, eh? They will be safer in your hands."

I was startled. "Mine?"

"Who will suspect there is anything of value in the possession of a cabin boy? No one!"

I shook my head. "No, sir, I lose things!"

"Like what?"

"Didn't I almost lose my life?"

The captain playfully lifted an eyebrow. "But your life was a trifle. These are emeralds!"

"What if I run away with them!"

"Run where? You are trapped, you know. I will have to trust you."

I looked again at the gems. Those two confounded stones in my pocket were going to weigh a ton. Then I gave a shrug. "Well, if I lose them, it'll be your funeral."

"No, shipmate, it will be your funeral."

With a sailmaker's needle, the captain sewed the emeralds into the bottom hem of my baggy blue coat. Only after I left the cabin did I pause to realize that Captain Gallows had shown uncommon courtesy. He had not once reminded me that I owed a thundering great favour—*The Giant Rat of Sumatra* had troubled to pluck me from the sea. I could trouble myself to walk around with a fortune in gems in the hem of my coat.

Chapter 7

In which a pile of rubble bursts apart,
and what jumps out

The captain's rancho spread from the sea cliffs to the bright mustard haze of foothills rising to the east. Together with a stout city official in a black frock coat and dusty boots, the captain stood on the cliff top studying an ink-drawn map of the property.

41

Waiting with Trot and Pukapuka, I watched from the nearby shade of the rambling adobe house, abandoned and silent. The men came armed for trouble on the roads with knives and wooden belaying pins from the ship. I tried to ignore the emeralds lurking in my coat, but they felt as bulky as cannonballs.

"Everything correct?" asked the official, blowing dust off his glasses. I didn't know who he was exactly, but he looked important.

"The property seems unnecessarily vast, Señor Machado."

"Yes," the official replied with a chuckle. "Our misfortune is that there is so much cactus land in California that the governor has trouble giving it away. The moment this rancho was available, I petitioned for it in your name."

"What happened to the owner?"

"Colonel Roberto, the Englishman? *Caramba*, his own Indians had turned on him. Another of the Indian rebellions. Everyone is in a temper these days. And him a loyal citizen of Mexico. We had almost forgotten he was an Englishman. And you? You cannot receive a grant of land if you are not a man of Mexico. Your letters assured me, sir—"

"The mission will have my records. I was brought here as a child on orders from the viceroy of Mexico himself. That should qualify me."

"Ah, yes, the poor orphans, given away like unwanted

puppies. You have risen in the world, Captain!"

"You have not used my true name?"

"You have not revealed it to me, sir. The grant is in the name of Captain Alejandro Gallows."

"That will serve."

"You understand you must live in this house, this hacienda, standing on your grant? And you must stock your land with cattle to hold your title?"

"I have already deposited funds with Judge Bomba, my agent of many years, to buy three thousand head of cattle."

"So great a herd to start?" replied Señor Machado. "You will make Don Simplicio himself jealous, may the fleas of a thousand dogs live in his beard."

"I remember the man well," said the captain with a cold shrug.

The official straightened his round shoulders. "Now you must throw stones into the four winds and declare that you are taking possession of El Rancho del Soledad."

Captain Gallows scratched around in the dirt until he had found stones to his liking. Then, as hard as he could throw, he cast one north, one east, then south and west. With a small, private smile, he said, "I take possession of El Rancho Candalaria."

"So?" remarked Señor Machado, making a note. "Named for your wife, Captain?"

The captain did not answer. The seamen and I looked at one another. If the tall Mexican had a wife, he had kept it a secret aboard ship.

The official smiled and shut his soiled book of documents. "The land is yours, Captain Gallows! Watch out for horse thieves, mountain lions, Americans, bandits, fleas, Indians—and your fellow Mexicans. *Suerte.*"

"Luck?" replied the captain, smiling. "I prefer to make my own."

The men led their rented horses to the well and began to fill the dry horse trough.

I poked around the abandoned ranch house. Here and there a small lizard scurried out of the way, like dust come to life. I paused to look through the window openings. Thieves had evidently carried off everything they could carry, including the window glass. The rooms were bare and lifeless, with walls a foot thick. What was the captain going to do with so many empty rooms. I wondered? One could get lost.

For the moment, it was good to feel solid land under my feet again and even to sniff dust in the air.

I found myself watching the waves as they flung themselves uselessly against the cliffs. They burst like pottery. Same as me, I thought, rushing eastward but stopped by these infernal Mexican cliffs.

A sound inside the house caught my ear. Did a door slam? I turned and looked down the long veranda that ran along the south side of the house. I wondered if I had just heard the sea wind banging a door, but I went inside the house to look around.

I glanced at the white stuccoed kitchen and the

adjoining rooms. Cobwebs hung like wispy ghosts from the ceiling beams. As I wandered along the gritty plank floors, room to room, I saw that my shoes were leaving footprints in the dust. And that's when I saw other footprints. Smaller ones.

Someone was in the house.

Someone in bare feet.

I opened another door and peered into a room with a shelfload of books scattered to the floor, evidently tossed aside as useless to the thieves. Footprints led my eyes to a pile of rubble where part of the roof had caved in. The cobwebs looked as if they had been roughly swept aside.

As I approached, a figure trailing cobwebs rose like a jack-in-the-box from the fallen roof tiles. I fell back astounded, as if confronted by a real ghost. But it was a girl and very much alive. She was yelling like something untamed and frightened. *"Aieee! Aieee!"*

She burst past me, her bare feet flying. She was wearing a rag of a red dress and shell bracelets. Like a surprised mouse, she was out the door and gone almost before I could get over my astonishment. She was shrieking in panic.

I rushed after her.

With the same sudden amazement, the captain and his men turned to see the girl as she burst outside. They spread out to stop her, but she dodged one and then another.

It would have been easier to catch a wild animal.

Pukapuka waved his tattooed arms wide to block her way. She darted under them, her eyes flaring white and terrified.

"Asesinos! Asesinos!" she was yelling.

What was she screaming, I wondered? It sounded like assassins. Assassins?

"Quiet, child!" commanded the captain. "No one is going to murder you!"

The men closed in and trapped her. The captain began talking to her in Spanish. She interrupted, *"Asesinos!"*

She flung out her hands as if to strike him, went limp, and fainted. Captain Gallows caught her. He picked her up and turned to carry her out of the sun and back into the house.

That's when I saw a small Indian woman wrapped in a shawl standing near the wall. She extended her arms. The captain shook his head and carried the girl into the kitchen.

I watched as the captain and the Indian woman talked rapidly in Spanish. The girl came to and wrapped herself in a tight ball. The woman, who later turned out to be her aunt, managed to calm her.

It was clear enough that they had been living in the deserted house, hiding from murderers and assassins. The captain told them that they could safely stay there. He offered to hire them and any other Indians who might be hiding. He intended to bring the rancho quickly back to life.

On the ride back to San Diego, he recounted what the older woman had told him in Spanish. "A rumour had sprung up that the Indians on the rancho were planning an uprising. There were sixty or seventy of them. They would kill the Englishman and steal all his cattle and sheep. *Dios mio!* Someone did. She crossed herself a dozen times to tell me it wasn't the Indians. But tempers caught fire among the Californios. They began hunting the Indians like wild animals. These revolts and chases have happened before. The young girl, who was eleven, and her aunt had survived at first by hiding in the ocean waves. Then they crept into the house. They've been hiding there since last winter."

The captain turned his head to make sure that I was following close behind on one of his rented horses. "Don't let that beast run away with you. Have you ever ridden a horse before?"

"No, sir."

"Hold the reins higher. Tighter."

I saw that the captain was keeping me always in the corner of his eye. The jewels had shackled us together.

Chapter 8

And then what happened

In the town plaza, two ragged soldiers from the old Spanish presidio on the hill were attempting to drill seven young men into a militia. The marching about only served to make me aware that the country was at war and that I was the enemy. I reminded myself not to open my American mouth in public, even though I was hearing English spoken everywhere.

Captain Gallows turned to me as if he could sense what I was thinking. "Aye, you Americans!" he said playfully, but with a touch of scorn. "Your Boston ships hold the foreign trade in the palms of your hands. And we are a trading port. So we were obliged to learn your language. You see, it is all your fault, Shipwreck!" The captain burst out laughing.

I gave back a skin-deep smile.

"When I was a boy you could hear English from San Diego to San Francisco," the captain continued. "If we lose this war, our tongues will hardly notice the difference!"

"Do you expect to lose?"

"Why not? Look at those men marching. Do you call that an army? The government in Mexico City is far, far away. They sent us what kind of soldiers? Convicts, most of them! When I was a boy, they raided everyone's gardens. Fight a war with what? Stolen figs? The capital has always looked at us as a curse and a burden, like barnacles on a ship."

My gaze returned to the militia marching under the full blaze of the sun. The soldiers might be convicts, but the young men looked enthusiastic and determined. I felt a certain safety in staying within the protection of Captain Gallows's long Mexican shadow.

"And you," he said suddenly. "What do I know about you? You have the look of an orphan."

"No, sir."

"It was your father who drowned, no?"

"Stepfather. My father was an actor."

"And your mother?"

"On the stage, too."

"To have a mother is a celebration," said Captain Gallows.

I gave a shrug. Maybe. I hoped so.

"And now you have begun life of your own, eh?" continued the captain. "That, too, is a celebration."

"Is it?"

"What will you make of it?"

I shrugged.

"The wide world is waiting for you."

I shrugged again. What was out there for me?

He broke into a smile. "Of course it is! I think the world is scratching its head at this very minute and wondering what it will make of that half-drowned boy, Shipwreck. Be patient, cabin boy. You will find out!"

I nodded and felt like smiling. "Maybe I'll become a pirate like you?"

"You think I am flattered? Shipwreck, I was born to set a bad example. If I find you in my footsteps, I will throw you back in the sea!"

We pulled up at a large whitewashed store and stables facing the bay. A huge and prickly clump of cactus stood in front like a dusty armed guard.

I was glad to get off the horse. I was sore and tender, and my first steps hurt. I noticed Captain Gallows rubbing

50

his back as if it had turned to pig iron.

The storekeeper came out to meet us. He included me in his first, friendly glance. He turned out to be Judge Bomba, justice of the peace. Shorter than Captain Gallows by inches, he wore a linen suit and a stand-up collar. He had smiling eyes.

"Judge," said the captain. "Did you make it known that I have deposited funds in your heavy safe to buy cattle?"

"I have already found you five hundred head. Good, scrawny California cows. A hundred sheep. And fifty hogs. Shall I keep buying?"

The captain nodded and grinned. "Tell me, what is Don Simplicio paying for cowhides?"

"That old miser? May the fleas of two thousand dogs—"

"Never mind the vermin. What is he paying?"

"Two dollars."

"Let it be known that I will pay four dollars."

"Each hide?"

"Each."

"Have you been dining on loco weed? Did something drive you crazy, my friend?"

"Make it known. The crazy sea captain is paying double for hides. Though make it known I will not do business with Don Simplicio Emilio Charro."

I found myself paying closer attention. I understood nothing about trade, but I could see that the captain would be taken for a thundering fool. The tall Mexican appeared unconcerned.

"Don Simplicio Emilio Charro will have fits," said the justice. "He will be forced to pay the same figure to buy hides. I have heard he is in debt."

"Unfortunate fellow," snapped Captain Gallows.

"*Si*. His last two ships vanished in the China Sea. Pirates, they say. Full cargoes of hides and candles! And a third ship is missing."

"Sunk, too, I can assure you. And Don Simplicio's tallow candles are worthless—too limp to stand under their own flame. The sea rovers did the world a good service."

"Buccaneers!" The storekeeper snorted and clicked his tongue as rapidly as castanets. "You are fortunate to have escaped the sea swine. They will ruin Don Simplicio."

"I pity the poor fleas. They must be starving in his bloodless chin," said Captain Gallows scornfully, and changed the subject. "Is it still customary when a trade ship anchors in the bay to put on a great ball for the townspeople?"

"Of course. It is our chief entertainment, especially if you have goods to sell. And how our young women dress up!"

"I have a cargo of China silks and porcelain dishes and even spices from Sumatra."

"Splendid, Captain! We are in need of a festival, with this shirt-tail war on our hands."

"Tomorrow?"

"So soon?"

"Will you oblige me by spreading the word?"

"Believe me," said Judge Bomba. "It will spread itself."

"What about musicians?"

"I will arrange it. Is there room on your ship for dancing?"

"We will make space on the quarterdeck."

"Then it is settled," declared the justice, smiling in anticipation.

"And perhaps you can recommend a *mayordomo*."

"A foreman? For the ship's ball?"

"For the Rancho Candalaria."

The judge paused and closed one eye thoughtfully. "Have you never forgotten that girl? That child? I wrote you, no one remembers her."

"I do," replied Captain Gallows, and quickly changed the subject. "I will need a *mayordomo*. To hire cooks and corn grinders and gardeners and weavers and candlemakers and vaqueros to work with the cattle. Someone to take charge. Someone to bring my hacienda back to life—quickly. In a week."

"A week! No *mayordomo* can do that!"

"Five days would be even better."

"Impossible," said the judge, and then added, running a finger inside his stiff collar, "unless Juan Largo cares to give up shooting horses. He is capable. He is in the store buying beans and sugar. Ask him yourself."

Captain Gallows looked doubtful. "He shoots horses?"

"Wild horses. *Si*. They have become pesky as crows and eat the grass out from under the grazing cows. So the ranches hired Juan Largo to thin out the wild ones. He is unhappy at the job."

"Long John?" muttered the captain. "I think I remember him."

At that moment, to the jingle of his silver spurs, a man with a weeping willow moustache walked out of the store. He carried a large sack of beans across his shoulder. He had legs as long and thin as a stork's.

"Juan Largo!" shouted the justice of the peace. "You once did service as Don Simplicio's *mayordomo*. Meet the sea captain, who has a preposterous offer to make."

Chapter 9

Containing various matters, including an unpleasant stowaway

On the night of the ball, but while it was still light, Captain Gallows transformed himself. He unpacked Mexican clothing tailored for him in Hong Kong. When he stepped out of his cabin, I hardly recognized him. Silver buttons ran down the sides of his trousers. His dark jacket was a swirl of embroidered gold. A silver pistol was stuck under a wide green sash around his waist and his bemused eyes were shaded by a wide-brimmed tan leather hat. "Behold!" he said to his crew. "Today I become Don Alejandro, eh?"

"Whatever you say, Cap'n," remarked Calcutta.

"Have the silks and dishes and spices been laid out for sale? You will be in charge. Chop Chop, did you sprinkle beach sand on the quarterdeck for dancing?"

"In a minute, Don Alejandro."

Trot was still gazing at the transformed captain. "Sir, is it proper to ask a lady to dance with a bloody pistol in your belt?"

"The bloody pistol is for the head of any pirate on deck who utters a bilgewater oath with visitors aboard."

"Gosh!" exclaimed Jimmy Pukapuka.

A boatload of musicians was the first to arrive. The men struggled with their instruments up the ship's rope ladder. They began to play at once, giving the first guests a festive welcome of fiddles and trumpet.

I watched from the mainmast ratlines as Don Alejandro, the silver pistol gone from his sash, welcomed whole boatloads of townspeople. It was Don Boniface this and Doña Victoria that and Señorita something else.

"Imagine!" I heard a man say, gesturing with a gold-headed cane at the bowsprit. "A trading ship with a rat for a figurehead! How curious. How mysterious are these ships from the Spice Islands!"

His companion replied. "Don Antonio, where in the world is Sumatra?"

I heard names. Bandini children chased Carrillo children around the decks and the Mexican governor himself, Pio Pico, pretended to catch them. Judge Bomba said, "Is it true, Governor, that on your rancho nearby you live in a house with nineteen rooms?"

"A lie!" exploded the governor, who then burst into a laugh. "There are twenty-two! I have many relatives!"

Soon the decks were crowded with chattering guests, who seemed overjoyed to escape their ranches for the excitement of the city. The younger men wore waistcoats decorated with spiderwebs of gold and silver thread to match their bell-like trouser cuffs. The women, in swirling skirts and wearing saucy feathers in their hats, were drawn to the dancing or to the cargo of China silks.

I had never laid eyes on a costume ball, but I'd read about them. I'd supposed this was as close as I could expect to come to such fairy-tale happenings. And then it crossed my mind not to forget that I was an enemy alien. I told myself to keep my American voice still. If I had to speak, I would confine my answers to *si* and *no*—especially in the presence of the governor. He appeared to be seeking relief from the war in a shipboard fiesta.

But my resolve almost gave way when I looked down from the ratlines as a big, coarse-looking man came aboard with his wife. I heard the man's name—Captain Henry Fitch.

Fitch? That was an English name. And his heavy, booming voice sounded American! Why didn't the Mexican authorities have him in manacles? Moving overhead, from ratlines to shrouds, I followed the man. His wife, as slim as a hummingbird, wanted to join the dancing on the quarterdeck.

"I'm too clumsy for that nonsense," he protested as Captain Gallows approached. "You, young feller, dance with my wife."

"I shall be delighted, Captain Fitch."

"You know who I am?"

"Doesn't everyone? A former sea captain yourself, the first American to make his home in San Diego, and by reputation an honest trader who knows everyone. And this is your charming wife Doña Josefa, one of Joaquin Carrillo's beautiful daughters."

The older man's eyes narrowed. "Who are you, sir?"

"What does it matter? I should like to ask you a question."

"I should like to dance," said Doña Josefa. "Listen to the trumpet!"

Said Captain Gallows, unwilling to be distracted by a trumpet in the sea air. "Perhaps you recall a girl from long ago, a girl named Candalaria. About twelve years old."

"There are many Candalarias."

"Not in San Diego. She was an orphan."

"Her last name might help, sir."

"She never told me," replied Captain Gallows.

"No?"

"I'm not sure she knew it herself."

"Ask Don Simplicio," advised the older man. "He was forever taking in orphans."

"Don Simplicio does not answer his mail."

"Perhaps that wrinkled old rogue has been dead all these years and is keeping it a secret from us!" Captain Fitch let out a booming laugh, and Don Alejandro accompanied the trader's wife to the dance floor.

I gave my head a slow tilt. It was now clear to me why Captain Gallows was so anxious to throw this party. Someone among the townspeople was bound to remember a twelve-year-old Candalaria. *The Giant Rat of Sumatra* had crossed the Pacific Ocean so that the captain could track her down.

"You up there!"

It was a moment before I realized that someone was yelling at me.

"You! In the yards!"

It was Captain Fitch shouting up at me.

"*Si.*" I said.

"Why are you following me around? Think I'm blind?"

"*No,*" I answered.

"What do you want?"

I retreated without another word through the shrouds and lines. When I banged my hand on a turnbuckle, I couldn't help letting out a yelp. "Ouch!"

I kept on my way and slipped through the fo'c'sle hatch. I tumbled down the ladder below decks to the safety of my bunk.

I pulled up sharply. I saw a stocky figure stretched out on my bunk.

I'd seen the man before. In the Red Dolphin. The harpooner who had joined One-Arm Ginger in the attack on Captain Gallows and been drowned. Now there he was, not drowned at all, but alive and breathing and smiling. Ozzie Twitch!

"We figured you couldn't swim!" I blurted out.

"Not a stroke!" replied the harpooner. "But a sea lion gave me a poke in the air, thankee. And I caught hold of the anchor chain and pulled meself up. Been hiding aboard ever since. Your one-armed shipmate swore there's tons of pirate treasure aboard. Be a good cabin boy and lead me to one of them green ship's eyes, and I'll be gone and happy. Where'd the captain hide the plunder?"

I was made quickly aware of the emeralds in the hem of my coat and almost gave them a reassuring tap. "If I knew, I wouldn't tell you, sir!"

"No? In that event, I'll be obliged to wring your cabin boy's neck."

"You'll have to wring mine first," bellowed Captain Fitch, who had come up from the shadows behind me.

At that, the harpooner leaped out of the bunk and bolted into the fo'c'sle darkness and was gone.

"What was that all about, lad?" asked Captain Fitch.

"He was a stowaway."

"A bad lot, stowaways."

"Yes, sir."

Said the captain, "I was bound to follow you."

"Me?"

"I heard you speak English."

I stood astonished. "Not me, sir!"

"No Mexican would yell 'ouch.' He would say '*ay!*'"

"I scraped my hand on a turnbuckle."

"You must be an American."

I fell silent.

"Don't worry," said the captain. "I am not going to turn you over to the Mexicans. They can't be bothered with an American cabin boy. Don't you know there are several of us Americans living here?"

"No, sir."

"We became citizens of Mexico and took Mexican wives. We are Californios, like our neighbours. So far the war has not touched us. Where are you from? Homesick?"

"Boston. Yes, I think so."

"Where is this ship bound for?"

"Nowhere," I said. "The captain has dropped the anchor here for good."

"Then how do you plan to get home?"

"I don't know, sir."

"That will call for patience, lad. There is no shortage of American ships out of sight in the Pacific. One year, the customs people logged in over six hundred traders and whalers! Imagine! Some ship's captain who hasn't heard we're in a war is bound to turn up for water and provisions. Watch for the Stars and Stripes! That'll be your voyage home!"

I burst into a smile. The Stars and Stripes! Yes, I'd keep my eyes peeled for flags.

Captain Fitch started back up the ladder but stopped for a backward glance. "If our eager militia gives you any trouble, lad, they mean well. Avoid the justice of the peace, who must go by the book. Send for a tavern keeper, Sam'l Spoons."

"Him?"

"You've met the devil?"

"I have, sir."

"Oh, he's on both sides of the law and never troubles himself with honour. But he can fix anything."

"I hope I will not have to trouble him," I declared.

"Good luck," said Captain Fitch in his rough voice, but with a broad and honest smile. I felt reassured to know a friendly face in this foreign town.

Chapter 10

In which appears the lady in velvet, and Captain Gallows loses his boots

A search of the ship was made, but the harpooner had vanished like a ghost. Calcutta thought he might have slipped in among the townspeople when they returned ashore in their crowded boats. Captain Gallows didn't seem concerned, hardly giving the matter a shrug.

He turned in early, obviously pleased with his great success as a host.

Morning arose in an orange fog of sunlight. Captain Gallows slept late. When he finally roused himself, we went ashore, saddled the rented horses, and started back up the coast.

The fog burned off, and the day now looked freshly washed and scrubbed.

My eyes kept scanning the flashing blue ocean to my left. There was no ship out there flying the American flag. There was no ship out there at all.

When we reached Rancho Candalaria, I saw the dead estate rising from its own ashes. Pigs were rooting in the pens. Black cattle had been turned loose to graze on the hills. Juan Largo had hired Indian vaqueros to round up wild horses and break them to the saddle. Gardeners were tending the neglected grapevines. Women sat in the shade of a pepper-tree and ground dried corn in three-legged granite mortars for tortillas. The kitchen chimney was cleaned and fresh fires started in the ovens. Cooks brought forth pots of pozole, a thick hominy soup smelling of pork, for the quickly growing population. I watched it all.

Captain Gallows was clearly impressed to see his moustached *mayordomo* quietly issuing orders in two languages. Without a wasted moment, Juan Largo hired an Indian blacksmith and a Mexican harness maker. He sent a cart to Los Angeles for glass to replace the stolen windows. As if decorating a festive cake, plasterers were already giving the house a fresh white icing.

"My compliments," said Captain Gallows.

"It is too early for compliments," said Juan Largo briskly. "And you are in my way. Manuel, we will start branding the cattle in the morning and shoeing the horses."

"But none of the rancheros brands cattle or shoes horses," said Manuel, pulling a sweat-stained rag down over his forehead.

"Then we will be the first," replied Juan Largo.

"My compliments, Juan Largo," the captain said again.

"I heard you the first time, Don Alejandro. And you are still in my way."

Captain Gallows burst out laughing and ambled off, clearly amused by the impudence of his stork-legged *mayordomo*.

Following along in Captain Gallows's dusty footsteps, I jingled the coins in my pocket. They weren't much, but I felt rich.

After the sale of the silks and spices and crockery aboard ship, the captain had ordered that the money be shared out. As cabin boy, I was entitled to a tiny share and now had a pocket jingling with heavy silver Mexican pesos. I had no idea what they were worth. I slept well, smiled a lot, and went days without thinking about home.

Outside the kitchen one morning, I caught sight of the frightened Indian girl cleaning a freshly caught barracuda.

I watched her for a while, relieved that she was no longer scared out of her wits and screaming.

I approached. I didn't know her language and she wouldn't understand me, but I wanted to say something. I said, "What's your name?"

"Oliviana."

"You understand English!"

"Not often," she answered simply, and carried the fish into the kitchen.

I climbed a dusty pepper-tree and watched Juan Largo looking over wild horses in the corral. The ranch manager chose five to be broken for use around the ranch. I saw Captain Gallows return from the house, wearing an old Mexican straw hat he had found. He looked over the saddle horses in the stable. He picked out a stallion, tall and black, for a gallop around his rancho.

I was told to climb down from the tree and to pick out an animal. I pointed to a smaller horse, tan as dirt, with a luxurious mane. The Indian vaquero said the beast was recently wild, but was now broken and tame as a chicken.

I eased myself into the saddle. The animal lost no time in reverting to his wild state. He leaped into the air. I could feel his back under me bending into a sudden horseshoe. I hung on. He snorted. He spun. I hung onto his mane. Then he gave a kick of his hind legs. That tossed me somersaulting through the dust.

"Shipwreck!" said the captain, grinning. "This is no time for play!" He made a chopping motion with his right hand. "Let's take these beasts for a ride. They need to know our voices!"

I didn't bother to dust myself off. I could feel the captain's impatient eyes on me. I hoped that Oliviana had remained in the kitchen and been unable to see me made a fool of by a dumb horse. She was almost as old as I was, and I bet she could ride any beast of a horse she wanted to.

I slipped my feet into the wooden stirrups. I had no choice but to try the horse again.

I shortened my grip on the reins and held them close and tight. I spoke firmly. Maybe he didn't understand English. He shook his head as if to jerk the reins out of my hand, but kept his legs still. I tried touching him with my heels. The horse ignored me. I tried again and made a sharp sound, like the cracking of a stick. That caught the attention of the horse. He took a gentle step forward. I was amazed. And then he took another step, as if he had only been trifling with me.

I didn't know whether to be pleased with myself or the horse. The captain rode out onto the rutted clay road. I followed.

We were quickly beyond sight of the ranch, picking our way through a fold in the hills. "Did you taste the hominy soup?" asked the captain.

"The pozole?"

"How do you know what it's called?"

"Is it a secret?"

"Ah, so you keep your ears open, Shipwreck. When I was a boy, in the old Spanish days, it was the smell of pozole that sometimes lured hungry Indians to the missions. The friars called it 'catching converts by the mouth.' But now all that is finished, *sí?* Now that Mexico is its own boss, it is the rancheros that catch them by the mouth. But at least we pay them, eh? Do you know what I am paying the Indian vaqueros?"

"Those horsemen?"

"Ah, the cleverest horsemen in the world! I will pay them a clever fifteen pesos a month."

I had counted my own pesos—I had twelve. Almost the equal of a vaquero! I could imagine the astonishment on my mother's face when I returned home and let the coins slide into her hand. Would she be impressed with me? The picture again rose in my mind of the festive orange parasol she had opened to see me off on the wild seas. Had her tears dried? Had there been any tears? I sometimes wondered if she had forgotten me before I was out of sight.

"Shipwreck!"

"Yes, sir."

"Stop dreaming. You will fall off that short-tempered horse."

"I'm awake."

"Were you dreaming of the young Indian girl? I saw you gazing at her. If you want to ask her name, I'll tell you how to say it in Spanish."

"I know her name."

"Indeed?"

"It's Oliviana," I said.

"Pretty name, eh?"

Then the captain made a sweep of his arm. "All this land is mine—I believe. Mine and the jackrabbits'!"

The birds stopped chirping. Rawhide lariats buzzed through the air and jerked the two of us out of our saddles. I felt myself flying in midair. "Hey!"

The horses, unburdened and so recently wild, ran free.

"Ah, señor! I have not had the honour of robbing you before! But I am new on these roads."

It was a woman's voice, as merry as a songbird's.

I found myself on my back. When I looked up, I saw a small woman in a feathered hat at the head of a ragged band of highwaymen. Their guns stuck out like the pins in a pincushion.

"Foreigners, it appears," she added in perfect English. "Such elegant boots!"

Captain Gallows brushed himself off and asked gallantly, "Shall we do you the courtesy of putting our hands in the air?"

"That formality won't be necessary," the woman replied. Her long hair hung over her shoulders in a glossy black fan. Mounted on a tall, rawboned horse, she was wearing velvet breeches, a green scarf around her waist, and a leather waistcoat. "But you may throw down your gun, if you wish."

"My dear woman, I would like to accommodate you—"

"I am not your dear woman," she interrupted sharply.

"I intended only to give you the benefit of the doubt," the captain said. "It is impossible for me to throw down my gun."

"Don't be absurd, sir."

"Alas, I failed to arm myself for this hazardous journey. I shall not be so forgetful again, madam."

"Miss," she said, again correcting him. "But no one travels empty-handed. I'm sure you won't mind making a contribution to the poor."

"I shall be delighted. What poor are we talking about?"

She turned a little smile on us. I couldn't help noticing that when she smiled her face was pretty, but tired. "You can see that my men are in little more than rags. Look at my father, Hernando. The poor man doesn't even own a pair of shoes. My brother Pedro, with his elbows sticking out, is in need of pesos. So I must trouble you for your valuables!"

"A family affair, I see," said the captain. He lifted his straw hat and pulled off a leather money pouch hung around his neck. He weighed it in his hand. "I suppose you have a name, señorita."

"Have you foreigners not yet heard of Señorita Wildcat?"

"You are mistaken. I am not a foreigner." The captain

cocked an eyebrow. "Señorita Wildcat? What an unseemly name to call yourself. It lacks elegance."

"It's what the rancheros have begun to call me. They are annoyed that we help ourselves to their cattle when we are driven by hunger. I was annoyed when a don himself grabbed me, and I scratched like a—"

"Wildcat. Have the rancheros no sense of chivalry?"

"None."

"I shall be honoured to contribute to the poor of your choosing." Captain Gallows tossed his money pouch from hand to hand. "But does it require so many bandits to rob one man and a boy? I have seen smaller armies."

"Señor, help is cheap in California—even among bandits. Throw down your money."

Captain Gallows tossed the pouch to the ground. If he was worried about the emeralds, his light and bantering manner revealed nothing.

A feeling came over me, like a sharp chill wind, that something was wrong. The emeralds. My right hand slid down to the hem of my jacket to reassure myself that the hard lumps were still there.

The emeralds were gone.

I had lost them!

My heart began to thunder. I looked at Captain Gallows. How could I tell him? I shrank back into myself, trying to become invisible. He'd hang me from the nearest tree.

Señorita Wildcat directed one of her men to pick up the pouch. "Now your jewellery."

"Señorita," the captain replied, confident and lighthearted. "As you can plainly see, I am not burdened with trinkets. Such trifles are not to the taste of a gentleman."

"Are you a gentleman?"

"A scoundrel by trade, a gentleman by instinct."

She gave her head a toss. "I have never met a gentleman who wasn't a scoundrel by instinct."

"Careful, Señorita Wildcat," the captain replied, with an air of mischief. "Wound the pride of a gentlemen and risk the consequences. The scoundrel may be obliged to challenge you to a duel."

She fired her pistol, almost winging his ear. "Because I am a woman, don't assume that I would decline. Was that close enough?"

I raised my eyes at the sound. Captain Gallows felt his ear to make sure it was still in place. "Quite close enough. I am charmed to have made your acquaintance, Señorita Wildcat." He made a chopping gesture with his hand. *"Buenos días."*

"Hold on, señor. Your red boots. They will fit my old father here with room to spare! Take them off."

From the captain's bantering manner, I was sure he thought his emeralds were safe in my coat. He sat on a fallen log and directed me to help pull off his boots.

I did what I was told, unable to look up. I couldn't swallow. My heart wouldn't stop pounding. Didn't he notice?

Old Hernando was overjoyed with this treasure. Señorita Wildcat looked at the captain in his stocking feet and smiled. "I'm sure you have many pairs of boots, señor. I will pray for you that we do not meet again."

"And I will light candles with the same happy thought, Señorita Wildcat."

She gave her men a shout. "*Vamanos!* Let's go!"

Off the bandits rattled through the willows and live oaks. As the gang disappeared, I caught sight of a slow smile bursting over Captain Gallows's face. "You see!" he exclaimed. "To a thief, a child has nothing in his pockets but marbles. As I suspected. You conducted yourself well. The emeralds are safe. Now then, I have not forgotten how to walk. *Vamanos!* Let's find our horses."

Chapter 11

In which the tall Mexican talks more than necessary

I stumbled after Captain Gallows. How could I tell him what had happened—that his emeralds were gone. Where could I run off to? Hide with the jackrabbits somewhere? Forever?

How could I have lost the stones? When the horse

threw me? Along the trail?

I saw that it amused the captain to again feel the earth between his toes. He'd pulled off his stockings, remarking that he'd spent the first fourteen years of his life on bare feet.

We came upon our horses, grazing on grass and buttercups a quarter of a mile away. He seemed almost reluctant to settle himself back into the hard saddle. Mounted again, we continued into the foothills. I was silent as a mouse, but he was full of talk.

"It seems, Shipwreck, that California grows bandits as abundantly as it grows cows," the captain mused. "Did you notice what a ragtag lot they were? Stealing boots! Imagine! These juiceless outlaws have no pride in their profession! And a woman, at that. When I was a child, bandits rode about like hidalgos! Like royalty!"

I was barely able to keep my mind on what he was saying. We rode a little farther before a flash of deep contempt rose into his voice, and I looked over at him. "Hidalgos! That's what Don Simplicio fancied himself to be. How he strutted! How he swaggered, eh? Like a peacock! You look pale. Sick?"

"No, sir," I muttered. "You were talking about Don Simplicio."

"May the fleas of a thousand dogs infest his beard," said Captain Gallows, giving the horse a touch of his heels. "Pay attention, Shipwreck. It relieves me of the embarrassment of talking to myself, eh? So. When I was your age and living under Don Simplicio's whip, I heard a rumour that in all of Southern California, nine boys went to school. Imagine! I thought they must be very special. But what did they learn in school? I found out they learned to read. So I tried to teach myself. When Don Simplicio caught me attempting to read a book, he personally whipped me. I still have the marks on my back and a chip on my shoulder, eh? You see, he knew the value of ignorance in those like me who worked his land. He worshipped ignorance. That's what kept us chained to his rancho. An educated peon was like a sea worm in the timbers of a ship, eh? So I ran off, and now I am back and I intend to out-hidalgo the hidalgos!"

Chapter 12

Containing an excess of villains and a kick in the dirt

Less than an hour later, the air filled with howls and wild shouts. I glanced around in amazement. Were we being held up a second time in a single morning?

"*Arriba las manos!* Up hands!"

Again horsemen flowed around us. Again I saw a pincushion of weapons, but these were arrows cocked in bowstrings. And these were bare-chested outlaws wearing headbands and dusty rawhide leggings. Indians!

The captain ripped off his straw hat and threw it to the ground. "Mangy, no-account, noisy rascals! Go to splintered lightning! Blast the lot of you! Mexican outlaws held us up an hour ago! Look!"

He pulled out his pockets and let them hang like dogs' tongues.

"Have you pesky highwaymen no sense of restraint? The pack of you look hungry enough to eat bark off a tree. Is everyone in Mexico out of work and pouncing upon strangers? Haven't you heard? They are hiring at Rancho Candalaria. Now, out of my sight!"

The captain defiantly kicked his horse, and I was quick to follow. The band of outlaws stood frozen and bewildered by the captain's bristling contempt.

The excitement of it all made me forget the emeralds. I was fearful of glancing behind as the captain advanced at an unhurried trot along the road. I hoped that the Indians were too numbed to follow. They had obviously never before met such a force of nature on two legs as this sea captain.

When I looked back, the Indians were fading away over the hills. The captain seemed afraid of no one. How had he grown up to be so fearless? I had watched the power of the captain's commanding presence freeze a flight of arrows. I wondered how I might grow up with that same bravado. I hadn't the courage to tell him what I had lost.

We turned back toward the rancho, riding in silence. Then he gave a sad shrug. "Unlucky devils," he said. "When I was a child, the Spanish missions made thousands of Indians work the orchards and herd the cattle for the hide trade. Shipwreck, I have seen mission lands the equal of small kingdoms! I remember when we pulled down the red-and-gold flag of Spain and raised the red, white, and green flag of Mexico. Did you see it on the flagpole in the plaza? Handsome, no? At last we had a country of our own. It was only fourteen years ago! Aye, and we took back the mission lands, except for a few acres. What could the padres do but turn the Indians loose, eh? What could the poor devils do but imitate what they saw so many Mexicans and foreigners do—steal cattle and take to the roads."

When we returned to Rancho Candalaria, I could hardly wait to dismount. I ran over to the corral where I had been thrown and started kicking through the dirt. I kicked and kicked. Finally Juan Largo noticed and came over.

"Lose something?"

"Anybody find anything?" I asked.

He shook his head and let me be. That's when I noticed Oliviana peering at me. Suddenly she rushed over and put a couple of rocks in my hand. The emeralds.

"When you were climbing in the pepper-tree," she

said, "I saw the marbles fall from your pocket! Such big marbles!"

I was speechless. I smiled and managed to call up a little Spanish. "Thank you. A thousand *gracias*-es."

"*Por nada,*" she answered, smiling back.

Chapter 13

In which I keep my eyes peeled, and the judge gives a hopeless shrug

"Shipwreck! Follow me!"

I was becoming accustomed to Captain Gallows's command. We were to return to town.

I had borrowed a needle and black thread from the seamstress and sewed the emeralds back in the coat with plenty of extra stitches. It was becoming too warm to wear the coat all the time, but I was relieved to put it back on. I figured that I was hardly any different from a pouch of valuables the pirate might keep around his neck.

I'd be glad to reach San Diego again. Ever since Captain Fitch had mentioned that an American ship might come blundering into the harbour, I had felt a renewed hope of finding myself a passage home. I'd keep my eyes peeled.

I didn't know exactly how I felt about the idea of leaving Rancho Candalaria and Captain Gallows. I found myself making machete chops with my hand, the way he did. And I even tried to imitate the captain's bold, fear-nothing walk.

When we reached San Diego, a few lean black cows were chewing weeds in the streets. Talk was in the air. Some fool was paying four dollars apiece for dried hides, and traders were arriving from the ranchos with hides by the wagonload.

"Where do you intend to store your goods?" asked the justice of the peace, lifting his hat and scratching through his black hair.

"I will rent a warehouse in La Playa," the captain said.

"You remember Sam'l Spoons at the Red Dolphin? He has a warehouse."

"I remember him," said Captain Gallows simply. "But, Judge, you must do something about the bandits on the roads. They are thick as fleas. Why don't your soldiers deal with them?"

I stood wondering how the captain, a bandit of the seas, could be feeling so righteous after being robbed by a bandit of the roads—and a tiny woman at that.

"Ah, the bandits," said Judge Bomba with a great, quivering sigh. "Our soldiers have hardly enough musket balls left to play a game of marbles—and not enough powder to fill a thimble. Months ago I petitioned General Castro to spare us a thousand musket balls and flints and powder. My pleadings have been ignored."

The bareheaded captain raised a hand to shade his eyes from the afternoon sun. "I will have shot and powder sent from my ship." And then he added with a shrug, "How do you expect to fight a war with the United States without ammunition?"

"We are hoping the Americans must have more important things to do than to invade us. Perhaps the army will be unable to find San Diego on the map."

"And if the American warships come by sea?"

The judge gave a hopeless shrug.

Chapter 14

In which Sam'l Spoons returns, and a dead man rises from the deep

Returning to the ship, Captain Gallows gave a whistle through his fingers and called the crew together.

"Calcutta, see how much powder and shot we have left aboard. What we can spare, send over to the militia. The rest of you, arm yourselves! Guns, knives, and belaying pins. First thing in the morning we're going to set a civilized example, now that we're landlubbers."

"Speak for yourself," said Chop Chop, standing with his powerful sea legs apart, the better to support his bulk.

Said the captain, "I promised to turn you into gentlemen, but that will have to wait. We're obliged to scare the daylights out of the impertinent rascals infesting the San Diego roads. One of them nipped my red boots!"

Then he pointed toward the La Playa shore.

"Chop Chop, go fetch Sam'l Spoons. You'll find him in the Red Dolphin. Cabin boy, polish me up another pair of London boots. The black ones."

I found the boots in the captain's quarters. Outside, settling myself in the shade against the deckhouse, I set to work with brushes. But the afternoon shade kept drifting away as the ship swung on its anchor chain. I had moved to the starboard side of the cabin when Chop Chop climbed aboard with Sam'l Spoons.

The tavern owner gazed at me with a flicker of recognition. "Ain't you—?"

I said nothing, polishing away with the shoe brush.

"You are! Me hat's off to you, lad! Loyal to your captain, you was! Escaped me clutches slick as an eel dipped in lard!"

The captain, who'd been below with Calcutta to direct

the gathering up of spare ammunition, appeared on deck and saw the tavernkeeper.

"Mr. Spoons, I'm surprised to find you still vertical, so to speak. Not dead yet? Hasn't anyone put a blade in your ribs in all these years?"

"Good day to you, Captain. Don't you see, I'm such a two-faced fellow that no one can creep up and surprise me."

"Come inside. Shipwreck, bring the boots and help me put them on."

Once inside the cabin, the captain seated himself in a Chinese red chair carved with dragons, and I began the labour of working on one of the long boots.

"Captain Gallows," the tavern owner was saying, "it gave me a fright, indeed it did, to listen while that officer of yours, Mr. Ginger, was plotting the other night to put out your lights and steal the coppers off your eyes."

"I'm sure you came heroically to my defence," said the captain with a scornful smile.

"Well, no. No, sir, can't say I did. Sam'l Spoons don't believe in putting his oar in other folks' business. But I reckoned that your one-armed, lowdown barnacle of a chief mate couldn't beat you in a fair fight. Or an unfair one. Even with all the help he brought along. I had the utmost confidence in you, sir."

The captain, growing impatient with the bar-keeper's flattery, gave his hand a chop and changed the subject. "I want to settle accounts."

Sam'l Spoons lowered his voice to a conspiratorial whisper. "You want to talk in front of your cabin boy?"

"Do you have anything to say you're ashamed of?"

"Not me! Not me, sir!" Then the tavernkeeper lowered his voice again and wiped his mouth on the back of his hand. He seemed to choose his words carefully, as if he were paying for them by the ounce. "Can I assume my messages found you, roundabout?"

Captain Gallows nodded. "Roundabout, aye."

"Nothing faster'n them China clipper ships."

"I presume this will settle accounts, eh?" The captain tossed a small pouch of coins into the tavern owner's lap.

"I won't bother to count it," said Sam'l Spoons. "You was born generous. Glad to be of service. Now ain't it a pity how Don Simplicio's hide ships get plundered? Spice Islands sea pirates, I hear."

"Pity."

"Is it true you're buying hides at four dollars each?"

"True."

"That's not going to go down easy with Don Simplicio. He's loading his last ship—the *Serrano* there, out the window. She holds forty thousand hides. But his cattle are stolen right and left—without any help from me, may I add—and I hear he needs another five thousand hides to fill the cargo hold."

"You hear a lot."

"Don't I!" The tavern owner laughed. "Well, I don't

think Don Simplicio can pay your price. I heard he's already down to his last pesos."

"The skinflint was always down to his last pesos."

"Of course. You'd know better than I."

I finished with the captain's other boot and gave both of them final touches of the brush. It was clear as window glass that Sam'l Spoons had been spying for the captain and getting messages to him. *The Giant Rat of Sumatra* must have lain in wait in the Philippines for Don Simplicio's last hide ship to come lumbering along off Manila.

"Mr. Spoons," said the captain, "I will need to rent warehouse space. At your usual dishonest rates?"

"It will be a pleasure."

Captain Gallows rose, exercising his feet in his boots, and Sam'l Spoons humbly backed toward the door.

"Good day, Captain. Do you know the boy there put himself at risk to warn you of the mischief afoot? If I hadn't locked him up, One-Arm Ginger would have croaked the lad with his good hand, for sure. Still might."

"Sadly drowned, is Mr. Ginger," remarked Captain Gallows.

"You don't say? Why, he was in my tavern not an hour ago."

The captain lowered an eyebrow. I froze. The air stopped short in my lungs. That mangy Mr. Ginger still alive?

"If he wasn't alive," said Sam'l Spoons, "he was giving a fine imitation. And he carries a grudge. If I was you, lad, I wouldn't turn my back to the dark."

Chapter 15

A whaling ship blunders in, and I peel off my jacket

I was not the first to spy the squat, three-masted whaling ship entering the harbour. She was heavy in the water and clearly homeward bound. An American flag, bright as fireworks, was flying from her stern.

"Look at that empty-headed fool!" shouted Sam'l Spoons, waiting for Chop Chop to appear and row him ashore. "Don't he know there's a war?"

My heart took a leap. There was my passage home!

I began stripping off my coat as I ran back to the master's cabin. But the captain was no longer inside. I threw the coat, with its heavy emeralds, across the lacquered Chinese chair. For an instant, I thought I heard a small snort from the captain's bunk.

"Who's there?" I called out.

Silence. I peered all around the cabin. I shrugged. There was no one there but me and my imagination.

When I returned on deck, Sam'l Spoons had found a speaking trumpet and was shouting at the whaler as she came alongside.

"Ahoy, you American blockhead! Where d'ya think you're going! You can't anchor here! Turn that windbag around! Don't you know you're at war with Mexico?"

I discovered Captain Gallows standing behind me.

"You planning to jump ship, cabin boy?"

"Look how heavy in the water she is!" I said. "She must be full and heading home!"

"The coat?"

"In your quarters."

"See, amigo?" said the captain. "I told you I could trust you. Shipwreck, I will be sorry to lose you."

"You won't need a cabin boy on your ranch. You'll have plenty of help."

"True. But who will look after you?"

"I can look after myself."

"Also true. You are learning the ship's ropes, but the world has other ropes. I was beginning to teach you, wasn't I? When you first came aboard, your chin was down to your stomach. Now you hold it up, like me, like a bowsprit, no?"

I took my eyes off the approaching whaler to face the captain. I think I must have puffed up my chest just a little. "Reckon so. Reckon I do."

"Who will I have to mutter to? Someone who has read a book or two, eh? A captain has his four ignorant walls for conversation. So I shall miss your company."

I was astonished. The captain would miss me? My own feelings rose and began to tumble about. Would I miss the captain's company? I would. But there before my eyes stood a homeward-bound ship. With a gulp in my throat, I gazed back up at the captain.

Sam'l Spoons, waving his arms, had caught the attention of the long-bearded captain of the whaler. "Head back to sea, you dunce! You'll be mousetrapped."

I saw the whaling captain begin to shout orders to his crew. Men were climbing up the ratlines. The helmsman spun the wheel into a blur. The ship came about sharply in the channel, a stone's throw off our port side.

"Have a safe trip home, Shipwreck," said Captain Gallows, grasping the speaking trumpet from the tavern owner, who took a moment to cross himself.

"Ahoy, Captain! Hold on. I have a passenger for you to take aboard!"

The captain of the whaler lifted a speaking trumpet of his own. "What's all this confounded shouting ashore? A war with Mexico? Great guns, sir! Have you lost your wits? Why aren't you shooting at us!"

"That can be arranged, Captain!" replied Captain Gallows. "Meanwhile, will you take an American passenger aboard? We'll send him alongside."

"Glad to oblige."

Captain Gallows turned to me, but I was already on the run. I was in and out of his cabin quicker'n scat. I reappeared slipping into the blue coat with the buttons down the front and the emeralds in the lining. I would stick to the captain awhile longer.

A smile, faint but firm, appeared in the captain's eyes when he saw me. He lifted the speaking trumpet to his lips again. "Belay that, sir! But do head out to sea. The militia boys ashore aren't practiced shots, so they just might hit you."

Chapter 16

Containing a full account of the notorious duel and how it ended

O n horses and saddles rented for a peso a day, half the crew of *The Giant Rat of Sumatra* followed Captain Gallows and me north. They remained more or less out of sight, lagging by a quarter of a mile.

"Shipmates!" Captain Gallows had instructed them.

"If bandits stop to make our acquaintance, I shall fire a shot. That will be your signal to rush forward and join the fight. We're obliged to make honest men of them!"

But it wasn't a man who confronted us on the beach road. Bursting out of a stand of wind-twisted pines came Señorita Wildcat.

"*Arriba las manos!*" she sang out, giving her loose black hair a toss. Several men behind her remained in the trees, their guns drawn. I could clearly see the bandit Hernando in his new maroon boots.

Captain Gallows held his fire. "Señorita Wildcat," he said. "I shall hate to make an unpleasant example of you. It doesn't seem chivalrous."

"Never mind chivalry or unpleasantness," she replied, straightening as she sat on her tall, rawboned horse. "Hands up."

"Seeking another pair of boots, are you?"

"This time, perhaps your stockings as well."

"And if I refuse?"

"As a matter of principle, I shall have to shoot you," she said.

"Is that ladylike, señorita? And what if I shoot you first?"

"A gentleman would not shoot first," she declared, smiling faintly.

"I do recall that you are a very good shot," said Captain Gallows. "I almost lost an ear the last time we met. But you are right. A gentleman, I suppose, would insist upon a duel."

"Do you think I would refuse because I am a woman?"

"I fear I am about to find out."

Her eyes flamed up. "I accept your challenge!" With a toss of her head, she slipped off her horse and planted her feet on the ground. She was touchy as gunpowder, I thought. And how tiny she was! "For honour or stakes, sir? What shall it be?"

"Why not both? If I fall, this young man will lead you to gems in my possession beyond your dreams. What have you to put up against such a treasure?"

I folded my arms as if to lock on the blue coat. What folly was the captain getting himself into?

She gave him a doubting look. "Let me see the jewels."

"You don't think I am stupid enough to carry them around like ship's cargo, señorita. On these roads? You have my word. What will you put up? Hernando's new London boots?"

"You may command my band of hungry outlaws!" she snapped. "Yours to feed and care for—if, after the duel, you are still standing! Most unlikely, sir!"

The captain turned to me. "Shipwreck, you witnessed the terms, did you not? If I am still standing, I win!"

I said nothing. The captain was regarding the duel as a lark. The bandit had already displayed her aim with a pistol. He'd seen how dangerous she was.

But almost as disturbing was the sudden thought that

Captain Gallows might fire his pistol at a woman. No gentleman would consider such a bloody act! On the other hand, he wasn't really a gentleman. He was a pirate.

"Ready, sir?" Señorita Wildcat sang out, bristling with confidence. "Shall we begin?"

"A certain attention to details is called for. What weapons do you prefer?"

She shrugged. "Pistols will be fine."

Captain Gallows got off his horse. "Do you care to choose a duelling spot?"

"What's wrong with this?"

The captain kicked a toe into the land. "One could mis-step in this beach sand. Will you allow me to select the place for our exchange of tempers?"

"Please yourself."

Captain Gallows looked into her eyes. "It is agreed, then? I have the privilege of choosing the spot?"

"Do you wish it in writing?" she asked scornfully.

"Your word will be good enough, señorita."

"Choose any silly place you wish."

"Splendid." Captain Gallows pointed his left arm straight out to sea. "We will hold our duel thirty paces due west!"

"Idiot," she muttered.

"That way!"

"You are pointing to the water."

"Indeed, I am. Thirty paces into the sea, Señorita Wildcat, and we may fire our volleys. Shall we begin?"

The surf was breaking noisily and trimming itself with white lace. I saw at once how the duel would end. The captain was tall. Señorita Wildcat was short.

"One!" called out Captain Gallows.

"Uno!" echoed Señorita Wildcat.

They began to march into the surf.

"Two!"

"Dos!"

"Three!"

Her voice had not lost its fire, even though she must have seen what might lay ahead. The bottom was falling away. The water would grow deeper. *"Tres!"*

"Four!

"Cuatro!"

When the waves began to break around her hips, Señorita Wildcat lifted her pistol high to keep it dry. The counting advanced as they ventured deeper into the ocean. Soon Señorita Wildcat was up to her elbows in water, but she refused to quit.

"Fifteen!"

"Quince!"

"Sixteen!"

When the captain reached the count of twenty-five, the water was at Señorita Wildcat's chin. She held her head high, full of pride and fury and defiance. She marched boldly deeper through the surf.

At thirty, she was stubbornly underwater.

But her arm was held high, and she pulled the trigger.

The pistol flashed in the general direction of the captain.

I tightened my eyes against the glare off the ocean. I barely saw the pistol fire. But I heard the bang of the shot.

The lead ball went wild. The captain was still standing, his head wet but above water. I didn't realize until that moment that I had held my breath. And when I let my air out, a ragged little laugh escaped with it. Protected underwater, the captain had seen that he'd be in no great danger from Señorita Wildcat below the surface. And if he chose to fire—

He raised the barrel to the blue heavens and pulled the trigger.

"I appeared to have missed you, señorita."

She wasn't listening. She was trying to swim back to shallow water.

The captain caught her by the waist and pushed her ahead of him through the surf. She fell onto the dry sand, catching her breath, and then turned her head to look at him.

"Scoundrel! If we duel again, we shall wait for the tide to go out!"

The tall Mexican said, "Notice that I am still standing. That was the sole condition agreed upon. You still have your honour, Señorita Wildcat. But, alas, you have lost the wager."

Alerted by the gunshot, the ship's crew came galloping up. They began waving the ship's belaying pins like war clubs and firing their weapons. The outlaw band took one look and fled through the trees.

Captain Gallows held up a hand to stop the noise.

"Belay that, shipmates! Those highwaymen are now under my command!"

"They will not take orders from you!" exclaimed Señorita Wildcat defiantly.

"They will from you. Tell them they may work these roads, but only by holding up other bandits."

"That's nonsense," replied the young woman. She tipped her head to allow seawater to run out of her ear.

"I can assure you, it is a profitable strategy."

"And if my men refuse?"

"*My* men, Señorita Wildcat. Mine. You're not going back on your word, are you?"

She flamed up. "I keep my promises!"

"So do I. Warn these rascals that if they defy these orders, my sea ruffians will hoist them from the yardarms of *The Giant Rat of Sumatra*. Seagulls will pluck out their eyes! As for you, Señorita Wildcat—"

But she was no longer listening. Striding to her rawboned horse, she threw herself into the saddle and started away. The bewildered band of outlaws rejoined her, but not before Hernando turned in his saddle.

"Señor, you want your boots back?"

"Keep them, with the compliments of Captain Gallows."

Chapter 17

*Containing a sprinkle of rain
and news of Candalaria*

For the first time, I saw Oliviana laugh. With dark clouds moving in from the ocean, an early summer shower fell over Rancho Candalaria like an unexpected visitor. Everyone ran for shelter, including me. I had been counting pigs in the willow-branch pens for Juan Largo.

Oliviana had been outside the kitchen, grinding corn for the noon tortillas, when the sudden gust of rain caught her. She sheltered the meal with her red apron, opened her mouth to the flinging drops, and laughed.

So I opened my mouth to the rain and laughed, too. "Tastes good, doesn't it?"

"Is clean," she replied, closing her eyes against the raindrops.

"Did you hear the mountain lion last night? Juan Largo said he found tracks this morning."

"My uncle was killed by a mountain lion," she said.

"I'll be thundered."

"Now I have left only my aunt, Mariana. There in the kitchen. I used to have a dog, Pablo."

"What happened to him?"

"Gone." She gave a shrug. "Gone."

Her aunt leaned out of the kitchen door and called to her in their own language. Oliviana wiped the rain dripping off her nose, picked up the bowl of ground corn, and went inside.

Juan Largo came by on his stork's legs and paused. "How many pigs did you count?"

"I forgot to keep track. The rain."

"You call this rain? I've wrung more water out of my socks. Let's make sure we're not missing a hog. We can't have a cougar carrying off our livestock."

"I'll count again."

"Candle maker!" the *mayordomo* shouted to a grey-bearded Mexican crossing to a work shed. "Felix! Don't make us candles like the ones Don Simplicio sells! *Comprende?* Full of air bubbles. And his candles are limp as slugs! Light a match to the wick and they bend over. Give our candles some pride, *sí?* Some backbone?"

"If you will render me some hard fat to add to the tallow, my candles will stand like cathedrals!"

"You shall have it!"

Before my eyes, I was seeing Rancho Candalaria transformed into a small village able to take care of itself. Indian women were making hard soap for the rancho and more for Don Alejandro to sell. A harness maker had set to work. Mexican brick makers were moulding adobe bricks, and masons were repairing the walls of old rooms. I supposed that Captain Gallows meant to have a rancho as bold and self-sufficient as the ones he had envied in his childhood.

Juan Largo kept hiring new help, and I was certain that I recognized a couple of bandits among them—Indians in worn rawhide leggings, who had been scared off weeks before by Captain Gallows's blustering manner. They were put to work below the cliffs to catch fresh fish for the ranch.

Captain Gallows now wore his Mexican clothes every day and was pleased when anyone addressed him as Don Alejandro. When he rode off without me, as he did to examine the records in the old Spanish mission, he warned me not to stray off the ranch. "No harm can come to you here. Jimmy Pukapuka will keep an eye on you, *sí?*"

Don Alejandro returned from the mission bursting with happiness. "She kept her promise!" he shouted on the veranda, needing to tell anyone and everyone.

"Who?" I asked. I could easily guess. Candalaria?

"Candalaria! She did not marry! I asked the priests to search again. Nor did they bury one, except a white-haired Candalaria with a limp! We looked through the mission records. Nothing! Old Padre Jaime recalled that my Candalaria ran away from Don Simplicio and vanished like a puff of wind years ago."

"Your sister, sir?" I stopped to realize that I had no idea who Candalaria really was. "Your wife?"

"Wife? She was eleven years old! We were orphans together in Mexico City. We were transported here together into the hands of Don Simplicio. When I ran away, I swore to her I would be back for her and make her a queen. And here I am!"

He lowered his voice and bent closer. "Don't lose the emeralds, eh? They are for her!"

Chapter 18

Enter the man with fleas in his beard

The road was still damp from the summer shower when a carriage drawn by four matched horses pulled into the courtyard of the Rancho Candalaria. Chickens flew out of the way as if shot from a cannon. The harness maker paused to admire the carriage's oiled leather trappings. Oliviana's aunt, in the kitchen doorway, crossed herself and shut the door.

I had picked up a deep sliver, a cactus needle, in my left hand that Captain Gallows insisted on prying out himself. Through the window I watched the carriage arrive. A moment later, Calcutta, who had taken a fancy to a Mexican hat with a brim as wide as his shoulders, came into the main room. "Some old man wants to see you," he announced.

"Then don't keep him waiting," said the captain.

"He's carrying a walking stick big enough to brain you with."

"He looks angry enough to use it, does he?"

"Aye. Steam coming out of his nose, like a bull."

"I've been expecting him."

Moments later a man with coarse white hair walked briskly into the room and pointed his walking stick at Captain Gallows. "Are you the imbecile paying four dollars for cowhides?"

"I am."

"I am Don Simplicio."

"I know who you are."

Don Simplicio lowered his cane. "Then you know the business of my ranch! Hides!"

"El Rancho Buena Vista? So much land the coyotes get lost in it. *Sí*, I know it well. Hides. Is something troubling you, Don Simplicio? One would think you had fleas in your beard."

"If you were on my land, and I were not a civilized

man, I would have you horsewhipped."

"Oh, you did, señor, many times."

The old man narrowed his eyes and looked down his leathery, suntanned nose. "Who are you?"

"A cattle rancher and dealer in hides and tallow and candles and soap. Like you, Don Simplicio."

The eyes of the old man were smouldering. "See here, young man, I was dealing in hides before you were born. I have a ship half loaded for China. My cattle are gone. But no one will sell me hides to fill my ship's holds. They are selling to you. You must quit this nonsense. You will ruin us both, señor!"

"I think not."

"I assure you! If I have to meet your price, you will ruin me."

"You have ruined others." Captain Gallows didn't bother to look up from his project of endlessly extracting the cactus needle from my thumb.

"What? Who are you, señor?"

"Orphans grow up, Don Simplicio."

"Eh?"

"Don't you remember a boy fresh from Mexico City? A boy named Alejandro?"

"I do not."

"How quickly we forget those we mistreat, true? But you mistreated so many of us. I have come to settle the score."

Don Simplicio stiffened. He froze. His eyes dulled.

He appeared as if his mind had gone spinning backward through the years. And then, without another word, he turned on his polished heels and left the room.

Don Alejandro pulled out the cactus needle.

I said, "Ouch!"

Chapter 19

In which news arrives and I leave

Jimmy Pukapuka raced to Rancho Candalaria with the news that an American warship had been sighted off the headland.

"Her bottom is stuck in the shoals! She's waiting for the tide to rise! The war is in our lap! And some Mexican general has come aboard *The Giant Rat*, and he's giving orders, but none of us understands him!"

Captain Gallows's eyes shot around for a saddled horse. Juan Largo, mounted on a grey stallion, was almost at the gate. The captain whistled him back and replaced him in the saddle. He shoved his boots into the blocky wood stirrups. "Is there time to take *The Giant Rat* out to sea? To safety?"

"No. Yes. Maybe," replied Jimmy Pukapuka.

Without another word, Captain Gallows kicked and raced the stallion out of the courtyard.

I watched him disappear into the trees, dirt flying from the horse's hooves. I was left behind. Had Captain Gallows forgotten that I was standing there? That I existed? If *The Giant Rat of Sumatra* was setting out to sea, shouldn't I be along?

Picking out a fresh mount and transferring the sweat-stained saddle, Jimmy Pukapuka went flying after the captain.

I was surprised at my own feeling of abandonment. The captain might have spared me a glance. A quick word. Had he expected me to remain on the ranch?

I shrugged with uncertainty. I'd become accustomed to following along where the captain went. What if the tall Mexican and *The Giant Rat of Sumatra* didn't return? What was I supposed to do with the confounded emeralds in my coat?

For the first time in a week, I thought about home. Where did I belong? On Rancho Candalaria? In Boston?

I discovered Oliviana staring at me as she carried a tub of water for the kitchen. I turned away and walked into the house.

I watched the ocean outside the windows, half expecting to see a fleet of American warships on the horizon. Later, when I discovered Captain Gallows's pistol lying on a chest, I ignored the thing. The captain had been in such a rush, he had forgotten to arm himself.

But then I was drawn back to the pistol. If the American warship was attacking, wouldn't the captain need his firearm? I picked it up. I wasn't sure what good a small pistol might be against a ship's cannons, but my decision was swift.

I stuck the pistol in the top of my trousers. It was a hot day to wear my coat buttoned, but I buttoned it over the pistol. I strode outside, making hand gestures to the Indian vaqueros to saddle my horse.

I looked back. Juan Largo was nowhere in sight. But Oliviana was still watching me. She seemed aware that I needed watching.

I gave her an innocent smile, and the moment the horse was saddled, I slipped my foot into the stirrup. I'd bring Captain Gallows his pistol, whether he needed it or not.

I allowed the horse to walk out the gate so as not to attract attention to myself. Once into the trees, I dug in my heels, and the horse began to rattle away.

Chapter 20

In which villains spring forth and amazements abound

I couldn't catch up. The captain and Jimmy Pukapuka were nowhere in sight over the brown hills and beyond the cliffs toward San Diego. When my horse began to blow, I took pity, slipped to the ground, and walked the animal along the rutted road.

"But don't take your time catching your breath!" I told the beast. "I'm still in a hurry."

My mind kept leaping ahead. I just might present myself to the American sea captain and ask to be taken aboard the warship. The Americans would see I got home to Boston, wouldn't they? How much would Captain Gallows care that I was gone? In the way of seafaring men, he'd give a wave and a smile and forget me quickly, I thought.

I heard running water and found a small brook flowing out to the cliffs and down to the sea. I fell on my stomach and drank. The horse didn't have to be told.

"My eyes! If it ain't the ship's cabin boy himself!"

The familiar voice sent a shiver through me. I slowly turned my head. Against the blazing sun, I saw One-Arm Ginger and the harpooner standing over me.

"If you're looking for Captain Gallows, sir, you missed him," I said, hardly moving a muscle. "He must be clear to San Diego by now."

"Oh, we saw him ploughin' by, all sails hoisted."

"It's not him we're looking for," added the harpooner.

"No, lad," said One-Arm Ginger. "The captain can go to blazes with me best compliments. It's you we're after, lad. You, cabin boy."

Sprawled and frozen, I slid them another look. I could hear the water rushing below my cheek. "You must be mistaken," I said, surprised at the steadiness of my own voice.

"No mistake about it!" replied One-Arm Ginger. "Mr. Ozzie Twitch here, he was hid about *The Giant Rat* where no one would think to look for him. Hid in the captain's own quarters, he was! Aye, and he saw you rip off your coat, did he not? You felt the lumpy lining with your fingers, did you not? And then you fled back on deck."

"I did and he did," said the harpooner proudly. "And out I pops to have a look, and what do you suppose I find? Now, who would sew common rocks in his coat, I ask ye?"

Said the one-armed man, "Mr. Twitch had the wit to pull apart the stitches enough to see a flash of green. He was about to make off with your coat—"

"But in again you pops and grabs the infernal coat and off you rushes back out."

I clearly remembered the moment when an American whaler had come blundering into port. I'd changed my mind about deserting Captain Gallows and leaving the coat behind.

One-Arm Ginger ran a scuffed finger under his nose. "Now, the moment Mr. Twitch told me about that sparkle of green, I calculated what it signalled. Emeralds is green, ain't they, lad? And just what green emeralds might they be, eh, cabin boy? Why, the eyes of the blinded *Giant Rat of Sumatra* herself! Am I correct? And now we overhauled ye at last, wearing the very coat buttoned to your neck!"

I could feel the pistol concealed against my stomach. I remained flat to the ground, wondering what Captain

Gallows would expect me to do. But the moment I felt One-Arm Ginger's fingers grasp at the coat, I spun over. Rolling to my back, I drew the pistol from my waist and held it firmly with both hands.

"Back off, sir!"

One-Arm Ginger sprang back with astonishment. And then his red-nosed face cracked a smile. "Lawful mercy, lad! That was cleverly done! Slick as butter! Why, I do believe you'd explode that trifle and send yur old friend to red-hot perdition!"

"You're no friend of mine. And you'd best back off."

"Certainly, lad. Come 'long, Twitch. The boy's hoisted a battle flag, and I say we salute it."

He gave a small, clumsy salute and turned his back to me. For a moment my muscles eased up. But the next moment, One-Arm Ginger gave a sharp backward kick with the heel of his boot. Loose dirt flew and struck my face.

I sprang up, half blinded. But Twitch was already charging into me. I felt One-Arm Ginger's powerful fingers closing around my small fist and the pistol. I held on with all my strength, and the gun fired.

For an instant, I think his muscles froze as well as mine. When it became clear that the shot had gone wild and that neither of us was shot, One-Arm Ginger chuckled with a burst of scorn. "My patience, lad! Don't you know I catch pistol balls between me teeth and spit 'em out?"

I bit the man's thumb even as the harpooner caught

my legs and brought me to earth. The pistol went flying like a pulled tooth and gave a twist in the air. It tumbled down the cliff, kicking up puffs of dust.

My heart sank.

One-Arm Ginger gave his thumb a hard shake. "Now, that wasn't a polite thing to do, lad. Me patience's at an end! Let's have that infernal coat!"

Mr. Twitch began pulling at the coat sleeve while One-Arm Ginger caught the collar. I reckoned that I was beaten, but a fury rose in me and I stubbornly folded my arms to lock the coat to my chest. Isn't that what Captain Gallows himself would have done?

The men tugged on the coat, then stopped short.

"Arriba las manos!" came a shout in the air. "Hands up!"

I gazed up at men on horseback surrounding us, their guns drawn and teeth bared like the dreadful jaws on the figurehead of *The Giant Rat of Sumatra*. My heart gave an awful leap and began to thunder. And then I recognized the voice of their leader. I took a breath, hugely relieved to see Señorita Wildcat on her tall, rawboned horse.

Chapter 21

Being full of derring-do and daring don't

"Is that how you foreigners rob travellers?" exclaimed Señorita Wildcat. "And a mere boy at that! You give dishonesty a bad name."

"Señorita," said One-Arm Ginger, attempting to brush himself off. "Miss, if you plan to empty our pockets, you'll find nothing but dust and a live flea or two. So we'll lift anchor, if you don't mind."

She made a short chop with her hand as she turned to her men. "Wrap them up like sausages," she said. "We'll deliver them to the jail. I keep my promises, even the foolish ones."

I stood transfixed. Had she seen Captain Gallows give his hand a chop the way she had just done?

Rawhide ropes were thrown out even as the harpooner attempted to run. I slipped down the shallow cliff and found the pistol. After scrambling back up, I hesitated while the two men were being disarmed.

"Ramón, my father," she called out. "See that they are wrapped tight. Help him, Luis, my brother."

My eyes fixed on Señorita Wildcat. Her father, Ramón? When she'd taken Captain Gallows's boots, hadn't she called her father Hernando? How many old fathers did she have?

"Thank you, miss," I said.

"You speak like an American," she replied, flashing me a smile.

"I am."

"We are at war. Then perhaps I should deliver you to jail as well."

"I'd be obliged if you don't. That thing you did with your hand, do Mexicans do that?"

"What thing?"

I sliced my hand through the air. "Like that."

"Like a machete, you mean? Do I still do that?" She

gave a little laugh. "Yes, something I must have learned as a child."

"The captain does the same thing."

"Who?"

"The man you fought the duel with. Captain Gallows."

"Well, you may tell your Captain Gallows that I have caught him a pair of bandits. That was our bargain."

I found myself studying her like a puzzle. She had one too many fathers. "Maybe you'll want to tell him yourself," I said. "Did you notice that ship in the bay, miss? The ship with the figurehead of a rat? If he's not there, I guess he'll turn up at the ranch."

"He has a ranch?"

"Rancho Candalaria."

She paused. "What a curious name."

"Is it?"

"But common," she added.

After tying One-Arm Ginger and the harpooner to their saddles, the men remounted. Señorita Wildcat gave the merest nod of her head, and the horsemen spurred their horses. She lingered a moment and then started after them.

Words rose to my throat without any help from me. Astonishment rose with them. Where had such a windblown thought come from?

"Good-bye, Candalaria," I called out.

That would stop her in her tracks, wouldn't it? Unless she wasn't Candalaria and rode on.

She rode on. I felt crushed. I had made a wrong and stupid guess. She wasn't an orphan. She was just Señorita Wildcat, fathers and all.

But then she hauled up on the reins, as if unable to resist a second thought. Her horse reared on its hind legs and spun around. She gazed at me. I hoped she would advance toward me. And she'd say, "How do you know my name?"

But she just peered at me. And then she turned the horse back around and rode off after her men.

Chapter 22

How the bold Giant Rat of Sumatra met her fate, and history was made

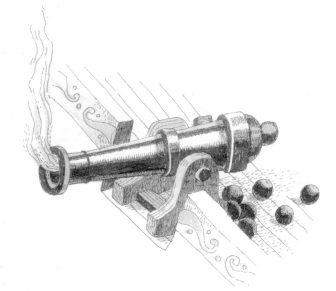

I saw the warship for myself. She had the sails raised on all three masts as she tried to blow herself off the shallows. Her row of square gun ports were open on her lee side, and the mouths of brass cannons gleamed in the mid-afternoon sun.

Closer in, *The Giant Rat of Sumatra* still lay at anchor. I could see Captain Gallows and Jimmy Pukapuka climbing up the jack ladder to deck.

Without losing a moment, I pounded on the door of the Red Dolphin, but Sam'l Spoons had locked it and fled the war. Others I saw standing on the roofs of the hide houses, peering at the warship stuck in the mud.

I ran around to the back, found the oars where I'd left them my first night ashore, and again borrowed Sam'l Spoons's rowboat.

With my hands on the oars and my back to the ship, I had a clear view of the small Mexican militia advancing along the bay road.

I was soon at the side of *The Giant Rat,* even as the crew began to rotate the squealing capstan and raise the anchor. I tied off the boat to steady it in the swells of the incoming tide so that I could catch the jack ladder. Up I went and on deck. Not ten feet away stood Captain Gallows, still in his Mexican trousers with the silver buttons down the sides.

He was shouting orders, while at the same time angrily addressing a Mexican officer with sleepy eyes and thick sideburns that swept under his nose like fishtails.

"Amigos! Raise all the canvas you can! General Castro, I have no interest in helping you escape. Sahibs! Man the guns! General, I am putting you off! Shipwreck, what are you doing here? Take the general ashore."

The officer was sputtering with anger. His gold collar

had popped open. "But the Americans are looking for the commanding general. If they find me, I will have to surrender."

"Without a fight?" snapped Captain Gallows.

"The cannons in the fort were spiked years ago! Fight with what? Look at the warship out there! The *Cyana* herself! Count those twenty-two guns!"

"I have," replied Captain Gallows.

"Clear the bay while you can, or she will blow you apart!"

"But what a disgrace for Mexico that nobody fights for her. Ah, cabin boy, is that my pistol? *Gracias*. Now, if you will be so kind as to take General José Castro ashore."

My eyes must have flared. "But I want to stay aboard!"

"This is not your fight. Quickly, now!"

"No, sir," I said.

"What's this? Mutiny from a cabin boy? I shall have to hang you, eh?"

"Sir—"

The captain turned his back to me and lent a hand at the capstan. The general tightened his collar angrily and led the way down the jack ladder to the rowboat. I followed.

We reached the beach as the militia came marching in. The general immediately took command and turned them around to escort him back to town.

I climbed to the roof of the Red Dolphin for a better

view of the warship. I saw the sails rising on *The Giant Rat,* but the ship remained tethered. The anchor chain looked stiff as a pole.

I could make out Captain Gallows and Jimmy Pukapuka and Calcutta struggling at the long handles of the capstan. Then it dawned on me. The anchor was fouled. Caught below. *The Giant Rat of Sumatra* could go nowhere.

It gave me a sense of relief. Captain Gallows wouldn't be so headstrong as to engage in a fight at such a disadvantage.

As I watched him shouting orders, it struck me that we now were obliged to regard ourselves as enemies.

I belonged to the other side. To the Americans. I no longer had any business aboard *The Giant Rat of Sumatra,* attempting to fight for the honour of Mexico.

The U.S.S. *Cyana* finally cleared the shoals. She turned and came cruising down the channel, taking in sails.

The Giant Rat of Sumatra fired off two of her deck cannons in blossoms of white smoke. For a moment the Americans might have taken it for a two-gun salute. I saw the cannonballs fall short, creating great splashes.

The warship fired back, taking down the sea rover's tall mainmast.

The sight of it falling stopped my breath. Captain Gallows was as often in the rigging as elsewhere aboard the ship. He might have been hit.

No. There he was, like a jack-in-the-box, making a

chop with his hand. *The Giant Rat* lit off another cannon. The ball came hurling high in the air. In an instant, the warship let fly another volley. The pirate ship lost another mast. She sat wounded and disabled, but afloat.

I saw Captain Gallows rise again from a great spiderweb of shrouds and ropes and fallen ratlines. He straightened and gave the American captain a salute and a smile. I took it to be one of admiration for the artistry of its gunners. But it was just as clear to me that the smile was for himself. No one could say that Mexico had given up without a gallant broadside. He fired off a final volley of cannonballs.

The warship found an anchorage and lowered a launch. A marine guard, some still visibly seasick from the voyage, steered for San Diego itself. I lost sight of them, but under the blue sky I could make out the tall flagpole in the plaza across the bay.

I saw the Mexican flag come down. San Diego had been captured. I watched the American flag rise and billow out like a sail in the late afternoon sea breeze. I felt immediately closer to home.

But how could I regard Captain Gallows as anything but a friend?

Chapter 23

Containing all manner of things, including the secret of Don Simplicio

C aptain Gallows came ashore with several of his crew. None of them bore more than a battle smudge of gunpowder here and there or a new rip in his clothing. They looked up curiously at the American flag snapping above the windy plaza. The entire village seemed to have come outdoors, even the few Americans, with all eyes gazing at the foreign flag. Everyone seemed to be talking at once and muttering the same thought. So! Is the battle finished? Does San Diego no longer belong to Mexico?

"Captain Gallows," said Judge Bomba, carrying his white linen coat hooked from a finger over his shoulder. "I am afraid you must regard yourself as under arrest."

"On what charge?" replied the captain, lengthening the stirrups on his horse.

"A young woman covered in church veils has delivered into our hands two road bandits as tightly bound as mummies. The one-armed ruffian declares that you are a notorious pirate. A buccaneer, amigo! And you our sudden hero! We saw you thumb your nose at the American warship. Of course, the charge against you is nonsense, but the villain is prepared to swear to his charge."

"But it's true," said Captain Gallows with a simple shrug. "I have a modest fame as a rogue and a villain in waters across the world."

The justice scraped his jaw thoughtfully with the back of his hand. "It saddens me to hear that. But we don't have room in our little jail for three."

"I give you *The Giant Rat of Sumatra*. Her sailing days are finished. She will make you a fine jail."

"And a splendid fine can be charged against you, paid in full," replied the judge, a smile rising like dawn on his face. "But it occurs to me that I cannot arrest you for piracy in oceans across the world. Those longitudes are beyond my jurisdiction! I am afraid you will be obliged to be judge and jury in your case and punish yourself."

"I shall be merciless," said Captain Gallows, only half jokingly, it seemed to me.

"I would give some legal weight to those broadsides you fired at the Americans! You appear to have survived the battle without a scratch!"

It was a wonder, I thought. And since *The Giant Rat of Sumatra* was in ruins, and now given away, I reckoned that Captain Gallows's pirate days had ended.

It was only then that big Captain Henry Fitch joined everyone at the flagpole, carrying a puppy in his arm.

"No one seems too upset to be under the American flag, have you noticed?" he said.

"I think some would have preferred the British," remarked the justice.

"Almost anyone would do, yes," remarked the big trader. "Our government in Mexico City neglected us like an unwanted child. They viewed California as fit only for Indians, jackrabbits, and missionaries! And speaking of the unwanted, this pup is the last of the litter. I promised my wife I'd find a home for the rascal." He turned to the justice. "How about you, Judge Bomba?"

When the justice shook his head, I spoke up. "I'll take him, sir."

"Done!" said the trader, handing over the dog before I could change my mind. "His name is Señor Behind-the-

Oven, which is where he was born, but call him what you wish."

"Yes, sir," I said.

Without a pause, Captain Fitch turned to the judge. "Your honour, I promised Don Simplicio I would fetch you. He's dying, you know."

Even as I snugged the pup at my elbow, I saw Captain Gallows's head snap around. "What's that?"

"Dying," repeated Captain Fitch. "As justice of the peace, Bomba, you're the only one he trusts to notarise his will. Not that he has anything left in his estate."

"You must be mistaken," said Captain Gallows crisply.

"I assure you, I am not. When his wife died, his heavy sorrows turned the old scoundrel inside out. How could he join her in heaven, you see? He tracked down those he had mistreated and provided them with land and cattle of their own—those he could find."

"He never tracked me down!" Captain Gallows exploded.

"Who could? And secretly he has been building orphanages where they are needed most, from San Blas to Monterrey to Mexico City. Never did he permit his name to be used. It was his punishment. And who would have believed the old miser had a beating heart? He even borrowed funds from me to keep building. Now his last peso is gone. He ruined himself."

I saw the colour drain from Captain Gallows's face.

"No," he said icily. "I ruined him."

He turned away from the flagpole and I followed him, clutching the dog but thinking of the four-dollar hides. Mounting his horse, the captain called to the justice that he was no longer buying hides at any price.

Several members of the crew of *The Giant Rat of Sumatra* decided to remain in San Diego until they could find another ship to their taste. Calcutta and Trot and Jimmy Pukapuka joined Captain Gallows on the march back to the rancho. Three pack mules bore their many sea chests.

I carried the puppy, fat as butter and only a little darker, clutched under my coat.

"Captain Gallows—" called out Jimmy Pukapuka.

"Don't call me that!" replied the captain in a cheerless voice. "Captain Gallows is no longer. I am Don Alejandro."

Don Alejandro sat gloomily and silently in his creaking saddle. Riding beside him, I gave him only one uneasy glance and quickly looked away. I sensed how tormented he was by what he'd just learned regarding Don Simplicio Emilio Charro. The captain had lavished years of hatred on a man who should have commanded his respect.

Wrapping his hands around the reins, Don Alejandro turned the horse around sharply and decisively and, without a word, began a flying gallop toward San Diego.

No words were necessary. I knew that he was racing

back to stand before the dying ranchero and make his solemn apologies.

Chapter 24

In which Candalaria returns, and surprises lurk about

I was eager to reach the ranch at last and to pull the surprise from under my coat. "His name's Señor Behind-the-Oven, because that's where he was born, but you'll want to change it," I said, handing the golden puppy over to Oliviana.

"Mine? To keep?"

"Sure, to keep. Does he look anything like the dog you lost?"

"No, but I will love him anyway!"

She had come in from the old garden with a basket of carrots. The dog began mopping her face, and I said, "He likes you."

"*Sí!* But don't you want to keep him for yourself?"

"I'll be leaving," I said.

Her expression darkened and she let out a small whimper. *"Aieee!"*

"I have a home. It's far away."

"Good-bye."

"I'm not going yet. I'll have to wait for an American ship. There should be lots, now that our flag is flying."

"Going to a home like this?" she asked, with a wave of her hand that seemed to embrace the entire ranch.

"Not like this."

She peered at me as if I must have lost my wits to turn my back on such a place.

"I have a mother in Boston. I want to see her again."

"A mother."

"I need to show her that I'm still alive. And then I'll see."

"See?"

"I want to know if she has an old orange parasol. Sometimes I wonder if it was someone near her, someone else I saw opening it up as my ship was leaving. We had already drifted quite a way from the wharf. Could have been someone else."

"I don't understand," said Oliviana, cuddling the dog and then holding him in the air. *"Gracias! Mil gracias!"*

"You're welcome. I may get back here someday, and that dog'll be grown! What are you going to call him?"

"I need to think."

"Plenty of time," I said, picking out a carrot and taking a bite. I started toward the door. Only then did I notice the tall, rawboned horse approaching.

Candalaria, wearing lace over her hair and shoulders, remained seated in the saddle. "You remember me?"

"You're Candalaria," I said.

"I think I am wasting my time. There are Candalarias all over Mexico!"

She seemed on the verge of turning the horse to gallop back the way she had come. What was she afraid of finding out? Quickly I held up the carrot to the horse. It turned its long face and picked up the carrot between its yellowing teeth.

"Don Alejandro just returned," I said. "Let me get him."

"Is that what he calls himself?"

"That's his name. Maybe you should come in."

"I choose to wait here."

I was sorry to leave her mounted, ready to flee at any moment. With fingers crossed, I hurried inside and found Don Alejandro standing at the windows, gazing at the sea.

"Candalaria is outside," I said in a bold voice.

Don Alejandro didn't bother to turn. "This is no moment for mischief."

"I'm sure it's her!"

"Don't be loco."

"It's Señorita Wildcat!"

The tall Mexican remained motionless. "Señorita Wildcat?"

"She looks ready to run. You'd better hurry outside, sir!"

"No need to hurry," said Candalaria.

I turned to see her standing inside the open doorway. Then she swept into the room like a typhoon wrapped in lace and winds of her own motion.

"Señor, why are you shouting my name about?" she asked. "What do you want?"

"Nothing, if your name is not Candalaria."

I saw her eyes flare with impatience. She stood, folding her arms and taking his measure from head to toe. "Who are you?"

"Do you remember a young Alejandro from Mexico City?"

"I don't recall."

"Let me look at you."

"Have you done anything but examine me since I stepped in?" she asked. "Like a jeweller through his eyepiece."

"I see no ring on your finger. You have never married?

Shall I assume you have been waiting for someone?"

"You may assume what you wish!"

"You recall being an orphan, señorita?"

"I do not."

Don Alejandro took a step closer. "It's been years, but Candalaria could have grown up to look like Señorita Wildcat. Like you. There is a resemblance. I see it now."

"Look more closely and you will find no resemblance. I have never been in Mexico City. I am not an orphan. I have not been waiting for anyone. And lately I ply my trade along the roads. Keep looking for your Candalaria. It is not me!"

With a sharp and final chop of her hand, she turned and flew through the door. It shut after her as if slammed by a gust of wind.

I looked at Don Alejandro. Don Alejandro gazed after her. And then he began to chuckle softly.

"I am going to marry that woman."

"Señorita Wildcat?"

"Soon. As soon as possible!"

"I'm sorry I was wrong," I said. "I was sure she was the Candalaria you're looking for. Did you notice what she did with her hand? Just like you. And I figured she just called every old man 'father.' "

"You were not mistaken. She is Candalaria. My Candalaria."

My spirits began to fill like a balloon. "You think so?"

"I could tell by the way her eyes examined me, still

looking for the fourteen-year-old Alejandro who left, swearing to return for her. She waited all these years. And today she found him. Me."

I gave a small, hopeful nod. I crossed to one of the windows and caught sight of Candalaria riding off under the pepper-trees.

"I don't think she liked you, sir. She said she wasn't an orphan and that she'd never been in Mexico City."

"Think! I returned to discover her a petty criminal, stealing boots and trinkets. How humiliating, *no*? Candalaria will deny everything until I get her to the altar."

I was anxious to be convinced. But a sudden cloud blew across my mind. "Señorita Wildcat'll be caught. She'll have to go to jail!"

"True, and there's a most uncomfortable prison in San Blas, I'm told. But Señorita Wildcat broke Mexican laws. You saw what happened today. We are now under new laws! American laws!"

"But what if she breaks them!"

"We must stop her before she does anything so foolish." He threw open the door. "Calcutta! Jimmy Pukapuka! Hang it all, Juan Largo! Whistle up your vaqueros and bring that señorita back wrapped up in rawhide like a tortilla. Careful. She may bite!"

Then Don Alejandro turned back to me. "I must now trouble you for the eyes of *The Giant Rat of Sumatra*."

I was glad to be relieved of them at last. I ripped open

the stitches at the bottom of my coat, and out tumbled the emeralds. It was almost August, and at last I didn't need to wear the warm, gosh-awful blue coat.

Chapter 25

Being full of emeralds and punishments and a scruffy ship homeward bound

Standing on the adobe wall, I watched as the United States troops, landed a week before in San Diego, now marched past Rancho Candalaria. They were on their way north to plant the American flag in Los Angeles.

I jumped down from the wall. Everywhere I looked, new things were happening around the hacienda. A blacksmith had set up his forge near the horse trough. A tailor had measured me for new clothes in the Mexican style, with silver buttons down the sides of the legs. Three seamstresses were at work making a wedding dress out of White China silk. Señorita Wildcat herself, in a room of her own, was making a summer hat she would wear after the wedding.

"I learned to make hats in New Orleans!" she burst out cheerfully at dinner one night. I listened quietly as her story quickly followed. Like Don Alejandro, she had run away from Don Simplicio. She had moved from mission to mission, finally running away from the Mission San Juan Bautista to the north. She had travelled to Texas and then New Orleans. There she had learned French, English, and how to make hats. Only weeks before, drawn to where she had grown up, she had returned with a trunkload of hats in the latest style to sell in San Diego.

But on the road, in a heavy rain, she had been stopped by highwaymen. Hoping to find something to eat, they had overturned the trunk in the mud.

"I had not imagined bandits could be so ragged and incompetent. But they were starving. They couldn't eat my hats, already ruined in the mud. Couldn't they see a feast of cattle grazing on the hills? Had they no imagination? Were they so afraid of the hidalgos? I decided with a snap of the fingers to make these poor fools equal to their profession.

'Follow me!' I commanded, and I learned to become a bandit. But truth to tell, the roads are empty, and a pair of maroon London boots was our greatest success!"

Day by day, war news drifted in. The white-bearded Mexican governor, Pio Pico, had fled, and all of California was falling to the Americans.

The morning arrived when I got dressed in my new clothes, pausing only a moment before a mirror to see if I recognized myself. Señorita Wildcat, in her wedding gown, stepped into the courtyard. Carriages were waiting to take everyone to the old mission in San Diego.

Hours later, shortly after noon, Señorita Wildcat stepped back into the bright sunlight under a new name. She was now Doña Candalaria. Large emeralds swung from her ears, as bright as green stars.

I heard a whisper. "Glass, of course." I lifted my eyebrows and smiled to myself.

The gems were so heavy on Doña Candalaria's ears that once the wedding party left the mission doors and reached the carriage, she fingered them as if she might pull them off.

"Doña Candalaria!" the judge exclaimed, after embracing the new bride. "You are free of the law! What can I charge you with? I am powerless! And what evidence do you offer? A pair of boots!"

"But handsome maroon boots. Made in London. Surely a serious offence," said Don Alejandro.

"All right," exclaimed the judge with a patient smile.

"We have a new jail. That ship in the bay with the lovely rat for a figurehead. Let yourselves in! Stay in jail as long as your conscience demands. Two weeks? A bit of hard labour clearing the debris? Yes, that will be your punishment. And then you may let yourselves out. And let that be a lesson to both of you!"

"I will learn my lesson well," said Doña Candalaria, at last pulling off the two large emeralds dangling from her ears.

Aboard *The Giant Rat of Sumatra*, the freshly married couple served out their sentences by clearing the war rubble from the decks. Doña Candalaria took her punishment seriously, scrubbing and polishing. Then it got into her head to climb below the bowsprit and give the giant rat a fresh coat of yellow paint. She wouldn't allow me to help her.

I remained aboard *The Giant Rat of Sumatra*, waiting for an American trading ship to turn up.

Don Alejandro offered to pay my passage, but I refused. I needed to make my own way home. I needed to prove to the lingering voice of my stepfather that I could manage for myself. To my mother, too.

I was almost sorry to see the *Sea Horse* enter the bay under the Stars and Stripes and drop anchor. Her cargo deck was piled high and covered with canvas. A scruffy sea freighter, I saw, and I quickly found out that she was heading for New York and Boston with her hold packed with Chinese rugs and fireworks.

The master of the *Sea Horse,* a Captain Fred B. Kinne, said he might take me on as cabin boy. "Do you get seasick?"

"No, sir."

"You will, aboard the *Sea Horse.* She bucks and rolls something fierce."

"Yes, sir."

"She leaks. You won't mind bailing out?"

"No, sir."

"Food's terrible."

"I'm not hungry, sir."

Captain Kinne grinned. "You'll do. Sign here. The *Sea Horse* is speedy. Quicker'n lightning. Why, I'll have you home in five months!"

The time came for me to move my few things to a fo'c'sle bunk aboard the *Sea Horse.*

Don Alejandro forced a small money pouch on me. "For your education. I pass on the gift that was made to me when I was a cabin boy, *sí?* Remember the hen ship? Someday, Shipwreck, I expect you to command a ship of your own!"

I knew I must be blushing. A burst of pride made my face feel warm. I didn't want to disappoint the tall Mexican.

I wouldn't.

Doña Candalaria embraced me. "Come back to us."

My emotions were churning. I avoided the sight of the *Sea Horse* nearby in the bay. Why was I leaving the

Rancho Candalaria?

I had to. Because I had to, I told myself.

The moment came to leave Don Alejandro and Doña Candalaria. I couldn't think of what I wanted to say—that I loved them as I wished I loved the woman under the orange parasol? But maybe that, too, would happen. I would find out. What I heard myself say was, "I wonder what Oliviana is going to name her dog?"

Then I turned and climbed aboard the *Sea Horse*. Lines were thrown off. Shouts and commands filled the air. Canvas rose to catch the wind. I took a last look at *The Giant Rat of Sumatra* and the tall Mexican and his wife I was leaving behind. I found my hand making a small, hesitant chop.

Then I heard a command. "Cabin boy!"

Author's Note

In which the ink-stained writer confesses, and a trilogy is revealed before your eyes

N ovels are not plucked out of thin air.

This one began with a question. What was wrong with the year 1846? Why were other writers ignoring it?

That was the year during the war with Mexico that

a twenty-two-gun American warship sailed into the vast blue bay at San Diego. It captured the town, lowered the Mexican flag, raised the Stars and Stripes; and soon California found itself on the United States map. It was not an insignificant event.

But was it a good story idea? Depends. Something was missing. Well, how about those rancho days, as they're called today, when California was a patchwork of Mexican cattle ranches the size of small kingdoms. In 1846 that feudal way of life was about to disappear.

That tempted me. I looked around for a place to open the curtains on the events of that momentous year. I might still be looking, except for a passing conversation.

I was having my eyes examined when Dr. Larry Garwood, one of the few doctors I know who reads novels, asked me if I knew about the giant rat of Sumatra. "Kind of," I answered. "Dimly. Refresh my memory."

Dr. Watson, who often boasted of the cases Sherlock Holmes had broken, mentions in "The Sussex Vampire" an affair involving the giant rat of Sumatra. What intrigues scholars is that Sir Arthur Conan Doyle never got around to scribbling a tale about that intriguing rodent.

I wasn't interested in writing a detective story, but I was amused and captured by the exotic image. What might the giant rat have been? A carved and valuable temple statue? A pirate ship in the Far East, with a figurehead of a huge rat with jewelled eyes?

Yes!

I reached home with dilated eyes, turned on the computer, and began. I had in mind only the opening scene for a tale of the last days of Mexico in California. On a foggy night, an owl forebodingly rings the church bells. A pirate ship, baring the rodent's teeth of its carved figurehead, enters the San Diego bay in the fog and drops anchor at stage centre.

Ten months later, I had the last scene. And the novel would complete a trilogy dealing with the chaotic years surrounding the California gold rush, begun with the sunny *By the Great Horn Spoon!*, continued by the darker *Bandit's Moon,* and completed now in the pages of *The Giant Rat of Sumatra.*

—*Santa Monica, California*